John Urquhart

The New Biblical Guide

John Urquhart

The New Biblical Guide

ISBN/EAN: 9783742810359

Manufactured in Europe, USA, Canada, Australia, Japa

Cover: Foto ©Andreas Hilbeck / pixelio.de

Manufactured and distributed by brebook publishing software
(www.brebook.com)

John Urquhart

The New Biblical Guide

THE NEW

BIBLICAL GUIDE.

VOL. VIII.

(Concluding Volume.)

BY

REV. JOHN URQUHART,

Author of

" *What are we to Believe ?* "   " *Modern Discoveries and the Bible ;* "
" *The Inspiration and Accuracy of the Holy Scriptures ;* " *&c.*
Member of the Society of Biblical Archæology,
and Associate of the The Victoria Institute.

London:

S. W. PARTRIDGE & Co.,

8 & 9, PATERNOSTER ROW, E.C.

Taunton:

E. GOODMAN AND SON, PHŒNIX PRINTING WORKS.

CONTENTS.

THE BOOK OF THE PROPHET ISAIAH.

CHAPTER I.

THE BOOK AND THE CRITICS.

CHAPTER II.

THE ARGUMENT FOR " THE SECOND ISAIAH " DRAWN FROM LANGUAGE.

CHAPTER III.

THE TESTIMONY OF THE LANGUAGE, STYLE, AND CONTENTS OF CHAPTERS XL.-LXVI.

CHAPTER IV.

Is the Babylonian Standpoint Inconsistent with Isaiah's Authorship?

CHAPTER V.

External and New Testament Witness to the Unity of Isaiah.

CHAPTER VI.

The Unity of Isaiah Proved by Old Testament Quotations and the Contents of the Book.

THE BOOK OF THE PROPHET JEREMIAH.

Ezekiel's Prophecy Regarding Egypt—Was it Fulfilled?

THE BOOK OF JONAH.

CHAPTER I.

The Date and Character of the Book.

CHAPTER II.

Was it Possible for the Whale to Swallow Jonah?

CHAPTER III.

Why Jonah Fled.

CHAPTER IV.

Proofs of the Historical Character of the Book.

The Prophecy of Nahum—When was it Written?

THE BOOK OF DANIEL.

CHAPTER I.

THE BOOK AND THE CRITICS.

CHAPTER II.

THE DATE FIXED BY THE LANGUAGES USED IN THE BOOK.

CHAPTER III.

THE MIRACLES IN THE BOOK OF DANIEL.

CHAPTER IV.

DANIEL'S CAPTIVITY.

CHAPTER V.

THE PALACE SCHOOL AT BABYLON.

CHAPTER VI.

THE NAMES OF DANIEL AND HIS CONTEMPORARIES.

CHAPTER VII.

THE REFERENCES IN DANIEL TO " THE CHALDEANS."

CHAPTER VIII.

BABYLONIAN COURT PATRONAGE OF MAGIC.

CHAPTER IX.

NEBUCHADNEZZAR'S DREAM.

THE NEW TESTAMENT HISTORY.

CHAPTER II.

The Church's Existence a Testimony to the Truth of Christianity.

CHAPTER III.

Ancient Heathen Testimonies to the Facts of the Gospel.

CHAPTER IV.

When Were Our Gospels Written? External Testimony.

CHAPTER V.

The Language Used in Judea and Galilee in the Time of Our Lord.

CHAPTER VI.

THE LANGUAGES OF THE BIBLE.

CHAPTER VII.

THE NEW TESTAMENT AUTHORSHIP—WAS IT APOSTOLIC ?

THE FOUR GOSPELS.

CHAPTER I.

WHENCE HAVE OUR GOSPELS COME?

CHAPTER II.

THE PROBLEM SOLVED.

CHAPTER III.

WHY HAVE WE FOUR GOSPELS?

CHAPTER X.

What these Things Mean.

THE BOOK OF THE PROPHET
ISAIAH.

to the Babylonians or to
the just punishment of
cities of Judæa, the T
severities of the exile
long time ; deliverance
already obtained great
Babylon and give libe
returned to their count
the temple, and enjoy a
Such is the state of thi
addition to what we ha
note also that the aut
the Israelitish kings, tl
fices, occupies himself
duties, such as the ob
the fasts, which were
outside of Palestine. ˙
us assign chapters xl.-
Babylonian captivity.
knows exactly the exte
disposition of the exil
tendencies are which
alternations of joy or
hand, in those twent
text is able to give the
for their author Isaia
other prophet earlier
this is ! "*

These illustrations i
conclude with a notic

* *Histoire critique des livre*

Colleges. It is fearlessly applied by him to the breaking up of "the first Isaiah." In chapters xiii. and xiv. there is a marvellous picture of the fall of Babylon, which is represented as having been the splendid, proud, arrogant, and cruel master of the nations. "How hath the oppressor ceased!" exclaims the prophet, "the golden city ceased! The Lord hath broken the staff of the wicked, and the sceptre of the rulers. He who smote the people in wrath with a continual stroke, he that ruled the nations in anger, is persecuted, and none hindereth" (xiv. 4-6). In the introductory note to these chapters the children in our public and private schools, who desire to pass the Cambridge Examination, are told : "That neither the passage as a whole nor either of its component parts was written by Isaiah appears from the following considerations: (a) In Isaiah's time Babylon was either a subject province of the Assyrian Empire or engaged in unsuccessful revolt against it. Here she is represented as the supreme world power, the glory of kingdoms, intoxicated with her own success, and exercising a cruel tyranny over many nations. (b) In particular she is the power that has long held Israel in the thraldom of exile; an event which might conceivably have been foreseen by Isaiah, but which he could not have assumed as known to the men of his time. . . . The prophecy, therefore, must have been unintelligible to the contemporaries of Isaiah ; and on the principle that the prophet always addresses himself primarily to the circumstances of his own time, we must assign these

chapters to the c
captivity." *

This is the positi
school. Vatke, Kı
tions upon the sa
picture events, an
stances, which lay
of Isaiah," says Vat
had as yet no exi
625 B.C.; how, th
able to represent i
larly Knobel says:
was not able to a
captivity by Cyru
captivity had no
which Cyrus is call
not naturally the v
in advance either
or the deliveranc
Kuenen expatiates
the historic situat
our chapters has a
attaches all his ex
speak, the point of
to the future of
expositors give th
in recognising tl
ordinarily to the
moment at which

* Vol. i., p. 104.   † E
§ *Histoire*

rejection of chapters xl.-xlvi., which shows how fully even the most moderate of our home critics have adopted in this matter the position of the so-called extremists. Dr. Driver admits that this is a continuous and great prophecy. But he says: "Three independent lines of argument converge to show that this prophecy is not the work of Isaiah, but . . . . has for its author a prophet writing towards the close of the Babylonian captivity." * The reason is that the picture presented is the picture of that time. It is assumed that that time could not have been foreseen by Isaiah. We shall return to the consideration of these statements, and shall inspect this foundation principle of the higher criticism. Meanwhile we shall test the various other so-called proofs which have been brought forward to show that the Book must have had more than one author.

CHAPTER II.

THE ARGUMENT FOR "THE SECOND ISAIAH" DRAWN FROM LANGUAGE.

MUCH was made, in the early stages of the controversy, of the diversities of language and style which were imagined to distinguish the latter chapters of Isaiah from the first. Dr. Driver still clings to these as supports for his belief in the "two

Isaiahs." But with others little reliance is now placed upon these assertions. Prof. Cheyne says distinctly : " My own opinion is that the peculiar expressions of the latter prophecies are, on the whole, not such as to necessitate a different linguistic stage from the historical Isaiah; and that, consequently, the decision of the critical question will mainly depend on other than purely linguistic questions." *

The word *bachar*—" to choose "—was at first said to be peculiar to the latter part of Isaiah. But it was at once pointed out that it occurred four times in the first part. Dr. Driver has amended this objection.† He says that in the sense of "*to choose*, of God's choice of Israel it is peculiar to the second part." But this is mere trifling. The word, in the sense of " to choose," is not peculiar to the second part. It occurs in the following passages : i. 49—" the gardens that ye have chosen ;" vii. 15—" to refuse the evil and choose the good ;" and vii. 16—" the child shall know . . . to choose the good." The use of this word in the very phrase of the second part occurs (as Dr. Driver himself admits) in xiv. 1 : " For the Lord . . . will yet choose Israel." What more natural than that, when the prophet has to picture Israel's coming restoration and the fulfilment of this promise, this word, already in Isaiah's vocabulary, should be as frequently used as it is ?

Dr. Driver's second point is that *tehillah*—" praise " —and *halal*—" to praise "—appear in the second part and not in the first. It may be mentioned that *halal*

---

* *Commentary on Isaiah*, vol. ii., p. 234 (third edition). † *Introduction*, p. 225.

occurs twice only; but if it had occurred with greater
frequency that would not have helped the critical case.
What is implied in this argument is that these words
were called for in the first part of the Book but were
not used, because they did not belong to the genuine
Isaiah's vocabulary. This Dr. Driver does not attempt
to prove, and the attempt would be vain even if he
made it. Nor does he show that these are late words,
appearing only in the Hebrew of the time of the exile
and not in the earlier Books. *Tehillah* (praise) is
found in Zephaniah iii. 19 and iii. 20, and this prophet
is admitted by Dr. Driver to have lived not very long
after Isaiah, and long before the termination of the
exile. *Halal* (to praise) is found in Joel ii. 26; and
he, though he is now put down to a late date merely
because he prophesies the dispersion of Israel, was
believed by the older critics to have prophesied nearly
100 years before Isaiah.

His third point that *tsemach*, "to shoot," or
"spring forth," especially in "a metaphorical sense,"
"of a moral state," and "of an event manifesting
itself in history" is peculiar to the second part. The
word does occur a number of times in these senses in
the latter part, and there is good reason why it should
occur there. The passages in which it is met with are
all Messianic; and the name of the Messiah, by which
the first part of the Book is so greatly distinguished,
is this very name *tsemach*, the "Branch," the new
springing life in the midst of a dead humanity. And
when we turn to the passage in which this title is
first of all applied to the Christ, we find an explanation

of the after use of the word. " In that day," says the prophet, "shall the Branch *(tsemach)* of the Lord be beautiful and glorious, and the fruit of the earth shall be excellent and comely for them that are escaped of Israel. And it shall come to pass, that he that is left in Zion, and he that remaineth in Jerusalem, shall be called holy, even every one that is written among the living in Jerusalem" (iv. 2, 3). The whole of the remaining three verses of this brief chapter expands the picture of the moral regeneration of Israel, which will come to her through this new upspringing Life— the Branch. What more natural than that, when this regeneration had to be pictured, this very word should be employed ? That use of the word is really one of those pregnant hints which are so marked a feature of the Scriptures. It indicates that Israel's temporal and spiritual prosperity and glory are to be found in and through Christ alone. The presence of this word *tsemach* (the "Branch") in the fourth chapter of Isaiah is now found to be such a trouble that some critics propose to assign the chapter to a later writer ! It will not be at all surprising if that contention is finally accepted. It is the critics' way to kill off awkward testimony. When facts are against them, it is always, sooner or later, so much the worse for the facts.

His fourth point is the use of the the word *patsach* ("to break forth" into singing, or into joy). It is used to indicate a transport of gladness and praise ; and where should we expect to find such a term used but in those predictions which set forth so gloriously

Israel's deliverance? But it is not correct to say that its use is confined to the five occasions in which it is met with in the second part. It is found also in the first part of the Book, where we read in the description of the earth's deliverance from the stroke of Babylon : "The whole earth is at rest, and is quiet : they *break forth into singing* " (xiv. 7). It is true that the fourteenth chapter is set aside as impossible to Isaiah. But that is simply on the ground of this prediction, and not on the ground of language. The word is Isaiah's word, here and elsewhere, because it is the fit expression of his message.

It would tax the reader's patience to follow Prof. Driver through the whole of his list ; but lest it might be imagined that he puts his weakest arguments in the beginning, and keeps his weightiest for the end, let us glance at the three last on the list. The first is the use of the phrase, "the arm *(zerōa)* of Jehovah." This is said to be confined to the second part, with a grudging admission that it is not confined to the second part, seeing that it is also found in xxx. 30. But what though it had been confined to the second part, where the power of God in the final and stupendous deliverance of His people and of the earth is celebrated so magnificently? Where should we be reminded of "the arm of Jehovah" if not there? But the pitiableness of the attempt to degrade "the Scriptures of truth " becomes evident the moment the facts are looked at. The same thought and words are in xxxiii. 2 : "O Lord, be gracious unto us ; we have waited for Thee : BE THOU THEIR ARM every morning,

our salvation in the time of trouble." In xxx. 30 the
figure is equally marked: "And the Lord shall cause
His glorious voice to be heard, and shall shew the
lighting down of His arm, with the indignation of His
anger, and with the flame of a devouring fire, with
scattering, and tempest, and hailstones."

The next is *"to deck (pa-ër)* or (in the reflexive
conjugation) *to deck oneself,* that is, *to glory,* especially
of Jehovah, either glorifying Israel, or glorying Himself in Israel: xliv. 23; xl. 3; lv. 5; lx. 7, 9, 13, 21;
lxi. 3. In Isaiah, only x. 15 of the saw *vaunting
itself* against its user." * Dr. Driver appears to think
that when he admits a difficulty he has answered it.
This last passage (x. 15) quite disposes of his pretended
distinction. He says that the use of the verb *pa-ēr* in
this sense of "to glorify," or "to glorify oneself," is
confined to the second part of the Book; and, nevertheless, in the face of this, he himself mentions an
instance of this very use—of a saw's glorifying itself
against the user of it—in the first part of the Book!
How many times must a word occur in the first part
before Dr. Driver will cease to assert that the use of
that word is confined to the second part? And if
Isaiah uses, as Dr. Driver admits that Isaiah does
use, this word in that very sense in x. 15, why should
he not also use it in the other passages which Dr.
Driver indicates? But this is not the whole of the
misrepresentation which is concealed in the above
quotation. He mentions Isaiah lxi. 3. Here *p'ēr* is
used in the sense of "beauty," or rather "head-

---

* Page 226.

dress " ("to give unto them beauty for ashes "). The
ashes were sprinkled on the head ; and now a "head-
dress " will be given for ashes. The word occurs also
in this same sense in verse 10—"As a bridegroom
decketh himself with ornaments" *(p'ēr)*, rather,
"with a head-dress." This use of the word, I repeat,
is given here by Dr. Driver as a peculiarity of "the
second Isaiah." Will the reader credit the statement
that *p'ēr* is used in this very sense by "the first
Isaiah "? Yet the statement is true. In iii. 20 it
stands in the original, where, in our translation, we
have the word "bonnets," that is, head-dresses. In
addition to this, other forms of the same word are
common to the first and second parts of the Book,
proving, what is abundantly proved otherwise, that
both the parts have only one vocabulary.

I now come to the last of this array of peculiarities
whose serried front has no doubt often struck with
dismay the believer in the Bible who has looked into
Dr. Driver's *Introduction.* He says: "The future
gracious relation of Jehovah to Israel is represented
as a *covenant :* xlii. 6 (=xlix. 8) ; liv. 10 ; lv. 3 ; lix. 21 ;
lxi. 8. In xxviii. 15, 18 ; xxxiii. 8 the word is used
merely in the sense of a treaty, or compact. Isaiah, often
as he speaks of a future state of grace, to be enjoyed
by his people, never represents it under the form of a
covenant." * Here we are confronted again with the
peculiarities of the critical logic and treatment of
facts. In these three last passages which he names,
he admits that the real Isaiah used the word *berīth*

("covenant"). The phrases in which it occurs are
as follow: "We have made a covenant with death"
(xxviii. 15); "And your covenant with death shall be
disannulled" (verse 18); "The Lord is exalted . . .
the highways lie waste, the way-faring man ceaseth;
HE HATH BROKEN THE COVENANT, he hath despised
the cities, he regardeth no man" (xxxiii. 5, 8). The
two former passages prove that Isaiah used the word
berīth in the sense of covenant; and consequently it
was and could be no peculiarity that it was used in
that sense in "the second Isaiah." But, says Dr.
Driver, it is used to represent there "the future
gracious relation of Jehovah to Israel." And why
should not a word, which was already used in the first
part, be used again in the second part, when that
covenant relationship had to be described? The
critical judgment seems to be considerably removed
from what is ordinarily called common-sense. But,
whatever might seem to be left to this representation,
that it is used by "the second Isaiah" of "the future
gracious relation of Jehovah to Israel" is swept
away by the last instance which he admits. When
the prophet says, "He hath despised the covenant,"
the covenant he speaks of is simply the past "gracious
relation of Jehovah to Israel." And the same use of
the word is met with in another passage "in the first
Isaiah" which Dr. Driver does not mention. In
xxiv. 5 we read of "the everlasting covenant." Here
again we have the past "gracious relation of Jehovah
to Israel" indicated by this word. And not only is
this true; but the phrase shows also that the very idea

which comes out so gloriously in the second part of
the Book, is already present in the mind of the writer
of the first part. God's gracious relation to Israel is
an "everlasting covenant"—literally, "a covenant
of eternity." It is broken for a moment by Israel's
perverseness. But, being eternal, it will be restored,
and it shall then abide for evermore.

But, if Isaiah is the author of the second part of
his Book as well as of the first, then traces of that
unity of authorship will be left upon the work. Are
there such traces? Is the hand of Isaiah as plainly
manifest in the last twenty-seven chapters as in the
first thirty-nine? When we turn to such a book, for
example, as that of Professor Birks, we encounter a
very different array of proofs of the unity of Isaiah
from that which Dr. Driver presents in favour of the
disruption of the Book. The proofs of the unity of
Isaiah are, in fact, so numerous that he limits himself
to words beginning with the first letter of the Hebrew
alphabet—the letter *aleph*, which answers to our letter
"a." He cites forty of these words, and from these
I make the following selection :

The word *āhābh* (to be willing), which occurs three
times in the first part (i. 19 ; xxviii. 12 ; xxx. 9, 15), is
found also in the second part (xlii. 24). It is never
found in the later prophets.

Ebhyōn (needy), used four times in the first part
(xiv. 30; xxv. 4; xxix. 19; xxxii. 7), is used also in the
second part. It is not met with in the later prophets.

Anam (a pool) occurs in xiv. 23 ; xix. 10 (translated
" ponds " in our version), and xxxv. 7. It is used also

by " the second Isaiah " in xli. 18 and xlii. 25. This word yields a peculiarly convincing testimony; for, except in these passages which are common to the first and second parts of the Book, it is never used in this sense anywhere in the entire Hebrew Bible. That is a proof of unity of authorship which is hard to be overcome.

The word *ohel* (a tent) is used in the singular form three times in the first part (xvi. 5 ; xxxiii. 20 ; xxxviii. 12), and twice in the second (xl. 22 ; liv. 2). The word appears in the later prophets, but only *in the plural.* The singular form, which is used with almost equal frequency in both parts of the Book, does not occur in any later prophet.

There is one word *ōr* (light), and *ōr* (to shine, to kindle), the use of which is a most marked feature in both parts of the prophecy. This word occurs only once in a later prophet—Zechariah, xiv. 6. " The Light of Israel," as a Divine title, occurs twice in the first part (ix. 2 ; x. 7), twice in the second part (lx. 1, 20), and nowhere else in Scripture.

Ēmer (a word) is met with in xxxii. 7, and in xli. 26, and never in any later prophet than Isaiah. *Assir* (a prisoner) occurs in x. 4 ; xxiv. 22 ; and in xlii. 7. It is found in this form in these three texts only.

I need not further multiply instances. These words are taken from those only which begin with the first letter of the Hebrew alphabet. Other lists could be drawn up. But those given here, instead of proving that the second part of the Book came from a different pen from that which wrote the first, are irreconcilable

with any such theory. Hebrew scholarship, when
questioned on this matter, refuses to uphold the
fashionable theory, and upholds the old belief and the
distinct testimony of the Scriptures.

CHAPTER III.

The Testimony of the Language, Style, and Contents of Chapters xl.-lxvi.

THE late Professor A. B. Davidson, when review-
ing Nägelsbach's *Isaiah*, in which the latter
writer maintained the unity of the Book, said : " The
merest glance into the vocabulary (of Nägelsbach)
will show how large the number of words is that are
peculiar to the second half of the book. But it is
not words so much as the peculiar use of them, and
not individual terms at all so much as phrases or
combinations of terms, and not even this so much as
the peculiar articulation of sentences and the move-
ment of the whole discourse, by which an impression
is produced, so unlike the impression produced by the
earlier portions of the book. It is quite possible to
subject this impression to the crucible and dissolve
it, reasoning it away bit by bit, and then to assert
that the testimony of style is worth nothing. Any
impression which is produced by the combined force
of many elements can be disposed of in this way.

But when the tide of logic recedes, the impression remains as distinct as ever." *

These last words betray a striking impatience of scrutiny. The critic has received an impression; but we must not press the question as to what it was that conveyed that impression; and, above all, we must not subject his reply to the test of reason. We must not argue as to whether he drew warrantable inferences from the facts which he observed, or as to whether there were other, and quite as important, facts which he ought to have looked at, and which would have altered his impressions. We are warned that if we attempt to reason with him our labour will be thrown away. He will say to us: "Yes, it is quite possible to subject this impression to the crucible . . . . but when the tide of logic recedes, the impression will remain as distinct as ever." One might sum up this in the words:

> " Critics convinced against their will,
> Are of the same opinion still."

Strange impression this, which it is said facts made, but which we are now told no fresh facts, or better observed facts, will ever be able to alter. If that is criticism, where shall we look for obstinate and determined dogmatism?

Fortunately, however, there are critics who have given reasons for the impression that is on them, and who have presented them for our inspection. Kuenen says: "There are diversities of language and of style which compel us to distinguish the

---

author of chapters xl.-lxvi. from Isaiah himself.
The Deutero-Isaiah uses a certain number of words
foreign to Isaiah, or rather which are employed by
him in a different sense. Thus Jehovah, for the
Deutero-Isaiah, is He who *formed* Israel (xliii. 1, &c.)
He is the *creator* (xliii. 1, 15) ; the *saviour* (xlv. 15, &c.) ;
the *redeemer* (xli. 14, &c.) ; the *comforter* (li. 12) of
Israel ; He *has mercy* on His people (xlix. 10). In the
authentic prophecies of Isaiah, Jehovah bears none
of these names, any more than one finds the expressions *as nothing* (xl. 17, &c.) ; *all flesh* (xlix. 26, &c.) ;
and a multitude of others. *Zedek* and *Zedeka* (righteous, righteousness) have indeed preserved, with
the Deutero-Isaiah, their primitive sense, which is
that of justice ; only it is he, and not Isaiah, who
attaches to it the thought of recompense, of special
blessing, of entitling to the natural fruit of justice,
just as he similarly modifies the significance of
mishpat " (judgment).

No one will seek to deny that the words and
phrases which Kuenen here names occur in chapters
xl.-lxvi. with more frequency than in the earlier
chapters ; but that finds a full explanation, not in
difference of authorship, but in change of subject.
The opening chapters are, in the main, upbraidings
of Israel, attempts to show the people their sins, to
warn them of coming judgment, and to prepare them
for it. The closing chapters behold that judgment
fallen and Israel beaten down to the earth. The
prophet's ministry is now one of consolation. God
has afflicted not in wrath but in mercy ; and now

hope must be revived, and the broken in heart must be healed. Why should there not be differences in language and in style with so radically different missions? But while this is so, there would, with the same authorship, be limits to these differences. We could not imagine the writer using words in the second part in a different sense from that in which he used the same words in the first part. We should expect, too, that he would still draw upon the same vocabulary so much of which he has made known to us in the thirty-nine chapters of the first part. This fact Kuenen in the above criticism has either over-looked or ignored. In addition to this, the above extract will deepen the distrust with which students have learned to regard critical statements. He says "the second Isaiah" " uses a certain number of words foreign to Isaiah " (that is, to the first thirty-nine chapters), " or, rather, which are employed by him in a different sense." He then gives the above list of the words which he here refers to. Of these there is not one that is not found in the first thirty-nine chapters; and, consequently, the statement that they are foreign to Isaiah ought not to have been made. But are they "used by him in a different sense?" The reply to this is also a distinct negative. Take the first, God as " He who *formed* Israel." The word *(yatsar)* means to shape as a potter shapes the clay. This, says Kuenen, is foreign to Isaiah: and yet we find it, for example, in Isaiah xxvii. 11 in this very sense, and in this very connection: " He that formed them (Israel) will show them no favour."

The representation that God as " Creator " is foreign
to the conceptions of Isaiah is likewise met by
Isa. iv. 5, 6 : "And the Lord will create *(bara)* upon
every dwelling place of mount Zion, and upon her
assemblies, a cloud and smoke by day, and the shining
of a flaming fire by night : for upon all the glory
shall be a defence. And there shall be a tabernacle
for a shadow in the daytime from the heat, and for
a place of refuge, and for a covert from storm and
rain." This very connection in which the word
stands forms a remarkable parallel to the first passage
to which Kuenen refers : " But now saith the Lord
that created thee, O Jacob, and He that formed thee, O
Israel, Fear not : for I have redeemed thee, I have
called thee by thy name ; thou art Mine " (xliii. 1).
It is only the creative power of God which can
restore Israel and give back its ancient splendour.

Still less can be said for the statement that the idea
of God as "Saviour" is foreign to the first part of
the Book. If the name is not there, the work which
the name tells us God does is expressed abundantly :
"Because thou hast forgotten the God of thy salvation " (xvii. 10) ; "Behold, God is my salvation . . .
for the Lord Jehovah is my strength and my song ;
He also is become my salvation " (xii. 2). Here the
same word is employed, so that neither the word nor
the sense in which it is used is "foreign to Isaiah."
He says the notion of God as Redeemer is also unknown to "the first Isaiah ;" and yet we find in
xxxv. 9, 10 the words : " The redeemed shall walk
there : And the ransomed of the Lord shall return,

and come to Zion with songs and everlasting joy upon their heads." In the same way it is denied that Isaiah knows God as the Comforter; and, nevertheless, Kuenen might have read in xii. 1 these words : "And in that day thou shalt say, O Lord, I will praise Thee: though Thou wast angry with me, Thine anger is turned away, and Thou comfortedst me." Here, as in the preceding instances, there is the identical use of the Hebrew word which Kuenen says Isaiah did not know or use in this sense. This last instance is all the more striking that the word *nacham* is used in the Hebrew Bible in two senses of " repenting " and of " comforting." It is used in the sense of " repent " in the earlier and in the later Books. Jeremiah, for example, whom Professor George Adam Smith is inclined to identify with "the second Isaiah," so uses it. But in that sense it never occurs in Isaiah. The earlier and the later chapters agree in using it in the sense of " to comfort." It fares similarly with Kuenen's other examples. They give way beneath the foot of investigation like rotten timber.

What Dr. Driver describes as " a remarkable instance " of the use of a word which points " to a later period of the language than Isaiah's age " " is afforded," he says, " by lxv. 25, which is a condensed quotation from xi. 6-9, and where *yachdav*, the common Hebrew word for *together*, is replaced by *k'echad*," an expression which, he affirms, "is found o ily in the latest books of the Old Testament." Many of his readers—one might venture to say the vast majority of them—must have felt that a fact of that kind settled this question. What could be a more decided proof that the second Isaiah was quite as late as the critics say he is? Why else should he have exchanged the earlier *yachdav* for the later *k'echad?* But, let us suppose that Dr. Driver had also informed them that the supposed earlier *yachdav* is not confined to the earlier chapters: that it is found in the later chapters as well; that, indeed, it occurs more than twice as often in the last twenty-seven chapters than in the first thirty-nine, the numbers being eight times for chapters i.-xxxix., and seventeen times for chapters xl.-lxvi.—would not the impression have been entirely dissipated? Would not the readers have said: "Isaiah did not, then, exchange *yachdav* for *k'echad,* because the readers of the last twenty-seven chapters could not understand the words used in the first thirty-nine?" And, seeing that they would have come to this conclusion, was it right to conceal so important a fact from them? Was it fair to entrap them into giving a verdict which would not have been given if they had known the facts?

This "remarkable instance" becomes still more remarkable when we test the other statements. *K'echad* is *not* a word the use of which is confined to the later Books of the Old Testament. It means simply "as one;" and, when applied to a gathering or a union, means more than that those so gathered or united are "together." It indicates a harmony, a unanimity, a oneness, which takes us far beyond any

meaning which can be drawn from the word "together." It is quite evident that the Hebrew could
not at any time have afforded to be without a word of
the kind; and, as a matter of fact, it is not a late
word at all. It is found in Genesis, Judges, 1st and
2nd Samuel, and in Obadiah. Dr. Driver argues that
there is a marked diversity in style between the
earlier and the later chapters. The general reliability
of such statements may be judged from the preceding.
The result of the prolonged discussion on these points
has left a very different impression upon the minds of
many of the members of Dr. Driver's school. To these
the similarity between the two parts of the Book is
so striking that their conclusion is that "the second
Isaiah" has imitated the first! "No other prophet,"
says one of them, "has so maintained the spirit of
Isaiah as the author of chapters xl.-xlvi. With no
other do we find his characteristic manner of speaking
so well reproduced."* Orelli expresses a similar
opinion. He assigns the origin of the last twenty-
seven chapters to the close of the captivity. But he
confesses that "the points of contact" between the
two parts of the Book "lead to this conclusion, that
if the author "of the second part" is not identical
with Isaiah, he has assumed his form in this book."†
Geseuius has made a similar admission. He says
that the second part, "by the sublimity of the descriptions, the freshness of the images, the vivacity and
the force of the exhortations, is able to be placed by

---

* L. Seinecke, *Der Evangelist des A. T.*
† *Die Propheten Jesaiah und Jeremiah.*

the side of the authentic Isaiah." * Cheyne's opinion upon this matter I have already quoted. In the face of these confessions, it is no longer possible to contend that an honest and capable investigator is unable to believe that the entire Book came from one and the same pen. The difficulty is entirely upon the other side. The ordinary reader of the Bible feels that there is nothing in the whole of Scripture which so closely resembles these last chapters of Isaiah as the first do. These two parts to him display the same features, and are invested with the same glory of majesty and of tenderness. And now the critics, after scorning the common notion, and with their heaped-up piles of words, and phrases, and " movements of thought "—they, too, confess that they cannot escape from the same conviction. If the second Isaiah, say they, " is not identical with the first, he has assumed his form " !

And there are other facts which complete the demonstration that this long-sustained assault against the Scripture has had nothing to justify it. The Hebrew of the second part of Isaiah was, for one thing, impossible at the close of the exile. A writer, brought up in Babylonia, and daily speaking a language full of the terms current in that district, would have left us a writing as distinctly marked by Aramaisms as those of Ezekiel and of Daniel. But the language of these chapters is, on the contrary, among the very purest in the whole of the Old Testament. Besides this, when we scrutinise the

---

* *Commentar über den Jesaia,* II., p. 23.

figures and the allusions of the chapters, we discover that they were written not in Babylonia, but in Palestine, and not at the close of the exile, but long before the exile began. How else can we understand those words of upbraiding in chapter lvii. : " Thou wentest to the king with ointment, and didst increase thy perfumes, and didst send thy messengers far off, and didst debase thyself even unto hell " (verse 9) ? Here Judah is still an independent State. She has her ambassadors, and she is in search of alliances. The little kingdom is troubled with fears, and she believes she must strengthen herself by a strong confederacy ; and to secure this, there is nothing that she will not do to render herself agreeable to her new friends, and there is no degradation to which she will not stoop to obtain her object. That is not the condition of the Jews of the exile. One might as well seek to make England blush for the crimes of the Saxons as to have made the captives grieve over that forgetfulness of God which had marked the days of the later Jewish monarchy. It is to that time itself—to the people of the Jewish monarchy—that the prophet is appealing. And when we turn back to the history we discover that we are looking, in this verse, upon the days of Ahaz, the very days in which " the first Isaiah " pursued his ministry.

The same place and time are revealed in the preceding verses. The prophet upbraids the Jews with enflaming themselves " with idols under every green tree, slaying the children in the valleys under the clifts of the rocks. Among the smooth stones of the

stream," he says, "is thy portion. . . Upon a lofty
and high mountain thou hast set thy bed: even
thither wentest thou up to offer sacrifice " (ver. 5-7).
Where are the rocks and the high mountains of
Babylonia? Where are the Babylonian torrents,
with their beds of smooth stones? The Jews to
whom the prophet speaks are in Palestine, and not in
Chaldæa. The country which he and they are in-
habiting is a land of mountain, and valley, and rushing
streams. It is not the flat, level, mountainless, and
stoneless land in which their children were afterwards
to bear the burden of their own and of their fathers'
sins. So complete is this proof of a Palestinian
origin for many passages in these last twenty-seven
chapters, that "the second Isaiah " is now undergoing
the fate long since accorded to the first. One chapter
after another is declared to belong to an older time.
It seems too much to expect that the critics will be
instructed by these experiences, that they will confess
that they have blundered, and that they will join us in
thanking God for "the one Isaiah." Had their position rested upon the evidences of language, style, and
references, we might have hoped for such a return.
But their trouble with the Book lies deeper; and into
the grounds of that trouble we shall now inquire.

CHAPTER IV.

Is the Babylonian Standpoint Inconsistent with Isaiah's Authorship?

IN our opening chapters, when listening to the statement of the critical case against the Book of Isaiah, we noted the contention that no prophet could have so thrown himself into the times and the circumstances of the exile unless he had personally participated in its trials and sorrows. It cannot be denied that the writer of Isaiah does this. It is, in fact, the ministry of the last section of the Book. The command, " Comfort ye, comfort ye My people," is issued in full view of the desolation and the misery of the captives. It is equally undeniable that the prophet has also in full view the capture and the sack of Babylon itself. He sees the temples rifled, and the heavy idols of gold and silver being borne away. "Bel boweth down," he exclaims, " Nebo stoopeth, their idols were upon the beasts, and upon the cattle: your carriages were heavy loaden ; they are a burden to the weary beast. They stoop, they bow down together ; they could not deliver the burden, but themselves are gone into captivity" (xlvi. 1, 2).

With like clearness he sees the once proud masters of Israel in the depths of degrading servitude. "Come down," he cries, "and sit in the dust, O virgin daughter of Babylon, sit on the ground: there is no

D

throne, O daughter of the Chaldeans; for thou shalt
no more be called tender and delicate. Take the
millstones, and grind meal: uncover thy locks, make
bare the leg, uncover the thigh, pass over the rivers "
(xlvii. 1, 2). More than all this, he is a spectator of
the advent of Cyrus. He is acquainted with the great
Persian's history. He knows his name. " I have
raised up one from the north," said God, by His
servant, " and he shall come : from the rising of the
sun shall he call upon My name : and he shall come
upon princes as upon morter, and as the potter
treadeth clay " (xli. 25). And again : " Thus saith
the Lord . . . . . that saith of Cyrus, He is My
shepherd, and shall perform all My pleasure: even
saying unto Jerusalem, Thou shalt be built; and to
the temple, Thy foundation shall be laid" (xliv. 24-28).
Here, full in view, lies the holy city in her blackness
and desolation. The temple is destroyed. Its very
foundation has to be laid. But the advent of Cyrus
is equally present. The favour with which he will
regard the Jews and the city of their solemnities is
equally well known ; and, in a word, we are set down
at the close of the captivity.

The explanation of all this is more than hinted in
the Book itself. It is indicated that these are
prophetic outlooks. For instance, with the above
intimation about the man who shall come from the
east and the north with doom for Babylon and freedom for Israel, this question is asked : " Who hath
declared from the beginning, that we may know ?
And before time, that we may say, He is righteous "

(xli. 26) ? In immediate connection with the naming
of Cyrus, God describes Himself as He "that con-
firmeth the word of His servant, and performeth the
counsel of His messengers ; that saith to Jerusalem,
Thou shalt be inhabited ; and to the cities of Judah,
Ye shall be built, and I will raise up the decayed
places thereof" (xliv. 25). In connection, too, with
Cyrus' capture of Babylon, we find this strong appeal
to the men of Judah : "Remember this, and shew
yourselves men : bring it again to mind, O ye trans-
gressors. Remember the former things of old : for I
am God, and there is none else ; I am God, and there
is none like Me, declaring the end from the beginning,
and from ancient times the things that are not yet
done, saying, My counsel shall stand, and I will do
all my pleasure : calling a ravenous bird from the
east, the man that executeth My counsel from a far
country : yea, I have spoken it, I will also bring it to
pass ; I have purposed it, I will also do it " (xlvi. 8-
11). Here the Babylonian standpoint is explained.
It is God's outlook into the future : it is His knowledge
of, and provision for, His people's need.

It cannot be denied that we are here face to face
with the supernatural, and that the standpoint of
these later prophecies raises the whole question of
miracle. But there is another fact of which we must
also take account. During the seventy years' exile,
a change took place in the religious thought of the
children of Israel. It was a change which cannot be
described otherwise than as one of the most extraordinary and most momentous revolutions in all

national history. The Jews went down to Babylon
with what seemed to be an ineradicable tendency to
idolatry. They returned from it, what they have
remained to the present day, the most monotheistic
of the nations. What had happened in the interval
to accomplish that which all previous chastisements,
and prophetic wrestlings, and royal reformations, had
failed to perform? It is vain to look to the external
circumstances of the Israelites for the solution of this
mystery. We find nothing there which can possibly
account for the change. Had Israel's faith been
hopelessly lost, and had Abraham's descendants gone
finally back to the idolatry from which he had been
cut out, Babylon would have at once presented the
explanation. It was the hotbed of heathenism. Its
idols, altars, and shrines, which were well-nigh as old
as humanity, commanded the reverence of the nations.
But when we ask how, in spite of all its allurements,
Israel fully and finally threw away her idolatry,
Babylon has no answer.

But an answer there must be. No nation can
pass through a change like that—so universal, so deep,
and so enduring—except under some overpowering
conviction. It must have been that the nation at last
awoke to the fact that the gods of the nations were
lying vanities, and that Jehovah was the one living
and true God, the Creator of all things, the only Ruler
of the Universe, whose will is done among the armies
of heaven, and among the inhabitants of the earth.
What revealed this fact—what so revealed it that
every eye had to see it, and every heart to receive its

indelible impress? Let me indicate one probable cause. Say that these last twenty-seven chapters were indeed God's word through Isaiah. Say that Israel recognised to its amazement Isaiah's Babylonian standpoint: that they saw God in their midst: that they realised how all these horrors had lived before His thought, and so long held back His hand from judgment. Say that, informed by this revelation of things future, they had watched the political movements of the time, and had seen them develop exactly as the prediction had said they should develop; that they saw the power of Babylon decay; that they saw the Cyrus named here, well nigh two centuries before he appeared, marching at the head of his victorious Medes and Persians; and that they read his decree for the return and the re-building of the Temple. Say that, as these events succeeded one to another, the nation's heart was borne away from the midst of vain idolatries, as by the pressure of an omnipotent force, and was set in the light of God's presence. Say that the darkness of surrounding superstitions was smitten through, and slowly but surely scattered by the broadening conviction that they had to do with one only God—with Him in whose hand their breath was and all their ways. Would there not in that case be a sufficient answer? And should we not understand, then, the pathos and the intensity of those appeals to say who had made known these things of old, and "declared this from ancient time" (xlv. 21)?

And if these twenty-seven chapters raise the whole

question of the miraculous, they also provide an answer to the question. They place before us un-doubted, or at least indubitable, miracles of prophecy. Let us turn to chapter liii. We shall not inquire what the explanations of that chapter are which are now current among the critics. It is enough to note that the New Testament clearly and repeatedly applies it as predictive of the suffering of the Lord Jesus. The Christian Church has accepted the iden-tification with unanimous and undisturbed conviction; and the same confession has been wrung by the contents of this chapter from the older Jewish Rabbis. This Jewish application of the prophet's words to the Messiah has left its mark even upon the prayers of the Synagogue. One of these, which is used annually at the Passover, prays : " Make haste, my beloved, until the end of the vision dawn ; hasten and the shadows shall flee from hence. High and lifted up and exalted shall He be, that is despised. He shall deal prudently, and shall re-prove, and shall sprinkle many."[*] Another runs thus : " Messiah, our righteousness, hath turned away from us : we are terrified and there is none who can justify us. Our iniquities and the yoke of our transgressions He beareth ; and was Himself pierced because of our transgressions. He carried our sins on His shoulder to find forgiveness for our iniquities," &c.[†]

How impossible it is to escape from the conviction that the prolonged description of chap. liii. suits only

* Dr. A. Wünsche. *Die Leiden des Messias*, p. 49.   † Page 106.

one figure in all human history—the Man of Calvary
—will be seen from these following details, which are
all true of Him, and which in their totality cannot
by any possibility be applied to any other.* (1) He
comes in utter lowliness: He is "as a root out of a
dry ground," and "hath no form or comeliness."
(2) "He is despised and rejected of men . . . . He
was despised, and we esteemed Him not." (3) He
was the bearer of others' sins: "Surely He hath
borne our griefs, and carried our sorrows." (4) His
suffering was vicarious, and formed a remedy for sin:
"He was wounded for our transgressions, He was
bruised for our iniquities: the chastisement of our
peace was upon Him; and with His stripes we are
healed." (5) It was suffering in which God Himself
made a transfer of our guilt. "All we like sheep have
gone astray; we have turned every one to his own
way; and the Lord hath laid on Him the iniquity of
us all." (6) His absolute resignation under this
fearful affliction: "He was oppressed, and He was
afflicted, yet He opened not His mouth: He is
brought as a lamb to the slaughter, and as a sheep
before her shearers is dumb, so He openeth not His
mouth." (7) He died as a felon: "He was taken
from prison and from judgment." (8) He was cut
off prematurely: "And who shall declare His generation?"—who will consider His life?—"For He was
cut off out of the land of the living." (9) And yet
He personally was guiltless: "For the transgression
of my people was He stricken. . . He had done no

---

* See also *Speaker's Commentary*, vol. v., pp. 266-271.

violence, neither was any deceit in His mouth." (10)
He is to live after death: "When Thou shalt make
His soul an offering for sin, He shall see His seed."
(11) These last words ("He shall see His seed")
indicate that, after His resurrection, offspring shall
be given Him. He shall have a following so closely
connected with Him that they shall form His family:
they shall be His children. (12) He is, after this
death and resurrection, to have an enduring and
successful ministry: "He shall prolong His days, and
the pleasure of the Lord shall prosper in His hand."
(13) This offspring, and this successful ministry, will
be the outcome of His sufferings: "He shall see of
the travail of His soul, and shall be satisfied."

Is it possible to mistake the likeness? As trait
after trait is added, is it possible to write any other
name beneath the portrait than this—JESUS OF
NAZARETH? And when we recall the fact that this
portrait was drawn, and every trait filled in, at least
500 years—according to the critics themselves—
before Christ came, what shall we say? Is prediction, distinct and clear, a fact, or is it not? What
mind could have pictured this Sufferer, described
His condition, told His story—a story which, full of
unique and startling details, is exactly the story of
the Man of Sorrows, but to which no one before
Him answers, and no one since? Is that a miracle,
or is it not? If it is not a miracle, then we expect
the man, who avers that to so forecast the history of
a man yet unborn is quite an ordinary event, to give
us an example of the possession of such power by

mortal man, or to tell us where we may obtain such
an example. There will possibly be men, say in the
third generation after the present, who will make an
era in the history of their people, perhaps in the
history of the world. But who will affirm that such
an era *will* be made, and who will tell now the history
of the man who will make it? Is there one single
example anywhere outside the Bible of such a thing?
And will any sane man set himself to search for any
fact of the kind elsewhere? But if man has no eye
to read the future, then who read the future in this
case, and who gave us a description of the great
Sin-bearer, which is still the truest and the fullest
that can be found? If that is not an instance of the
supernatural, and a proof that this Book of Isaiah is
a Divine message, what is it?

But, if I may make a distinction where everything
is so wonderful, there is a still greater marvel in the
opening words of verse 9: "He made His grave
with the wicked, and with the rich in His death."
The words have had difficulties for expositors, and
critics have proposed to alter the text and to put the
words "grave" and "death" in what they judge to
be their natural order. But we shall find that they
yield so startling a sense when taken as they have
always stood, that we cannot doubt that the arrangement was designed. Hebraists are agreed that the
verb "made" is here impersonal, and that the words
mean "His grave was made," or, as the Revised
Version has it, "They made His grave" with the
wicked. By the Roman Law the body of the

crucified was left hanging to the cross till it disappeared through exposure. But in Judæa a change had to be made. The Law of Moses expressly enjoins that the body of no executed criminal was to be exposed after sunset. There was in this case also an additional reason. The following day, which began at sunset, was the commencement of the great Passover feast ; and, therefore, a Sabbath, "and an high day." That could not possibly be profaned. The Roman officials had, consequently, to make provision for the burial, as well as for the execution, of our Lord and the two malefactors. There were three graves as well as three crosses. These must have been nigh to the place of execution, if not actually at the feet of the crosses to which the three sufferers were fixed. And what, now, must have been the order of these contemplated burials ? The order, evidently, which was followed in the execution. Our Lord was crucified in the midst of the two thieves : and so it was doubtless arranged that He should also be buried between the two thieves. "They made His grave with the wicked." Yes, they had so arranged it, but God had not ordained that it should be thus ! Remember what happened. A thought sprang up within the breast of one who had hitherto been a secret disciple, but who in these last days, when all men were forsaking the Nazarene, was not afraid to declare himself. His soul revolted at the thought of the intended desecratian. This ruler, Joseph of Arimathæa, "went in boldly unto Pilate, and craved the body of Jesus" (Mark xv. 43).

It was a great thing to ask, and the Jewish ruler knew it. The reader will note the word "craved." Matthew and Luke also emphasise this. In both we are told that Joseph "begged" the body of Jesus. In John we read that he "besought Pilate that he might take away the body of Jesus" (xix. 38). It was a great thing to ask, and it was a great thing to grant. But the permission was given. The body was surrendered to Joseph. He had a new tomb ready, no doubt for himself, and one which wealth and art had prepared and adorned. There, touched with reverent hands, and enveloped in rich and fragrant ointments, the Redeemer's body was laid. That is the record of the Gospels; but lo! it is all written there 700 years before on the prophetic page! "They made His grave with the wicked, and with a rich man in His death." He has a felon's doom, but an honoured burial!

Let us now note one thing more. The words form a turning-point in the description. Up to the words, "they made His grave with the wicked," the story is one of deepening humiliation. It changes with those next words—"and with a rich man in His death." That is, when He was actually dead, and when all the penalty was paid, and the full atonement made, the story suddenly alters. It may be observed in passing that all this is emphasised by a difficulty which exercises the critics of to-day as it exercised the expositors of the past. "Death" is in the plural. He was with a rich man in, or at, "His deaths." What, it is asked, can the word mean? Can a man die more than once?

But is not the answer found in the entire description? This is the Sufferer for humanity. His death is literally "deaths," so that each believer can say that he died with Christ and is free from the terrors of broken Law. But when these deaths for "us all" have been suffered, there is no call for further degradation; for in Himself there is no room for condemnation, and so far as we are concerned all suffering has now been endured. The turning point in the story is therefore marked by the words : " He was with a rich man in His death ; because He had done no violence, neither was any deceit in His mouth." It is also repeated that He was there, simply and solely, as "an offering for sin." And now, from this point on, all is brightening glory and crowning triumph. Who drew that dividing line? Who was it that saw so clearly that, at the moment of burial, the humiliation should be arrested and the exaltation be begun? Who said this from of old, that though "they made His grave with the wicked," in that grave the Redeemer's body should not lie? Who was it that predicted that an interposition should be made just there? When we receive a merely natural explanation of this, we may believe this Book to be the forgery and the imposition which criticism would convince the world that it is. But, till then, reason and experience, mind and conscience, demand that we receive it as the Word of the living God.

It will now be seen that the critical law for the dating of the various portions of this and of other parts of Scripture goes to pieces upon a fact of that kind. The critics practically exclude the idea of prophecy. The prophet, they tell us, always speaks to and for his contemporaries, and nothing that he says or writes can contain what is not intelligible to them. The New Testament gives an entirely different —I might say, an exactly opposite—account. It tells us that the prophets had to study their own predictions in the hope of understanding "what or what manner of time the Spirit of Christ which was in then did signify . . . . unto whom it was revealed, that not unto themselves, but unto us, they did minister " (I. Peter i. 11, 12). This fifty-third chapter was a prediction of the very kind here indicated. In vain did the prophet and the men of his time look around them for the Man of whom these great things could be true. In vain must they have tried to imagine the whence, and how, and when of that wondrous history. Yet everything in the picture is exact, and everything in it is in order. If Isaiah could thus have told the story of Christ, what was there to prevent him naming Cyrus? And since this and similar predictions of the Christ form so marked a feature of the Book, it is not true that a prediction, revealing men and events of a period removed by two centuries from the prophet's time, is out of keeping with the character of the Book. In other words, the entire fabric of the critical readjustment of Isaiah lies in the dust.

CHAPTER V.

EXTERNAL AND NEW TESTAMENT WITNESS TO THE UNITY OF ISAIAH.

S O far we have encountered nothing which lends even an appearance of serious support to the critical theory.   But though the critics had succeeded in placing their hypothesis of "two Isaiahs" upon a better basis, there are facts which I have not yet mentioned that would have overturned it.

The apocryphal book of Ecclesiasticus, written by an ancient Jerusalem rabbi, Jesus the son of Sirach, and quoted by the rabbis under the name of "Ben Sirach," was written in the third century before Christ.   It is not doubted that he possessed in the Hebrew Bible of his day the so-called "Second Isaiah" bound up with, and part of, the first Isaiah.   There are many phrases in the recovered Hebrew of his book which show that to him the last chapters were revered Scripture, the language of which he loved to copy.*   And there is one clear passage which leaves us in no doubt whatever as to the position assigned to the last chapters in the third century B.C.   In xlviii. 22-25 he says: "Hezekiah did that which was pleasing to the Lord, and was strong in the ways of David his father, which Isaiah the prophet commanded, who

---

* *The Wisdom of Ben Sira*, Drs. Schechter and Taylor.

was great and faithful in his vision. In his days the
sun went backward: and he added life to the king.
He saw by an excellent spirit what should come to
pass at the last ; and he comforted them that mourn
in Zion. He showed the things that should be to
the end of time, and the hidden things or ever they
came." Here the reference to these closing chapters
of the prophecy is too plain to be mistaken. "From
the end of chapter xlviii." [of Ben Sirach], says Dr.
Taylor, "it was sufficiently obvious that he credited
one author with the book of Isaiah as a whole; but
the Hebrew was wanted to show that in speaking
of 'exactness of balances and weights' (chapter
xlii. 4) he appropriated a phrase from Isaiah xl. 15,
'The nations are counted as the small dust of the
balance.'" * For Ben Sirach and the men of the third
century B.C. there was but one Isaiah, and for them,
as for us, the prophet's glory rested mainly upon the
closing chapters of his Book.

A statement of Josephus, which brings into relief a
passage, which is met with both in Chronicles and in
Ezra, takes us farther. He says : † " In the first year
of the reign of Cyrus, which was the seventieth
from the day that our people were removed out of
their own land into Babylon, God commiserated the
captivity and calamity of these poor people, according
as He had foretold to them by Jeremiah the prophet,
before the destruction of the city, that after they had
served Nebuchadnezzar and his posterity, and after
they had undergone that servitude seventy years, He

---

* *Ben Sira*, p. ix.   † *Antiquities*, IX. 1.

would restore them again to the land of their fathers, and they should build the temple and enjoy their ancient prosperity ; and these things God did afford them ; for He stirred up the mind of Cyrus, and made him write this throughout all Asia : ' Thus saith Cyrus the king :—since God Almighty hath appointed me to be the king of the habitable earth, I believe that He is that God whom the nation of the Israelites worship ; for, indeed, He foretold my name by the prophets, and that I should build Him a house at Jerusalem, in the country of Judæa.' "

"This was well known to Cyrus," Josephus continues, " by his reading the book which Isaiah left behind him of his prophecies." It will possibly be felt that too much reliance may be placed upon these words of the Jewish historian. It may be said that he is only echoing the Scripture, and is not supporting it by any external testimony. He is only doing, it may be urged, what an ardent believer might do to-day—not bringing forward any independent ancient tradition, but putting his own interpretation upon the Scriptures. In the present state of our knowledge we cannot meet that objection. But the same thing cannot be said of the decree of Cyrus to which he refers. We have already noted, in the previous volume, the testimony of Assyriology to the Hebrew phraseology, which forms such a striking feature in Cyrus's inscriptions. If the Hebrew prophets, and specially among these Isaiah, had attracted his attention, and if he had perused them with interest, this strange fact would be fully explained. But, in addition to this, the decree which gave the Jews permission to return and to rebuild the Temple makes special mention of the fact that he had been "charged" to do this thing: "Thus saith Cyrus king of Persia, All the kingdoms of the earth hath the Lord God of heaven given me; and He hath charged me to build Him an house in Jerusalem, which is in Judah" (2 Chronicles xxxvi. 23).

The usual critical chemistry, at the touch of which the most solid statements of Scripture history vanish into thin air, cannot be applied here. This is not a late tradition. There is no time for the manufacture of myth, or for the strange metamorphoses and inventions of folk-lore. Chronicles and Ezra, in both of which Books the statement appears, belong to the beginning of the Persian dominion. They are contemporary documents. The decree of Cyrus, without which there could have been neither return of the people nor rebuilding of the Temple, must have been in the possession of the Jewish authorities, and must have been well known to all the people for whom these Books were written; and there can be no doubt that the Decree ran in those terms. When and how, then, was Cyrus thus "charged?" What has impelled him to declare to the world and to Israel that the Lord God of heaven hath charged him to build Him a Temple in Jerusalem? Say that this Book of Isaiah has been placed in the conqueror's hands; that he and his learned Counsellors have read in manuscripts, whose age cannot be doubted, these words: "Thus saith the Lord . . . that saith of Cyrus, He is My

E

Shepherd, and shall perform all My pleasure : saying
to Jerusalem, Thou shalt be built ; and to the temple,
Thy foundation shall be laid" (Isaiah xliv. 24, 28);
say that Cyrus read these words, and those which
immediately follow, which speak again of the king
by name, and describe him as God's "Anointed," and
which say : " For Jacob My servant's sake, and Israel
Mine elect, I have even called thee by Thy name : I
have surnamed thee, though thou hast not known ·
Me "—would not the message come to king Cyrus
as a voice direct from heaven ?   And would not the
terms of the Decree be fully explained ?   But, in any
case, the presence of these words in Chronicles and
Ezra is unmistakable evidence that these last chapters
of Isaiah were held at the end of the captivity to be
already ancient Scripture.   In other words, "the
second Isaiah" was identical with the first.

It is interesting to note, in passing, the terms of
the prophecy.   Cyrus says, in the Decree, that he is
charged "to build" the Temple.   The prophet say
that Cyrus will say to it : " Thy foundation shall be
laid."   Cyrus did not build the Temple.   The adversaries of the Jews hindered the work, and finally had
it stopped by a decree of the false Smerdis.   " Then
ceased the work of the house of God which is at
Jerusalem.   So it ceased unto the second year of the
reign of Darius king of Persia."   How marvellous in
its exactitude, then, is this prediction ?   The idea of
" verbal inspiration," that is, of an inspiration that
has had to do with the choice of the words of Scripture, is spurned as too ridiculous for discussion.   But

what of this, which is simply one out of thousands of instances ? How came that word to be placed there, so that, if studied, it would have modified Jewish expectations, and have prepared the men of Israel for coming trouble ? Was not the Spirit of God concerned in the very phrasing of the promise, so that it should run thus, and only thus : "saying . . . to the Temple, Thy foundation shall be laid ?"

There is one more external testimony : The Book of Isaiah, as we have it to-day—the first and the second parts bound together, and under the one name of Isaiah, was in the Jewish Canon. The Canon is regarded by the critics as a fiction. They take it for granted that there was among the Jews no special guardianship of the sacred writings. There is apparently no use in arguing that the Pentateuch alleges that the practice was inaugurated by Moses, in accordance with the Divine command, of placing the sacred documents in the Tabernacle, and under the care of the High Priest. It seems equally vain to inquire how the Jews came to have a collection of sacred books, distinct from Jewish literature, unless there had been some such authoritative custody of them. But though such interrogations are slighted, the fact remains. Standing out distinct from all other Jewish writings was this sacred collection. It was clearly defined, and was universally known and accepted. There were no competing collections. There was no collection that diminished the number of Books—and these were numerous ; and there was no collection that added to the number. The notion,

that the Sadducees admitted only the Law, is now
known to be a mistake. From the closing of the
Canon, there was one collection only, always, and
everywhere, whether in Judæa, or in Galilee, or
among the Jews of the dispersion. Can anyone, in full
view of that fact, believe that a collection of writings,
which formed the civil and religious Statute-book of
the nation, which contained laws for the priesthood
and the Temple-service, and which constituted what
was held to be God's message to the Jewish people,
was under no guardianship, and that no authoritative
copy was placed under the care of the chief of the
priesthood?

But there are some statements in the writings of
Josephus which have an important bearing upon this
question. He gives an elaborate description of the
triumphal procession of Vespasian and of Titus
through the streets of Rome, in celebration of their
conquests. The gorgeous pageant spread, under the
eyes of the Roman populace, the almost fabulous
wealth of the time. Huge structures were borne
along, three and four stories high, picturing the
places and the incidents of the Roman victories.
"The magnificence also of their structure," says
Josephus, "afforded one both pleasure and surprise;
for upon many of them were laid carpets of gold.
There was also wrought gold and ivory fastened
about them all. . . . Moreover there followed those
pageants a great number of ships; and for the other
spoils they were carried in great plenty. But for
those that were taken in the Temple of Jerusalem,

they made the greatest figure of them all ; that is the golden table, of the weight of many talents; the candlestick also, that was made of gold, though its construction was now changed from that which we made use of; for its middle shaft was fixed upon a basis, and the small branches were produced out of it to a great length, having the likeness of a trident in their position, and had every one a socket made of brass for a lamp at the top of them. These lamps were in number seven, and represented the dignity of the number seven among the Jews; and the last of all the spoils was carried, THE LAW OF THE JEWS."*

He then tells us that, after the triumph, Vespasian erected a temple to Peace. Into this he gathered "all such rarities as men aforetime used to wander all over the habitable world to see. . . He also laid up therein, as ensigns of his glory," continues Josephus, "those golden vessels and instruments that were taken out of the Jewish temple. But still," he adds, "he gave order that they should lay up their Law, and the purple veils of the holy place, in the royal palace itself, and keep them there." † There was, therefore, beyond doubt, a Temple copy of "the Law." It was carried along with the other treasures found in the Holy Place by the Romans, and was plainly included with them in the triumphal display for the reason that it had been found with them in that sacred repository. But, it will be asked, what is meant by "the Law." Was it only the Pentateuch that was treasured as a sacred possession? The

---

* *Wars of the Jews,* V. 5. † V. 7.

meaning of the word "Law," the expressed will of
God, the Divinely-given direction for Israel's life,
would make it hazardous to argue that "the Law"
carried in the Triumph embraced the Pentateuch
only. Besides, too, the New Testament use of the
term shows that it frequently embraced the whole
of the Old Testament Scripture. Our Lord asked
the Jews: "Is it not written in your law, I said, Ye
are gods" (John x. 34)? This quotation is from
Ps. lxxxii. 6. The expression "the Law," therefore,
embraced the Psalms, and evidently the whole of the
sacred Books. In other words, "the Law" was the
Hebrew Bible. We have also a proof that the term
covered these very prophecies of Isaiah with which we
are now dealing. Paul, writing to the Corinthians,
says: "In the law it is written, With men of other
tongues and other lips will I speak unto this people ;
and yet for all that will they not hear Me, saith the
Lord " (1. Corinthians xiv. 21). The words are quoted
from Isa. xxviii. 11, 12. But all doubt on this point
is removed by Josephus himself. He tells us, in his
autobiography, that Titus afterwards gave him this
Temple copy as a mark of his special favour. His
words are: "I had also the holy Books by Titus's
concession." * By "the Law," therefore, Josephus
meant "the holy Books," those which he has
enumerated elsewhere, and shown to embrace the
Prophets and all the Books which make up the
Hebrew Bible of to-day.

This testimony disposes of the critical theory. With

* *Life,* 75.

any careful custody, such as this, of the sacred Books, it was a simple impossibility that anonymous prophecies should be received, or that writings should be ascribed to a prophet from whom they had not come. But let us now look for a moment at the New Testament witness to these last twenty-seven chapters. The first, in order of time, is the testimony of John the Baptist. Questioned by the Pharisees as to who he was, he replied : " I am the voice of one crying in the wilderness, Make straight the way of the Lord, as saith the prophet Esaias " (John i. 23). The reference is to the fortieth chapter, the opening words of the so-called "second Isaiah." This is but one of a number of similar passages in which these last twenty-seven chapters are cited as the words of Isaiah. Professor George Adam Smith admits that there are nine of these quotations by name (Matthew iii. 3 ; viii. 17 ; xii. 17 ; Luke iii. 4 ; iv. 17 ; John i. 23 ; xii. 38 ; Acts viii. 28 ; Romans x. 16-20). "A second fact in Scripture," he says, " which seems at first sight to make strongly for the unity of the Book of Isaiah, is that, in the New Testament, portions of the disputed chapters are quoted by Isaiah's name, just as are portions of his admitted prophecies. These citations are nine in number. None is by our Lord Himself. They occur in the Gospels, Acts, and Paul. Now, if any of these quotations were given in answer to the question, did Isaiah write chapters xl.-lxvi. of the Book called by his name ? or if the use of his name along with them were involved in the arguments which they are borrowed to illustrate (as, for instance,

is the case with David's name in the quotation made
by our Lord from Psalm cx.), then those who deny
the unity of the Book of Isaiah would be face to face
with a very serious problem indeed. But in none of
the nine cases is the authorship of the Book of Isaiah
in question. In none of the nine cases is there
anything in the argument, for the purpose of which
the quotation has been made, that depends on the
quoted words being by Isaiah."*

We feel obliged to Professor Smith for this array
of reasons. Such a fact as he here deals with is too
often passed by the critics with a silence which is
suggestive of contempt. His argument seems to rest
upon these three facts :—

(1) None of these citations by name is made by
our Lord Himself. But there are statements made
by our Lord which oppose the critical theories
regarding the origin of the Pentateuch. He quotes
from these Books, and ascribes the words to Moses.
He distinctly assigns to him the authorship of the
entire Law. That fact has not been permitted to
interfere with, or to modify in the slightest degree,
the critical finding. Wellhausen and his fellows are
followed, and our Lord is ignored. Those who have
treated the Lord's testimony so lightly in regard to
the authorship of the Pentateuch are not likely to
have paid more attention to it in regard to the
authorship of the last chapters of Isaiah.

(2) The testimony is confined to the Servants of
Jesus: it occurs "in the Gospels, Acts, and Paul."

* *The Book of Isaiah*, vol. ii., p. 6.

But what then ? Is the Spirit of Christ less authoritative than Christ ? The Lord said to these disciples that they who heard them heard Him. Do we honour a king when we refuse to listen to his ambassador ? Are we honouring Jesus when we head a revolt against the Apostles and Evangelists who have delivered to us His words ? Those who draw this distinction, and say it would be serious to set aside the witness of the Master, but who imply that the ignoring of the witness of His servants need not cost us a thought, have flung away the belief on which the Church of Christ and all the doctrines of Grace are founded. Inspiration is discarded as a myth.

(3) Isaiah's name is not involved in the argument : nothing depends upon the words being by Isaiah ("as is the case with David's name in the quotation . . . . from Psalm cx.") rather than by any other ; and none of them are "in answer to the question, Did Isaiah write chapters xl.-lxvi. ? " The reference to Psalm cx. is unfortunate : it recalls how it has fared with the Lord's authority there. We have been told that the Lord's statement does not prove the Davidic authorship of the psalm, but only that the Lord adopted the view of an uncritical time. The critics would have been hindered quite as little had any one of these quotations been in answer to the question, Did Isaiah write the chapters ?

Such are the three reasons, but by none of them is the force of this nine-fold citation of the later prophecies as Isaiah's removed or lessened. It is taken for granted that there was no purpose in citing the words as Isaiah's, and that the name of the prophet is mentioned merely for reference. Are we certain that it is so? Are we sure that the Spirit of God has no purpose in reminding the reader that these words are from Isaiah, the great evangelic prophet in whose inspiring promises the Jewish people and the Christian Church have alike rejoiced? May there not be a suggestion that the words, which had waited for 700 years, were at last fulfilled, or that they stand imbedded in words, so many of which God has already vindicated, and not one of which shall fail to find its accomplishment? But let it be that there is no such suggestion in the mention of the name, and that Isaiah's name is mentioned only by way of reference, are we to believe and to teach that the Spirit of God assigns words to a man who never wrote them? Deny the inspiration of the New Testament, and there may be nothing in this testimony; but let it be explained at the same time how this uninspired New Testament stands peerless amid all the literature of the Christian ages. Grant the inspiration of the New Testament, and this nine-fold witness is final.

CHAPTER VI.

The Unity of Isaiah proved by Old Testament Quotations and the Contents of the Book.

IN view of the facts which we are now to notice it is hard to understand how the notion of the non-Isaianic authorship of the last chapters has prolonged its existence. The critical theory is, that these chapters were written about the end of the exile. But quotations are made from them which show that they were in existence long before. These quotations also prove that the last chapters of Isaiah had already been recognised as Scripture, and were so familiar to the people that their words were used by the Spirit of God to enrich a fresh message.

The authenticity of Zephaniah is not questioned. He prophesied in the reign of Josiah, while Judah was still a kingdom. Driver says: "It may be inferred, with tolerable certainty, that the period of Josiah's reign during which Zephaniah wrote was prior to the great reformation of his eighteenth year (B.C. 621)." * In the fifteenth verse of the second chapter of his prophecy there is a quotation from Isaiah xlvii. 8, 10. The words refer to Nineveh.

" This is the rejoicing city that dwelt carelessly, that said in her heart, I am, and there is none beside me " (Zephaniah ii. 15).

" Therefore hear now this, thou that art given to pleasures, that dwellest carelessly, that sayest in thine heart, I am, and none else beside me " (Isaiah xlvii. 8).

" Thou hast said in thine heart, I am, and none else beside me " (verse 10).

These words, "I am, and there is none beside me," are identical in the Hebrew. These three passages are distinguished also by the use of the

---

word *aphsi*—"none besides"—which appears nowhere else in the Hebrew Bible. The reader will
also note the use of these four phrases, and the order
in which they appear: (1) "rejoicing city"—city
"given to pleasures;" (2) dwelling "carelessly;"
(3) saying in the heart; (4) "I am, and there is
none beside me." The description given in Isaiah
of the coming judgment upon Babylon is applied by
Zephaniah to the nearer judgment upon Nineveh.
It is thus indicated by the Spirit of God that these
cities, alike in their arrogance and in their crimes,
were to be alike in their punishment. That is shown
by the fact of the quotation. But for the quotation
to have been made, "the second Isaiah" must have
already been received as Scripture before the time of
Zephaniah. In other words, chap. xlvii. was already,
in 621 B.C., part of the first—and the only—Isaiah.

We find a similar quotation in the prophet Nahum,
who lived not long after Isaiah.

"Behold upon the mountains the feet of him that bringeth good tidings, that publisheth peace!" (Nahum i. 15).

"How beautiful upon the mountains are the feet of him that bringeth good tidings, that publisheth peace" (Isa. lii. 7).

Here, again, with the exception of the words
"Behold," and "How beautiful," the words in the
Hebrew are identical in the two prophecies. The
reader will again note the expressions, and the order
of them. (1) "The mountains;" (2) "the feet;"
(3) the bringing of good tidings; and (4) the publishing of peace. As in the preceding case, the fact

of quotation is undoubted. Even if it were merely a question of expressions, these are not ordinary: they are singular and striking. The figure of the looked-for messenger coming into view on the mountain ridge, and speeding down the mountain-side to bear the tidings to the beleagured town below that there is peace, once noted, could never be forgotten. But it is not only the fact of this figure being reproduced in Zephaniah which we have to take account of. There are also these four distinct parts of the description, all appearing, and all appearing in the same order. Once more, therefore, "the second Isaiah" is in existence shortly after the close of Isaiah's ministry, and is already recognised as Scripture.

To these a third quotation may be added, this time from Jeremiah. I append the two passages:—

"Thus saith the Lord . . . who divideth the sea when the waves thereof roar: The Lord of hosts is His name " (Jer. xxxi. 35).

"I am the Lord God, that divideth the sea, whose waves roared: The Lord of hosts is His name " (Isaiah li. 15).

Here again the resemblance is too marked to be treated as accidental. The connection in both passages is similar. Jeremiah gives a pledge of God's fidelity to Israel; and here, in this reference to the miracle by which a way of escape was opened to the fleeing Israelites, when that stormy sea raged in front of them as their enemies raged behind them, there comes the mightiest possible assurance to God's people in future deadly peril, when it may seem as if the nation must go down under the hate of the foe.

The connection in Isaiah, when noted, lends fresh force to the words in Jeremiah. It was in view of those very last crises in the nation's fate that the prophetic words were originally spoken. The prophet calls upon Israel, evidently in the throes of her last great trial, to remember her destiny. " Who art thou," he asks, "that thou shouldest be afraid of a man that shall die?" Israel is asked to lift up her eyes and mark the coming deliverance: "The captive exile hasteneth that he may be loosed, and that he should not die in the pit, nor that his bread should fail" (li. 12, 14); and now God, as it were, appends His signature to this promise in the words: " I am the Lord thy God, that divided the sea, whose waves roared—the Lord of hosts—the Lord of armies— is His name." Jeremiah's quotation has accordingly this suggestion in it—so far from deserting His people and letting them finally succumb under their foes, He has solemnly pledged Himself by this name to deliver in that last and supremest trial.

The reader will mark here also the identity of the phrases and of their order in each passage. We have (1) the dividing of the sea (the Hebrew is the same again in both passages—*rōga hayyām*). (2) The waves thereof roaring, the Hebrew in both passages being again the same—*vay-yěhěmu găllaiv*. (3) "The Lord of hosts is His name," the Hebrew again being identical. That this is a quotation cannot be doubted; and only one suggestion promises a refuge to the critic. " The second Isaiah" may have quoted from Jeremiah! But a little reflection will send this hunted and doomed fiction once more into the open. Whatever may have been said of "the second Isaiah," poverty of imagination or of language has never been attributed to him. In both of these respects he has been assigned the noblest place in all the prophetic band. And the words are in Isaiah's style. They form but a single sentence in one of the grandest outbursts of consolation to be found in the whole of Scripture, where everything is in accord, and where everything is marked by the same glow and grandeur. But, if Isaiah did not quote Jeremiah, then Jeremiah quoted Isaiah, and the second part of the Book was from the beginning bound up with the first.

Professor Margoliouth, in summing up his learned and acute discussion of the two-Isaiah theory, says :

" The ' second Isaiah ' employs words only known otherwise to the first Isaiah, of which the meaning was lost by Jeremiah's time.

" The second Isaiah shows himself otherwise possessed of a scientific and technical vocabulary which the first Isaiah only shares with him.

" Is there, then, nothing in the splitting theories ? To my mind, nothing at all." * To this I may add that there was never any reason for drawing a dividing line at the close of chapter xxxix. It is quite true that those four chapters, xxxvi. to xxxix., are history ; and that the transition from the calm narrative, which is concluded in chapter xxxix., to the grand prophetic outburst in chap. xl. is startling. But to be guided, or even influenced, by a sensation

---

* *Lines of Defence of the Biblical Revelation,* p. 136.

of that sort, is not study of the Book.   What of the
prophecies which precede chapter xxxv. ?   Let us, for
the moment, leave out this historical portion, and
compare the prophecies which go before with those
which come after.   Do they, or do they not, bear the
impress of the same mind ?   Are they messages which
have come from the same lips ?   or, to put it in another
way, do they show us the same vocabulary ?   " In
xxxiv. 15, and twice in lix. 5," says Prof. Margoliouth,
"a verb (meaning, literally, ' to split ') is used of
hatching serpents' eggs; it does not occur elsewhere
in this sense.   In xxxiv. 15 a special verb is used for
' to be delivered of,' ' produce,' which only occurs in
lxvi. 7 besides. . . . Now, the author of xxxiv. seems
on other grounds identical with the ' second Isaiah ;'
the reference to Edom and Bozrah in verse 5 cannot,
with any probability, be separated from that in lxiii. 1,
and the address to the ' nations and peoples' in
xxxiv. 1 is evidently in the style of the author of xli. 1.
The threat in xxxiv. 3 closely resembles that with which
the Book of Isaiah closes.   Chapter xxxv. also cannot,
with any probability, be separated from chap. xl.-lxvi.;
both the thought and the language are closely akin to,
and in part identical with, those of the ' second Isaiah.'
On the other hand, it is by no means easy to separate
xxxv. from what precedes; verse 5 takes us back to
xxix. 18, and verse 4 to xxxii. 4." *

A real student will also ask whether there is any
apparent reason why the historical episodes in those
four middle chapters—xxxvi.-xxxix.— should have

* Pages 132, 133.

been introduced. When that question is once
seriously asked, the reply will soon reveal itself. In
xxxvi. and xxxvii. we see Jerusalem besieged, and
her strong enemy judged. On the other hand, we
see the godly in Israel, represented by Hezekiah, overwhelmed, but clinging to God for help. Remember
the mission of the Book—recall the fact that in these
last chapters its object is to console ; and have these
facts no obvious typical significance? Do they not
form a historical starting-point for the men of Isaiah's
time, and a historical background to our own time of
immense importance to the one and to the other ?
Chapter xxxviii. tells of Hezekiah's mortal sickness
and miraculous recovery. The prophet is sent with
the sentence of death. "Set thine house in order,"
said the prophet; "for thou shalt die, and not live."
But when Hezekiah pours out his soul before God,
the prophet is sent back with the promise of a
lengthened life-span. And to what does it all lead ?
To a political alliance in which God's counsel is not
sought, and to the captivity in Babylon (see xxxix) !
If chapters xxxvi. and xxxvii. form a starting-point
and background for the consolations, do not chapters
xxxviii. and xxxix. indicate why the consolations are
needed ? In the order in which the events are here
put, we see that Judah, delivered from the Assyrian,
has a revival. It is to the nation as life from the
grave—a resurrection. And to what will it lead ? To
walking with God, and being in deed and in truth His
people ? Nay, but to fresh stumbling, to trust in the
arm of flesh, and to the old pollution of conformity to

F

the godless world around it. And this again—to what
does it lead ? To Babylon—to ruin, in which political
and religious institutions will go down, and the people
will be plucked up from their inheritance and cast
away. Is not all this, from the entry of Sennacherib
upon the historical stage to Isaiah's prediction of the
exile to Hezekiah, the real beginning of the second
part of the Book?

And when we read chapter xxxix. the last vestige of
the critics' case vanishes. It is urged against chapters
xl.-lxvi. that in them the prophet occupies a Babylonian view-point. But already in chapter xxxix. we
have the Babylonian view-point. When we have been
told of the coming of the Babylonian ambassadors,
and of Hezekiah's response, the prophetic message is
spoken : " Behold the days come, that all that is in
thine house, and that which thy fathers have laid up
in store until this day, shall be carried to Babylon ;
nothing shall be left, saith the Lord. And of thy
sons which shall issue from thee, which thou shalt
beget, shall they take away; and they shall be
eunuchs in the palace of the king of Babylon." Here,
then, we are already looking on towards Babylon. We
are, indeed, borne into it. We are confronted with the
incidents of the exile. We see the young Judæan
princes, " eunuchs in the palace of the king of
Babylon." We are looking upon Daniel and his
companions. Is it to be believed that " the first," or
any, Isaiah could stop there? Was there no other
word to be spoken to Judah as it stands before that
lifted veil ? Were God's people to be left with that

ghastly ruin, that degrading bondage, and with that alone, in front of them? The first Isaiah has here done too much not to become straightway the second Isaiah.

And even that is not all. Has the reader noticed the last words of the so-called "first Isaiah?" They are these: "Then said Hezekiah to Isaiah, Good is the word of the Lord which thou hast spoken. He said moreover, For there shall be peace in my days" (xxxix. 8). It is here indicated that Isaiah had conveyed a fuller message to Hezekiah. The king had been assured that he himself would go to his grave in peace. In other words, Hezekiah had received his consolation. But what of the people of the captivity? The king in his palace has been comforted: is there never a word of consolation for those who will need consolation more? Here, in the very next words, comes the answer in that glorious outburst: "Comfort ye, comfort ye MY PEOPLE, saith your God" (xl. 1). The close of chapter xxxix. makes the opening words of chapter xl.—the next words in the Book—a necessity. And criticism has never so certainly and so fully ensured its own final condemnation as when it ventured to draw its great dividing line between the close of chapter xxxix. and the opening of chapter xl.

THE BOOK OF THE PROPHET JEREMIAH.

CHAPTER I.

THE MAN AND HIS MISSION.

WE have already noticed the provision which God had stored up in the prophecies of Isaiah for Judah's coming trial. The hope and consolation of those last twenty-seven chapters of his Book were set among the commonplaces of the Jewish faith long before the blow fell and those days of heavy trial began.

But we have now to mark a more astonishing display of Divine activity. It has been said that the thirty years' war killed faith among the German people. They cried for deliverance from that fearful scourge, and no deliverance was given. The Protestants hoped for special intervention, but no intervention came. Their enemies were not slow to hurl the taunt at them—"Where is thy God?" Stricken Germany had no reply. Protestantism everywhere is wrestling now in a life-and-death struggle with the unbelief which sprang from that despair. There was a like peril in this crisis of Judah's fate. The people, already all too prone to cast away the faith of their fathers, might have triumphantly pointed to God's judgments as the proof of His powerlessness, or even of His non-existence. "Where," they might have asked, "is the God of whom our fathers have told us?

Where is He who chose Israel for Himself, and who pledged Himself to be a wall of defence round about her?" These questions, or rather the unbelief at which they hinted, would have fallen with the more crushing force, seeing that the people were now making a great display of their faith in God. They trampled, indeed, upon His commandments and did not hesitate to defy Him by worshipping other gods; yet they, nevertheless, made a great and imposing show of entreating God's mercy and help at this very time. They were no doubt quite sincere in their desire to be saved from their foes, though they were resolved that nothing should be permitted to save them from their sins. They had their fasts, and their sacrifices, and their solemn Temple services; and thus the inevitable outcome of the chastisement would have been a conviction that Jehovah had been tried and had been found wanting. The unbelieving would have triumphed, and the faithful would have had to wrestle, in the depression and wretchedness of external calamities, with the thought that God had despised His inheritance and had utterly rejected His people.

To save the men of Judah from this fate, the entire field was occupied by some of the most brilliant prophetic ministries which Israel had ever known. Three men were raised up who seem never to have forgotten their mission even for a single day. Jeremiah prophesied among the remnant left in Jerusalem and in Judah. Ezekiel was raised up among the captives in Babylonia. Daniel carried the testimony for God into the presence of the kings who swayed the

destinies of a world-wide empire. The conqueror
and master of the Jew was taught to fear the God of
Israel.

The work of both of the latter prophets will come
before us in due course; we confine ourselves now to
that of Jeremiah. He belonged to the priesthood, one
of whose cities, Anathoth of Benjamin, was the birth-
place and the early residence of the prophet. It is
somewhat less than three miles from Jerusalem, and
it must, both by the duties of its inhabitants as well
as by its nearness to the capital, have been brought
into special contact with the life and the events of that
stirring time. The prophet appears to have been early
summoned to take his lonely stand for God, and his
service seems to have covered a period of at least
sixty years. The call came with the assurance that
God had designed him for this high mission even
before his birth (i. 5). The call was met with that
timidity and crushing sense of unfitness, which, as in
the case of Moses, have not seldom been the heralds
of coming greatness. "Then said I, Ah, Lord God!
behold, I cannot speak: for I am a child" (verse 6).
This consciousness of inefficiency kept him continually in the presence of God, his only refuge; and never
was there a bolder ministry, or a more unflinching
testimony than his. "Be not afraid of their faces,"
said the Lord, "for I am with thee to deliver thee."
It was a ministry that was marked, too, by absolute
consecration. It was a prolonged martyrdom: but,
though the burden pressed him down, it was never
thrown away. When the prophet counselled his dis-

ciple Baruch not to seek great things for himself, the young noble had before his eyes one whose entire life was a comment upon the words. When Jerusalem had fallen, the Babylonian general offered Jeremiah a safe asylum and an honourable maintenance in Babylon. But Jeremiah had still to live with the wretched remnant of his people, to bear with their manners in Judæa and in Egypt, and to interpret to the rebellious the judgments of the Lord.

This is not the place to tell the prophet's story, but it is well for us to note what this distinguished service meant. He was surrounded by sickening corruption and hypocrisy. " Run ye to and fro through the streets of Jerusalem," said God through the prophet, " and see now, and know, and seek in the broad places thereof, if ye can find a man, if there be any that executeth judgment, that seeketh the truth ; and I will pardon it " (v. 1). A spectacle such as that takes the heart out of service ; but the prophet laboured on. He kept with God, and God's Word was spoken. He was withstood by the false prophets, the heroes of the hour. He was even denounced by them in the name of the Lord. One of them sought from the midst of the very captivity in Babylon to accomplish Jeremiah's destruction. Shemaiah the Nehelamite sent letters " unto all the people that are at Jerusalem, and to Zephaniah the son of Maaseiah the priest, and to all the priests, saying, The Lord hath made thee priest in the stead of Jehoiada the priest, that ye should be officers in the house of the Lord, for every man that is mad, and maketh himself a prophet, that thou shouldest put him in prison, and in the stocks. Now therefore why hast thou not reproved Jeremiah of Anathoth, who maketh himself a prophet to you ?" (xxix. 25-27). He was imprisoned and threatened with death by those to whom his words were the bitterest of inflictions. But no message which the Lord sent was left unspoken ; and thus, labouring with God, he worked for all time. Jeremiah, the prophet of chastised Judah, has become one of the mightiest prophets of humanity.

His ministry is a striking display of the Divine wisdom and mercy. Those disasters, under which Judah succumbed, might have been, as we have said, grievously misread. It might have been imagined that God, instead of His people, had been tried and been found wanting. Here, therefore, God had to make provision for Israel and for us. His prophet remains in the midst of a rebellious and gainsaying people. The utter vanity of their loudly-professed reverence and fidelity is shown in their rejection of him. The stubborn and unfaithful heart reveals itself, and leaves its mark on many a rebellious word and deed. That was one needful service both for them and for those who should come after them. The sin with which God was dealing was stripped of all pretence, and was disclosed in the hideousness of that revolting hate. Then each successive disaster was revealed as a stroke from the hand of God. The false prophets predicted peace, Hananiah, for example, broke the yoke that Jeremiah wore upon his neck, and said: " Thus saith the Lord ; Even so will I

break the yoke of Nebuchadnezzar king of Babylon
. . . within the space of two full years " (xxviii. 11).
Jeremiah had at the moment no word from the Lord
in reply. He could only say that he who prophesied
peace would be justified when the prediction was fulfilled ; and, having thus delivered his soul, he retired.
But the word of the Lord soon came, and was fearlessly spoken to a people that loved smooth things,
and hated the bearer of evil tidings. The yoke of
wood which Hananiah had broken would be replaced,
he said, by a yoke of iron, " For thus saith the Lord
of Hosts, the Lord God of Israel ; I have put a yoke
of iron upon the neck of all these nations, that they
may serve Nebuchadnezzar king of Babylon ; and
they shall serve him " (verses 12-14). A sign was also
given of the genuineness of this Divine message. The
false prophet who had dared to speak a lie in the name
of the Lord should bear the burden of his daring
blasphemy. The Jews were called upon to note that
he should die within the year.

God and rebellious Israel were thus brought face to
face. That time became the era of Israel's chastisement, the blows falling like the measured strokes of
a scourge. The Jews in Jerusalem were told of the
fate which awaited them. The veil was lifted even
from the tragic future of their king. Those who had
been already led into captivity were told to cast away
the vain hope of speedy release. " Thus said the Lord
of Hosts, the God of Israel, unto all that are carried
away captives, whom I have caused to be carried
away from Jerusalem unto Babylon ; Build ye houses,

and dwell in them; and plant gardens, and eat the
fruit of them; take ye wives, and beget sons and
daughters; and take wives for your sons, and give your
daughters to husbands, that they may bear sons and
daughters; that ye may be increased there, and not
diminished. And seek the peace of the city whither
I have caused you to be carried away captives, and
pray unto the Lord for it: for in the peace thereof
shall ye have peace" (xxix. 4-7). These, too, were
also in this way shut in with God. The fulfilment of
this prediction, in the permanence of their captivity,
revealed God's livingness and truth. It was a
revelation to them and to their children that Jehovah
was the Master of their destinies even in the land of
the enemy.

And there was given to God's servant a still nobler
ministry. He revealed God's mercy. The Lord had
not cast away His people. They were not cast out
of the land for ever. The time was coming when
Judæa should cease to be a desolation, and when it
should be again possessed by its rightful owners.
While Anathoth was in the grip of the Chaldæans,
Jeremiah purchased his cousin's field, and gave orders
to have the title-deeds put into an earthenware
receptacle, that they might be preserved many days;
and this symbolic act was followed by the words:
"For thus saith the . . . God of Israel; Houses and
fields and vineyards shall be possessed again in this
land" (xxxii. 15). The time, too, of the return was
appointed. The limit had been set when the fearful-
ness of the coming judgment was revealed. "This

whole land," said the prophet, "shall be a desolation, and an astonishment; and these nations shall serve the king of Babylon seventy years" (xxv. 11). They were told also how their deliverance was to come. It was not to spring from any relenting on the part of their Babylonian masters. It was to arise from their judgment. "And it shall come to pass, when seventy years are accomplished, that I will punish the king of Babylon, and that nation, saith the Lord, for their iniquity" (verse 12). And the mission of consolation went still further. God was chastening, not punishing. Even in this dark hour He was remembering His covenant. "Thus saith the Lord; If ye can break My covenant of the day, and My covenant of the night, and that there should not be day and night in their season . . . If My covenant be not with day and night, and if I have not appointed the ordinances of heaven and earth; then will I cast away the seed of Jacob, and David My servant" (xxxiii. 20-26). "Thus saith the Lord; If heaven above can be measured, and the foundations of the earth searched out beneath, I will also cast off all the seed of Israel for all that they have done" (xxxi. 37).

This mission of consolation abides for Israel. There are promises in this Book which pass beyond the return from the Babylonish captivity, and which touch the Jew in his exile to-day. "Thus saith the Lord, which giveth the sun for a light by day, and the ordinances of the moon and of the stars for a light by night . . . if those ordinances depart from before Me, saith the Lord, then the seed of Israel also shall cease from being a nation before Me for ever" (xxxi. 35, 36). These words have been strikingly fulfilled. Eighteen hundred years of exile, scattering, and fierce persecution find the Jews to-day a numerous people, more thoroughly separated from the peoples among whom they dwell than any nationality besides is separated from another. That preservation is the pledge that other predictions in this Book, which speak of restoration to the land of promise, and of blessing for Israel there such as their fathers never knew, will also be accomplished in due time.

CHAPTER II.

THE GENUINENESS OF THE CONCLUDING PROPHECY
OF JEREMIAH.

THE prophecies of Jeremiah are so pervaded by the characteristics of the writer that, speaking generally, no doubt is entertained about the genuineness of the Book. Criticism, however, has touched nothing in the Bible which it has not marred, and it has left its sign-manual here also. The closing prediction, which is contained in chapters l. and li., was found to be opposed to critical belief as to the nature of prophecy, and the facts were forthwith brought into conformity with the critical theories. Those two chapters give us a picture of the whole of Babylon's future; and, if the critical theory as to prophetic limitations is true, then it is clear enough that such words could not have been spoken by any man living in Jeremiah's time. To the critic, the only possible conclusion in such circumstances was that the words were not spoken by Jeremiah, but were composed by some one writing at a later period. They were consequently rejected by Eichhorn, the inventor of that now very familiar title, "the higher criticism;" and the rejection is still maintained by Dr. Driver, the most recent, and also esteemed the most moderate, of our leading British critics.

If the reader will turn to the chapters he will find that they are carefully marked as Jeremiah's. The prediction opens with the statement: "The word that the Lord spake against Babylon and against the land of the Chaldeans by Jeremiah the prophet " (l. 1); and it closes with the similar statement: "Thus far are the words of Jeremiah." Between these two assurances chapters l. and li. are clasped. The long prediction regarding the doom of the then mistress of the nations is thus bound up, tied round, so to say, and sealed, as God's decree delivered by His servant Jeremiah. There is no other portion of the Book so carefully authenticated; and yet, it is this very part which, with characteristic daring, the critics set aside. The authentication is treated as of no account. It is plain to them, they say, that Jeremiah is not the author of the words.

Beside noting the statements which begin and conclude these two chapters, the reader will also observe that the prophecy is carefully dated. Jeremiah

is directed to give, by a symbolical act, God's solemn
assurance that all that is here predicted will be fulfilled.
Zedekiah, the king of Judah, went to Babylon in the
fourth year of his reign. In the king's suite was a
prince named Seraiah. "So Jeremiah wrote in a
book all the evil that should come upon Babylon, even
all these words that are written against Babylon.
And Jeremiah said to Seraiah, When thou comest to
Babylon, and shalt see, and shalt read all these words;
then shalt thou say, O Lord, Thou hast spoken against
this place, to cut it off, that none shall remain in it,
neither man nor beast, but that it shall be desolate
for ever. And it shall be, when thou hast made an
end of reading this book, that thou shalt bind a stone
to it, and cast it into the midst of Euphrates: and
thou shalt say, Thus shall Babylon sink, and shall not
rise from the evil that I shall bring upon her: and they
shall be weary. Thus far are the words of Jeremiah"
(li. 60-64).

So completely has mistrust taken the place of faith
among the critics, that a statement of this kind at
once excites their suspicion. Reuss, who has cut
these chapters out, and placed them in a different
volume, in his translation of the Bible, says: "The
historic note, added to the end of the discourse, claims
to refer it to the fourth year of king Zedekiah, that is
to say, to the seventh year before the destruction of
Jerusalem. Jeremiah commits it to a person who goes
to Babylon, enjoining him to read it—it is not said to
whom—then to attach a stone to it, and to cast it into
the Euphrates, saying: Thus shall Babylon be cast

G

into the abyss. There are several remarks to be made
here : First, it is of importance to remember that, in
the Book of the prophet Jeremiah, other discourses
are found, whether of this same fourth year of Zedekiah, or, speaking generally, of the first years of his
reign, which express in the most formal manner the
certainty that the Babylonian power will subsist for
a long time still ; that the present generation must
not flatter itself with illusory hopes as to a near return ;
that the captives should, on the contrary, resign themselves to their fate ; create establishments, cultivate
the fields, and found families in their new father-land.
Far from then foreseeing the advent of Persia and
the victories of Cyrus, he predicts, on the contrary,
the ruin of that country (Jeremiah xlix. 34). And
lest one should say that the whole of this prophecy is
relegating to a distant future the catastrophe which
must at length lead to the deliverance of Israel, he is
able to predict it at the very time when he recom-
mended patience and submission to his unfortunate
brethren. The text is opposed to this combination ;
for the two elements are not reconcilable with one
another, as they must have been according to this
supposition. They are separated, independent of one
another, and the second, that which offers the perspec-
tive of a better future, addressed to the generation
which should have profited by it, is hidden from its
knowledge, cast to the bottom of the Euphrates, more
than half-a-century before its accomplishment, and
by this very act as not future." *

---

* *Les Prophetes*, t. II., pp. 181, 182.

This is a typical passage. The reader is amazed, and possibly overwhelmed, by assurances of irreconcilable contradictions, and by extraordinary statements that are urged with all the weight of critical authority. Prof. Reuss here tells us that Seraiah's act, in casting the prophecy into the river, showed that the prophecy was not future! What was it then? Was it already accomplished? Did not everything in that imposing ceremony point to the prophecy as both future and sure; and that, just as the parchment bound to the stone sank beneath the water and was lost to sight, so would Babylon sink and pass away from the world's view? Everything, in fact, in Seraiah's action was an emphatic declaration of a coming doom; and yet Reuss can somehow see in it a declaration that the doom was not future, and that the words were not prophecy at all, although Seraiah is directed to say when he has thrown the loaded book into the river: "Thus shall Babylon sink, and shall not rise from the evil that I will bring upon her"!

The assertion which precedes this may certainly be described as childish. He says that by casting this prediction into the Euphrates it was hid away from the very generation which should have profited by it. How, then, is it that we are able to read it now? The prophecy was embodied, as we see, in Jeremiah's Book, and that Book was placed in the hands of the captives of Babylon, for we know that it was in the possession of Daniel, who pleads with God because the end of the seventy years, prophesied by Jeremiah as the duration of the captivity, had come. When we recall that fact, we understand the significance of Seraiah's act. It would excite eager curiosity among the captives as to what this prediction was, and the assurance of Babylon's coming downfall would be graven in their memories, would sustain them in their sufferings, and keep them in expectation of the Divine intervention.

Reuss's other statements need hardly detain us. There is no contradiction between the prophecies. Jeremiah's counsel to the captives, to make up their minds for a prolonged sojourn in Babylonia, was intended as a correction to the delusive hopes of an immediate return, which were being excited by the false prophets. At the same time he is led by the Spirit to convey to them the assurance that there will be a return, and that God has limited the captivity to seventy years. The prophecies in chapters l. and li. complete this prediction ; for they show how the gates will be opened for imprisoned Israel, and the judgment which will eventually overwhelm their present oppressors. Reuss's reference to Jeremiah xlix. 34 is even more unfortunate, if that can be. This prediction relates to Elam: but Elam is not Persia. And even though Jeremiah had foretold the ultimate ruin of that latter country, this would not have interfered with its temporary triumph meanwhile.

But what, the reader may ask, of the language and the style of the chapters ? Is it not because these are so different from the language and the style of Jeremiah that the critics feel themselves compelled to reject the chapters, although they bring in other reasons to sustain their rejection of them ? It is indeed hard to believe, after all the lofty claims made by this so-called "devout scholarship," and after all the praises and reverential references showered upon it by obsequious ecclesiastics, that criticism is the arbitrary and wayward thing it really is. But whatever the reader's final impression may be as to this, let him note now that no attempt is made to show that in language or in style these chapters differ from what is admitted to be the prophet's work. Graf says : " This prophecy" (against Babylon) "contains nothing which Jeremiah was not able to write in the fourth year of the reign of Zedekiah, and the style presents all the characters of the special style of that prophet." That fact weighed with Graf, and he admitted the authenticity of the chapters. "This oracle is then," he writes, "wholly his work, as well as the other oracles against the foreign peoples." * And though Ewald refuses to admit the chapters to be Jeremiah's for a reason which we shall immediately notice, he says quite frankly : " This long section regarding Babel has, in common with Jeremiah, many words, phrases, and thoughts : it is, in fact, entirely in the same style."† Kuenen makes similar admissions. "Assuredly," he says, "the prophecies of Jeremiah present numerous passages parallel to chapters l. and li. One is able to assert that in the use of certain characteristic expressions, such as, 'Thus saith the Lord God of Hosts, the God of Israel,' 'saith the king, whose name is the LORD of Hosts,' 'They shall depart both man and

---

* *Commentar* (see chapter l.)   † *Die Propheten*, III., p. 140 (1868).

beast,' 'the Lord, the hope of Israel,' 'and of great
destruction,' 'the time of their visitation,' 'every
one to his people,' 'desolate for ever'—one is able
to assert that, in the use of the like phrases, the author
of chapters l. and li. resembles no one so much as the
prophet Jeremiah."*

But if there is no ground in language and in style
for rejecting these chapters as Jeremiah's, what
ground do the critics allege for their rejection of
them? Simply and solely that the destruction of
Babylon was too far removed from Jeremiah's time!
Dr. Driver, while he endeavours to conceal the naked
rationalism of this conclusion, is after all compelled
to avow it. He says: "The standpoint of the
prophecy is later than Zedekiah's fourth year."†
Here inspiration is simply ignored. That a prophet
might be placed by the Spirit of God in full vision of
things to come, so that the prophet's standpoint would
be in the midst of these still future things, is apparently not to be imagined for a moment. He, indeed,
separates himself from the critics who declare frankly
their belief that these chapters were written *after* the
event, and that they are, therefore, merely pretended
prophecies, or, in plain terms, rank imposture. He
says that he does not believe that they were written
after the event. The probable account of the chapters,
he suggests, is that they were written by a disciple of
Jeremiah's just as Babylon was about to fall; that
this disciple copied the style of his master; and that
the prophecies were bound up with Jeremiah's. It is

---

* *Histoire Critique de l'Anc.*, Test. ii., pp. 295, 296.   † *Introduction*, p. 250.

very doubtful, indeed, whether that attempt to save the character of those two chapters is really worth the labour and expense which it cost to place it before the public. What amount of honesty would be left to them, if we were to admit that they were written by a man who copied Jeremiah's style, and who headed his production with this description : " The word that the Lord spake against Babylon and against the land of the Chaldeans BY JEREMIAH THE PROPHET"?

It will, therefore, be noted that the chapters are called in question solely on account of their contents. We shall immediately see whether these contents vindicate the authenticity of the chapters or not. But it is meanwhile clear, from the chapters themselves, that they are deeply marked by Jeremiah's style, and that there is no reason, apart from their prophetic claims, to set them aside as having been mistakenly bound up with his prophecies.

CHAPTER III.

CHAPTERS L. AND LI. PROVED TO BE GENUINE BY THEIR PROPHETIC CHARACTER.

"IT does not seem," writes Dr. Driver, "that this prophecy (l. 1-li. 58) is Jeremiah's. . . . . The standpoint of the prophecy is later than Zedekiah's fourth year. The destruction of the *Temple* is presupposed; the Jews are in exile, suffering for their

sins; but Jehovah is now ready to pardon and deliver
them; the hour of retribution is at hand for their
foes, and they themselves are bidden prepare to leave
Babylon. But in B.C. 593 it was the measure of
Israel's wickedness which, in Jer.'s estimation,
was not yet filled up; the Chaldæans had yet to
complete against Jerusalem the work allotted to
them by Providence; only when this has been
accomplished does the prophet expect the end of the
Babylonian monarchy, and the restoration of Israel.
Thus the *situation* postulated by the prophecy—
Israel's sin forgiven and the Chaldæans' work
accomplished—had *not arrived* while Zedekiah was
still reigning: on the other hand, the coming
destruction of Jerusalem, which is foremost in
Jer.'s thoughts throughout the prophecies belonging to Zedekiah's reign, and which he views
as necessarily *preceding* the restoration, is here
alluded to as *past.*" *

This contraction of the prophet's name is perhaps a
small matter; but it seems to call for notice. It is
continued throughout a long paragraph. Why should
Jeremiah be given as " Jer.," and "Zedekiah," which
frequently occurs, not be indicated by "Zed.?" It may
be replied that no slight is intended by the abbreviation,
an assurance which I should at once accept ; but why
should it be indulged in? I imagine that, should I
refer to Dr. Driver as "Dri.," I should certainly
expose myself to a charge of lack of due respect for
the Oxford Regius Professor of Hebrew. But let us
deal with the contention which runs throughout the

---

* *Introduction*, pp. 250, 251.

above paragraph. Jeremiah, he says, had a certain standpoint in the fourth year of Zedekiah's reign. He had before him then the coming siege and destruction of Jerusalem. But, he contends, the standpoint in chapters l. and li. is different from this. The prophet sees the Jews already in exile—a situation which had "not arrived while Zedekiah was still reigning." Therefore, he concludes that these chapters could not have been written by Jeremiah.

The reader may have difficulty in following the Professor's reasoning. He admits the possibility of a prophetic outlook—provided that it be within a certain "measurable distance." But, small though the admission is, it is valuable. Seven years after the fourth year of Zedekiah's reign, Jerusalem is taken. Zedekiah is captured after an attempted flight. The temple is burned, "and the king's house, and all the houses of Jerusalem." The walls of the city were broken down round about, and the people are carried away into captivity. Now that is a very distinct "situation." It is one also which "had not arrived" seven years before, in the fourth year of king Zedekiah's reign. And yet, although this "situation" belongs entirely to the then future, Dr. Driver admits that Jeremiah occupies it. Why, then, should not this power be still more fully manifested, and Israel be seen in captivity, and Babylon be seen as judged, even in the reign of Zedekiah?

Possibly the reply would be that Jeremiah is not limited on the prophetic side, but on what we may call the ministering side. His words are meant for

the people of his own time, and his standpoint must
be limited by theirs. That is, if he speaks of future
things to the men of Zedekiah's time, these must be
things which those men are to see. But that is a
limitation of prophetic ministry which is utterly
opposed to the facts. Were these men, or Jeremiah
himself, to see the coming of the Christ and the
earth's full redemption? And all this full redemption
is still predicted to us, although we, like our fathers,
may not see it even in the last days of our earthly
pilgrimage. Yet who will assert that these things are
not depicted in Jeremiah's prophecies? The thirty-
third chapter is admitted by Dr. Driver to be genuine.
Yet there we read as follows : " Behold, the days
come, saith the Lord, that I will perform that good
thing which I have promised unto the house of Israel
and to the house of Judah. In those days, and at
that time, will I cause the Branch of Righteousness
to grow up unto David ; and He shall execute judgment and righteousness in the land (earth). In those
days shall Judah be saved, and Jerusalem shall dwell
safely : and this is the name wherewith she shall be
called, THE LORD OUR RIGHTEOUSNESS " (xxxiii. 14-
16). Jerusalem has never yet borne that name. The
Branch of Righteousness has not yet sat down in the
throne of His father David. He has not yet set aside
man's executive, and executed judgment and righteousness in the earth. Judah is not yet saved, either
temporally or spiritually. This earlier description is
also equally in the future : " I will cause the captivity
of Judah and the captivity of Israel to return, and

will build them, as at the first. And I will cleanse them from all their iniquity, whereby they have sinned against Me; and I will pardon all their iniquities, whereby they have sinned, and whereby they have transgressed against Me. And it shall be to Me a name of joy, a praise and an honour before all the nations of the earth, which shall hear all the good that I do unto them : and they shall fear and tremble for all the goodness and for all the prosperity that I procure unto it " (verses 7-9). And yet we now possess assurances, in this very gospel light in which we walk and live, that these words shall be gloriously redeemed. If Jeremiah could thus occupy " a situation " twenty-five centuries at least in advance of his own time, what shall we say of this critical rule that no prophecy shall be accounted his which was not for the men of his day ?

Chapter xxxi. is equally admitted by Dr. Driver to be Jeremiah's. There we read the well-known and memorable words : " Behold, the days come, saith the Lord, that I will make a new covenant with the house of Israel, and with the house of Judah. . . . . After those days, saith the Lord, I will put My law in their inward parts, and write it in their hearts; and will be their God, and they shall be My people. And they shall teach no more every man his neighbour, and every man his brother, saying, Know the Lord : for they shall all know Me, from the least of them unto the greatest of them, saith the Lord : for I will forgive their iniquity, and I will remember their sin no more " (verses 31-34). But though those

days are still beyond us, a sign is given that the words
are not forgotten. The Jews, we are told in this
immediate connection, shall be preserved as a distinct
race until the time of the fulfilment of this promise.
God says (verse 35) that till sun, and moon and stars
cease to yield their light Israel shall not " cease from
being a nation before Me for ever. Thus saith the
Lord ; If heaven above can be measured, and the
foundations of the earth searched out beneath, I will
also cast off all the seed of Israel for all that they have
done, saith the Lord " (36, 37). Israel's preservation
and separateness stamp that promise as Divine ; and,
nevertheless, the prophet's vision sweeps down
through our own times, and beyond them, to the day
of Israel's full and lasting restoration.

But Dr. Driver's contention is equally impossible
in view of the very chapters to which it is applied.
" The prophecy," he says, " is the work of a follower
of Jeremiah, familiar with his writings, and accustomed to the use of similar phraseology, who wrote
no very long time before the fall of Babylon." * This,
however, does not explain the miracle of foresight
which is exhibited in the chapters. The forecast is a
very distant one—so very distant that to bring the
prophecy some fifty or sixty years nearer the event
lends no help whatever in any attempt to explain the
prediction by natural means. This will be evident
even upon a brief inspection of the prophet's words.
As one instance, take these in chapter l. 14-16 :

" Put yourselves in array against Babylon round

---

about: all ye that bend the bow, shoot at her, spare no arrows: for she hath sinned against the Lord. Shout against her round about: she hath given her hand: her foundations are fallen, her walls are thrown down. . . Cut off the sower from Babylon, and him that handleth the sickle in the time of harvest; for fear of the oppressing sword they shall turn every one to his people, and they shall flee everyone to his own land."

Now, these words found no fulfilment in the conquest of Babylon by Cyrus. We now know that, after the storming of the palace in the night surprise, the surrender of the great city proceeded in comparative peace. It was a transfer rather than a conquest. The foundations did not fall. The walls were not thrown down. Neither sower nor reaper were cut off from Babylon. She was not deserted by her population. The city was still so great that, when it rebelled against Darius Hystaspis, it had to be besieged with an immense army. When Alexander the Great, two centuries after, conquered the Persian dominion, Babylon was filled with a vast multitude, and was still possessed of much besides that had pertained to her ancient greatness. A new capital was built in her vicinity—Seleucia—under one of Alexander's successors, and Babylon's population and greatness suffered a gradual decline. About the beginning of the Christian era a small part of Babylon was still inhabited; but the sower and the reaper were even then still busy within the ancient walls, for we are told that the huge area of the ancient city was then under cultivation.

The words, therefore, were not fulfilled for more than five centuries after the later date which Dr. Driver would attribute to them. Were they, then, bolts shot at random ? Were they mere angry male-dictions forced from a Jewish patriot's lips by the sight of the grievous oppression of his people? When the vail was lifted from Babylon by modern research, the words were seen to have had an awful fulfilment. "Her foundations are fallen, her walls are thrown down." The sower is cut off from Baby-lon, and him that handleth the sickle in the time of harvest. No one can read these chapters, and listen to Babylon's long history, and to the description of what the ancient capital and the land of Chaldæa are to-day, and believe that. These things were foreseen; for the details of the description are numerous, exact, and unique. They suit no other country, and they form the most accurate picture of this as it is to-day. It is only when we compare the Scripture with a far-off fulfilment like that, that we see how utterly foolish this rule of criticism is. The prophet, the critics tell us, cannot escape from his environment. The "situation" supposed by any prophecy, they say, must be the situation occupied by the prophet and his contemporaries at that very time. These two chapters cannot be Jeremiah's, argues Dr. Driver, "because the standpoint of the prophecy is later than Zedekiah's fourth year." But where shall we find a standpoint for a prophecy not fulfilled till long after the beginning of the Christian era, and yet then so marvellously accomplished that no other possible description can so well picture the reality? The standpoint was really the standpoint of omniscience. In other words, Jeremiah's prediction was the Word of God; and the critical attempt to break up the Scripture, and to affix dates to the fragments, on any theory of human limitations, is merely a proof that they fatally misunderstand the Book, regarding which they are seeking to enlighten mankind.

CHAPTER IV.

"THE BRICKKILN AT THE ENTRY OF PHARAOH'S HOUSE AT TAHPANHES."

THE Word of God had predicted the utter desolation of Judæa during the seventy years' captivity; but, as has often happened, the prediction seemed to lack a full accomplishment. There was still a considerable number of the poor of the people and of others left in the country; and over these Gedaliah, the son of Ahikam, had been made Governor by the king of Babylon. A nucleus of a population was thus preserved, and it promised to increase. Those who had been scattered over the country, and others who had taken refuge in Moab and in the adjacent countries, "even all the Jews returned out of all places whither they were driven,

and came to the land of Judah, to Gedaliah, unto
Mizpah, and gathered wine and summer fruits very
much " (Jeremiah xl. 12).

Everything seemed full of promise. The tree had,
indeed, been cut down to the roots; but it appeared
as if it would now put forth some vigorous shoots,
and gradually cover the land once more with its
shadow. But, alas! what may turn aside the Divine
decree, or ensure prosperity to men of falsehood and
blood ? Ishmael, who belonged to the Judæan royal
house, and who no doubt imagined that he had
more right to the governorship than Gedaliah,
treacherously slew him and plunged everything into
confusion. The Jews, dreading that this insurrection
against the Babylonian authority would be imputed
to them, decided, in opposition to the Divine counsel
obtained for them by Jeremiah, to go down to Egypt
in a body, and to seek an asylum from the Pharaoh.
" So they came into the land of Egypt: for they
obeyed not the voice of the Lord : thus came they
even to Tahpanhes " (xliii. 7).

When they had reached their place of supposed
refuge God had a word for them. We have already
seen that Jeremiah's and Ezekiel's missions were
alike in this: that they had to interpret God's dealings
to their rebellious generation, and make them clearly
behold His hand in their punishments. So we read :
" Then came the word of the Lord unto Jeremiah in
Tahpanhes, saying, Take great stones in thine hand,
and hide them in the clay in the brickkiln, which is
at the entry of Pharaoh's house in Tahpanhes, in the

sight of the men of Judah; and say unto them,
Thus saith the Lord of hosts, the God of Israel;
Behold, I will send and take Nebuchadrezzar the
king of Babylon, My servant, and will set his throne
upon these stones that I have hid; and he shall
spread his royal pavilion over them. And when he
cometh, he shall smite the land of Egypt, and
deliver such as are for death to death; and such as
are for captivity to captivity; and such as are for the
sword to the sword. And I will kindle a fire in the
houses of the gods of Egypt; and he shall burn
them, and carry them away captives; and he shall
array himself with the land of Egypt, as a shepherd
putteth on his garment; and he shall go forth from
thence in peace. He shall break also the images of
Beth-shemesh, that is in the land of Egypt; and the
houses of the gods of the Egyptians shall he burn
with fire" (verses 8-13).

The following chapter will deal with the similar
prophecy in Ezekiel. We shall confine our attention
now to this reference to "the brickkiln." An unexpected and remarkable discovery has furnished us
with a valuable comment upon this passage, and with
a proof of the minute accuracy and historical
character of these prophecies. To begin with, it
will strike the reflecting reader that to have a "brickkiln" "at the entry" of a royal palace was a peculiar
arrangement. This would have been a most unsightly
intrusion into the beauty and orderliness which must
have prevailed throughout the whole of the royal
precincts. The Revised Version is in this instance

H

more happy than the Authorised. It renders:
" Hide them in mortar in the brickwork ; " and
in the margin it gives another translation : " Lay
them with mortar in the pavement (or square)."
That last suggestion, " or square," and indeed one
may say the same of " pavement," shows how much
even the revisers needed the light which was to spring
from a discovery made the year after the publication
of the New Version of the Old Testament. And it
ought also to be said that, if the Authorised Version
erred in this matter, it erred in good company. Even
Gesenius, in the latest editions of his Hebrew
Dictionary, has no other translation to suggest for
malbēn than " brickkiln." The *Vulgate,* in its desire
to interpret this obscure passage, ventured upon an
explanation, and went farther wrong. Its translation
runs : " Take great stones in thy hand, and hide
them in the crypt (or vault) which is under the brick-
wall which is at the gate of the house of the Pharaoh
at Taphnes." The best translation of *malbēn,* as we
shall see, is " brick-work."

I shall now let Dr. Flinders Petrie tell the story of
his discovery. "When I was exploring," he says,
" in the marshy desert about Tanis, I saw from the
top of a mound—Tell Ginn—a shimmering grey
swell on the horizon through the haze ; and that I
was told was Tell Defenneh, or rather Def'neh, as it
is called. It was generally supposed to be the
Pelusiac Daphnæ of Herodotus, and the Tahpanhes
of the Old Testament ; but nothing definite was
known about it, and as it lies in the midst of the

desert, between the Delta and the Suez Canal, twelve miles from either, it was not very accessible." After some time, Dr. Petrie made arrangements for the carrying on of the work in which he was then engaged, called for volunteers for the new enterprise, and formed a camp near the new scene of operations. The camp contained seventy men, boys, and girls.

The place was " a wide, flat plain, bordering on the river, strewn all over with pottery, and with a mound of mud-brick building in the midst of it." This mound was a most conspicuous object. He asked the name of the mound and was struck by the reply. The name was *Kasr bint el Yehudi*—" the palace of the Jew's daughter." " This at once," says Dr. Petrie, " brought Tahpanhes to my mind. Can there be any tradition here? I thought. I turned to Jeremiah, and there read how he came, with Johanan, the son of Kareah, and all the officers, and the king's daughters, down to Tahpanhes and dwelt there. We can hardly believe that the only place in Egypt, where a celebrated daughter of a Jewish king lived, was called in later times 'the Palace of the Jew's daughter' by accident, especially as such a name is only known here." The next inquiry was, how the place had come by its Greek name " Daphnæ." The excavations soon supplied an answer. Abundance of ancient Greek pottery was found, with many Greek remains and very few Egyptian. It was plain that this had been a Greek camp. " This, then," continues our explorer, " was the camp of the Ionians, described by Herodotus as having been founded by

Psammetichos I. on the Pelusiac branch; and on reaching down to the foundation of the fort I there took out the tablets with the name of Psamtik I. as the founder."

The place seems "to have been an old fort on the Syrian frontier guarding the road out of Egypt. . . The fort was a square mass of brick-work, with deep domed chambers or cells in it, which were opened from the top; this sustained the actual dwellings at about forty feet above the plain, so that a clear view of the distant towns and the desert could be seen over the camp wall, to some ten or twenty miles. The camp was defended by a wall forty feet thick, and probably as high; but this is now completely swept away down to the ground by the winds and rains. . . This fort was enlarged by chambers added to it during a couple of generations later; and it must have been over that threshold, which still lies in the doorway, that the Jewish fugitives entered, when Hophra gave them an asylum from the Assyrian scourge. We cannot doubt that Tahpanhes—the first place on the road into Egypt—was a constant refuge for the Jews during the series of Assyrian invasions; especially as they met here, not the exclusive Egyptians, but a mixed foreign population, mostly Greeks. Here, then, was a ready source for the introduction of Greek words and names into Hebrew, long before the Alexandrine age; and even before the fall of Jerusalem the Greek names of musical instruments, and other words, may have been heard in the courts of Solomon's temple."

It will be of importance to recall that fact, when we speak, as we shall soon do, of the Book of Daniel. But what of "the brick-kiln," or "brick-work," or " pavement?" Was anything found which threw light upon this? Dr. Petrie says: "Another remarkable connection with the account given by Jeremiah was found on clearing around the fort. The entrance was in the side of a block of building projecting from the fort; and in front of it, on the opposite side of its roadway, similarly projecting from the fort, was a large platform, or pavement, of brick-work, suitable for outdoor business, such as loading goods, pitching tents, &c.—just what is now called a *mastaba*. Now, Jeremiah writes of 'the pavement (or brick-work) which is at the entry of Pharaoh's house in Tahpanhes;' this passage, which has been an unexplained stumbling-block to translators hitherto, is the exact description of the *mastaba* which I found; and this would be the most likely place for Nebuchadrezzar to pitch his royal tent, as stated by Jeremiah." *

In an earlier notice in *The Times* of 18th June, 1886, Dr. Petrie indicates that this *mastaba* seems to have been about three feet high. And in another work he says: "This platform, or *mastaba*, is therefore unmistakably the *brickwork, or pavement, which is at the entry of Pharaoh's House in Tahpanhes.* Here the ceremony described by Jeremiah took place before the chiefs of the fugitives assembled on the platform, and here Nebuchadrezzar *spread his royal*

---

* *Ten Years' Digging in Egypt*, pp. 50-54.

pavilion. The very nature of the site is precisely applicable to all the events." *

Ezekiel's Prophecy Regarding Egypt— Was it Fulfilled?

THE peculiar imagery of the prophecies of Ezekiel receives a complete explanation when we recall the representations which were constantly before the eyes of the captives in Babylonia. We limit ourselves now, however, to one prediction, which was confidently declared not to have been accomplished, but on which research has now shed some welcome light.

Chapters xxix.-xxxii. are a great prophetic picture of the judgments which are to fall upon Egypt, Israel's ancient oppressor, and, in the last days of the Jewish kingdom, her deceitful ally. The prolonged description opens with the two prophecies in chapter xxix. The first of these is a summary of the blows which are to fall, and of the long enduring humiliation to which they are the prelude. This message, the prophet tells us, came to him "in the tenth year, in the twelfth month, in the twelfth day of the month" (verse 1). It concludes with these words :—

"Therefore thus saith the Lord God; Behold, I will bring a sword upon thee, and cut off man and

---

* *Tanis.* Part II.

beast out of thee. And the land of Egypt shall be
desolate and waste; and they shall know that I am
the Lord: because he hath said, The river is mine,
and I have made it. Behold, therefore I am against
thee, and against thy rivers, and I will make the land
of Egypt utterly waste and desolate, from the tower
of Syene even unto the border of Ethiopia. No foot
of man shall pass through it, nor foot of beast shall
pass through it, neither shall it be inhabited forty
years. And I will make the land of Egypt desolate
in the midst of the countries that are desolate, and
her cities among the cities that are laid waste shall be
desolate forty years: and I will scatter the Egyptians
among the nations, and will disperse them through
the countries.

"Yet thus saith the Lord God; At the end of
forty years will I gather the Egyptians from the
people whither they were scattered: and I will bring
again the captivity of Egypt, and will cause them to
return into the land of Pathros, into the land of
their habitation; and they shall be there a base
kingdom. It shall be the basest of the kingdoms;
neither shall it exalt itself any more above the nations:
for I will diminish them, that they shall no more rule
over the nations" (verses 8-15).

In the five last verses of the chapter we have a
second prediction. Let me ask the reader to mark
the date with which it begins, and to note also that,
though it is placed with the foregoing in the same
chapter, the two predictions are nevertheless quite
distinct.

"And it came to pass in the seven and twentieth

year, in the first month, in the first day of the month, the word of the Lord came unto me, saying, Son of man, Nebuchadrezzar king of Babylon caused his army to serve a great service against Tyrus: every head was made bald, and every shoulder was peeled: yet had he no wages, nor his army, for Tyrus, for the service that he had served against it: Therefore thus saith the Lord God; Behold, I will give the land of Egypt unto Nebuchadrezzar king of Baby-lon; and he shall take her multitude, and take her spoil, and take her prey; and it shall be the wages for his army. I have given him the land of Egypt for his labour wherewith he served against it, because they wrought for Me, saith the Lord God" (v. 17-20).

It has been imagined that those, who look upon the prophecies as mere forecasts, more or less far-seeing, made by patriotic politicians, have here a strong case. These, we are told, are predictions that were not ful-filled. There was (1), they say, no invasion of Egypt by Nebuchadnezzar; and (2) there was no depopula-tion of the country, and no forty years' desolation at that time. On the contrary, it is urged that the reign of Amasis, who succeeded Pharaoh-Hophra, the Apries of the Greeks, was one of marked pros-perity. "There is another discrepancy," says *The Speaker's Commentary*, "between the narrative of Herodotus and the prophecy of Ezekiel. The pro-phecy speaks of the utter desolation of Egypt; the historian says that in the reign of Amasis the land was most flourishing, ' both with regard to the advan-tages conferred by the river on the soil, and by the soil on the inhabitants,' and that the country ' could boast no less than 20,000 inhabited cities ' (*Herodotus* ii. 177). This is also confirmed by the existence of many monuments bearing the mark of this reign, which attest the wealth and luxury of the inhabitants" (Wilkinson, *The Ancient Egyptians* i. 180). The writer seeks to explain the discrepancy by remarking that the fulfilment of the prophecy was gradual ; although it is somewhat hard to understand how that can explain a forty years' desolation.

It is astonishing to note how complete an answer lay at hand in the very distinction which I have asked the reader to note. The prophecy, summing up the after history of Egypt, is entirely distinct from this in which Nebuchadnezzar's name is mentioned. The first prediction was uttered in the tenth year of the captivity ; the second in the twenty-seventh —seventeen years afterwards ! If the predictions of the prophets are carefully scanned, it will be seen that, when a general prophetic survey, a burden of doom on any land or people, is given, it frequently happens that a near and distinct event is also predicted, and appended to this as a sign that the other and more distant prophecy shall also be accomplished. That is the place filled by this prediction concerning the invasion by Nebuchadrezzar. It is not a repetition of the previous prophecy. It is merely God's seal attesting that this previous prophecy will surely be fulfilled. The temporary desolation of forty years' duration performs a similar service. It is another seal affirming the certainty of the coming and long-enduring humiliation. In our

present ignorance, with regard to the after history of
the country, we cannot yet say at what point this
forty years' captivity occurred. But, if we cannot
discover this seal, we can now look upon that greater
evil whose coming it proclaimed—we can test whether
this was God's Word by looking upon God's act.
From that point downwards, Egypt declined; and
now, in our own day, the words have found a full accomplishment: "They shall be there a base kingdom. It
shall be the basest of the kingdoms; neither shall it
exalt itself any more above the nations; for I will
diminish them, that they shall no more rule over the
nations" (xxix. 14, 15). The prophecy implied that
the Egyptians, unlike the Assyrians and other ancient
peoples, should continue: and they have continued.
It equally implied that it should continue a kingdom:
and it is a kingdom now, as it has continued to be all
through its history. But there is not a more degraded
sovereignty on the face of the earth to-day. The
Khedive has no control. Strangers levy, collect, and
spend, the Egyptian taxes. Strangers pay him, his
ministers, and his officials, their salaries; and neither
he nor his ministers dare interfere with these strangers,
nor even criticise their actions. If there is a
sovereignty more deeply humiliated than this upon
the earth's surface, and that yet continues to be a
sovereignty, I know not where to find it.

Let us now turn to the predicted conquest by
Nebuchadnezzar. "The Bible," says Mr. Budge,*
"contains one allusion to Apries under the name

Pharaoh Hophra, and the prophet Jeremiah (xliv. 30) speaking in the name of the Lord, says : ' Behold, I will give Pharaoh Hophra king of Egypt into the hand of his enemies, and into the hand of them that seek his life; as I gave Zedekiah king of Judah into the hand of Nebuchadrezzar king of Babylon, his enemy, and that sought his life.' In another place the prophet Ezekiel (xxix. 18-xxx. 1 *ff.*) declares that Egypt shall be given unto Nebuchadnezzar (II.) as a reward for the work which he had done for the Lord God of Israel in connection with the ' great service against Tyrus.' "

Of the minute fulfilment of Jeremiah's prediction regarding Pharaoh Hophra, Mr. Budge himself, though he does not seem to notice it, presents the fullest proof. According to Herodotus, Hophra was kept in prison for a time until his enemies among the nobility compelled Amasis to strangle him. The monuments cited by Mr. Budge tell a somewhat different story. There was anarchy in the country. Amasis left his old master Hophra undisturbed. The result was that the country was covered with Greek mercenaries, who " in numbers which cannot be told, are going about throughout the North (that is, the Delta) as if the country had no master." * The result was two battles, fought at an interval of six months, in the second of which Hophra was overtaken in a boat by the soldiers of Amasis and slain. The reader will have noticed that Jeremiah does not say that Hophra will be delivered into the hand of Nebuchad-

---

* Page 17.

nezzar. He says that of Zedekiah; but this is Hophra's fate—he will be given, in like manner, "into the hand of *them* that seek his life;" and the monuments now tell us that it was the soldiers who revolted against Hophra, who used Amasis that they might get their revenge upon Hophra, and who stirred up the man of their choice to deliver one battle after another—it was they, who sought his life, into whose hands, as the Scripture said, Pharaoh Hophra was delivered.

But, if Mr. Budge is silent about the striking fulfilment of this prediction, he distinctly challenges that which declared that Nebuchadnezzar should invade Egypt, and enrich himself and his army with its treasures. "The prophet Jeremiah," he says, "speaking (xliii. 10) in the name of the Lord God, said, ' Behold, I will send and take Nebuchadrezzar the king of Babylon, My servant, and will set his throne upon these stones that I have hid ' (that is, the stones which God told Jeremiah to hide in the brick wall at the entrance to Pharaoh's house at Tahpanhes) 'and he shall spread his royal pavilion over them.' That Nebuchadnezzar advanced as far as this frontier city, on the east of the Delta, there is no reason whatever to doubt, but there is also no reason whatsoever for believing that he entered Egypt proper, or even that he conquered any part of it."

Josephus, however, expressly states that Egypt was successfully invaded by Nebuchadnezzar. He says: "On the fifth year after the destruction of Jerusalem, which was the twenty-third of the reign of Nebuchadnezzar, he made an expedition against Cœlesyria; and when he had possessed himself of it, he made war against the Ammonites and Moabites; and when he had brought all those nations under subjection, he fell upon Egypt in order to overthrow it; and he slew the king that then reigned, and set up another."*

Josephus is here certainly mistaken when he says that the king of Egypt was slain by Nebuchadnezzar, for we have already seen that Hophra lived for some time after Amasis had taken the throne. Besides, too, it is equally clear that Hophra reigned for twelve years after the twenty-third year of Nebuchadnezzar. The latter began to reign in Babylon in 604 B.C., and continued to 561 B.C. His reign therefore lasted forty-three years, and his twenty-third year was 582 B.C. Hophra reigned from 591 B.C. to 570 B.C.

This is certainly not in favour of the absolute exactitude of Josephus; but the facts are nevertheless equally opposed to the conclusion of Mr. Budge that Nebuchadnezzar never invaded Egypt. He does indeed refer to the inscription of Nes-Hor, or Nes-Heru, as he prefers to read the name. But he represents it as describing a mere insurrection of foreign troops engaged in the Egyptian service. Even that is an advance compared with the note which appears in *The Records of the Past*, vol. vi., pp. 79-84, in which it is stated that the Apries mentioned in the inscription is not the Hophra of the Bible. That assertion Mr. Budge does not confirm. There is no longer any question as to the fact that Nes-Hor was

---

* *Antiquities*, x., ix. 7.

a great official in the service of the king Hophra of
the Bible. The monument has long been known. It
represents Nes-Hor, who is Hophra's governor of the
south of Egypt, as kneeling and adoring the three
gods—the Egyptian Triad—worshipped at the Cata-
racts, and whose effigy he is holding in his hands.
On the pillar on which his back is leaning is an
inscription in which we read the following lines:

> I have caused my statue to be erected; through it
> my name will always endure; it will not perish in
> the temple, because I have taken care of the house
> [of the gods] when it had to suffer from the foreign
> troops of the Amu [of the Semites], from the peoples
> of the North, from those of Asia, the wretches . . .
> who [have wrought evil in their thought] ; for to
> over-run and to ravage the higher land [Upper
> Egypt] was in their thought. The fear *which they
> had* of his Majesty was small. They executed the
> plans which their hearts had conceived. I did not
> permit them to reach quite to Ta-Kems [the country
> adjoining the first cataract of the Nile] ; I made
> them approach the place where his Majesty was; his
> Majesty had prepared for them a defeat.*

This is plainly a planned campaign, and one which
was largely successful. The army was also composed
of the very kind of troops of which Nebuchadnezzar's
army must have been composed—Semites, Asiatics,
and the people of the North. They besieged Elephan-
tine, and worked havoc in the temple of Khnoum, in
which Nes-Hor subsequently erected his statue.

* A. Wiedemann, *Der Zug Nebucadnezar's gegen Aegypten* (quoted in vigouroux),
Zeitschrift fur Egyptische Sprache, 1878, p. 4.

There are two other possible traces of this campaign. Two Babylonian cylinders have been found which have been described by J. Menant.* They are the only two yet known which bear an Egyptian inscription. Both of them bear the name of Hophra, in Egyptian hieroglyphics. It seems likely that these cylinders were executed by Egyptian prisoners carried off to Babylon in this campaign. The date given by Ezekiel, too, as the time when his prophecy was uttered falls quite into line with the facts. The captivity seems to have begun in 606 B.C. The twenty-seventh year, when the promise is made to Nebuchadnezzar of the pillage of Egypt, would be 580 B.C. This is ten years before Hophra ceases to reign, and Nes-Hor shows us that king certainly driven back before the invaders, but still possessed of full power over his own soldiers, and using them with apparent success in preventing the further advance of the Babylonian army. The time also agrees with the prediction in Jeremiah. Jerusalem fell in July, 586 B.C. Not very long after this, the attempt to care for, and to replant, the remnant in Judæa came to an end in the assassination of Gedaliah. The Jews passed down into Egypt, and Jeremiah hides the great stones in the *Mastaba* and foretells the same expedition of Nebuchadnezzar against Egypt.

But when did the expedition actually take place? Ezekiel's prophecy helps us to furnish a reply. The march into Egypt began apparently upon the fall of Tyre, which had been besieged for thirteen years—

---

* *Notice sur quelques cylindres Orientaux,* No. III., pp. 10, 11.

from 585 to 573 B.C. While Jeremiah's prophecy, therefore, was being spoken, Nebuchadnezzar's battering-rams were thundering against the walls of Tyre; and the Egyptians, and those Jews who had sought refuge among them, were no doubt rejoicing in that city's stubborn resistance, and imagining that the conqueror's path was effectually barred. In 580, when Ezekiel's prediction was uttered, the siege had lasted five years. The confidence of Egypt had increased; and there was, no doubt, corresponding disheartenment among the Babylonians. These are now encouraged. The siege will, indeed, go on till every head is bald and every shoulder is peeled; and when they capture the city they will only find an empty shell. But their reward awaits them in Egypt. Thither they advanced in 572, just two years before Hophra is deposed. His defeat, no doubt, led to the rebellion of his soldiery, and to the choice of a new king, Amasis, from among his generals.

These facts and dates are confirmed by two Babylonian documents. "The name of a city, Sûru, which," says Dr. Pinches, "is probably Tyre, occurs on a tablet dated in Nebuchadnezzar's thirty-fifth year (569 B.C.—four years after that city was taken). It refers to a transaction in which Sesame is sold, an official of the city being a party to the contract. Later on, in the fortieth year of Nebuchadnezzar, a contract was entered into between Milki-idiri, governor of Kidis (Kedesh), with regard to some cattle. This document is dated at Tyre (Surru) on the 22nd of the month Tammuz. Not only Tyre, therefore, but the whole district, owned the dominion of Nebuchadnezzar at this time."* And plainly this was a dominion undisturbed by either hopes or fears of any Egyptian interference. That country had also felt the weight of the hammer which had crushed the nations.

---

* *The Old Testament*, &c., p. 401.

THE BOOK OF JONAH.

CHAPTER I.

The Date and Character of the Book.

W HEN we pass from the historical Books of the
Old Testament, and enter the region of the
poetical and prophetic Books, we are surrounded by
comparative quiet. The critics are at work, indeed,
even here. The microscope fixes its piercing gaze in
the best artificial light which can be had, and the
dissecting knife is applied with such defiant reckless-
ness, that one is inevitably reminded of that Chinese
punishment in which the victim is condemned to be
cut into "a thousand pieces." But, speaking generally, the historical character of these Books is not
assailed with the fierceness which has characterised
the assault upon the Books with which we have
already dealt. And the reason for this comparative
quiet is evident enough. The dates claimed for the
poetical and prophetic Books do not, with the exception of that of the Psalms, materially interfere with
the critical theories regarding the gradual and quite
natural development of the religion of Israel. They
are supposed rather to assist them, and hence the
measure of favour with which they have been treated.

But to this general statement there are two glaring
exceptions. To the Book of Daniel no quarter has
been given, and the Book of Jonah has met with a

similar fate. Attempts have been made to show that
the latter Book is of late date, and that, consequently,
it could not have been written by its alleged author.
It is urged that this is shown by the presence of
Syrian forms in the Hebrew of Jonah. The same
argument is levelled against the Song of Solomon;
but it is really founded upon our ignorance, as we are
not aware to what extent the Hebrew of the ten tribes
had suffered through their freer intercourse with the
Syrians and the neighbouring nations. Judging by
what is told us in the Scripture of the two kingdoms
of Judah and Israel, the intercourse of the latter with
the peoples of Syria was much more marked, and the
language of the Israelites would naturally, therefore,
be correspondingly modified. Another argument for
the late date of the Book is founded upon the words,
"Now Nineveh was an exceeding great city" (iii. 3).
This, it is said, plainly shows that Nineveh had ceased
to exist when the words were written—for, otherwise,
the sentence would have run : " Now Nineveh *is* an
exceeding great city." The argument seems to have
weight, and it is urged with proportionate confidence
in critical works as finally disposing of the belief that
the Book could have been written by Jonah, or by any
writer till after the fall of Nineveh, an event that took
place about two and a-half centuries later than the
incidents which the Book records. Will it be believed
that this argument was exploded by the critics
themselves, almost a century ago? De Wette, an
accomplished Hebraist and critic, who desired few
things more than to discover proofs of the late date

of the Book of Jonah, sets this argument definitely aside. In a note to paragraph 237 of his *Introduction*, he says: "The statement respecting the size of Nineveh (iii. 3) is of no importance in determining its date." The justice of this remark has been recognised by later Hebraists. The narrative being in the past tense, this verb "was" had, in accordance with the requirements of Hebrew grammar, to be in the past tense also. As to the rest, there is no reason whatever for doubt as to Jonah himself being the writer of the Book, notwithstanding his writing in the third person. Hosea's authorship of the Book which bears his name is not disputed; and yet we find that the opening words run thus: "And the Lord said to Hosea, Go and take . . . so he went and took," etc.

But our business at present is to show how very specially the statements of the Book have been confirmed by recent research; and therefore, first of all, to note how it has been assailed. The early Church had to encounter the ridicule of the nimble-witted Greeks, and their Roman and other pupils, proud of their philosophical knowledge, yet attracted to the gatherings of the believers of the new and now popular faith. Augustine says, with regard to Jonah's imprisonment in the belly of the fish: "I have heard this kind of inquiry ridiculed by pagans with great laughter." Theophylact bears similar testimony. He writes: "Jonah is therefore swallowed by a whale, and the prophet remains in it three days and the same number of nights; which appears to be beyond the power of the hearers to believe, chiefly of those who come to this history fresh from the schools of the Greeks and their wise teaching."

The objection sprang up again with the deism of the eighteenth century. It was equally unable to imagine a man's existing three days and three nights in the belly of a whale. It is in vain to reply that this was no more wonderful than the raising of a man from the dead, or the turning of water into wine, or the increase of the five barley loaves and the two small fishes, which were made to suffice for five thousand men, besides women and children, and to yield in addition thirteen baskets filled with the frag-ments. This does not clear away the difficulty, or stifle the laughter. These men believe in no miracle ; and, when they are pressed to say how life began upon the earth, or how it was undeniably and clearly predicted for ages that in the seed of Abraham—that is, in a Jew—men of all nationalities should find sal-vation, they have no reply. Miracles may be laughed at, and nevertheless be realities. But modern scepti-cism has added a buttress or two to the old unbelief. The objection no longer stalks about in the nakedness of its incredulity : it is now arrayed in the robe of superior knowledge. It speaks in the name of science, and tells us that there is no whale in the seas that could have swallowed Jonah ; that the throat of the whale, huge animal though it be, and, consequently, to an uninstructed mind entirely capable of such a feat as the Scripture records, is only about two inches in diameter !

This has been stated again and again to be a result of

scientific research; and it has been received as entirely disposing of the alleged miracle and of the claims of the Book. This assertion of scientific men has, as usual, also imposed upon Biblical scholars. There was, consequently, an immediate stampede from the whale, and a hurried attempt to find some other tenant of the ocean with reference to which the scientists could not urge the same objection. We were reminded by those, to whom we looked for help in a trying moment, that the Scripture did not say that it was a whale which swallowed Jonah, and that the expression is "a big fish." We were further informed that there were denizens of the deep which quite answered to this description, and which were also quite able to swallow the prophet. This is the line taken by so judicious and helpful a commentator as Keil, who says: "The great fish . . . which is not more precisely defined, was not a whale, because this is extremely rare in the Mediterranean, and has too small a throat to swallow a man, but a large shark, or sea-dog . . . . . which is very common in the Mediterranean, and has so large a throat, that it can swallow a living man whole." *

When such an impression was made upon orthodox scholarship, the panic among those who labour to retain the educated public within the Church, and who are constantly throwing overboard everything to which a scientist can object, may be imagined. Some declared that the Book must go. Others contended that only its historical character need be surrendered.

* *The Minor Prophets*, vol. i., p. 398.

Professor Reuss, of Strasburg, gives the following
account of how the earlier rationalism struggled to
get rid of the miraculous element in the Book.   He
says: " The most adventurous and the most absurd
interpretations took the place of the Biblical narrative.   Sometimes the scenes of the ship and of the
fish were accounted for as a dream of the prophet ;
sometimes Jonah, thrown into the sea, had the chance
of saving himself on the carcase of a dead whale.
At other times this [the whale] was changed into a
ship which bore that name and chanced to be passing ;
or possibly the whole of this part of the history was
merely the reflection of the hesitations, the want of
courage, the torments of conscience, of the dis-
obedient missionary.   Others pretended that they
recognised here a foreign myth, touched up, re-cast ;
for example, that of Andromeda, bound to a rock
near Joppa, and rescued by a sea monster; or that
of Hesione, delivered from a like peril by Hercules,
who on this occasion entered into the belly of the
animal; or, finally, that of Oannes, who, according
to the Babylonian mythology, taught the peoples the
arts and the sciences.   One sees without difficulty
that there is no resemblance between any of these
Greek or eastern fables and the substance of our
Book, in which the fish is only an accessory element
and which is certainly never in the slightest degree
identified with the prophet." *   Instructed, apparently, by these failures, Professor Reuss has cut the
knot which they tried to loose.   He has put the

* *La Bible, Philosophie Religieuse*, pp. 565, 566.

Book of Jonah outside the Canon, and has placed it in a collection which he calls *contes moraux,* " moral tales." * " Without troubling ourselves in the least," he says, " to criticise the miracle, we arrive at the conclusion that we have here before us a moral tale." †

Such is the short and easy method of the higher criticism with the Bible miracles. The older rationalism did think it had to save in some way the honour of the Bible. Its unbelief had not then attained the hardihood to thrust the claims of Scripture contemptuously aside, not to say to scout them openly. But to Prof. Reuss and his friends the Bible has no longer any honour to save. Ideas of its inspiration, and even of its historical accuracy, have long since been swept away before the unclouded sun of an infidelity that has all the scholarship and insight of finality. This is shown in the after criticism of the Book. Professor Kuenen deals in similar fashion with its history. "*A priori,*" he says, in his *Critical History of the Old Testament,* " nothing is able to inspire us with confidence in the credibility of the Book of Jonah. . In examining it more closely, one soon discovers how indefensible is the hypothesis according to which we have to do here with a historical writing. Here are the principal difficulties which present themselves. To begin with, can we figure to ourselves all the inhabitants of Nineveh converted *en masse* to Jehovah, after having listened for a single day to the preaching of an Israelitish prophet ? Admitting that he spoke their language, how would he be able

---

to attain this high authority over a people strangers
to the worship of Jehovah? If the Ninevites had
really been converted, would not pains have been
taken to instruct them in their new faith?" And
again: "Let us note the general tone of the narrative. Of the principal personage we learn merely the
name. As to 'the king of Nineveh' we know neither
how he is called, nor at what epoch he reigned. Nor
is anything more told of us of the ultimate fate of the
city, after iii. 10: 'And God repented of the evil that
He had said He would do unto them, and He did
it not'! Finally, we leave Jonah seated outside
Nineveh. Did he return into his fatherland? Did
he learn to bless the Divine mercy towards the
Ninevites? There is absolute silence upon all these
questions."

In other words, the Scripture must be written in
accordance with Professor Kuenen's ideas, and must
contain answers to all his questions, on pain of being
rejected at the critical tribunal. "The madness of
the prophet" is a Scriptural expression; we shall
have to place by the side of it this other—"the madness of the critic" who will no longer suffer God to
place us at His point of view, or permit Him to
emphasise those truths by speech and silence which
He desires us to consider! Our home criticism has
followed closely in the steps of that of the Continent.
We are here told on all hands that Jonah is an alle-
gory. It represents the swallowing up of Israel by
the Gentile nations, &c. "The author . . . takes a
traditional story about Jonah," says a writer who

has announced a gratifying change of view in some other matters, and who may also have now modified the belief to which he here gives expression—he takes the story, he says, "to convey through it a theological lesson of the utmost value. . . . . While we have no reason for regarding the historical part of the book as a narration of facts, we have every reason for treating the theology of the book as a revelation of God." In another passage he explains the reason for this representation. "If you start," he says, "with the demand that the episode of the fish is a matter of faith, you at once close the book and its message to the modern mind."

Dean Farrar, after a reference to the mention of Jonah in 2 Kings, writes: "We know nothing farther about him from the historic books, nor is it possible to tell whether this anonymous narrative of uncertain date was intended to represent fact or psychological fiction."* Finding, however, that it can be made to teach a lesson, he counsels that we cease "to pore over the whale and forget God." Dr. C. H. H. Wright, in his *Biblical Essays*, has contended strongly that the Book is allegorical, an opinion to which the writer on Jonah, in Dr. Wright's "International Teachers' Bible," is inclined to lean. Prof. George Adam Smith, with characteristic strenuousness, not only maintains the same view, but actually anathematises all who persist in accepting the Book as history, and in taking, as he says, God's "poetry as prose." But Jonah was at least a historical person. He is

---

* *The Supremacy of the Bible*, p. 234.

described in the opening words of the Book as "Jonah the son of Amittai;" and in 2 Kings xiv. 25 we read that Jeroboam II. "restored the coast of Israel from the entering of Hamath unto the sea of the plain, according to the word of the Lord God of Israel, which he spake by the hand of his servant Jonah, the son of Amittai, the prophet, who was of Gath-hepher." He was consequently a prophet as well known in Israel in that age as Isaiah and Jeremiah were in Judah in later times.

And the references of our Lord to the narrative leave us in no doubt as to its character. Its incidents are assumed to be history, and neither parable, nor fiction. Our Lord refers to the very feature in the history which excites to-day the fiercest derision: "For as Jonas was three days and three nights in the whale's belly; so shall the Son of Man be three days and three nights in the heart of the earth " (Matthew xii. 40). This reference may be explained away. It may be said that it is possible for us to illustrate a real incident by a fictitious one; but common-sense will always enter its protest against such an exposition of the words. It will ask also whether it is consistent with those words which immediately precede: "An evil and adulterous generation seeketh after a sign, and there shall no sign be given to it, but the sign of the prophet Jonas" (verse 39). Here it is plainly implied that Jonah had been a sign; in other words, that the experience had been actually endured by the prophet, and had attracted the attention of Israel. In Luke xi. 30 we learn also that the sign extended to the men of Nineveh—" For as Jonas was a sign unto the Ninevites, so shall also the Son of Man be to this generation." And, though all these passages might be successfully wrestled with, the victory would be fruitless. For it is simply impossible by any sophistry to escape the force of the following words : "The men of Nineveh shall rise in judgment with this generation, and shall condemn it ; because they repented at the preaching of Jonas ; and, behold, a greater than Jonas is here " (Matthew xii. 41). The contemporaries of Jesus, who treated so lightly the invitations and the warnings of the Son of God, could scarcely be condemned by a fiction ; and the words that follow allow no escape. The men of Nineveh "repented at the preaching of Jonas." There is no possible means of stating a fact more absolutely than is done in that expression. The Scripture stands or falls with the historical character of the Book of Jonah.

CHAPTER II.

WAS IT POSSIBLE FOR THE WHALE TO SWALLOW JONAH ?

IN touching now upon the miracle of Jonah's preservation, I shall limit myself to what those who spoke in the much-abused name of science have contradicted. It has often been asked how Jonah's life was preserved during the three days and the three

nights in which he was imprisoned within the whale.
How did he find air to breathe, or power to withstand
the animal's internal heat ?   To these, as to all such
questions, there is but one possible reply.   The
preservation of the prophet was part of the miracle.
It was part of God's marvellous working, with
regard to which, though it passes our power to understand it, our reason is, nevertheless, perfectly satisfied.
For the Cause of all causes is there; and all our
questionings die down in utter restfulness before Him
of whom we have known enough to understand that
He is marvellous in counsel, and His ways past
finding out.   I cannot tell how Christ was raised
from the dead; but I know that His resurrection is a
fact.   The new apostolic manhood tells me that, and
a world renewed proclaims it.   I cannot tell how the
heavens and the earth were created; nor is science
able to explain to me how matter was brought into
being, its ultimate atoms "manufactured," and life
afterwards introduced upon our earth.   Yet science
assures me that the ultimate atoms of matter are
really "manufactured articles," and that life has also
been created.   And now, where science is dumb, and
can tell me nothing more, I am satisfied; for all
these mysteries find their explanations in the infinite
wisdom and power of God.   "Through faith we
understand that the worlds were framed by the word
of God" (Hebrews xi. 3).

I therefore leave all that, without any attempt to
pierce a veil which no man can penetrate; and I
confine myself to the statement that the Scripture

shows ignorance when it implies, as it plainly does, that the whale was able to swallow Jonah.

The *Speaker's Commentary* had in this, as in so much besides, struck the right track. Prebendary Huxtable, to whom this Book was assigned, has the following note which deserves reproduction. " The observation has been frequently repeated that the whale has so small a throat, as to be incapable of swallowing a man. That is, beyond question, true in respect to the *True*, or *Greenland Whale* (the Arctic Right Whale, the *Balæna Mysticetus* of Cuvier and other naturalists); but it is not true of all species of whales. The natural history of these monsters of the deep, whom it is not very easy to subject to investigation, is invested with much uncertainty ; their classification, indeed, has varied in the hands of successive naturalists so greatly, as to make it extremely difficult even to name some of them with precision. The one kind which, next to the *Greenland Whale*, we know the most about, is the *Great Spermaceti Whale* (the *Physeter Catodon* of Linnæus, the *Cachalot Macrocephalus* of Cuvier and Lacépède) ; whose natural history has been elucidated by one, who enjoyed ample opportunities of studying it, in a work entirely devoted to the subject *(Observations on the Natural History of the Spermaceti Whale*, by Thomas Beale, surgeon, London, 1839; and in page 294 of his work Mr. Beale expressly observes : 'The throat is capacious enough to give passage to the body of a man, presenting a strong contrast to the contracted gullet of the Greenland whale.' The presence of these *Physeters* in the Mediterranean is

K

expressly asserted by Cuvier in his *Regne Animal*,
vol. i., p. 342."

The reply indicated in Beale's book has now been
put upon a broader basis by Mr. Frank Bullen in his
Cruise of the Cachalot. In this charming book, he
describes a struggle with a huge sperm whale, or
cachalot. After telling of its capture, he writes:
' During the conflict I had not noticed what now,
claimed attention—several great masses of white,
semi-transparent-looking substance floating about, of
huge size and irregular shape. But one of these
curious lumps came floating by, as we lay, tugged at
by several fish, and I immediately asked the mate if
he could tell me what it was, and where it came from.
He told me that, when dying, the cachalot always
ejected the contents of his stomach, which were invariably composed of such masses as we saw before
us; that he believed the stuff to be portions of big
cuttle-fish, bitten off by the whale for the purpose of
swallowing, but he wasn't sure. Anyhow, I could
bring this piece alongside now, if I liked, and see.
Secretly wondering at the indifference shown by this
officer of forty years' whaling experience to such a
wonderful fact as appeared to be here presented, I
thanked him, and, sticking the boat-hook into the
lump, drew it alongside. It was at once evident that
it was a massive fragment of cuttle-fish—tentacle or
arm—as thick as a stout man's body, and with six or
seven sucking discs, or *acetabula* on it. These were
about as large as a saucer, and on their inner edge
were thickly set with hooks or claws all round the

rim, sharp as needles, and almost the shape and size of a tiger's.

" To what manner of awful monster this portion of limb belonged I could only faintly imagine; but of course I remembered, as any sailor would, that from my earliest sea-going I had been told that the cuttle-fish was the biggest in the sea, although I never even began to think that it might be true until now. I asked the mate if he had ever seen such creatures as this piece belonged to alive and kicking. He answered, languidly, 'Wall, I guess so; but I don't take any stock in fish, 'cept for provisions er ile—en thet's a fact.' It will be readily believed that I vividly recalled this conversation when, many years after, I read an account by the prince of Monaco of *his* discovery of a gigantic squid to which his naturalist gave the name of *lepido-teuthis grimaldii!* Truly the indifference and apathy manifested by whalers generally to everything except commercial matters is wonderful—hardly to be credited. However, this was a mighty revelation to me. For the first time, it was possible to understand that, contrary to the usual notion of a whale's being unable to swallow a herring, here was a kind of whale that could swallow—well, a block four or five feet square, apparently; who lived upon creatures as large as himself, if one might judge of their bulk by the sample to hand; but being unable, from only possessing teeth in one jaw, to masticate his food, was com-pelled to tear it in sizable pieces, bolt it whole, and leave his commissariat department to do the rest." [*]

---

[*] *The Cruise of the Cachalot*, by Frank Bullen, pp. 77-79.

Describing another specimen, he says : " The lower jaw of this whale measured exactly nineteen feet in length from the opening of the mouth, or, say the last of the teeth, to the point, and carried twenty-eight teeth on each side." *   But both of these were put in the shade by a subsequent capture.   Of this he says : "The ejected food was in masses of enormous size, larger than any we had yet seen on the voyage, some of them being estimated to be of the size of the hatch-house, *viz.*, eight feet by six feet into six feet." †
In other words, this whale had swallowed, and afterwards, when dying, had vomited up in its entirety, a mass which was two feet longer than a tall man, and whose other dimensions were about thirty-six feet square, or equal in breadth and width to the bodies of six very stout men rolled into one !

The question has been partly answered already as to whence these huge masses come. Mr. Bullen was privileged, however, to behold a startling spectacle which fully solved that problem.   " There was a violent commotion," he writes, " in the sea, right where the moon's rays were concentrated, so great that, remembering our position, I was at first inclined to alarm all hands ; for I had often heard of volcanic islands suddenly lifting their heads from the depths below, or disappearing in a moment, and with the Sumatra's chain of active volcanoes so near, I felt doubtful indeed of what was now happening. Getting the night-glasses out of the cabin, where they always hung in readiness, I focussed them on the troubled spot, perfectly satisfied that neither volcanoes nor earthquakes had anything to do with what was going on; yet so vast were the forces engaged that I might well have been excused for my first supposition.

"A very large sperm whale was locked in deadly conflict with a cuttle-fish, or squid, almost as large as himself, whose interminable tentacles seemed to enlace the whole of his great body. The head of the whale especially seemed a perfect network of writhing arms—naturally, I suppose, for it appeared as if the whale had the tail part of the mollusc in his jaws, and in a business-like, methodical way, was sawing through it. By the side of the black columnar head of the whale appeared the head of the great squid, as awful an object as one could well imagine even in a fevered dream. Judging as carefully as possible, I estimated it to be at least as large as one of our barrels (pyxes), which contained 350 gallons; but it may have been, and probably was, a good deal larger. The eyes were very remarkable from their size and blackness, which, contrasted with the livid whiteness of the head, made their appearance all the more striking. They were at least a foot in diameter, and, seen under such conditions, looked exceedingly eerie and hobgoblin-like. All around the combatants were numerous sharks, like jackals round a lion, ready to share the feast, and apparently assisting in the destruction of the huge cephalopod. So the Titanic struggle went on, in perfect silence, so far as we were concerned, because, had there been any noise, our distance from the scene of conflict would not have permitted us to hear it." *

These facts make an end of the objection that no whale could have swallowed Jonah. The scientists who said that, and the critics and others who repeated it, were speaking not from their knowledge but from their ignorance. There are over sixty kinds of whales; and every one of them, with the solitary exception of the Greenland whale, has a gullet in proportion to its size. Scientists were arguing from the exception to the rule. A most interesting, though humiliating, volume might be written about the mistakes of science, which, unlike the alleged mistakes of the Bible, have been very real, and not seldom very terrible. Medicine, for example, has had sometimes to revolutionise its beliefs, and to completely reverse its treatment. It has had to acknowledge that, instead of fighting against disease, and along with the natural forces operating for the patient's recovery, it had been doing the exact opposite. These things would make some sad chapters; but I do not know that, seen in the light of eternity, there would be one sadder than that which would tell how men, in the name of science, falsely so called, have belied that only fountain of light and life for humanity—the Bible.

* Pages 143, 144.

CHAPTER III.

Why Jonah Fled.

———

THE statement that "Jonah rose up to flee unto Tarshish from the presence of the Lord" (i. 3) has brought down upon the Book the critical condemnation. God is here conceived of, it is urged, as confined to the land occupied by the tribes of Israel. If Jonah were only once well away from Palestine— if he can escape, for example, to Tarshish—it is imagined, we are told, that he will dwell in peace. The command of the Lord to go to Nineveh, or anywhere besides, will not trouble him there! How unworthy a conception of God, say they, is this. And they indicate that little besides is required to justify such action as that of Prof. Reuss in placing the Book outside the Canon of Scripture.

But critics, like more ordinary mortals, do not always remember everything. How does this supposed crude conception of God agree with the late date to which they assign the Book of Jonah? At the time when they say it was written, they themselves tell us, the thought of Israel regarding God had widened. The older and grosser conceptions had passed away. Israel then recognised Jehovah as the Creator of heaven and earth, omnipotent and omnipresent. But if all that be so, whence comes this conception which they condemn? It is quite clear that one of two conclusions must be admitted by any logical critic. Either Israel was *not* then delivered from its crude notions about God, seeing that even a prophet can imagine that Tarshish is outside the sphere of God's presence,—or the Book of Jonah was written in an earlier and darker time.

To one of these two conclusions their reading of these words must bind them. But, for our own part, we meet overwhelming evidence that Israel knew of God's omnipresence from the first ; and, instead of discovering any contrary belief in these words, we find in them the key to what have seemed to be the enigmas of the Book. One wonders whether these men, all of whom are more or less connected with the ministry of the Gospel, have ever entreated their hearers to "come to God," or to "come to Christ." Have they never at any time spoken about a sinner "returning to God"? And what would they say or think, if, at the close of such an address, some one were to wait upon them and express astonishment at their crude conceptions of the Deity? And if the protesting hearer went on to inquire how he could be asked "to return to God," or "to come to God," seeing that we are never at any moment outside God's presence, would they not conclude that the man was either a lunatic or an idiot? There is plainly another, and that a very real, sense in which Jonah could go from God's presence.

Is there anything, then, in the circumstances of the time which throws light upon the prophet's action? When that question is asked, an evident reply suggests

itself. Assyria had been laying her hand for some
generations upon the nations on the Mediterranean
coast, and it was the hand of a fierce and ferocious
mastery. No considerations of pity were permitted
to stand in the way of Assyrian policy. It could
not afford to garrison its conquests, and it practised
a plan which largely dispensed with the necessity for
leaving garrisons behind the Assyrian armies. There
was unsparing slaughter to begin with. The kings
seem to gloat in their inscriptions over the spectacle
presented by the field of battle. They describe how
it was covered with the corpses of the vanquished.
This carnage was followed up by fiendish inflictions
upon individual cities. The leading men, as at
Lachish when Sennacherib had conquered that city,
were led forth, seized by the executioners, and subjected to various punishments, all of them filled to
the brim with horror. Some of the victims were
held down while one of the band of torturers, who
are pourtrayed upon the monuments gloating fiend-
ishly over their fearful work, inserts his hand into
the victim's mouth, grips his tongue, and wrenches
it out by the roots. In another spot pegs are driven
into the ground. To these, another victim's wrists
are fixed with cords. His ankles are similarly made
fast, and the man is stretched out, unable to move a
muscle. The executioner then applies himself to his
task; and, beginning at the accustomed spot, the
sharp knife makes its incision, the skin is raised inch
by inch till the man is flayed alive. These skins are
then stretched out upon the city walls, or otherwise

disposed of, so as to terrify the people and leave behind long-enduring impressions of Assyrian vengeance. For others, long sharp poles are prepared. The sufferer, taken like all the rest from the leading men of the city, is laid down ; the sharpened end of the pole is driven in through the lower part of the chest ; the pole is then raised, bearing the writhing victim aloft ; it is planted in the hole dug for it, and the man is left to die.

No man in Israel was ignorant of these things. Jonah may have witnessed them. Without doubt, too, Jonah knew that Assyria, this spoiler of the nations, was the appointed executioner of God's vengeance upon the ten tribes. It was not hid from the prophets of Judah that their people were to fall under the hand of a nation that had not yet risen to supreme power. They knew that Babylon was to pour out upon Judah the fierceness of God's wrath. In like manner did God deal with the prophets of God in Israel who had a harder task than that, heavy though it was, of their Judæan fellow-labourers. Hosea predicts clearly that Israel shall be rooted up and "eat unclean things in Assyria." Now, say that this counsel of Jehovah had been revealed to Jonah, can we not understand his action? The word of the Lord came: "Arise, go to Nineveh, that great city, and cry against it ; for their wickedness is come up before Me " (i. 2). Nineveh's cup, then, was full. The Judge had ascended the tribunal. The cause had been placed before Him. Sentence was about to be pronounced. Gladder news than this, Jonah's ears had never heard. If Nineveh perished, Israel was saved! This fearful scourge would be tossed into the fire, before it had time tò fall upon poor Israel's already bleeding shoulders. There was only one thing to be feared: God's mercy might arrest the smiting of God's justice. Jonah knew that He was a merciful God, and that, if even Nineveh cried to Him, Assyria might be saved, and then Israel would perish. But what if Nineveh were left without warning? What if she and her princes were now abandoned to reap the reward of their fearful atrocities?

It was a choice between vengeance on him, a rebellious prophet, and vengeance on his people. He would sacrifice himself, let Nineveh perish, and so save Israel! That seems to have been Jonah's purpose and the reason of his sorrow at Nineveh's escape. Paul said he was willing even to be accursed —cast out from God's presence—if by that means Israel could be saved. It was Christ's resolve when He saved us; for He was made a curse for us. The Lord has told us that Jonah was a type of Himself. The type may have begun there. The expression that Jonah " fled from the presence of the Lord " is repeated in i. 10. It is this fact which makes the mightiest impression upon his fellow-voyagers. "Then were the men exceedingly afraid, and said unto him, Why hast thou done this? For the men knew that he fled from the presence of the Lord, because he had told them." And it will be noticed that Jonah, though he confesses to these men, makes no confession to God. When he is cast overboard, there is no prayer, no cry to the Lord, from the prophet's lips. He has counted the cost. He has put himself outside God's mercy. He has made himself a curse for his people's sake; and, in the calmness of that eternal sacrifice, he resigns himself to his fate. The time has come to pay the price; and he pays it!

CHAPTER IV.

PROOFS OF THE HISTORICAL CHARACTER OF THE BOOK.

IT is impossible for any writer, who alludes to the circumstances of his own time, not to leave the mark of the age upon his work. He writes out of a full acquaintance and actual contact with the time which no mere description, however full, can possibly convey to a later author. The Book of Jonah, much as its claims to be ranked as history have been scouted, may be cited as an example and illustration of this universal law.

There are several allusions, for instance, to the extraordinary extent of the Assyrian capital. The Book begins with the words: "Now the word of the Lord came unto Jonah the son of Amittai, saying, Arise, go to Nineveh, that great city" (i. 1, 2). We meet, in iii. 3, the statement: "Now Nineveh was an exceeding great city of three days' journey;"

and the Book ends with the question addressed by
God to the prophet: "And should not I spare
Nineveh, that great city, wherein are more than
sixscore thousand persons that cannot discern between their right hand and their left hand; and
also much cattle?" (iv. 11). This last statement
implies a large population—not less than a million—
and an enormous extent for the city. The walled
towns of Babylonia seem to have enclosed large
spaces for cultivation and pasture, so that they were
able to stand a prolonged siege. That Nineveh was
a city of this kind is indicated by the reference to its
"much cattle."

This allusion, which has excited the smiles of
unbelief, has startled the rationalistic Assyriologist.
Schrader has directed attention to the fact that
Nineveh was really signalised by this extraordinary
extent. He says, it is true, that the full compass was
not attained till Sargon, the father of Sennacherib,
had erected a certain quarter of it, and this at a
period somewhat subsequent to the time of Jonah.
It is not unlikely, however, that Sargon built upon
an old site, and did not alter the huge lines of the
older fortifications. The city, as it stood in Sargon's
day, *was ninety miles in circumference,* and was, literally, "an exceeding great city of three days' journey."

As we have already seen, the critics have asked
whether it is at all likely that the people of Nineveh
would have been so moved by the preaching of
a foreign prophet. But, if Nineveh was at that
very time filled with apprehensions of approaching

calamity, we can well understand how, as the spark
thrown among dried wood produces a speedy conflagration, the excited fears of Nineveh might, with
this new incident, have issued in just such a deep
and universal repentance as the Scripture describes.
Was there anything, then, in Nineveh's position at
that time which sheds light upon this matter? Prof.
Rawlinson has long ago pointed out that, just at the
time of Jonah, Nineveh was undergoing what seemed
likely to be a final eclipse. "With Iva-lush IV.," he
writes, " the glories of the Nimrod line of monarchs
came to a close, and Assyrian history is once more
shrouded in darkness for a space of nearly forty
years, from B.C. 781 to B.C. 744. . . In the declining
condition of Assyria, under the kings who followed
Iva-lush IV., there was naturally a growth of power
and independence among the border countries.
Babylon, repenting of the submission which she had
made, either to Iva-lush IV., or to his father Shamas-
Iva, once more vindicated her right to freedom,
and resumed the position of a separate and hostile
monarchy. Samaria, Damascus, Judæa, ceased to
pay tribute. Enterprising kings like Jeroboam the
Second and Menahem, taking advantage of Assyria's
weakness, did not content themselves with merely
throwing off her yoke, but proceeded to enlarge their
dominions at the expense of her feudatories. Judging
of the unknown from the known, we may assume
that, on the north and east there were similar defec-
tions to those on the west and south—that the tribes
of Armenia and of the Zagros range rose in revolt,

and that the Assyrian boundaries were thus contracted in every quarter." *

It is equally plain from the Scripture narrative, as
Professor Rawlinson here indicates, that this was a
time when the Assyrian power was experiencing an
alarming decline. No fear of Assyrian reprisals
weighed upon the Israelitish king or people, and no
hope of Assyrian succour enabled the neighbouring
peoples to withstand the advance of the armies of
Israel. Jeroboam II., the king in whose reign Jonah
seems to have lived, "restored the coast of Israel
from the entering of Hamath unto the sea of the
plain." This means that the hand and the terror of
Assyria were for the time withdrawn. The wounded
lion seems to have been driven back to his lair. The
hunters were closing in upon him, and the fear that, as
former powers had passed away, so Assyria's final hour
was come, was already whispering its forebodings of
overthrow and massacre. Jonah's message was one
for which the time was ripe. It gave utterance to the
burdened spirit, and the hearts of the thousands of
Nineveh were bowed as the heart of one man.

But was it at all likely that the State would interfere in this matter, and that a royal edict would be
issued enjoining a prolonged fast? Was action of
that kind at all in accord with Assyrian custom? We
know what the higher criticism thinks of it, and what
rationalism has thought of it all along—for to them
it has seemed one of the big improbabilities of the
story—but what has the Assyriologist, who has got

* *Ancient Monarchies*, vol. ii., pp. 379, 380.

back through one discovery after another to this ancient people and to these very times, to say of it? Here is the reply. "It is just such a fast," says Professor Sayce, "as was ordained by Esarhaddon II. when the northern foe was gathering against the Assyrian empire, and prayers were raised to the sungod to 'remove the sin' of the king and his people. 'From this day,' runs the inscription, 'from the third day of this month, even the month Iyyar, to the fifteenth day of Ab of this year, for these hundred days (and) hundred nights the prophets have proclaimed (a period of supplication).' The prophets of Nineveh had declared that it was needful to appease the anger of heaven, and the king accordingly issued his proclamation enjoining the solemn service of humiliation for one hundred days."[*]

There was one feature, however, in the fast mentioned in Scripture, which is not repeated in the above decree. The very beasts were to share in this humiliation before God. "And he caused it to be proclaimed and published through Nineveh by the decree of the king and his nobles, saying, Let neither man nor beast, herd nor flock, taste any thing: let them not feed, nor drink water: but let man and beast be covered with sackcloth, and cry mightily unto God" (iii. 7, 8). There is no notice of such an extension of the humiliation in the Assyrian decree just quoted. The idea of it is not one that would occur to us in any circumstances; and, judging from the utter silence of the Scriptures, it is a notion which was equally strange to the

[*] *The Higher Criticism versus the Monuments*, pp. 489, 490.

Israelitish people. But was it as far removed from the customs of the Assyrians; or were they likely, in a moment of supreme peril, to resort to just such an act as this? Herodotus has answered that question long ago. He tells us that, when the Persian armies were in Greece, a battle was fought in which a general, endeared to the whole army, was slain. "On their arrival at the camp," says Herodotus, "the death of Masistius spread a general sorrow through the army, and greatly afflicted Mardonius himself. They cut off the hair from themselves, their horses, and their beasts of burden, and all Bœotia resounded with their cries and lamentations. The man they had lost was, next to Mardonius, most esteemed by the Persians and the king. Thus the barbarians *in their manner* honoured the deceased Masistius." * Strange as was the practice to the Jews, and strange as it is to ourselves, it was not strange "to the barbarians," the men who had come from those very regions in which the Assyrians had lived, and over which they had ruled. It was "their manner," and was naturally resorted to in a time of deadly peril for man and beast.

There is one other thing with a notice of which this chapter and this extended reference to the Book of Jonah may fitly close. A word was spoken by our Lord, which no treatment of the Book of Jonah ought to overlook. He said that His generation sought a sign—a sign that would end their doubt and their hesitation, and show them once for all that

* IX. 24.

L

this was the Christ. He declared that no such sign as they desired should be given them. But, said He, they should nevertheless have a sign, and that, "the sign of the Prophet Jonas." What did the words mean? Look back over those well-nigh nineteen centuries, and you will read the answer. When Jonah, having become a curse for his people, came back, as it were, from the dead, whither did he carry the word of the Lord? To Israel? No; to the Gentile city of Nineveh. And there he beheld what he had in vain longed and prayed to see among his own people—the turning of a whole city to God —the leaders leading for once in the right direction, and the entire people following and seeking God with purpose of heart. When Christ came back from the grave, and the word of the Lord was once more to be proclaimed, whither was it carried? It was borne to the Gentiles. And how fared it with the message there? The Word of Life, which Israel had rejected, these received. Age after age the Jew has been confronted with that sign. He asked whether this was, or was not, the Christ. Jesus said the reply would be found in the sign of the prophet Jonas. And this is the enigma of enigmas to the Jew. He has never been able to get away from it. He is confronted with it to-day. He killed the Messiah—in ignorance, and at the impulse of the evil heart that is in us all, he did it. And out of the grave of the Crucified has come this power that has tamed the barbarian, changed the savage, cleansed and raised the hopelessly debased, brought back the outcast races into the brotherhood of man, and given to all who have received the message, the nobleness, the spiritual insight, the compassions, and the purity of the children of God. He, who said that the Jew should have that sign, read the future. He gave a promise, and rising from His grave, He has kept it. He has proved His claim to be the Son of God and the world's Saviour. He has attested the Book of Jonah; He has attested the entire Scripture; and for us that attestation is final.

THE PROPHECY OF NAHUM—WHEN WAS IT WRITTEN ?

THE brief prophecy of Nahum, consisting of three short chapters, 47 verses in all, has awakened the admiration of the rationalistic critics. De Wette, for instance, the unemotional character of whose writing was admitted even by his friends, becomes warm in his description of *Nahum*. "The reader of taste and sensibility," he says, "will be affected by the entire structure of the poem, by the agreeable manner in which the ideas are brought forward, by the flexibility of the expressions, the roundness of his phrases, the delicacy of his figures, by the strength and delicacy, and the expression of sympathy and greatness which diffuse themselves over the whole subject." The poetic power and beauty of the Book have similarly impressed all who have studied it.

But when we ask where the prophet lived, and at what time his prophecy was written, we encounter the most conflicting replies. The title of the Book is: " The Burden of Nineveh : the Book of the vision of Nahum the Elkoshite." This seems to settle the question of place. Nahum was a native of Elkosh. But, when we have noted that fact, we are merely entering upon our difficulties. For, when we inquire where Elkosh was situated, we receive various answers between which most people find it difficult to decide. There was an ancient Jewish tradition that it was Alkush in Assyria. That town was situated on the eastern bank of the Tigris, a mile or two above Mosul. It was natural for the Jews, after the dispersion at the beginning of the Christian era, when they were prohibited from entering Palestine, and when Babylon was an important Jewish centre, to multiply sacred shrines in that neighbourhood. The notion, however, has been received favourably by some, who have imagined that Nahum's parents may have been Israelitish captives, carried away in the reign of Tiglath-pileser. Another identification has, however, been received with greater favour. Jerome was shown a place in Galilee which bore this name; and it has been remarked that Capernaum means, literally, "the village of Nahum." The opinion has consequently been general that he was a native of Galilee. In any case, he would seem, from references in the Prophecy, to have lived in Palestine.

We are now concerned, however, with the question as to *when* the Prophecy was written. On this point views have been widely different both in ancient and in modern times. "Attempts have been made," says a writer, "to fix the date with precision, from the allusion to the destruction of No-Ammon, or Thebes, in Egypt; but as it is uncertain when this event took place, Eichhorn and others have conjectured that it was near the beginning of the reign of Hezekiah, or about B.C. 720, as about this time Sargon, king of Assyria, waged an unsuccessful war against Egypt (Isaiah xx.)"

Fortunately, we are now able to remove all doubt upon this point, and so to fix an approximate date for the prophecy. The following is the passage in which the reference occurs. The prophet, addressing Nineveh, asks: "Art thou better than populous No *(No-Amōn)*, that was situate among the rivers *(yeorim)*, that had the waters round about it, whose rampart was the sea, and her wall was from the sea? Ethiopia and Egypt were her strength, and it was infinite; Put and Lubim were thy helpers. Yet was she carried away, she went into captivity: her young children also were dashed in pieces at the top of all the streets: and they cast lots for all her honourable men, and all her great men were bound in chains" (iii. 8-10).

Of what importance the help is which has been derived from recent research is shown by the above quotation. "Populous No" is a rendering of the Hebrew which was the best that our translators could give at the time. They were not aware that *Amōn* was not a Hebrew word, but was, on the contrary, an

Egyptian term, the name, indeed, of the great Egyptian divinity. But it is with this god Amōn that we have here to do, and the *No-Amōn* in the Hebrew text means simply the dwelling or place of the god Amōn. *Yeorim*, translated "rivers," is the plural of the Egyptian name for the Nile. That river was also frequently spoken of as the sea; and this use of the word, which was unknown to ancient translators and commentators, misled them in the identification of the ancient city here referred to. It is said that "her rampart is the sea," and that "her wall was from the sea." It seemed clear from this that No-Amōn must have been on the coast; and so Jerome inserted in his Latin translation (the Vulgate) Alexandria for No-Amōn. It was only slowly that even Archæologists were led to the correct identification. Champollion, for example, said, in his *Egypt under the Pharaohs:* "The description which the prophet gives of No-Amon agrees, in all respects, with Diospolis in Lower Egypt."* The identification of the great city with Thebes, which had already been suggested, he distinctly set aside.

The Assyrian monuments have now, however, closed this discussion. They have settled, first of all, the identity of No-Amōn. No, or rather, Ni'a, which exactly corresponds to the form in the original Hebrew, is the name applied to Thebes in the Assyrian inscriptions. "Thebes, called No," says Mariette, is "*the* city *par excellence.*" The name "No-Amon"—the city of the god Amon—in Nahum

---

indicates its special sacredness in the eyes of the Egyptians, and indeed of the then civilised world. Oppert says: * "Thebes was the seat of the special worship of the god *Amoun*, whom Herodotus (II. 42) identifies with the Greek *Zeus*, and so the name which the Greeks gave to the great Egyptian city was *Diospolis*," that is, "the city of God." The Bible description of the ancient and famous capital of southern Egypt is absolutely correct in other respects as well. It was in the midst of the waters, being built on both banks of the Nile, and having no doubt canals led round the whole extent of the fortifications. Her "rampart" also "was the sea"—the huge river that flowed through its midst; and "her wall was from the sea," going down on each side to the water's edge. "Ethiopia and Egypt were her strength." She lay on the border land of both countries, then among the very mightiest in the world. Help could be summoned from Egypt on the north, and from Ethiopia on the south.

But Assyriology has done more than assist us to identify the place. It has also recorded the time and the manner of its overthrow. Assurbanipal, the conqueror of Thebes, has himself told the story which Assyriology has now recovered and interpreted for us. He says :—

> In my second campaign, towards Egypt and Ethiopia
>
> I directed my march. Urduman

---

* *Mémoire sur les Rapports de l'Egypte et de L'Assyrie,* p. 620.

heard of the progress of my expedition and that
    I had crossed
the frontiers of Egypt.   He abandoned Memphis,
    and,
to save his life, he fled to Thebes.
The kings, the chiefs, and the governors whom I
    had established in Egypt
came into my presence and embraced my feet.
I followed the route which Urduman had taken,
I went to Thebes, the strong city.
He saw the approach of my mighty army and he
    abandoned Thebes,
and he fled to Kip-kip.   This city (Thebes)
in its entirety, for the service of Assur and of
    Istar, my hands took it ;
the silver, the gold, the precious stones, its palace
    furniture, everything which it contained,
male and female slaves,
two lofty obelisks, covered with beautiful sculp-
    tures,
2,500 talents * were their weight, set up before
    the gate of a temple,
from their place I raised them and transported
    them into Assyria.
A booty great and countless I carried away from
    the midst of Thebes.+

Another inscription indicates how completely
Thebes was sacked and destroyed.   One line says :

They carried away everything from the city and
    destroyed it like a flood.

---

* " Over ninety tons," remarks Mr. Geo. Smith.
| See Geo. Smith, *Assyrian Discoveries*, pp. 328, 329, and Alden Smith, *Die Keilschrifttexte Assurbanipal's*, I. 12-15.

This invasion took place in 664 or 663 B.C. Everyone has admitted that the Book of Nahum refers to this as a quite recent event, and it must therefore have been written shortly after this date. Nineveh fell about 608 B.C.; it fell as Nahum had predicted, and was desolated (just as he had pictured) by fire and by water: and it fell for ever. "The Lord hath given a commandment concerning thee," wrote the prophet of the oppressor, "that no more of thy name be sown: out of the house of thy gods will I cut off the graven image and the molten: I will make thy grave; for thou art vile" (i. 14). And again: "There is no healing of thy bruise; thy wound is grievous: all that hear the bruit of thee shall clap the hands over thee: for upon whom hath not thy wickedness passed continually" (iii. 19)?

The date of the prediction is, therefore, fixed by this discovery of Assurbanipal's inscription. It must have been composed about 660 B.C. But we must not miss the lesson yielded by the long-continued doubt as to the period in which the Book was written. Eichhorn believed, as we have seen, that Nahum must have prophesied about 720 B.C. De Wette and Knobel suggested 710 B.C. But the remarkable fact in connection with these discussions is the attempts made by all alike to get hold of some *historical* basis. On the mere evidence of language and of style the critics proceed to cut up the Pentateuch. They know, to a year, they assure us, when this or that portion must have been composed or inserted; and because of their so-called "results" the Churches are now asked to revolutionise their views of the Scripture and to revise their creeds. But in regard to Nahum it was universally admitted that no appeal to language or to style was able to fix the date of the composition. The purity of the language lent countenance, indeed, but nothing more, to the belief that Nahum must have been a contemporary of Isaiah. And now even that notion has been swept away by the discovery to which I have just referred. If language and style, therefore, afford no foundation, or only a fallacious foundation, for ascertaining the date of Nahum, how can we be asked by rational and honest men to accept these as absolutely sufficient for the partition and the desecration of the Books of Moses?

THE BOOK OF DANIEL.

CHAPTER I.

The Book and the Critics.

WHEN the Jews were torn away from the land of promise, and were left in Chaldæan bondage, signs were given that in wrath God remembered mercy. Two prophets were assigned to them, who spent their lives with and for their afflicted brethren. Ezekiel was devoted entirely to the prophetic service, and communicated the word of the Lord to the great body of the captives, whom even their terrible chastisements had not severed from their sins. To Daniel another vocation was assigned. Like a second Joseph, he carried immense and Divinely-given administrative capacity into the cabinets of the world's rulers, and, by his services, paved the way for his nation's acceptance with their Gentile sovereigns, and to the favour which eventually led to their return. But to Daniel further grace was given. The statesman became a prophet. Revelations were given him in which he has set before his people, and the Christian Church, the chart of the world's entire history. The great world-wide dominions are set before us. They are to come in a certain order which is definitely stated. There are to be four of them, and four only. The fifth universal kingdom is to be the Lord's; and His coming, and the sufferings and the struggles which will precede it, are set before us in words which have become clearer as the ages have rolled on, and which will, no doubt, yet shine out like the pillar of fire when the last darkness falls.

What the Church would lose were this Book snatched away from it, this glance at its mission will indicate. It is significant of the Book's value, as ministering to the Church's hope, that it has been singled out for special assault almost from the first. Jerome has the following reference to the objections urged by Porphyry, a heathen opponent of early Christianity. "Porphyry," he says, "wrote his twelfth book against Daniel the Prophet, wishing to prove that the Book was not written by him with whose name it is inscribed, but by someone who had been in Judæa, in the time of Antiochus Epiphanes, and that the Book of Daniel did not so much foretell things which were to come, as relate events which had taken place; and, finally, that whatever was related of the times before Antiochus was true history, but when he attempted to go beyond this, his remarks were false, because he was ignorant of the future. Eusebius, Appolinaris, and Methodius," he adds, "replied to these arguments."

These objections were revived first by the English deists of the seventeenth century, and then by the higher criticism. De Wette speaks of Daniel as "fiction," and states the critical hypothesis in words which criticism still accepts. "At the time of Antiochus Epiphanes, when prophecy," he says, "was quite extinct, a Jewish patriot wished to excite his suffering and struggling countrymen, and to strengthen them by predictions of the approaching triumph of the theocracy. For the sake of obtaining the more ready belief, as well as to compensate for the want of credibility in the predictions themselves, he ascribed them to the old prophet Daniel, of whom, perhaps, some legends were still in circulation." *

It is remarkable how clear and complete critical theories are to begin with. This Antiochus Epiphanes theory was regarded, and is still represented in such unreliable handbooks as Cornill's as a triumphant demonstration. Dr. Driver, however, finds that the explanation fails in some important points. Cornill is certain that the Book was written in 164 B.C.; because, says he, up till that point the eleventh chapter of Daniel gives a continuous and clear account of the proceedings of this oppressor of the Jewish people, while from that point all is suddenly misty, and the history and the so-called prophecy no longer march together. The poor theological student, into whose hands this precious contribution is thrust by strong professorial and other commendations, imagines that here he has reached the solid bed-rock of fact, and that he can now be certain at least of this, that *Daniel* was written at the very time when an acute criticism has discovered that history is exchanged for prophecy. But when he turns to Driver he finds that Cornill's confidence is not justified. While certain that the Book is a forgery, the learned Canon cannot fix upon a date for the composition of the Book. "In face of the facts presented by the Book of Daniel," he says, "the opinion that it is the

* *Introduction,* §. 257.

work of Daniel himself cannot be sustained. Internal evidence shows, with a cogency that cannot be resisted, that it must have been written not earlier than about 300 B.C., and in Palestine ; and that it is at least *probable* that it was composed under the persecution of Antiochus Epiphanes, B.C. 168 or 167." *

Though unconvinced by the arguments which have led so many of the critics to fix the date as low as the latter part of the second century before the birth of our Lord, Dr. Driver has no hesitation in accepting the critical position. The Book was a late production, and written, according to him, in Palestine, and not in Babylonia. This is the position assumed by all shades of the higher criticism. Kuenen asks whether the conclusion can be resisted that the Book was written in the year 165 B.C. Nöldeke declares that † "the Book is not authentic, and the majority of the incidents recorded are fabulous and impossible. The judgment passed upon the Book," he says, "has been established by modern criticism with more certainty than for the majority of the other Books. With the exception of some ardent apologists, all men of science have long since been agreed on all essential points concerning the Book of Daniel."

Whether that is a judgment which ought to be passed, we shall immediately inquire. If the Book contained nothing besides its prediction of the year of our Lord's coming, its inspiration would be proved. And what true science has to say regarding the date of the Book and the place in which it was written

* *Introduction*, p. 467.   † *Histoire Littéraire de l'Ancien Test.*

may be meanwhile gathered from the following touching confession, made by one of the very greatest Assyriologists of his time. " I must confess," says François Lenormant, "that one part of the arguments cited by Corrodi, Eichhorn, Jahn, Gesenius, De Wette, Lengerke, Ewald, and Hitzig (against the Book of Daniel) long appeared to me to be unanswerable. I accepted their opinion, and I have even published it. . . . Reasons purely and exclusively scientific. . . have led me to change that opinion. . . and to return to those handed down by tradition. . . My new conviction is based upon the study of the cuneiform texts, the guidance of which was wanting to the judgment, which, I believe it is now necessary to revise. In fact, the testimony of these texts is an indispensable element in the debate. *

CHAPTER II.

THE DATE FIXED BY THE LANGUAGE USED IN
THE BOOK.

BEFORE we proceed to cite the testimonies to the genuineness of the Book which modern discovery has accumulated so rapidly, it may be well to note that, quite apart from this evidence, the critical theory labours under immense difficulties. We are told, as we have just seen, that the Book was composed in Palestine, and in a time when the Greek tongue and Greek civilisation and customs had long been

---

* *La Divination et la Science des Presages*, pp. 170, 171.

familiar to Palestine in common with the entire East. The universal conviction, on the other hand, for more than 2,000 years has been that it was written by a man who had spent his youth and manhood in Babylon, and that it was written for a people who had shared the experiences of his exile, and who with him had breathed the air and lived the life of that same place and time. We can point to scores of indications that the Book was written by such a man, and for just such readers. The critics, on the other hand, though straining to the utmost their ingenuity and their undoubted imaginative ability, have failed to find (with the solitary exception of three alleged Greek names of musical instruments) a single Greek word or official title, or the slightest reflection of the civilisation of this Greek period. Must not this seem, even to the critics, an extraordinary thing? We have had a hitherto undisturbed belief that the Authorised Version of the Bible was published in the reign of James VI. of Scotland and I. of England, and in the year 1611. But let us imagine for a moment that it is now alleged that this belief is merely a devout imagination, and that the translation was really made and published at the passing of Catholic Emancipation in 1829. Let us further suppose that the two events are said to throw new and most instructive light upon each other, and that the theory has been largely accepted. But when that theory had won its triumph, its difficulties would begin. Assuming the place of a fact, it would necessarily have to adjust itself to other things which are also facts; for the human mind is impatient of discord there, and makes an imperious demand for harmony. "We see," it would be said, "marks enough that the Version is really King James's, as it is said to be. It speaks the language, and its tongue has the very accent of that time. We can find no trace, on the contrary, of its having been cast in a nineteenth century mould." What answer could the theorists give? And if they could not reply, would their theory be able to live? In that very inability to adjust itself to undoubted facts, any man might read its fate and foretell its expulsion from the realm of accepted beliefs. And a theory as to the origin of the Book of Daniel can no more live under such a burden than a theory as to the date of the Authorised Version.

When we examine the contents of the Book, the difficulties of the higher criticism become still graver. Daniel is marked by a striking feature; for it is written in two languages. From the fourth verse of chapter ii. to the end of chapter vii. the Book is in the Aramaic tongue. All the rest of it is in Hebrew. The symbolic use, which is made of language in the Scripture, enables us to understand a variation which at first sight is sufficiently perplexing. For the explanation which is naturally suggested in reading ii. 4: "Then spake the Chaldeans to the king in Syriack," will not stand investigation. It is by no means certain that the Chaldæans spake in Syriac, or rather, Aramaic; and, even if they did, that would not account for their language being continued long after the report of what they said is finished. The original, too, does not say that they spoke in Aramaic. The words run:

"Then spake the Chaldeans—*Aramith*—O king, live for ever!" The word *Aramith*, that is, Aramaic, is interjected to call the reader's attention to the fact that what follows is not in Hebrew but in the Aramæan tongue.

This throws us back, however, upon the question why this sudden change from one language to another should have been made. I have said that the Scripture use of languages gives us a clue. The reader is aware that while, apart from this and other two similar exceptions in Ezra and Jeremiah, the whole of the Old Testament is in Hebrew, the entire New Testament, on the other hand, is in Greek. There is no exception made, even when the Jewish Churches are written to ; for the epistle to the Hebrews is also in Greek. This is the more to be wondered at when we recall the fact that all the writers were Hebrews, and that Greek was to all of them (with the possible exception of Paul and Luke) a foreign tongue. Was there any great purpose to be served, then, by the use of the Greek tongue— a purpose so great that neither the writers, nor even (in one case at any rate) the original readers, were considered ? Remember that, while Hebrew was the language of God's ancient people, Greek was the universal Gentile tongue—the medium of communication, at the time, between all nations—and the significance of the choice will become apparent. It signified the deposition of the Jew. His spiritual leadership was, for the time, to cease. The kingdom of God was taken from him and given to another people. Now the Aramæan was, in the time of

Jeremiah, Daniel, and Ezra, what Greek was in the days of the Apostles. It was the language of commerce and of diplomacy over the whole known world—the common language of the Gentile peoples. Is not the passing, then, from the language of the Jew to the common language of the Gentiles an indication of a change in the relative positions of Jew and Gentile? When we examine the contents of the Aramaic portion of Daniel, this suggestion receives signal confirmation. The prophecies relate to the Gentile supremacy over Israel—the four great world-empires. When that point in the world's future is reached (vii. 24, 25), at which the Antichrist appears, and the hour has come (according to other predictions of the Scripture) for God to visit once more His ancient people, the Aramæan ends, and the Hebrew is resumed in chapter viii.

But we are concerned, now, less with why the two languages are used than with the fact that the Book is written half in Hebrew and half in Aramæan. The free use of both tongues plainly indicates, that when the Book was written, both were understood by the Jewish people. Now this suits the time of Daniel, but cannot suit even the year 300 B.C., the highest possible date that Dr. Driver will allow for the production of the Book, about two and a half-centuries after the time of Daniel. The reader will remember that the Hebrew officials, in the time of Hezekiah, said to the Rab-shakeh : "Speak, I pray thee, to thy servants in the Syrian language; for we understand it : and talk not with us in the Jews' language in the ears of the people that are on the wall" (2 Kings xviii. 26).

Here, it is clearly indicated, that to the Jews generally, the Aramæan was a foreign tongue, and that if the Assyrian ambassador used it, his communication would no longer be understood by the people that were on the wall. On the other hand, when the people return from the exile, and the Law is read publicly to them, it has to be explained. Attempts have been made to deny that this is the correct interpretation of the words : " So they read in the Book, in the Law of God, distinctly, and gave the sense, and caused them to understand the reading" (Nehemiah viii. 8). But the objection would hardly occur to anyone not burdened with a theory. Why should the sense have had to be given after the Hebrew of the Law had been read? If Hebrew was then the language in daily use among the people, was the language of the Scripture not simple enough, and could any fitter words have been found to convey God's message? Now this was done in 444 B.C.; so that about a century and a half before Dr. Driver's earliest possible date for the Book of Daniel the Jews had ceased to understand Hebrew. And so, according to him and his fellow-critics, quite half of the Book is written in a language that the people could not understand! The writer, according to them, desires ardently to bring consolation to his fellow-countrymen, and to strengthen them, so that they may endure the fiercest persecution to which they had ever been subjected : and nevertheless, he wraps up the consolation and the strength in a language which they cannot read!

That theory cannot be shaken into harmony with

the facts. What, then, of the Jewish and Christian belief—what of the theory which simply accepts *Daniel* as an honest Book? The facts are, that before the time of Daniel, the Jews did not understand Aramæan ; and after the time of Daniel they ceased to understand Hebrew. In the time of Daniel *they knew both languages.* The belief that just at this time both languages were used to communicate God's revelation to the Jews is in absolute accord with the facts—in such absolute accord, in fact, that the agreement is a strong testimony to the genuineness of the Book. Should the critics reply that the Hebrew was used by a writer who pretended to be the prophet Daniel, so that by using the ancient sacred language, he might the more easily find acceptance for his work, they will rush upon another difficulty. For why, then, should he have also used the Aramæan? He would, in this, have wantonly broken the spell, and have raised questionings which would have wrecked his chance of imposing upon the people. By using the Hebrew, this critical phantom, their supposed forger of the Book, would have shown himself a knave ; and, by also using the Aramæan, he would have proved himself a fool.

CHAPTER III.

The Miracles in the Book of Daniel.

THESE prefatory words to our study of one of
the most important prophetic Books of the Old
Testament would be regrettably incomplete without
some reference to the miracles recorded in it—miracles
which must have made the mightiest impression both
upon the Babylonians and the Jews, and which have
strongly appealed to the imagination and the heart
of every subsequent age. This is an element of the
Scripture with which rationalism is in the deadliest
antagonism, and to its prominence in Daniel the
critical hostility to the Book is largely, if not wholly,
due.

This is manifest throughout the whole critical
attack. After enumerating the objections raised to
the contents of the Book, ending with Daniel's
deliverance from the lions' den, Eichhorn exclaims:
" What a host of difficulties ! " De Wette bases his
conclusion, that the Book is spurious, first of all on
" its legendary contents," and in the summary of
these the miracles are mentioned with special scorn.
Dr. Samuel Davidson says : " The miracles recorded
in the Book are lavishly accumulated without any
apparent object, and differ from those elsewhere related. Their prodigal expenditure is unworthy of the
Deity. They are also of a colossal nature, imposing

and over-awing in form." * Davidson here, as usual, is repeating the arguments of his German masters. Hengstenberg sums them up in similar fashion. He represents men, whose names are now strange even to critics, but who were leaders of the critical host in the earlier time, as saying : " We find in Daniel an aimless profusion of miracles. Of what use was it to Nebuchadnezzar to know who would be his successors, or to be acquainted with the revolutions that were to take place afterwards in his monarchy ? Was it worth such a manifold variety of miracles to satisfy his political curiosity ? What was the object of making known to Belshazzar, by a writing which nobody but Daniel could read, that the Medes and Persians were to be masters of his capital? etc. This want of any adequate aim in miracles, altogether surpassing the common course of nature, must perplex even the most candid inquirer." Hitzig declared the Book to be "irrational and impossible." Nöldeke's antagonism to the miracles cannot be concealed any more than that of the others. "The Book of Daniel," he says, "is not authentic," and at the head of his reasons for its rejection he places the following: "First of all, the majority of the facts recorded in the Book belong to the category of fable, and could not have happened." He makes special mention of "the three young men cast into the fire, and the other marvels quite as extravagant." †

Behind all this there lies, as has been already re-

---

* *Introduction to the Old Testament*, vol. iii., p. 174.
† *Histoire literaire de l'Ancien Testament*, p. 330.

marked, the disbelief in the miraculous. Into this fundamental question I do not now enter. It is enough to remark that the inquirer into God's works is brought face to face with miracle as certainly as the reader of God's Word. The matter out of which our planetary system and all the stars of heaven have been made, with its ultimate atoms, which the chemist can only fitly describe as " manufactured articles " is a miracle. The introduction of life upon the earth is a miracle. The arrangement of our planetary universe, of the bones in the human hand, of the lenses and the muscles of the human eye, are all of them miracles. That is, there is nothing in purely natural causes to explain how they came to be planned so wondrously. The Bible, supremely alone in the world of books, is a miracle. Every fulfilled prediction, and of these there are scores in its pages, is a miracle. To this I may add that Jewish tradition shows that the gifts of the Spirit and the miracles of the first Christian age were actual experiences.

But I do not now argue this great question. The matter to which our attention is, for the moment, directed, is, did *these* miracles happen, and do they exhibit the wisdom, as well as the power, of God ? One, as yet unanswered, argument for their genuineness is that they account for phenomena in Jewish history which nothing else can explain. The Jews were led away to Babylon incorrigible idolaters. They returned from it the most purely and sternly monotheistic people which the world has ever seen. We are all aware that the current critical explanation is, that latterly, they came into contact there with the Persians: that the Persians were quite as firm believers in the existence of One only living and true God : that the Jews, who had refused to believe their own prophets who had preached this truth, were struck and capti- vated by it as soon as they heard it from the lips of the Persian people ; and that then it was at last possible for Israel to write, and to receive the words: "Hear, O Israel, the Lord thy God is one Lord." But this dream has been thoroughly dispelled. The Persians knew nothing of this stern monotheism. Cyrus and the kings who followed him on the Persian throne were idolaters. Consequently there was absolutely no nation in Babylonia from whom the Jews could have received this teaching, and to whose influence their conversion can be attributed. But a national change like this, so extensive, so deep and thorough, and so long-enduring, must have had some adequate cause. What then was it ?

Here is an answer—the only one that has ever been given. This sudden, radical, and universal change in Jewish belief and practice, *occurred during the very period covered by the Book of Daniel.* When the Jews went down with, and after, Daniel, idolatry was the apparently ineradicable vice of the people. Their hearts were with the beliefs and the religious obser- vances of the surrounding peoples. When they return under Ezra and Nehemiah this entire tendency has disappeared as by magic. Neither of these leaders has to entreat the multitude to deliver up their gods, or to cease provoking Jehovah by their idolatries.

It never enters, apparently, into the mind of either
leader that there is the slightest call for such a course.
The entire people, I repeat, are convinced and well-
established believers in the one living and true God,
the alone Creator of heaven and earth, the sea and
all that in them is. And here is the reason. God had
now disclosed Himself to the children, as He had
disclosed Himself to their fathers in Egypt and in the
wilderness. Once more had He made bare His arm
and worked stupendous deliverances. He had paved
the way, and had opened with His own hands the
gates, so that His servant might have to enter into
the counsels and the friendship of Babylonian, and
Median, and Persian kings. God had once more raised
up a prophet in Israel who told them the secrets
of these years of waiting. They were instructed in
the politics of the future. They knew, before the
Persian power had begun to lay its hand upon the
nations, that it was to succeed the Babylonian. The
other prophecies treasured up for this day of trial
were now bathed in new light, and were read with new
intelligence and interest. The people were shut in
with God's word as they had never been in all their
previous history. They were watching and anticipating the advent of the events of predicted history.
They knew, from the pages of Isaiah, the very name
of their appointed deliverer; and when Cyrus did appear, named all the world over by the very name with
which God had hailed him nearly 200 years before,
doubt was changed to adoration. It was thence forward impossible for the Jew not to believe in Jehovah,

the only God, with all the ardour of a soul that had been stirred to its deepest depths. Monotheism now ran in the very blood of the Jew; and it ran there because those miracles of God, and the ministry of His servant Daniel, were alike realities.

This has also answered our further question as to whether these miracles displayed the wisdom of God. One mark of Divine intervention is that it reveals the need of the time. Such a revelation were those miracles in Egypt, when the mightiest and proudest empire of the period learned that God was establishing Israel as His own people. Such were those in the wilderness when the faith of that people had to be established in the livingness and nearness, the righteousness, and might, and pitifulness of the Creator of heaven and earth. Such were those of Elijah and Elisha when the faith of the ten tribes was going down under a fashionable, powerful, and unscrupulous idolatry. And such a revelation were these miracles in Babylonia. Nebuchadnezzar and his people believed that Jehovah had been conquered by Merodach, Nebuchadnezzar's favoured idol, and by the other gods of Babylon. And now they were taught by deeds that the God of Israel was God of all the earth. Israel, on the other hand, broken and despairing, had to be comforted. It might be said that comfort had already been provided in the prophecies which had this very time in view. But they needed to be convinced that these predictions with their comfort were really meant for them. These miracles, proving so astoundingly that Jehovah was their God as really as He had been the God of their fathers in the days of the Exodus, sent this conviction home, and unsealed for them the fountains of Scripture consolations. And thus the very things, at which the unbelief of to-day stumbles, brought grace to Jew and Gentile.

<hr />

CHAPTER IV.

DANIEL'S CAPTIVITY.

——

THIS conflict "for hearth and altar" into which, in the Providence of God, we are thrust to-day, frequently rages round minute points, which, in themselves may seem of small importance. This has been the fate of many a contest. The historic farm upon the field at Waterloo, whose high brick walls show to-day where the French bullets tore their way along, was the key to the British position. During that fearful storm of shot and shell, it was assaulted and assaulted again; but the British troops triumphed there, and their victory preserved the formation of the British army, and heralded the complete overthrow of the foe.

Such a point is the date noted in the opening words of the Book of Daniel: "In the third year of the reign of Jehoiakim king of Judah came (Hebrew, *Ba)* Nebuchadnezzar king of Babylon unto Jerusalem, and besieged it. And the Lord gave Jehoiakim king of Judah into his hand, with part of the vessels of the house of God: which he carried into the land of Shinar to the house of his god; and he brought the vessels into the treasure house of his god " (i. 1, 2). On this, Dr. Driver says: "That Nebuchadnezzar besieged Jerusalem, and carried away some of the sacred vessels in " the *third* year of Jehoiakim, though it cannot, strictly speaking, be disproved, is highly improbable: not only is the Book of Kings silent, but Jeremiah *in the following year* (chapter xxv., &c.) speaks of the Chaldæans in a manner which appears directly to imply that their arms had not yet been seen in Judah." *

This entirely ignores the question, raised long since, whether in the opening words of Daniel the Hebrew *ba* is quite correctly translated by "came." It has frequently the sense of " went," or "marched." This has been denied by the critics. Dr. Samuel Davidson says expressly: The verb *bô* does not mean *to set out* . . . but *to arrive at.*" † This is a melancholy, but instructive, specimen of the shallow and utterly misleading dogmatism of the higher criticism. We read, for instance, that Jonah "went down to Joppa, and he found a ship going to Tarshish " (i. 3). The verb which is here translated "going" is this very verb *bô,* which Dr. Davidson says "does not mean *to set out,* but always *to arrive at.*" According to this critical rule, then, the translation ought to run: " Jonah . . . went down to Joppa, and he found a ship arriving at Tarshish !" In this way, Jonah would have discovered a happy solution of all his difficulties.

That fearful Mediterranean tempest would have been escaped, as well as all his after experiences. Coming to Joppa, he found a ship arriving at Tarshish, stepped on board, and was already there! Had this been a solitary instance of the use of *bō*, the mistake might have been overlooked, though the dogmatism would even then have been unpardonable. But the use of the Hebrew verb in the sense of "go" is actually frequent, and is found from Genesis to Malachi. Pharaoh, for instance, commands Joseph to say to his brethren: "Go, get you into the land of Canaan" (Genesis xlv. 17). The verb translated "get you" is *bō*, and the words unquestionably mean, "Proceed ye into the land of Canaan." We are forced to render it in the same way in Exodus vi. 11 : "Go in *(bō)*, speak unto Pharaoh king of Egypt." These are samples out of a multitude of instances. *Bō* is used in the sense of "to set out" in every Book of the Pentateuch, in Joshua, Judges, Ruth, 1st and 2nd Samuel, 1st and 2nd Kings, 2nd Chronicles Ezra, Nehemiah, Esther, Job, the Psalms, Proverbs, Isaiah, Jeremiah, Ezekiel, and in six out of the twelve Minor Prophets. Such is the well-nigh incredible ignorance and criminal rashness of this so-called "scholarship!"

Now, taking the word in this sense of "set out," "went," or "marched," the statement in Daniel not only becomes perfectly intelligible, but is also found to be a valuable contribution to the history of the time. Nebuchadnezzar *set out*, or *marched*, from Baby-lon in the third year of Jehoiakim, but did not arrive at Jerusalem and besiege it till the fourth year of that king's reign. The difference between the two dates of "the third year" and "the fourth" may have meant only a month or two. A modern traveller might easily have left Babylon in December, say, of 1903, and not arrive in Jerusalem till February or March, 1904. His time of arrival would depend largely upon what he had to do in the course of his journey.

But was there a military expedition undertaken by Nebuchadnezzar in even the fourth year of Jehoiakim, which might embrace Jerusalem within the scope of its operations? Dr. Driver distinctly implies that this, too, would be a historical blunder. He tells us that in that very year Jeremiah speaks in chapter xxv. of his prophecies in a way which indicates that the Babylonians had not yet invaded Judah. But why is Dr. Driver silent about Jeremiah xlvi. 2? There we are distinctly told that there *was* just such a military expedition by Nebuchadnezzar, followed by a crushing defeat of the Egyptian army in *the fourth year* of Jehoiakim, king of Judah. His words are : " The word of the Lord which came to Jeremiah the prophet against the Gentiles ; against Egypt ; against the army of Pharaoh-necho king of Egypt, which was by the river Euphrates in Carchemish, which Nebuchadrezzar king of Babylon smote in the fourth year of Jehoiakim the son of Josiah king of Judah" (verses 1, 2).

To make the course of events quite plain, let me remind the reader of Pharaoh-necho's march to the

N

Euphrates. That occurred in the last year of king Josiah, who met his death in a loyal, but futile attempt to help his over-lord, the king of Assyria. Nineveh was tottering to its fall, and the eagles of Babylon, Media, and Egypt were hurrying to the prey. Pharaoh saw a chance of recovering Syria for Egypt, and of rivalling the glories of the ancient Egyptian kings. He drove before him what Assyrian forces were on the west of the Euphrates, and seized and garrisoned Carchemish, the ancient Hittite city, and the key to Syria upon its eastern side. But Nebuchadnezzar, in concert with his father Nabopolassar, resolved to assert his claim to the world-empire which the Assyrians had now lost. He set out, therefore, in the third year of Jehoiakim, and evidently at the end of it, to wrest Carchemish from the Egyptians. It was now the fourth year of Jehoiakim (and probably the commencement of it) when the first successes of the campaign were reaped, and the Egyptian army was smitten.

Here, then, in the fourth year of Jehoiakim, the victorious Babylonians are in Carchemish. Is it likely that they are to content themselves with the possession of that city? They have now the key in their hands which opens to them Syria and the west : shall they not enter in and take possession? No one who knows the military capacity, and the promptitude, of the Babylonian people, will hesitate as to the answer. But we know that, as a matter of fact, Nebuchadnezzar did pursue his advantage. "The key of Syria," says Professor Rawlinson, "at this

time was Carchemish. . . Here the forces of Neco
were drawn up to protect his conquests, and here
Nebuchadnezzar proceeded boldly to attack them. A
great battle was fought in the immediate vicinity of
the river, which was utterly disastrous to the
Egyptians, who 'fled away' in confusion, and seem
not to have ventured on making a second stand.
Nebuchadnezzar rapidly recovered the lost territory,
received the submission of Jehoiakim, king of Judah,
restored the old frontier line, and probably pressed on
into Egypt itself, hoping to cripple, or even to crush,
his presumptuous adversary. But at this point he was
compelled to pause. News arrived from Babylon that
Nabopolassar was dead; and the Babylonian prince,
who feared a disputed succession, having first concluded a hasty arrangement with Neco, returned at
his best speed to his capital." *

It will now be abundantly plain that a siege of
Jerusalem in the fourth year of Jehoiachim king of
Judah was not merely a probability: it was an actual
military necessity. The whole of Syria had to be
wrenched from Egypt; and Judah and Jerusalem
could not possibly be neglected. Necho had asserted
his lordship over them, and from a like necessity
Nebuchadnezzar had to demand their allegiance. And
a careful perusal of the Scripture makes it quite
plain that the siege actually occurred. This is referred to both in Kings and in Chronicles in their very
brief summaries of the events of this monarch's reign.
The former says: "In his days Nebuchadnezzar king

---

* *Ancient Monarchies*, vol. iii., pp. 488, 489.

of Babylon came up, and Jehoiakim became his servant three years" (xxiv. 1). After these three years, we are told, he rebelled, and, instead of sending an expedition from Babylon for the punishment of this turbulent, but comparatively contemptible vassal, Nebuchadnezzar sent his commission to the neighbouring peoples, who with a small Babylonian force wasted the country. "Then," continues the Scripture, "he (Jehoiakim) turned and rebelled against him. And the Lord sent against him bands of the Chaldeans, and bands of the Syrians, and bands of the Moabites, and bands of the children of Ammon, and sent them against Judah to destroy it" (verses 1, 2). The country was destroyed probably up to the very neighbourhood of Jerusalem. Jehoiakim died in his eleventh year, and his son Jehoiachin had reigned only three months, when the city was again besieged by the Babylonian armies. "At that time the servants of Nebuchadnezzar king of Babylon came up against Jerusalem, and the city was beseiged. And Nebuchadnezzar king of Babylon came against the city, and his servants did besiege it. And Jehoiachin the king of Judah went out to the king of Babylon, he, and his mother, and his servants, and his princes, and his officers. . . . And he (the king of Babylon) carried away all Jerusalem, and all the princes, and all the mighty men of valour, even ten thousand captives, and all the craftsmen and smiths: none remained, save the poorest sort of the people of the land" (2 Kings xxiv. 10-14). Here, then, are two sieges of Jerusalem, the second three months after

Jehoiakim's death, the first undated, but described as happening at a time which allowed for the three years' subjection to Babylon, the revolt of Jehoiakim, and his evidently prolonged punishment by letting loose those predatory bands upon the territory of Judah. The entire reign of Jehoiakim was only eleven years. It is not at all unlikely that the siege happened in this very fourth year of the king's reign. And yet Dr. Driver can mislead all who take him as an authority by the words: "Not only is the Book of Kings silent "! The Book of Kings is not silent. On the contrary, it makes a statement which has a direct and important bearing upon the subject, and which no one deciding a question of this kind ought to have over-looked.

The course of events of that time of trouble will now be clear. In the fourth year of Jehoiakim, Jerusalem is besieged. This is clear from the statement in Jeremiah xlvi. 2 and that in 2 Kings xxiv. 1. This event is also recorded in 2 Chronicles xxxvi. 6, 7: "Against him (Jehoiakim) came up Nebuchadnezzar king of Babylon, and bound him in fetters, to carry him away to Babylon. Nebuchadnezzar also carried of the vessels of the house of the Lord to Babylon, and put them in his temple at Babylon." Here, it will be noted, is an identical statement with that in Daniel about Nebuchadnezzar's carrying off after this siege "part of the vessels of the house of God." The purpose of transporting the king seems not to have been carried out. Probably in his humiliation Jehoiakim entreated mercy, and terms were consequently

made with him. We are told that he served Nebuchadnezzar three years. This brings us to the seventh
year of his reign. The measures taken for his punishment and the ravaging of Judah seem to have occupied
the remaining four years. And all this is in complete
accord with the prophecies of Jeremiah in the name
of which Dr. Driver stamps the opening statement of
Daniel as unhistorical. He says, as we have seen,
that in the fourth year of Jehoiakim Jeremiah "speaks
of the Chaldæans in a manner which appears distinctly
to imply that their arms had not yet been seen in
Judah." Dr. Driver, in making this statement, refers
to the twenty-fifth chapter of Jeremiah. In the first
verse the prophecy is carefully dated " in the fourth
year of Jehoiakim the son of Josiah king of Judah,
that was the first year of Nebuchadrezzar king of
Babylon." We are further told that it was a word
for "all the people of Judah " and "all the inhabitants
of Jerusalem." It recounts what God had done in
sending "all His servants the prophets, rising early
and sending them " (verse 4). It reminds them that
all God's warnings had been in vain : "ye have not
hearkened nor inclined your ear to hear." And now
God pronounces judgment upon them. It is a doom
of utter desolation for the land, and of exile and captivity for the people. Now, suppose that all Judah
and Jerusalem know that Nebuchadnezzar has defeated
the forces of Egypt, and that his victorious army is
on its westward march, do not the terrors of King
and Court and people invest this judgment with an
awful solemnity ? Do we not see that a moment has

been chosen in which its words will be written indelibly upon every heart?

This is surely enough to suggest that this year is named because it is the year of the invasion in which the first blow of that terrible judgment fell. But this does not stand alone. God declares (verse 11): "This whole land shall be a desolation and an astonishment, and these nations shall serve the king of Babylon SEVENTY YEARS." *This very year,* the fourth of Jehoiakim, and the first of Nebuchadnezzar, *is the commencement of the seventy.* The servitude, therefore, commenced with it; and the siege of Jerusalem, implied in Jeremiah, and described in 2 Kings and 2 Chronicles, occurred in the conclusion of that very expedition which Daniel describes as marching from Babylon "in the third year of the reign of Jehoiakim king of Judah." We now understand also the double dating of this prediction of Jeremiah's. We are struck by the association of a Jewish and a Gentile king—"In the fourth year of Jehoiakim the son of Josiah king of Judah, that was the first year of Nebuchadrezzar king of Babylon." The Jews must have been still more impressed by it. If we ask what it meant, Daniel and the other passages which we have looked at suggest a reply. God had given the Jews a new master. He had handed them over to the king of Babylon. The siege and capture of the city had virtually ended the Jewish monarchy. The captivity was begun.

Popularisers of the higher criticism tell us that " the chief instrument of the higher criticism is *the com-*

parison of Scripture with Scripture. Never, probably, has there been such a thorough, careful comparison ; never, since the days of the Massoretes, such minute painstaking study of every sentence, every clause, every word of Holy Writ." * As a comment upon that claim, let me ask the reader to place beside it the above quotation from Dr. Driver and the following statement. " We know by the Book of Jeremiah," says Kuenen, " that no such event " (he is referring to the siege of Jerusalem spoken of in Daniel i. 1) "took place in the reign of Jehoiakim." † The claim is only one more addition to daring misrepresentations, the temporary triumph of which will be avenged by deep and enduring dishonour.

CHAPTER V.

THE PALACE SCHOOL AT BABYLON.

THE story of Daniel and of his three companions is introduced with the following explanation. King Nebuchadnezzar, we are told, "spake unto Ashpenaz the master of his eunuchs, that he should bring certain of the children of Israel, and (rather, both) of the king's seed, and of the princes; children in whom was no blemish, but well-favoured, and skilful in all wisdom, and cunning in knowledge, and under-

---

Rev. Alfred Holborn, M.A., *The Pentateuch in the Light of To-day*, pp. 7, 8.
†*Histoire critique de l'Ancien Testament*, t. II., p. 558.

standing science, and such as had ability in them to stand in the king's palace, and whom they might teach the learning and the tongue of the Chaldæans. And the king appointed them a daily provision of the king's meat, and of the wine which he drank; so nourishing them three years, that at the end thereof they might stand before the king" (Daniel i. 3-5).

I may mention that we are now able to amend our translation of the above passage in one particular. The great official to whom Nebuchadnezzar sent the above command was not "the master of his eunuchs." One, indeed, might have wondered what the master of the eunuchs, that is, the chief of the personal attendants of the palace, should have been doing so far away from the scene of his not unimportant duties. But our translation arose from treating a purely Assyrian and Babylonian official title as a Hebrew word. The so-called "master of the eunuchs" is none other than Nebuchadnezzar's "Rabsaris"— the second of the three great State officials mentioned in 2 Kings xviii. 17 : "And the king of Assyria sent Tartan, Rabsaris, and Rab-shakeh from Lachish to king Hezekiah." The presence here of that title, the meaning and significance of which were quite unknown to the later Jews, is one of the many proofs of the genuineness of the Book of Daniel.

But another and still more striking proof lies in the extraordinary suggestions of the verses which we have now quoted. For they plainly imply the existence of elaborate arrangements in Babylon for the education of youth. The lads are carefully selected from among those who have been already educated in Jerusalem and possibly elsewhere; and who have shown such aptitude for study that they are likely to profit by the further training in Babylon— "whom," says the Scripture, "they might teach the learning and the tongue of the Chaldeans." These words, "they might teach," imply the existence of a staff of instructors, who have, no doubt, been selected with at least equal care. Another circumstance in connection with this school is, that it is held within the royal buildings: it is a palace-school. They are to "stand in the king's palace," and their food is sent to them from the royal table: "the king appointed them a daily provision of the king's meat, and of the wine which he drank" (verse 5). The course extends to three years: "so nourishing them three years." All this, too, it will be noticed is preparatory to their entrance into the Babylonian State service: "So nourishing them three years, at the end thereof they might stand before the king." The great king is personally interested in the pupils gathered under his roof; and their final examination appears to have been conducted by the monarch himself. For when Daniel asks the Rabsaris for permission to refrain from using the royal food and wine, that official replies: "I fear my lord the king. . . for why should he see your faces worse liking than the children which are of your sort? Then shall ye make me endanger my head to the king." And we read also: "Now at the end of the days that the king had said that he should bring them in, then the Rabsaris brought them in before Nebuchadnezzar. And the king communed with them" (verses 18, 19).

Now, if these statements are pondered, there is much in them that cannot fail to seem remarkable. There is not a single hint in the Scriptures of such an institution existing either at Jerusalem or elsewhere. The student of history finds it equally new; and it retains its singularity when we pass under review the institutions of our own times. There is no such school in connection with any of the royal palaces in our own country; and, though our empire is of wide extent, embracing under its sway many chiefs and princes, the notion of selecting for special training any of their sons, and of afterwards giving them posts in our State service has apparently never occurred to a single British statesman. Is the Bible, then—our experiences have been of too sad a kind to admit of hesitation in putting the question so bluntly —is the Bible romancing in this introduction to the history of the great Jewish statesman and seer? Or was there really a custom of the very kind in the Babylon of the time?

To that question we are now able to give a reply astonishing both in its directness and fulness. This practice of selecting children of captive princes, and of training them for the service of the State was common to both Assyria and Babylon. An inscription of Sennacherib's informs us that that monarch had followed this very custom. He refers to a child taken from the home of a Babylonian noble, whom he had trained in his palace, and to whom he had

afterwards committed the vice-royalty of Chaldæa.
The inscription runs :

> Belibni, son of a learned man from the neigh-
> bourhood of Suanna (Babylon), who as a young
> child had been brought up in my palace, over the
> kingdom of Sumir and Accad I set him.

This devotion to literature had passed to Assyria
from Babylon, and when the Assyrian supremacy
came to an end it flourished once more in its ancient
home. "In Chaldæa," says Perrot, "the highest
social position and the first place appear to have
always been reserved for the members of the sacer-
dotal caste, called, *par excellence*, the Chaldæans.
These priests were the learned of the time. At first
magicians and astrologers, they soon became, as
much from curiosity as from necessity, attentive
observers and patient calculators. It is they, much
more than the Egyptians, who have created the first
methods and sketched the first theories of astronomical science." *

We are at present able to obtain the clearest view
of the Babylonian learning, and the rigorous training
necessary for its acquisition, from the records left by
their Assyrian imitators. Of what kind that training
and learning were will be plain from the following,
taken from Professor Sayce's small, but valuable,
work on *Babylonian Literature*. After stating that
ancient Babylon was the most literary of the nations,
he continues :

> "It is impossible to say when and where the first

---

* *Revue des deux Mondes,* 1st October, 1882.

library of Accad was founded. Berosus makes Pantibiblia, the town of books, the chief ante-diluvian city of Babylonia. . . The library of Erech, the modern Warka, was among the oldest in Chaldæa. . . . . Of the library of Cutha, all that remains is a legend of the Creation, and of a war of the giants; while that of Larsa, or Senkereh, has yielded several mathematical tablets, including tables of squares and cubes. But the most famous of all the libraries of Babylonia was that of Agané, a city near Sippara, founded by Sargon I., probably in the seventeenth century B.C. It was for this library that the great work on astronomy and astrology in seventy-two books was compiled, which Berosus, it would seem, translated into Greek. . .

" Sargon himself was a Semite, the first of the Semitic conquerors, perhaps, who patronised liter-ature. The language of Accad had already ceased to be the tongue of the people; here and there a Scribe might possibly be found who still knew how to speak it, but otherwise it was a learned dialect like the Latin of the middle ages. The books, therefore, with which the library was stocked were either trans-lated from Accadian originals, or else based on Accadian texts, and filled with technical words which belonged to the old language. Education, however, must have been widely spread; the catalogue of the astronomical works, in the library of Agané, enjoins the reader to write down the number of the tablet or book he needs, and the librarian will thereupon give him the tablet required. What stronger proof than this can we have of the development of literature and education, and of the existence of a considerable reading public? Every tablet had its number, and the tablets were ranged according to subject and contents. The arrangement adopted by Sargon's librarians, one of whom has left us a signet ring now in the British Museum, must have been the product of generations of former experience. They simply inherited the labours and wisdom of their Accadian predecessors, just as their monarch himself inherited the organised rule and royal prerogatives of the Accadian princes." *

After the Assyrians had subjected the Babylonians, the conquered (as afterwards happened with Greece and Rome) became the instructors of their masters, and the literature of Babylonia was gradually transferred to Assyria. "The first Assyrian library, of which we know was that of Calah, a city built by Shalmaneser I. about B.C. 1300, and restored by Assur-Natsir-pal in 885. It was after its second foundation that the library was established there, and among other books deposited in it was a copy of the great work on astronomy. The collection was presided over by Nabu-zukup-cinu, the son of Merodach-mubasa, 'the astronomer,' . . . . . and the work of copying and composing texts went on briskly.

"It remained for Assur-bani-pal, or Sardanapalus, the son of Esarhaddon, the "Grand Monarque" of Assyria, and the great patron of literature, to surpass his predecessors, and gather into his library at Nine-

---

* Pages 8-10.

veh or Kouyounyik the selected literary treasures of Babylonia and Assyria. Scribes were kept busily engaged in copying and translating earlier works, or in drawing up new ones, either in Assyrian or in extinct Accadian, the study of which was now revived. In fact, grammars, dictionaries, and phrase-books of the old language were compiled, the Assyrian equivalents being written interlineally or in the right-hand column. To facilitate the study of the li.erature, as well as to assist the strangers from Egypt or Cyprus or Lydia who thronged the court of Sardanapalus, syllabaries were made, in which the cuneiform charactres were classified and arranged. . . . . . With reiterated earnestness the king declares that Nebo, the ' prophet ' god of literature, and his wife Tasmit, ' the hearer,' had made broad his ears and given sight to his eyes so that he had ' regard to the engraved character of the tablets ; ' and the writing which none of the kings before him had cared for, even ' the secrets of Nebo, the literature of the library,' ' or tablets,' he had ' written, engraved, and explained, and stored in the midst of his palace for the inspection ' of his ' subjects.' " *

The learning of Chaldæa embraced a wide circle of subjects. " Traces of a Chaldæan Euclid, with geometrical figures, have been met with. It was in the service of astronomy, however, that the lives of the Accadian men of science were mainly spent. Observatories were erected in every city, and fortnightly reports were sent in to the king by the astronomer royal." †

---

* Pages 12-14.   † Page 51.

But before citing the testimony which follows, let me call the reader's attention to the language of the Scripture. We are told in Daniel i. 4 what the special subjects of study were. These are "the learning," literally, "the books and the tongue of the Chaldæans." The language is named last. The acquiring of a knowledge of the language of the "Chaldæans," which points specially to the ancient Accadian, was of high importance. But the emphasis is laid upon "the books of the Chaldæans." There was plainly a huge literature to be mastered, as well as a new language and a new writing. How true this was we now know. The writing was of a specially difficult kind. Not only was there a multitude of signs to become acquainted with, but there were also confusing complications to be mastered. One sign had more than one sound, and sometimes it represented no sound at all, but stood as a symbol for an idea or an object. It consequently required careful instruction on the master's part, and intense application on that of the pupils, for a pupil to be able to read the ancient texts with ease and certainty.

"Besides learning the syllabary," writes Prof. Sayce, "the Babylonian boy had to learn the extinct language of Accad and Sumer. For this purpose he was pro-vided with lists of words or vocabularies in which the Accadian word was explained in Semitic Assyrian, with grammatical paradigms giving the forms of the Accadian verbs and post-positions, with the explan-ations of difficult phrases, with extracts from ancient books translated into Assyrian, notes being sometimes added upon obscure and important words, along with interlinear and parallel translations of long and complete texts. The student was also encouraged to write himself in this literary Latin of Chaldæa ; and numerous works exist which show by their age, their idioms, and sometimes even their errors, that they must have been the work of Semitic Scribes. The Accadian of the subjects of Nebuchadnezzar could be as faulty as monkish or schoolboy's Latin. . . But there were other things besides languages which the young student in the schools of Babylonia and Assyria was called upon to learn. Geography, history, the names and nature of plants, birds, animals, and stones, as well as the elements of law and religion, were all objects of instruction. The British Museum possesses what may be called the historical exercises of some Babylonian lad in the age of Nebuchadnezzar or Cyrus, consisting of a list of the kings belonging to one of the early dynasties, which he had been required to learn by heart." *

Here, then, a civilisation, which had passed away centuries before the critics tell us the Book of Daniel was written, and concerning which there was the profoundest ignorance—an ignorance which endured to our own day—has now come forth from the tomb to testify that the critical date for the origin of the Book, and the critical theory as to its character, are sheer impossibilities. The opening words of the Book prove it to be history. They are written in full view of a state of things which soon afterwards ceased to be. They

---

* *Social Life among the Assyrians and Babylonians*, pp. 36-39.

imply the existence of a huge Chaldæan literature; and that literature was there. They refer to a language which called for special and prolonged study; and such was the language in which this literature was embalmed. They speak of a fully organised system for instruction in both language and literature; and that fully organised system was a feature of the Babylon of Daniel's time. And, last of all, they show that a palace-school was one of the well-known institutions of the place and period; and that palace school, as we have now seen, was there. If we had nothing more to go upon than these opening words, they are more than enough to wreck the critical case.

CHAPTER VI.

THE NAMES OF DANIEL AND HIS CONTEMPORARIES.

THE reader who has perused this and the preceding volumes of *The Guide* is aware to what an enormous extent we are indebted to Assyriology for our ability to repel the present attack upon the Bible. There are also very few labourers in that field to whom we owe so much as to Professor Sayce. This makes it the more regrettable that in the present chapter we have to see him not with ourselves, but leading the foe in their attack upon this portion of the Word of God.

Dr. Sayce has made still further advance since he definitely separated himself from the higher critics by the publication of his book upon *The Verdict of the Monuments;* and it is possible that the contentions which I am about to notice would now be withdrawn. But, seeing that they have been published, and have been naturally enough used by those who seek to discredit the Book of Daniel, it is needful to reply. He says:—

> The first two chapters afford evidences of a compiler of a later age than that of a contemporary of Nebuchadrezzar. The name of the great Babylonian monarch is mis-spelt. Nebuchadrezzar—Nabiu-kudurri-utsur in the cuneiform—has been corrupted into Nebuchadnezzar. The other Babylonian names mentioned in the chapters are equally incorrect. Belteshazzar, we are told, was the name given to Daniel after his adoption among the "wise men" of Babylon. Now, Bilat-sarra-utsur, "O Beltis, defend the king," is a good Babylonian name. But in the Book of Daniel the name is written, not with a *tau*, as would be required by the word Bilat, but with a *teth*, so that the first word in it is transformed into the Assyrian word *ballidh*, "he caused to live." The result is a compound which has no sense, and would be impossible in the Babylonian language.

> Abed-Nego, again, is a corrupted form. Abed, "servant," must be followed by the name of a deity, and the word Nego does not exist in Babylonian. The name ought to be Abed-Nebo, "Servant of Nebo," and its corruption indicates want of acquaintance with the language and the gods of Babylonia.[*]

He adds in a note: "I have found the name of

Abed-Nebo in an Aramaic inscription of the sixth or fifth century B.C. engraved on the sandstone rocks north of Silsilis in Upper Egypt." He also says that the names of Shadrach and Meshach have not been found, and that their termination is a very uncommon one in Assyria; and that Ashpenaz "is not Babylonian, whatever may be the explanation; and though Arioch (ii. 15) is found in the cuneiform inscriptions, it would not have been used in the age of Nebuchadrezzar."

In marshalling these supposed proofs of a later date Professor Sayce has simply repeated the opinions of a school which he was fortunately abandoning. A fuller consideration of some, at least, of these points will show him that there is good reason for separating himself from it in regard to Daniel as well as in regard to the Pentateuch. It is a school that is built on rash conclusions, and that favours boldness rather than thoroughness. Let us begin with what is here said about the name of Nebuchadnezzar. Here the real problem—for there is a problem connected with the name—is left untouched. The utter silence regarding it suggests, indeed, that the problem has not even been noticed. The facts, too, with a neglect that is characteristic of the higher criticism have not been stated, and perhaps have not been investigated. Daniel is not alone in the name which he applies to the Babylonian monarch. The Books of 2 Kings, 1 Chronicles, 2 Chronicles, Ezra, and Nehemiah all use the same form of the name as Daniel. Are they also, then, to be condemned as

late productions because they speak of Nebuchadnezzar instead of Nebuchadrezzar? The writer of
2 Kings so gives the name in the six references he
makes to the conqueror of Judah. The gravity of
this fact, as it affects this part of the critical position,
will be immediately apparent. The Book of 2 Kings
is not, the critics themselves admit, later than Daniel.
" The compiler of Kings," says Dr. Driver, " though
not, probably (as some have supposed), Jeremiah
himself, was, nevertheless, a man like-minded with
Jeremiah, and almost certainly a contemporary who
lived and wrote under the same influences." * But if
2 Kings uses the form Nebuchadnezzar, some fifty
years before the Book of Daniel was written, how
can the use of this name in the latter Book be a
proof that it could not have been written then, and
must, on the contrary, be held to have been produced
some three centuries later? And one is tempted to
ask farther whether such a bundle of loose and ill-
considered statements is entitled to call itself
" criticism " ?

But even this is not all. It has surely escaped the
recollection of the critics that the form of the name
given by Berossus is this very form which is rejected
so cavalierly as a blunder. If Berossus inserts the *n*
instead of the *r*, as he does in the name *Nabouchod-
onosoros*, it has to be remembered that he does not
write in ignorance of the testimony of the monuments. His history was compiled from them, and
no doubt he knew more of them, and could decipher

---

them more faultlessly than the best Assyriologist we
have yet had.   The spelling with *r* was known in the
West, for Abydenus, Megasthenes, and Strabo so give
the name.   When Berossus, then, inserted the *n*, it
is plain enough that, while he may have had some
special reason for doing so, there must have been at
least authority for the form which he selected.   In
other words, both forms of the name were in existence.   It is quite possible, and, in view of the use of
both names being found in the contemporary documents of the Bible and of the form adopted by the
Babylonian historian, exceedingly probable, that the
latter form will yet be found on the monuments.

The testimony of Berossus thus helps us in grap-
ling with a problem which criticism has hitherto
failed to notice.   Ezekiel refers to the king of Babylon
four times, and gives the name each time as Nebuchadrezzar.   Jeremiah mentions him with great
frequency, and is generally set down as spelling the
name with *r* instead of *n*.   But there are eight closely
connected passages in which the prophet makes a
distinct change, which he maintains till the section is
completed.   He drops the form with the *r*, which he
uses both before and after with no deviation except
this only, and he gives us the king's name spelled
with the *n* just as Daniel and the other historical
Books of the Bible have given it.   These chapters, in
which this striking deviation occurs (xxvii.-xxix.), have
passed the critical bar unchallenged.   Dr. Driver says:
"Chapters xxvii.-xxix. belong to the beginning of the
reign of Zedekiah."   In other words, we have the form

with *n* in a document written in the life-time of the great Babylonian king; so that Jeremiah, who is called as a witness against Daniel, really testifies in his favour.

But it is possible that he also does more. Why does Jeremiah change the name so suddenly, and keep to the change so persistently in these eight passages? Before chapter xxvii., he writes the name consistently with *r*. At the close of chapter xxix., and on to the end of his Book, he keeps to the same form without the slightest alteration. Why, then, is the change made here? And why is it kept to with equal consistency? When we scan the contents of these chapters we find that they set forth the utter subjection of Israel under the power of the Chaldæan king. The Jews are told not to listen to their false prophets, who are attempting to beguile them with hopes of a speedy deliverance. Nebuchadnezzar is their appointed master, and there will be no deliverance till seventy years have been fulfilled and the kingdom of Nebuchadnezzar is at an end. It would seem, therefore, that the form of the king's name with *n* had some significance which pointed to this unchallengeable mastery. This would explain the use of it in Daniel and the other historical Books of the Bible, which all refer to the captivity.

The name Belteshazzar is supposed by Professor Sayce to be an attempt by a late and ignorant writer to manufacture a name meaning "O Beltis, protect the king;" and he imagines that this ignorance made its inevitable blunder in misspelling the name Beltis.

This is a point which we must leave Assyriologists to answer. Schrader gives a quite different etymology. He renders it: "his life protect," and fails to find the name of Beltis in the word. He quite atones for this, however, in critical eyes, by supposing that the writer of Daniel made a mistake and took the first syllable, *Bel*, for the name of the Babylonian god. But we have now a much more recent reading of the name from one of the very highest authorities on the Babylonian writing and language. Dr. Pinches in his new book says: "The Babylonian name given to him (Daniel), Belteshazzar, is apparently an abbreviated form, which would be, in Babylonian, Balat-su-ûsur, 'Protect thou (O God), his life.' If this be the explanation, a better transcription of the Hebrew form would be Beletshazzar (making the first *sheva* vocal and the second silent, instead of the reverse). . it is probable that either the patron-deity of Babylon, Bêl, or else Nebo, the god of learning, may have preceded the first element as the name now stands. In the inscriptions of Babylonia and Assyria many examples of abbreviated names occur, on account of what we should consider their inordinate length, and to such an extent was this customary that one element only, out of three or four, might alone be used. Thus, in the contracts of the time of Nebuchadnezzar, at least fourteen persons of the name of Balatu, and seven of the name of Balatsu occur, and it may be safely taken that they are all abbreviations of names similar to that bestowed upon Daniel." [*]

Two points, therefore, in this supposed proof of a late origin of the Book are not only discredited, but are also changed into evidences of its genuineness. The names of Nebuchadnezzar and of Belteshazzar are names of the period, and show not a shadow of the ignorance of "a late compiler." What, then, of the rest? We are told that Abednego is a corrupted form of Abed-Nebo, "the servant of the god Nebo;" and this alleged correction has been adopted with surprising readiness by Biblical scholars. Even so, it may have been a transcriber's error, and not a mistake of the writer of the Book. But we bear in mind the poet's warning as to receiving the Trojans' gifts. It is somewhat early yet to assert that the Babylonian tongue can give us no interpretation of Abednego. The knowledge of Assyrian is continually extending; and there is nothing else in the passage to suggest a copyist's mistake. Shadrach and Meshach are set aside as not having an Assyrian termination. But that is an opinion with which Schrader does not agree. He says: "The name *Shadrach* is explained by Delitzsch with considerable probability as a Babylonian one, Sudur-Aku, 'command of Aku,' that is, of the Moon-god (Sin)." *

As has been already noticed, the final *u* is peculiar to the Babylonian, and the Hebrew is thus an absolutely faithful transcript of the Babylonian name. Meshak, may be, as Delitzsch also suggests, a similar compound ending with the name of the same divinity.

With regard to Arioch, we are told, in the passage

---

* *Cuneiform Inscriptions and the Old Testament,* vol. ii., pp. 125, 126.

in Dr. Sayce's book, to which I have referred, that it was a name which "would not have been used in Babylonia in the age of Nebuchadrezzar. . . It may have found its way into the Book of Daniel from the fourteenth chapter of Genesis." Schrader, a member of the school which Prof. Sayce has quitted, but also a leading Assyriologist, cannot suffer that suggestion to pass without chastisement. His words are these: "*Arioch.* There is no reason to suppose that this name has simply been borrowed from Genesis xiv. 1. The name Iri-Aku is a genuine Babylonian one, and may have been preserved in Babylonia up to the latest date with which we are here concerned." *

But, leaving the names, and coming to what is much more important—the arrangements and customs which the first chapter of Daniel speaks of as prevailing at the time—we find the Book most emphatically confirmed. Ashpenaz is spoken of as "Prince" or "Chief of the eunuchs." To him Daniel first of all makes his request that he and his companions may be assigned a simple vegetable diet. The very desire of this princely personage, that Daniel may have the developed and goodly form that will attract the royal favour, leads to a denial of his request. Daniel then presents a modified petition to Melzar, "whom the prince of the eunuchs had set over Daniel, Hananiah, Mishael, and Azariah," to try them with this diet for ten days only (i. 9-18). Were there such fuctionaries in the royal palace in Babylon? "These two functionaries . . . of the palace," says Fr. Lenor-

* Page 127.

mant, "are two personages well known from the original Assyrian documents, and the text sets them before us with great exactness in their real relationships. As for the second (of them), it uses the very form of his title in the Assyrian tongue. . . . For the first, the expression used, *rab hassarisim* or *sar has-sari-sim*, is conformed to that *rab-saris* which corresponds, in the other Books of the Bible, to the Assyrian qualification *rabbi-nar* or *rab-nar*, 'chief of the servants,' indicating the superintendence of the eunuchs over all the service in the interior of the palace." *

CHAPTER VII:

THE REFERENCES IN DANIEL TO THE CHALDEANS.

EVERY reader of Scripture is aware of the frequent mention in Daniel of "the Chaldeans." That is certainly, indeed, not a peculiarity of the Book, for the name occurs in the Old Testament from Genesis onwards. It is used in Jeremiah with great frequency, as is natural in a Book which has to say so much of this Divinely-appointed scourge of Judah. We meet with it also in Ezekiel, the contemporary, along with Jeremiah, of Daniel. In one passage of Ezekiel we have an implied distinction which is noteworthy in view of what I am about to say. While the prophet speaks of "the land of the

---

* *La Divination chez les Chaldéens*, pp. 196, 197.

Chaldeans " (i. 3, &c.), he clearly indicates that these are not the only inhabitants of it. We read (xxiii. 23) of "the Babylonians and all the Chaldeans." The Chaldeans (in the Hebrew, *Chasdim*) are, therefore, not Babylonians. The Chaldeans, who were Accadians, and who belonged to the south of Babylonia, were now the masters of the country; and the Babylonians, who were Semites like the Assyrians, were their subjects. As we shall see immediately, this distinction shows full acquaintance with the times.

But there is a sense in which the term Chaldean is used in Daniel which is peculiar to the Book. It is applied to the learned class. In the account of Nebuchadnezzar's attempt to have his dream re-called and interpreted, the term "Chaldeans" is used in this restricted sense no fewer than five times. We read (ii. 2) that "the king commanded to call the magicians, and the astrologers, and the sorcerers, and the Chaldeans, for to shew the king his dreams." The Chaldeans are plainly the acknowledged heads of this fraternity; for it is they only who address the king and to whom the king replies. "Then spake the Chaldeans to the king" (verse 7); "the king answered and said to the Chaldeans" (5); "the Chaldeans answered before the king, and said, There is not a man upon the earth that can shew the king's matter: therefore there is no king, lord, nor ruler, that asked such things at any magician, or astrologer, or Chaldean " (10).

It is undeniable, therefore, that the term "Chaldean" is used to designate a class. This has been eagerly seized upon as an incontrovertible proof that the Book could not have been written by Daniel; that it must have been composed long after his day; and that it is, therefore, the forgery which the critics assert it to be. " The 'Chaldeans,'" writes Prof. Driver, "are synonymous in Daniel (i. 4 ; ii. 2, &c.) with the caste of wise men." This sense, he says, quoting Schrader, is unknown to the monuments; and he adds : " It dates from a time when practically the only 'Chaldeans' known belonged to the caste in question." * Whatever responsibility is attached to this contention must rest equally at least upon some leading representatives of Assyriology. Dr. Driver was only repeating the words of Schrader, who says that the use of the name Chaldeans as meaning "'wise men,' that we meet with in the Book of Daniel, is foreign to Assyrio-Babylonian usage, and did not arise till after the fall of the Babylonian empire. This is in itself," he concludes, "a clear indication of the post-exilic date of the Book of Daniel." †

Professor Sayce, in his book which still preserved so much of his earlier critical attitude, brought this to bear against the claims of this part of Scripture with all his tact and strength. He writes : "'The Chaldæans' are coupled with the 'magicians,' the 'astrologers,' and the 'sorcerers,' just as they are in Horace or other classical writers of a similar age (Daniel ii. 2). . . But after the fall of the Babylonian empire the word Chaldæan gradually assumed a new

---

* *Introduction*, p. 468. † *The Cuneiform Inscriptions*, vol. ii., p. 125.

meaning. The people of the West ceased to be acquainted with the Babylonians through their political power or their commercial relations; the only 'Chaldæans' known to them were the wandering astrologers and fortune-tellers who professed to predict the future or practice magic by the help of ancient 'Chaldæan Books.' 'Chaldæans,' consequently, became synonymous with fortune-tellers; and fortune-tellers, moreover, who, like the Gypsies, or 'Egyptians' of to-day, were not considered of a very respectable character. *The term lost its national and territorial signification, and became the equivalent of 'sorcerer' and 'magician.'*

"It is in this sense," he continues, "that the term Kasdim is used in the Book of Daniel. It is a sense which was unknown in the age of Nebuchadrezzar or of Cyrus, and its employment implies, not only that the period was long since past when Babylonia enjoyed a political life of its own, but also that the period had come when a Jewish writer could assign to a Hebrew word a signification derived from its Greek equivalent. This last fact is of considerable importance if we would determine the age of the Book of Daniel. We are transported to a period later than that of Alexander the Great. . In the eyes of the Assyriologist the use of the word Kasdim in the Book of Daniel would alone be sufficient to indicate the date of the work with unerring certainty." *

This passage, and indeed his whole treatment of the Book of Daniel, is singularly wanting in those

---

* *The Higher Criticism, &c.*, pp. 533-535.

qualities of thoroughness and insight which have won
for Dr. Sayce the high position which he has long
held in the estimation of those acquainted with his
works. He adds, for instance, the following : "An
almost equally clear indication of date is furnished
by the statement that 'the Chaldæans' spoke to
Nebuchadrezzar 'in Syriac.'" Now, Dr. Sayce, as
a Hebrew and Aramaic scholar, ought to have known
that the Book says nothing of the kind. It makes
no statement whatever as to the language in which
the king was addressed by his hastily summoned
counsellors. There is simply one word—*Aramith*—
that is, "Aramæan," prefixed to this part of the
Book. It draws the reader's attention to the fact
that the language of the narrative *is now changed
consciously and intentionally.* That change continues
chapter after chapter, long after the Chaldeans and
their speech have been left behind us. It is the
language of one-half the Book, and it covers the
predictions that relate to the Gentile supremacy over
the Jewish people along with the related history; and,
when we come to those prophecies which relate to the
return and to the re-establishment of God's people,
the Hebrew is again resumed as the language of the
Book. As the whole of the New Testament is in
Greek, and is marked by that fact as being intended
for, and prophetic of, the period of the Gentile
Church—the supremacy of the Gentiles in the things
of God; so the change here from the Hebrew, the
language of God's people, to the Aramæan, the language
which was the means of political and commercial

intercourse among the Gentile peoples, has a similar symbolic message. That long-continued Gentile supremacy, which has come down unbroken to our own day, is recognised, and is indeed ordained, by God.

This fact, that the Aramæan is not confined to the speech of the Chaldeans, ought to have been noticed by Professor Sayce. But he makes another statement that is still harder to understand. He says that the Book of Daniel shows that, when it was written, the term Chaldean had "lost its national and territorial signification, and become the equivalent of 'sorcerer' and 'magician.'" The reader will peruse these words with astonishment. We turn to the very passage which Professor Sayce cites—Dan. ii. 2 —and we read : "Then the king commanded to call the magicians . . . and the sorcerers, and the Chaldeans for to shew the king his dream." Here, so far from the term being used in the sense of "sorcerer" and "magician," it is distinctly set apart from these as the name of a special and different class. This may not seem a great matter ; but it shows a lack of the distinguished Assyriologist's usual full and patient consideration of facts. The Chaldæans are certainly spoken of as a class; but they are a distinguished class. They are plainly the acknowledged leaders of the wise men of Babylon. It is they alone who address the king.

But the statement that in Daniel the term Chaldæan "had lost its national and territorial signification" is amazing. When we read in Daniel v. 30:

"In that night was Belshazzar the king of the Chaldeans slain," are we to believe that the term "Chaldean" is not used in "its national and territorial signification?" And are we to reject that as the meaning of the word in ix. 1, where we read that Darius "was made king over the realm of the Chaldeans?" No one, capable of understanding what words mean, will conclude that any argument is needed to show that the word is used here "in its national and territorial signification." The peculiarity of the Book of Daniel is that the term "Chaldeans" is used in both senses, and I now proceed to show that this, instead of being a mark of a late date, reflects the actual conditions of the time. The designation of Belshazzar, to begin with, as "the king of the Chaldeans," instead of "the king of Babylon," shows the closest acquaintance with the character of the dominion which then came to an end. The Chaldeans were distinct from the Babylonians. The latter were a Semitic people closely allied to the Assyrians in speech, religion, and customs. The Chaldeans, on the other hand, were inhabitants of the southern parts of the country bordering upon the Persian gulf. "To all appearance, the Babylonians themselves," says Dr. Pinches, "preferred the Assyrians to the semi-barbarous Chaldæans and Aramæans, with whom they were, in fact, in too close connection to have any great respect for. It is needless to say that this fell in with the ambition of the kings of Assyria." *

---

* *The Old Testament, &c.,* p. 371.

P

But this antipathy seems also to have had another explanation. The Chaldeans had been the ancient masters of Babylonia, and their claims to the dominion seem to have been acknowledged even after their power was overthrown. During the supremacy of the Elamitic conquerors, to whom Chedorlaomer belonged, one of them " married," says Maspero, "a princess of Chaldæan blood, and by this means legitimatised his usurpation in the eyes of his subjects." The insurrections in Babylonia, with which the Assyrian monarchs had to contend, were led by the Chaldean princes. It was one of these, Merodach-Baladan, who sent an embassy to Hezekiah ; and when the Assyrian power came at last to its end, it was a Chaldean who seized the falling sceptre. It is now generally agreed that Nabopolassar, the father of Nebuchadnezzar, belonged to this ancient people, and was probably the rightful representative of its royal house. The new Babylonian was literally, as the Book of Daniel distinctly implies, a Chaldean supremacy.

But they were a caste as well as a nationality. The caste may be said, in fact, to have represented the nation. They had retained the tongue, the writing, and the culture of their ancestors, and their great colleges won the admiration of the Greeks. Herodotus refers to them as the priests of Bel, and in a way that implies that their special pre-eminence was too well known to call for explanation. In describing the temple, and speaking of the sanctuary, he says that in its topmost tower : "There is no statue of any

kind set up in the place, nor is the chamber occupied
of nights by any one but a single native woman, who,
as the Chaldæans, the priests of this god, affirm, is
chosen for himself by the deity out of all the women
of the land." * On this, Rawlinson says : " It is
only recently that the darkness which has so long
enveloped the history of the Chaldæans has been
cleared up, but we are now able to present a tolerably
clear account of them." He then shows their identity
with the Akkadians, who spoke a Turanian tongue.
" With this race," he says, " originated the art of
writing, the building of cities, the institution of a
religious system, and the cultivation of all science,
and of astronomy in particular. . . In this primitive
Akkadian tongue . . were preserved all the scientific
treatises known to the Babylonians, long after the
Semitic element had become predominant in the
land. . . The mythological, astronomical, and other
scientific tablets found at Nineveh are exclusively in
the Akkadian language, and are thus shown to belong
to a priest-class, exactly answering to the Chaldæans
of profane history and of the Book of Daniel." †

This opinion has been fully confirmed by other in-
vestigators. I avail myself of the following from the
pages of Lenormant, which sets this question at rest :

"The superior and dominant caste," he says,
"entirely exclusive,was composed of the Chaldæans,
properly so-called, who . . . . were strangers, and
conquerors of the Turanian race. They had obtained possession of all priestly functions, and used

---

them so as to govern the state. Classical writers give us some details of their organisation, functions, and power.

" 'The Chaldæans,' says Diodorus Siculus, following Ctesias, who had seen them at Babylon, 'are the most ancient of the Babylonians; they formed in the state a body resembling the priests in Egypt. Set apart for following up the worship of the gods, they passed their whole life in meditation on philosophical subjects, and had acquired a great reputation in astrology; they especially devoted themselves to the science of divination, and to predictions of the future; they attempted to avert evil and procure good fortune, either by purification or by sacrifices, or by enchantments. They were accomplished in the art of predicting the future by observing the flight of birds; they explained dreams and prodigies. Skilled in the art of inspecting the entrails of victims, they were accounted capable of giving the true interpretation. But these branches of knowledge were not taught as among the Greeks. The learning of the Chaldæans was a family tradition; the son who inherited this from his father was exempt from all taxes. Having their relations for instructors, they had the double advantage of being taught everything without reserve, and that by masters in whose statements they could put implicit faith. Accustomed to work from infancy, they made great progress in the study of astrology, partly because learning is easy at an early age, and partly because they received a long course of instruction. . . The Chaldæans always remained at the same point in science, maintaining their traditions without alteration; the Greeks, on the contrary, thinking of nothing but profit, were constantly forming new schools, disputing among themselves as to the truth of the most important doctrines, confusing the minds of their disciples, who, tossed about in continual doubt, ended in believing nothing at all."

"We see by the Book of Daniel," continues Lenormant, "what were the functions of the Chaldæans; they composed many distinct classes, of more or less elevated rank in the hierarchy. Some of them were the sacred scribes, decipherers of writings; others the constructors of horoscopes, or interpreters of the stars, magicians who pronounced magical formulæ, conjurors who had power to avert malign influences. Their power of divination assured them great influence, as it made them, so to speak, masters of every one's destiny. They usually foretold in almanacks, a custom that seems to have lasted to our own time, all that our common almanacks now predict— fluctuations in the temperature, physical phenomena, and historical events. The Chaldæans were not confined to Babylon, but were spread over all Babylonia. They had schools in various places, more or less flourishing; according to Strabo, that at Borsippa was the most celebrated. That at Orchoe, or Erech, was also well-known, and maintained its reputation down to the times of the Romans. . . .

"But the Chaldæans did not confine themselves to the duties and positions of priests and astrologers, and to the unbounded influence derived from this position both over the State and over individuals. They became the absolute governing class in politics.

Members of this caste commanded armies, and held all the chief offices of the State. From them came all the royal families who ruled Babylon, whether vassals of Assyria, or, after the time of Phul, completely independent. At the head of the hierarchy and caste was an Archi-magus, whose national and proper title we do not yet know ; he was, next to the king, the chief personage of the empire ; he accompanied the sovereign everywhere, even in war, to direct all his actions according to the priestly rule and presage. When the king died, and the legitimate successor could not immediately assume the reins of power, this personage administered the government in the interim, as in the instance which occurred between the death of Nabopolassar and the arrival of Nebuchadnezzar." *

I need hardly add that here we have, as Lenormant confesses, the very state of things implied in the Book of Daniel. The Chaldeans were both a nationality and a caste ; and that they are spoken of in both relationships makes this Scripture, here as everywhere besides, a faithful mirror of the time.

CHAPTER VIII.

BABYLONIAN COURT-PATRONAGE OF MAGIC.

WE have just seen how it has fared with the contention that, because *Daniel* speaks of the Chaldeans as a caste, the Book is unhistorical. It

* *The Ancient History of the East,* vol. i., pp. 493-495.

would, on the contrary, have been a clear mark of
ignorance of the times had it, in dealing so closely
with the Babylonian priesthood, not described the
Chaldeans as a caste. The objection has detained
us, however, on what is merely the border of one of
the most conclusive proofs of the historical character
of the Book.

There is much in the Book which, because it deals
with a civilisation so utterly different from our own,
may strike a reader not only as extraordinary, but as
unreal. It is this fact that has seconded so well the
attempts which have been made to discredit its
claims; and that the description of this scene has
helped to form the impression there can be no doubt.
We are told that " Nebuchadnezzar dreamed dreams,
wherewith his spirit was troubled, and his sleep brake
from him " (ii. 1). In this there is nothing strange.
Nor are we surprised that he should immediately
seek the solace and help of counsellors; but we are
certainly astonished when we note to whom it is that
the call is sent. Neither friends nor counsellors are
summoned. He might certainly have sent for the
priests; but these are not described as ministers of
religion. He "commanded to call the magicians,
and the astronomers, and the sorcerers, and the
Chaldeans " (verse 2). Two other names are added—
" wise men," and " soothsayers." Here one epithet
is added to another, giving us an impression of a
public and extraordinary culture of magical arts.
This priesthood is thus fully occupied and identified
with a pursuit which we regard to-day as a hideous

superstition, and which, in earlier times, was looked
upon with horror as a commerce with the infernal
world. Is it credible that any nation, and especially
a nation that was the heir of one of the grandest of all
civilisations, could descend so low as openly to cultivate these arts, and to apply to them the venerated
name of religion? And was this true of the Babylon
in which Daniel lived? These are questions for
which we shall try to find an answer. And, if it is a
true description of the Babylonian faith, we shall be
met by another inquiry: are the classes named in
the second chapter those into which the learned and
priestly class was really divided?

A prolonged study of the Babylonian texts has
thrown increasing light upon the Babylonian religion.
In his re-study of the subject, the results of which
were made known in his recent *Gifford Lectures,** Prof.
Sayce contrasts the Israelitish and Babylonish re-
ligions. "How far," he says, "the Babylonian prophet
resembled the Hebrew prophet it is at present impossible to say. But there were certainly two important
points in which they differed. The Babylonian prophet
was, on the one side, a member of the priestly body;
the mere peasant could not become an 'utterer' of
the will of heaven without previous training and
consecration. There was, consequently, no such
distinction between the prophet and the priest as
prevailed in Israel; Babylonia was a theocratic, not
a democratic, State. On the other side, the prophet
was closely linked with the magician and necro-

---

mancer. Magic had been taken under the protection of the State religion, not repudiated and persecuted as among the Israelites. Hence, while the prophet was a priest to whom the rites of purification were specially entrusted, he was, at the same time, classed with the *sailu* who 'inquired' of the dead, the *masêlu* or necromancer, and the *makhkhu* or 'soothsayer.'"*

"The sacred books of Babylonia," he says on another page, "fall into three classes. We have, first, the so-called magical texts, or incantations, the object of which was to preserve the faithful from disease and mischief, to ward off death, and to defeat the evil arts of the witch and the sorcerer. Secondly, there are hymns to the gods; and, lastly, the penitential psalms, which resemble, in many respects, the psalms of the Old Testament." After speaking of "the ritual texts," he says these were "the framework in which the hymns and spells were set ; and they all formed together a single act of Divine worship, the several parts of which could not be separated without endangering the efficacy of the whole. That the incantations," he adds, "were the older portion of the sacred literature of Chaldæa, was perceived by Lenormant. They go back to the age of Animism, to the days when, as yet, the multitudinous spirits and demons of Sumerian" (Akkadian or Chaldæan) "belief had not made way for the gods of Semitic Babylonia, or the sorcerer and medicine-man for a hierarchy of priests. They transport us into a world that harmonises but badly with the decorous and

---

* Pages 465, 466.

orderly realms of the gods of light. . . . . Ea is no longer the creator and culture god, but a master of magic spells; and his son A'sari displays his goodness towards mankind by instructing them how to remove the sorceries in which they have been involved, and the witcheries with which they have been tormented." *

In a further description of the so-called sacred books, he says : " The official canon had been collected together from all sides. . . Up to the last, one of the classes into which the priesthood was divided was known as the Êni or 'Chanters,' whose name was derived from the Sumerian ên, 'an incantation.' It is this word which is prefixed to the charms and incantatory hymns that constitute so integral a part of the magical texts; and though in course of time it came to denote little more than ' recitation,' it was recitation which possessed magical powers, and for which, therefore, a special training was necessary. A single mistake in pronunciation or intonation, a single substitution of one word for another, was sufficient to destroy the charm and necessitate the repetition of the ceremony. Some of the incantations had even to be recited in a whisper, like certain parts of the Roman missal; and a whole series, or collection, is accordingly termed ' the ritual of the whispered charm,' reminding us of the passage in the Book of Isaiah where the prophet refers to ' the wizards that peep and mutter.' " In a note he adds: " The beginning, for instance, of the second book of the Maglû

---

* Pages 399-401.

collection had to be recited in a whisper before a wax image." *

On page 487 he speaks of "that dark background of magic and sorcery which distinguished and disfigured the religion of Babylonia up to the last. The Sumerian element," he proceeds, "continued to survive in the Babylonian people, and the magic which was its primitive religion survived also. It was never eliminated; behind the priest lurked the sorcerer; the spell and the incantation were but partially hidden beneath the prayer and the penitential psalm. One result of this was the exaggerated importance attached to rites and ceremonies, and the small space occupied by the moral element in the official Babylonian faith."

Here, it is abundantly evident, recent discovery has brought to the light of day the extraordinary features of the very worship revealed to us in the second chapter of Daniel. But there is one class mentioned in the Scripture—the astrologers—of which nothing has so far been said in these extracts. Was the lore of the stars as much prized and cultivated as the various enchantments? The work, from which I have just quoted, replies to this question also. "A hundred years ago, writers on the history or philosophy of religion had much to say about what they called Sabaism. The earliest form of idolatry was supposed to have been a worship of the heavenly bodies. . . . 'Sabaism' has long since fallen into disrepute. Anthropology has long since

* Pages 410, 411.

taught us that primitive religion is not confined to a worship of the stars. . . . Of late the tendency has been to discount it altogether as a factor in the history of religion.

"But the tendency," Prof. Sayce continues, "has gone too far. There was one religion, at all events, in which it played an important part. This was the religion of ancient Babylon and of those other countries which were influenced by Babylonian culture." After remarking how an insufficient acquaintance with the inscriptions had seemed to him, and others, to support the idea that this was a late development, he confesses that further discovery has corrected that impression. "The rise and growth," he says, "are of far earlier date than was formerly imagined. Astro-theology was not a mere learned scheme of allegorised science, the plaything of a school of pedants: it exercised a considerable influence upon the religion of Babylonia, and upon the history of its people." * And not only had it entered into the ancient religion, but there were also observatories in connection with the temples, whence the stars were constantly watched, and the seeming connections of the heavens with passing events were carefully recorded. There were seventy-two books which bore the name "The Illumination of Bel," and which contained the record of the astronomical observations of the past. The astrologers, as is plain from the title of those books— "The Illumination of Bel"—were among the most

* Pages 479, 480.

important sections of the Babylonian priesthood.

Here, then, is the reply to our first question. Magic and religion were mixed up in this very manner in the Babylon of Daniel's time. The description in the Scripture is neither a caricature nor an exaggeration. It is an exact representation of the religion of the time as it existed in this capital city of the world.

Let us now ask what answer research has procured to our second question. Has the Book of Daniel made us acquainted with the actual divisions of the priesthood? There are, in all, six classes named in Daniel. These are the *Chasdim*, or the Chaldeans; the *gazerim*, the "soothsayers" (see ii. 27); the *khakimim*, the "wise men" (ii. 12); the *khartumim*, the "magicians"; the *mekasheim*, the "sorcerers"; and the *assaphim*, the "astrologers." These names were the despair of scholars. The ancient rabbis made attempts to distinguish between them, which only showed that no real knowledge as to their meaning any longer existed. The Greek translators in the Septuagint Version were plainly as much in the dark in regard to this matter as their rabbinical successors. This latter fact has been rightly regarded as a very serious one for the critics. They assign the composition of the Book of Daniel to the times of the Maccabees— to the very times when those Alexandrian scholars were concluding their Greek translation of the Old Testament. But at this very time, as the translation shows, all knowledge of the meaning of these terms had perished. How was it possible, then, for a writer forging this Book, not only to know that the Baby-

lonian priesthood was divided into sections, but also
to give us the titles by which these sections were
known in the days of Nebuchadnezzar and of Daniel?
Of course, it is quite open to the critics to reply
that this description of the priesthood is a bow drawn
at a venture, and that the implied character of the
Babylonian religion, the existence of a priesthood, its
divisions, and the names of them are all pure inventions. This, indeed, seems to be the only alternative;
but it is one which is equally impossible. In regard to
three of these four points we have already discovered
that the description is exact. This was, in reality, the
character of the Babylonian religion. It was a religion
of magic. And it had a priesthood separated for
study, and for the practice of the religious ceremonies.
The long extract from Lenormant has also shown that
the writer of Daniel was fully informed as to there
being divisions in this priesthood. He says that "they
composed many distinct classes, of more or less
elevated rank in the hierarchy. Some of them were
the sacred scribes, decipherers of writings; others the
constructors of horoscopes, or interpreters of the
stars, magicians who pronounced magical formulæ,
conjurors who had power to avert malign influences."*
The quotations from Prof. Sayce's recent lectures
have made this equally clear. He speaks of "the
classes into which the priesthood was divided," and
has already given us several examples.

And now, what is still more surprising, Assyriology
is showing that, in the matter of the names, the

* *The Ancient History of the East,* vol. i., p. 494.

Scripture lifts the veil from this ancient superstition. The reader has noticed the term *Assaphim,*
which our English Version has translated by the word
"astrologers." This word has been found on the
monuments, and been discovered to mean "prophets."
"The *asi-pi* or 'prophets,'" writes Prof. Sayce, "constituted a class apart. . It was 'by order of the college
of prophets' that Assurbanipal purified the shrines of
Babylon after the capture of the city, and the prophet
accompanied even an army in the field. At times
they predicted the future; more often it was rather
an announcement of the will of Heaven which they
delivered to mankind. As they prophesied they
poured out libations; hence it is that the purification
of the shrines of Babylon were their special care, and
that an old ritual text commands the prophet to pour
out libations 'for three days at dawn and night during
the middle watch.' The word was borrowed by the
writer of the Book of Daniel (ii. 10), under the form
of *ashshâph,* which the Authorised Version renders
'astrologers.' But the Babylonian *asip* or 'prophet'
was not an astrologer; he left to others the interpretation of the stars, and contented himself with
counselling or foretelling the destinies of men." *
The word appears also in other connections, bearing
the same meaning. The gate of the chapel on the
top of the pyramid of Borsippa bore the name of
bab Assaput, "the gate of the oracle." The inscriptions also speak of *bit assaput,* "the house of the
oracle" in the pyramid of the royal city of Babylon.

* *Gifford Lectures,* p. 463.

This is, so far, the only absolute identification which Assyriology has made. There are indications, however, that Daniel is here in advance of our discoveries. The word *khartumim*, "magicians," seems to be connected with the name of the rod of office which these carried. This was called *kharutu*, "sceptre." "It was the special office of these men," says Mr. Fuller,*"to repulse by their incantations, and even imprecations, the demons and evil spirits." There are many examples of the exorcisms which they used. The word *gazerim*, of which the Septuagint translators could make no sense whatever, and which they rendered by turning the Hebrew letters into the corresponding letters of the Greek alphabet, seems to be connected with the Assyrian word *kazir* which is met with in the inscriptions. The kazir "collected the laws. . . . of astrological phenomena and portents, and pronounced upon them." †

I shall conclude by mentioning a still more striking fact. Fr. Lenormant, who made a special study of these ancient texts, and who has long been the leading authority upon them, makes a significant admission of the marvellous accuracy of these allusions to the Babylonian priesthood. When I mention that the critical delusion with regard to the alleged Greek words in the Book (which we shall notice in a subsequent chapter) was shared by Lenormant, the importance of the following confession will be felt. He says : "It is curious to notice that the three parts composing thus the great work on magic, of

---

‡ *The Speaker's Commentary*, vol. vi., p. 251. †*Ibid*, p. 253.

which Sir Henry Rawlinson has found the remains, correspond exactly to the three classes of Chaldæan doctors, which Daniel enumerates together with the astrologers and divines *(Kasdim* and *gazrim)*, that is, the *Khartumim*, or conjurors, the *Chakamim*, or physicians, and the *Asaphim*, or theosophists. The further we advance in the knowledge of the cuneiform texts, the greater does the necessity appear of reversing the condemnation much too prematurely pronounced by the German exegetical school against the date of the writings of the fourth of the greater prophets." * It will be felt that the foregoing study of the Babylonian religion and priesthood compels us all to share that judgment. It was simply impossible that a late writer could have cast aside the dense ignorance of his time and have so shown us, without effort and merely by the choice of his words and the moulding of his phrases, that religion and the divisions of its priesthood. Judged merely as a human composition, the Book belongs to the time.

CHAPTER IX.

NEBUCHADNEZZAR'S DREAM.

IF we are struck by the strangeness of the counsellors whom Nebuchadnezzar calls before him, the reason for the summons must seem still more extraordinary, not to say extravagant. The

---

* *Chaldæan Magic*, p. 14.

king is troubled by a dream, and is indeed so troubled
by it that these men must either recall and interpret
it, or die!

It need not be said that nowhere to-day could such
a scene occur in civilised and sane society. But it
may be thought that we can go still farther, and say
that such a scene was never possible anywhere. Could
we conceive of it as possible, say at the court of
Alexander the Great? In arguing in this way, however,
we assume that every civilisation must be after our
Western pattern, and that Eastern civilisation must
not differ from ours on pain of being pronounced
incredible. We are only rational when with open
mind we enquire what this Eastern civilisation really
was.

It may easily be shown that our modern ideas
regarding dreams differ materially from those of our
forefathers; but a glance at Herodotus or any other
ancient author, or even at the sceptical Bayle, is
enough to show that in former times importance was
universally attached to dreams. In his brief notice
of Majus, an author and teacher of languages in
Naples towards the end of the fifteenth century,
Bayle says: " He was the great *onirocritick* ('judge
of dreams') of his age: and people flocked to him
from all parts to know what such and such dreams
presaged. Many pretended that his answers to
them were very useful. This is not unworthy of
reflection."

In a long note appended to this last sentence,
Bayle, with his usual marvellous learning, deals with

the entire subject of dreams. The account of the
daily scene in Majus's chambers, with which he
begins his note, shows how dangerous it is to judge
even the fifteenth century of our own era by the
notions of to-day. "Alexander ab Alexandro," he
writes, "who had been his scholar, says wonderful
things of his knowledge in these matters. Every
morning the house of Majus was full of people who
came to tell him their dreams, that they might learn
from him the interpretation of them ; and among
them there were some persons of quality. He
answered them, not as the greatest part of others do,
in dark speeches and a few words, but clearly and
largely. Many persons, by following his advice,
secured themselves from death, and prevented sometimes very great troubles." After giving his own
explanation, he adds : " I desire also that it may be
observed that those, who maintain that there are
dreams of divination, need do no more but enervate
the objections of their adversaries, for they have an
infinite number of facts to allege for their opinion ;
and so have those also who maintain that there is
such a thing as magic. . . I ought also to take notice
that I do not pretend to excuse the ancient Pagans
either as to the care they took to relate so many
dreams in their histories, or as to the proceedings
that were consequent upon certain dreams. Sometimes they had no other foundation for appointing
certain ceremonies, or for condemning the accused.
. . . . One may justly laugh at the weakness of
Augustus, and much more at the Law, which enjoined

all private persons in certain countries, who had dreamed anything concerning the Republic, to declare it openly, either by setting up an advertisement or by a Crier."

These references are sufficient to indicate how widely the views of antiquity differ from those of the present time upon this matter. Artemidorus of Ephesus, a celebrated naturalist, who lived about the beginning of the Roman Empire, wrote an extensive work on the subject of dreams and their interpretation which still survives, and which has passed through several editions since the invention of printing. Herodotus details the repeated dream by which Xerxes was said to have been driven to invade Greece. He dreamed that he saw before him a man of unusual stature and beauty, who commanded him to resume his intention of subduing the Greeks. The effect of the vision disappeared under the expostulations of his wise counsellors, and he announced to the assembled princes and officials of the empire that the expedition was abandoned. But the vision was repeated. It appeared also to Artabanus, the king's uncle, who had strongly dissuaded him from this enterprise, and the result was the conversion of king and counsellor to a warlike policy.

Other instances related by Herodotus show that similar beliefs were entertained in the West. The inscriptions disclose the fact that the belief had a stronger hold upon Assyria and Babylonia than even these reports prepare us for. Kings do not in the least shrink from avowing to their subjects and to posterity that they regarded dreams as messages from the gods. Assurbanipal, king of Assyria, and not very far removed in point of time from Nebuchadnezzar himself, tells us that Gyges, king of Lydia, sent an embassy to him to say that in a dream the god Assur had appeared to him, commanding him to submit himself to the king of Assyria. But Assurbanipal also tells us of a message which came to himself through a vision. He records that while present at Arbela to observe the festival there in honour of Ishtar, he prayed to her and besought her help to save him from an Elamitic invasion which was then threatened. "In the night time of that night, in which I had prayed to her," he says, "a certain seer lay down and had a dream. In the midst of the night Ishtar appeared to him, and he related the vision to me thus: Ishtar who dwells in Arbela came unto me begirt right and left with flames, holding her bow in her hand, and riding in her open chariot as if going to the battle. And thou didst stand before her. She addressed thee as a mother would her child. She smiled upon thee, she Ishtar, the highest of the gods, and gave thee a command, Thus: Take (this bow) she said, to go to battle with! Wherever thy camp shall stand, I will come to it," &c.

Dreams were regarded as showing the special favour of the gods, and as the gateway between the soul of man and the Divinity. This we know from the monuments to have been specially the case in Babylon and in the life-time of Daniel. Nabonidus, a number of whose inscriptions have been recovered, speaks so frequently of these Divine favours vouchsafed to him that Winckler, in his recently-issued edition of Schrader's book on *The Cuneiform Inscriptions and the Old Testament*, says that he (Nabonidus) ascribes all his acts to revelations made to him in dreams. We might quite legitimately ask whether this does not support somewhat remarkably the accounts in Daniel. If it had really happened that such visions had entered into the experience, and influenced so notably the career of his great predecessor, we should at once have an explanation of the exceeding prominence given to dreams in the inscriptions of this last king of the Chaldean dynasty. But I ask only that the fact should be noted that this belief that dreams were sent from heaven, and were laden with Divine counsel not only for what concerned the king as an individual, but also for the well-being of the State, was a special feature of Daniel's time. This at once explains how God should have chosen this means to reveal His will to Nebuchadnezzar. In no other fashion could the conviction have been so powerfully impressed upon him that the message was from the God of Israel, the Creator of heaven and of earth. It also enables us to understand the king's desire to have the dream recalled and its message read.

But we have something more to go upon, in this instance, than this conclusive proof that the narrative is in the fullest accord with the times of which it speaks. We are able to show that the dream, the record of which has been preserved for us in the Scripture, was in very truth a revelation from God. I shall not enter into any minute exposition of the prophecy, for such it really was. A glance at some of its outstanding features will be enough to demonstrate how God has here affixed His seal to the Book. It was no doubt in accordance with the Divine purpose that the dream should have to be recalled to Nebuchadnezzar through Daniel's intervention. That was the Divine seal to him upon the communication that was to follow. For the message needed such an affirmation then, seeing that the events whose advent it announced were still future. To us, who look now from another standpoint, the affirmation comes in a different fashion. We ask—Has God fulfilled what God was then said to have revealed?

The great colossal statue which the king had seen was made up of four parts. There was (1) the head of gold interpreted to the king as representing his own empire, the Babylonian. (2) The breast and the arms (a two-fold power) were of silver. This was said to Nebuchadnezzar to represent another kingdom inferior to thee, which shall arise "after thee." (3) The belly and the thighs (margin, "sides") were of brass, and this was said to signify "another third kingdom of brass which shall bear rule over all the earth." (4) The legs of the image (another power of a two-fold character) were of iron; and this "fourth kingdom," said the prophet, "shall be strong as iron: forasmuch as iron breaketh in pieces and subdueth all things; and as iron that breaketh all these, shall it break it in pieces and bruise." (4a) Special attention is directed to the final condition of the fourth empire.

It is to be divided, and to be partly strong and partly weak. "His feet part of iron and part of clay;" that is, of brittle earthenware, which seems as hard as iron, but is smashed by a stroke into fragments which cannot be welded together again. This also receives its interpretation, and that, too, with special fulness. "And whereas thou sawest the feet and toes, part of potter's clay and part of iron, the kingdom shall be divided; but there shall be in it of the strength of the iron, forasmuch as thou sawest the iron mixed with miry clay. And as the toes of the feet were part of iron and part of clay, so the kingdom shall be partly strong, and partly broken " (margin, "brittle") [ii. 41, 42]. (5) The great image met its doom before the king's eyes in the night vision. "Thou sawest till that a stone was cut out without hands, which smote the image upon his feet that were of iron and clay, and brake them to pieces. Then was the iron, the clay, the brass, the silver, and the gold, broken to pieces together, and became like the chaff of the summer threshingfloors; and the wind carried them away, that no place was found for them : and the stone that smote the image became a great mountain, and filled the whole earth." The interpretation of this part of the dream is as follows : "And in the days of these kings " (the toes, therefore, represent "kings," or kingdoms, existing simultaneously) "shall the God of heaven set up a kingdom, which shall never be destroyed : and the kingdom shall not be left to other people, but it shall break in pieces and consume all these kingdoms, and it shall stand for ever. Forasmuch as thou sawest that the stone was cut out of the mountain without hands, and that it brake in pieces the iron, the brass, the clay, the silver, and the gold; the great God hath made known to the king what shall come to pass hereafter: and the dream is certain, and the interpretation thereof sure " (verses 34, 35, 44, 45).

CHAPTER X.

THE DREAM INTERPRETED.

HERE, then, we have the entire scheme of the world's history from the time of Nebuchad-nezzar to our own; and so triumphantly have the prophetic claims of this scheme been vindicated that the most strenuous efforts have been made to confuse the great dividing lines which are as conspicuous in the world's history as in the prophecy. Every possible variation has been tried to prevent the Roman Empire being included within the view of the Scripture. Dr. Pusey has summarised these attempts as follows :—*

(1) Nebuchadnezzar alone was made the first Empire; the weak descendants of his house, the second.

(2) The Medo-Persian Empire was divided, so that the Median should become the second empire, the Persian should be the third.

* *Lectures on Daniel the Prophet,* p. 101.

(3) Leaving both these in their integrity, the
Macedonian Empire was divided, Alexander alone
being made to constitute the third Empire ; his
successors, amid the weakness of their perpetual
divisions, the fourth. This was Porphyry's expe-
dient.

(4) Lastly, all three Empires were left entire, and
the Empire, which was subtracted at the end, was
replaced by one added on at the beginning. Ewald
was rightly dissatisfied with all those former solutions ; yet with the contempt for any evidence, which
so often characterises German theory, he assumed
that Daniel lived, not at Babylon, but at Nineveh;
and that " the winged lion traditionally meant the
Assyrian Empire." " The bear " then became "the
Babylonian symbol ; the leopard that of the Medes
and Persians ; while the fourth beast represented, as
is not uncommonly held," says Dr. Williams, " the
sway of Alexander." *

" Now, of these theories," continues Dr. Pusey,
" each concedes by turns so much of the truth as it
can afford. Out of the four theories, the adherents
of three concede, or contend, that the Babylonian
Empire in its integrity is one entire Empire ; three
maintain the same as to the Medo-Persian ; three, as
to Alexander and his successors. So that the traditional interpretation of, I may say, both the Jewish
and the Christian Church, nay, of the heathen world
before Christ, has, in each case, the support of three
out of the four parties who oppose it."

In other words, none of these expedients satisfies

---

* *Essays and Reviews*, p. 76.

the rationalists themselves. The late Dean Farrar
insisted that the Medes and the Persians formed the
second and the third Empires. But the Medes never
held what could by any possibility be described as a
world-wide dominion, and, above all, they were never
masters of Judæa and of the Jewish people. The
suggestion of Ewald that the Assyrian was the first
Empire was too daring in view of the words spoken
to Nebuchadnezzar: "Thou art this head of gold"
(verse 38). The remaining theories, which insist
that a distinction had to be made between Nebuchadnezzar and the after kings of the Chaldean Empire,
or between Alexander and his successors, were too
hopelessly absurd for adoption. But all those theories
are equally hopeless in view of the statements in
other portions of Daniel. The four Kingdoms are
seen again by the prophet as four beasts of prey; and
there the fourth beast receives the fullest description
of all. This has ten horns, and among the ten a
new horn makes its appearance, before which three
of the ten are plucked up by the roots. The new
"power" (for such is invariably the meaning of that
figure in Scripture) "made war with the saints, and
prevailed against them; until the Ancient of Days
came, and judgment was given to the saints of the
Most High; and the time came that the saints
possessed the kingdom " (vii. 21, 22).

The fourth Kingdom, therefore, is that which is to
go on till the end of the dominions of man and the
founding of the kingdom of God. There is to be no
other human dominion after it, but it is to endure in

its fragments until the Lord shall come in judgment
for the nations. The importance of this identification
will be felt; for if this is a veritable prophecy, we
should know something of the fourth Empire. The
second and the third Empires are also as distinctly
defined and named in the eighth chapter as that of
Babylon in the second. There we have the record of
another vision. The prophet beholds "a ram which
had two horns; but one was higher than the other,
and the higher came up last" (viii. 3). The reader
will remember the *two arms* of the image. This
Empire is represented, therefore, in both visions as
two-fold; and the interpretation granted to the
prophet removes every shadow of doubt as to the
Medo-Persian Empire being the second of the four
mentioned in chapter ii. "The ram," said the angel,
"which thou sawest having two horns, are the kings
of Media and Persia" (verse 20). The one figure
represents the combined peoples. Their united
strength is its arms, and is also symbolised by the
horns. The two "powers" are possessed by this
one dominion. This ram the prophet sees attacked
by a he-goat, which has one "notable horn between
his eyes" (verse 6). *After* his victory over the ram,
"the great horn was broken; and for it came up
four notable ones toward the four winds of heaven"
(verse 8). This is also explained. "The rough goat
which thou sawest is the king of Grecia; and the
great horn that is between his eyes is the first king.
Now that being broken, whereas four stood up for
it, four kingdoms shall stand up out of the nation, but

not in his power" (verses 21, 22). Here Alexander
and his successors form one Empire, represented by
the goat, and the Medes and the Persians form
another, represented by the ram. The attempts to
blot out, or to confuse those great dividing lines
have thus been providentially frustrated. The first is
named the Babylonian in chapter ii.; and in chap. viii.
the second is named the Medo-Persian, and the third
the Grecian with its unity and its after four-fold
division. The only remaining Empire is that which
inherited the dominions of these four; and that we
know was the Roman.

Now, even if we limit ourselves to this outline, is
it possible to explain it apart from miracle? This
Book says that there would be four great world-
empires *of man;* that there should be no more than
these four in all this world's after history; and that
the fifth should be the universal Empire of God.
These four have appeared. The fourth Empire was
in the fulness of its glory at the beginning of the
Christian era, a century and a-half after the time
when, according to the critics, this Book was completed, and when it contained everything which it
contains now. The Book said that the Roman
Empire would be succeeded by no other universal
dominion of man; and, strange to say, though
successors were found for the Empires of Babylon,
and of Persia, and of Greece, none have been found
for the Roman. The world's throne is vacant to-
day. I ask again, is it possible to explain this? We
account for it by saying that this fact is God's seal

to the Book of Daniel; that, in other words, this is God's Book revealing what He was to do in the coming time. That explanation satisfies. It meets the case. Is there any other explanation that will satisfy?

But take another glance at the prediction. The fourth Empire is represented as two-fold. Every one will recall the two consuls of Rome, and the later division of the Empire into two—the Eastern and the Western. Then this two-fold Empire is to continue in fragments, or further divisions, represented by the ten toes of the image. This has long been the political condition of Europe and of the eastern portion of the Empire. Turkey has Syria, the other Asiatic provinces and part of Europe. The rest is divided up among the Powers of the time. I might show how the latest political developments have been bringing us appreciably nearer to the time when these Powers will number exactly ten. But take only these two additional facts: (1) That the Fourth Empire was to be two-fold; and (2) that it was to exist latterly in a larger number of portions; can we explain that on naturalistic principles? Are we not compelled to acknowledge that there has been here a distinct reading of the future—an undeniable revelation of things to come such as God alone could have given?

CHAPTER XI.

THE SO-CALLED GREEK WORDS IN DANIEL.

THE reader will find a number of additional confirmations of the Book of Daniel in another work of mine.* To what will be found there recent research has added nothing further that is of importance; and, as I desire to touch upon some confirmations of the New Testament History, I limit myself now to the supposed Greek words in this Book of Daniel.

The occurrence of these words has been seized upon with the greatest eagerness; for a fact of that kind appeared to justify the critical contention that the Book was a late production, composed during the fierce persecution under Antiochus Epiphanes, and taking the name of Daniel in order to persuade the suffering Jews to continued resistance by imparting to them a strong, but also lying, assurance of speedy deliverance. The critics find in that imagination of theirs one of the most natural of all possible motives for the production of the Book; and here, in these Greek words, is the one apparently incontestable proof that they needed. Those Macedonian, or Greek, words, they argued, showed that Greek influence had, by the time the Book was written, spread over the East, and planted these words in the Hebrew speech

---

* *The Inspiration and Accuracy of the Holy Scriptures*, pp. 340-576 (Marshall Bros.)

of the time. And when could that have been done? Certainly, was their reply, not before the triumphant invasion of Alexander the Great in 332 B.C. And even that date was plainly too high. For it must have taken time, and close and long-continued intercourse with the new masters of the East and of Palestine to have thus invaded, so to speak, the language of the Jewish people, and to have left these words in their daily speech as the lasting monuments of their triumph and their presence. Could any demonstration be more overwhelming that the Book must have been written about 160 B.C.?

The above is no exaggeration of the critics' confidence and boasting in view of the alleged Greek words. Bertholdt said long ago: "We meet with Greek words in the Book of Daniel, and this circumstance excludes the idea of an earlier composition than (taking the highest, but still an improbable supposition) towards the middle of the reign of Darius Hystaspis, when Daniel could no longer be alive."* These supposed facts have, however, been steadily melting away under the scrutiny of scholars and the researches of explorers, till there is now, as we shall see immediately, merely a ghost of the old array: but notwithstanding, "the Greek words" are still the stay and the rejoicing of the critic's heart. Dr. Driver says, under the words "*Authorship and date:*" "In face of the facts presented by the Book of Daniel, the opinion that it is the work of Daniel himself cannot be sustained. Internal evidence

---

* Quoted by Hengstenberg, *The Genuineness of Daniel*, p. 9.

shows, with a cogency which cannot be resisted, that it must have been written not earlier than about 300 B.C., and in Palestine; and it is at least *probable* that it was composed under the persecution of Antiochus Epiphanes B.C. 168, or 167." *

The statement is followed up, three pages further on, by the following: " Daniel . . contains at least three *Greek* words: ' *kitharos=kitharis* ' (Greek for harp, the same word from which *guitar* is derived); ' *pesanterim = psalterion* ' (Greek); ' *sumphonyah= symphonia.*' Whatever may be the case with *kitharis*," continues Dr. Driver, " it is incredible that *psalterion* and *symphonia* can have reached Babylon about 550 B.C. Anyone who has studied Greek history knows what the condition of the Greek world was in that century, and is aware that the arts and inventions of civilised life streamed then into Greece from the East, not from Greece eastwards. Still, if the instruments named were of a primitive kind, such as the *kitharis* (in Homer), it is *just* possible that it might be an exception to the rule, and that the Babylonians might have been indebted for their knowledge of it to the Greeks; so that had *kitharis* stood alone, it could not, perhaps, have been pressed. But no such exception can be made in the case of *psalterion* and *symphonia,* both *derived* forms, the former used first by Aristotle, the latter first by Plato, and in the sense of concerted music (or, possibly, of a specific musical instrument) first by Polybius. These words, it may be confidently affirmed, could not have been used in the Book of Daniel unless it had been written *after the dissemination of Greek influences in Asia through the conquests of Alexander the Great."* *

The italics throughout the quotation are Dr. Driver's. He afterwards, in summing up his proof, clenches this argument with the following statement : " The Greek words *demand*, the Hebrew *supports*, and the Aramaic *permits*, a date *after the conquest of Palestine by Alexander the Great."* † But along with all this reiteration there is a surprising reticence. Dr. Driver does not tell half the story of these Greek words ; and if the ministers of the period are to content themselves with his book, they will miss an edifying tale. Here is how the account stood against the Book of Daniel as summed up by the earlier critics. " We meet with Greek words in the Book of Daniel," says Bertholdt, in his commentary ; " and this circumstance," he continues, " excludes the idea of an earlier composition than (taking the highest, but still an improbable supposition) towards the middle of the reign of Darius Hystaspis, when Daniel could no longer have been alive." He then cites the following list, which for more convenient reference I place in two columns, accompanied by their English meanings :

HEBREW AND ARAMAIC.	ENGLISH.	GREEK.	ENGLISH.
Parthĕmim,	nobles.	*Prōtimoi*,	first, chief men.
Pithgam,	writing, decree.	*Phthegma*,	a voice, a sound.

HEBREW AND ARAMAIC.	ENGLISH.	GREEK.	ENGLISH.
Kārōz,	a herald.	*Kērux,*	a herald.
Kiraz,	to proclaim.	*Kērussein,*	to be a herald, to proclaim.
Pattish,	a tunic.	*Petasos,*	a broad-brimmed hat.
Nibizbah,	a gift.	*Nomisma,*	a custom, a current coin.

Names of Musical Instruments.

Kītharos,	a harp.	*Kitharis,*	a harp.
Sabka,	a stringed instrument.	*Sambukē,*	a harp, a sackbut.
Sūmphoniah,	a musical instrument.	*Symphonia,*	a musical instrument.
Mashrokhitha,	a musical instrument.	*Syrinks,*	a musical instrument.
Pesantērīn,	a musical instrument.	*Psalterion,*	a musical instrument.

Such was the list of alleged proofs of the late date of Daniel. The first six have perished long ago, and no trace of them will now be found in critical works like Dr. Driver's. It is left to us to build their monument, and to inform posterity what they were and how it fared with them. But this silence of present-day critics is eloquent. It shows that this part of the critical case has been demolished so completely that any further attempt to cling to it would be disastrous. Let us take the words in the order in which they are given above.

(1) *Parthēmim,* "nobles," was identified with the Greek *prōtimoi,* said to mean chief. But in this

matter critical scholarship showed itself as defective in its Greek as in its Aramaic. The word which the Greeks used in this sense was *entimoi*, and not *prōtimoi.* The most that can be urged is that the word is Persian. It appears in the Persian cuneiform inscriptions as *Fratama.* There was a long and ancient connection between Babylonia and Persia, and such intercourse is always accompanied by borrowing of words. In addition to this, the Persian dominion was established in Babylonia before the end of Daniel's ministry, and before his Book was written.

(2) *Pithgam,* "a writing," was said to be the Greek *Phthegma,* "a voice "; but it would be impossible to show that the words had any other connection than that of a similarity in sound. It is impossible, too, to substitute the Greek word for the Aramaic word where it occurs in Daniel.

(3) and (4) *Kiraz,* "to proclaim," and *Kārōz,* "a herald." The critics were jubilant over these words. The Greek *Kērux* and *Kērussein* were too closely allied both in form and in sense to allow the identification to be contested. But never was confidence more misplaced. These words had actually been borrowed by the Greeks. They were found in the Assyrio-Babylonian inscriptions, and were thus proved to be words in ordinary use among Semitic writers long before the time of Daniel.

(5) *Pattish* comes from a Hebrew word, " to strike with a hammer," " to spread out." *Pattish* was, consequently, something hammered or spread out, and is believed to be the tiara worn by the Babylonian

courtiers. That there are in Greek the verb *patassō*, with a similar meaning, and *petasos* (something spread out), "a broad-brimmed hat," is simply one of the proofs that the Semitic and the Aryan languages have sprung from the same primal tongue. *Pattish*, "a hammer," is found in Isaiah xli. 7, and in Jeremiah xxiii. 29 and l. 23.

(6) *Nibizbah*, "rewards" ("ye shall receive of me gifts and rewards" [Daniel ii. 6]), was said to be derived from the Greek word *nomisma*, "money." This was soon set aside by more accurate scholarship. Gesenius in his dictionary expressed his belief that it was a Persian word. This took us far beyond the time of Alexander the Great, and made its use in Daniel quite in keeping with Daniel's authorship of the Book. But in his later and greatest work, the Thesaurus, Gesenius rejects the supposed Persian origin of the word, and expresses his belief that it is derived from an Aramaic verb, "to ask for," which is closely connected in form with *nibizbah*. But Fuerst takes us further still. He reminds us of the Hebrew verb *bazaz*, "to plunder," "to take for a prey," "to take away." There can be no doubt that the word was closely connected with this old Hebrew root, and that it had been in use in the Aramaic tongue long ages before the time of Daniel.

The critics understand the value of the Napoleonic plan of hurling masses upon some important part of the enemy's line. They point to their long lists of alleged proofs (before whose mere length, indeed, the faith of the weak has often fallen), and they tell us that it is the number of these, rather than the weight of anyone of them, upon which they rely. But how many nothings must one add together to get even a fraction of the smallest positive number? I imagine that no one has ever yet been met with who was foolish enough to heap together the contents of a long array of empty pockets in the hope of making a pound or a penny as the result of his labour. And all these proofs were merely ciphers. They have vanished like a dream; and the higher criticism of to-day dislikes exceedingly to be reminded of them.

A like fate has been pursuing the alleged Greek names of the musical instruments mentioned in Daniel iii. All the six were originally claimed and rejoiced over. I have given five in the list on page 243. The number is now reduced to three, and even to two; and to this remnant Dr. Driver clings as to the sheet anchor of the critical attack upon Daniel. The critics were not at first aware that the Greeks had themselves declined the honour of having supplied the East with the sackbut. Athenæus, the Greek Grammarian who lived in the third century of our era, says that the *sambukē* was "a Syriac invention." This we are also told by a still earlier authority. Strabo, who wrote his *Geography* in the opening years of the Christian era, says: "From the song, the rhythm, and the instruments, all Thracian music is supposed to be Asiatic. . . Those who regard the whole of Asia as far as India as consecrated to Bacchus, refer to that country as the origin of a great portion of the present music. One author speaks of 'striking forcibly the Asiatic chithara;' another calls the pipes Berecynthian and Phrygian. Some of the instruments have also barbarous names, as Nablus, Sambuke, Babitus, Magadis, and others." He follows up this by saying that "the Athenians always showed their admiration of foreign customs." *

Here the sackbut and the harp, the *sambukē* and the *kitharis* are distinctly wiped out of the list by authority which critics dare not question. And besides this, the very foundation of their argument is shattered by the same authority. They hold that the Greek instruments came into Babylon. Strabo, unswayed by any prejudice, and speaking from his observation and his reading, that is, from knowledge unobtainable now by the best learning that exists, is distinctly of the contrary opinion. Dr. Driver, however, clings to two out of the six names. "Whatever," he says, "may be the case with *kitharis*, it is incredible that that *psaltērion* and *symphōnia* can have reached Babylon about 550 B.C."

This strong assertion is founded upon the belief of the critics, including himself, that little came into the East from Greece before the time of Alexander the Great. But that conviction was due originally to our ignorance of the international relations at that early period, an ignorance which had been largely dissipated when Dr. Driver penned his *Introduction*. The results of Flinders Petrie's excavations of the ancient Greek cities in Egypt were

---

* X., c. III., c. 17, 18.

public property before that time, and his statement, in which he refers to the bearing his discovery had upon this very question, had long been accessible to Dr. Driver. The discoverer pointed out that at Daphne, or Tapanhes, on the eastern frontier of Egypt, Greek civilisation had long been in contact with Judah and the further east, and that musical Greek instruments could have been taken even into Babylonia from that side. But the old contention that Greece carried nothing to Babylonia before the time of Alexander the Great is now too absurd for serious discussion. We have learned that the old world was not slumbering; but that it was, on the contrary, fully awake, accomplished, learned, ingenious, active, and enterprising.

And it is quite in harmony with this that we should discover the trace of a very busy commercial intercourse between Greece and Babylonia about a century before the time when Daniel was written. It is surprising, however, that these discoveries should bring us so fully into the heart of the question with which we are now dealing. For it proves that a brisk trade was then carried on in musical instruments. The harp with seven strings was invented by Terpander, a Greek poet and musician. " He was the first person," says Strabo, " that used the lyre with seven instead of four strings, as is mentioned in the verses attributed to him : ' We have relinquished the song adapted to four strings, and shall cause new hymns to resound on a seven-stringed cithara.' " *

---

* B. XIII., c. ii. 4.

Terpander's harp was invented in 650 B.C. Assurbanipal, king of Assyria, died 625 B.C.; that is, only twenty-five years elapsed between the invention of the seven-stringed harp and the death of Assurbanipal. The significance of these figures will be seen when it is stated that this harp with seven strings is sculptured upon a monument of Assurbanipal's.* Within those twenty-five years harps of this kind had been carried from Greece into Babylonia and sold at the court of King Assurbanipal ! But the time has long since passed when any one who really knows this subject could honestly maintain the critical objection. In the fifteenth century before our era there was a Greek ambassador at Tyre, and Tyre and the whole of Phœnicia were even then in active and constant intercourse with Babylonia. Sargon, who captured Samaria in 722 B.C., knew of Greece, and in his inscriptions names the sea around the island of Cyprus, "the sea of Javan," that is of Ionia, or Greece. His son Sennacherib encountered the Greeks in Cilicia, obtained a victory over them, and raised a monument to commemorate his triumph. Berossus mentions that this king also had a Greek corps in his army. Sennacherib's son and grandson, Esarhaddon and Assurbanipal, were in direct contact with the Greeks ; for they mention among their tributaries several Greek kings in the Isle of Cyprus —Ituander, of Paphos; Irisu, of Sillu : Damasu, of Curium, &c. These kings are named in the same list in which the name appears of Manasseh king of

---

* Fr. Lenormant, *La Divination chez les Chaldéens*, p. 191.

Judah. And no doubt we have here a possible means by which Assurbanipal, a great patron of music, may have been able to obtain possession of Terpander's newly-invented harp. We have also a proof of the close relationship between the Babylon of Nebuchadnezzar and Greece in a notice by Alcæus, who is said to have been the inventor of Lyric poetry, and who flourished about 611 B.C. Strabo, speaking of Mitylene, says: "It formerly produced celebrated men, as Pittacus, one of the Seven Wise Men; Alcæus the poet, and his brother Antimenidas, who, according to Alcæus, when fighting on the side of the Babylonians, achieved a great exploit, and extricated them from their danger by killing

'a valiant warrior, the king's wrestler, who was four cubits in height.' " *

Greek musical instruments, carrying with them, of course, their Greek names, could therefore be, and no doubt were, in Babylon long before the time of Daniel. In addition to this, it should be noted that this very picture of the solemn gathering in the plain of Dura, in which music holds so prominent a place, has strongly impressed Fr. Lenormant, the great Assyriologist. He says: "An author, removed from the events by four centuries, would have been truly learned, as hardly any one else of that time could have been, if he had known this fact, attested by the texts and by the sculptured monuments, that instrumental music, very little used by the first Assyrian kings, had become, precisely at the opening of the

B. XIII., c. ii. 3.

seventh century B.C., a leading element in all religious and public ceremonies in Assyria and Babylonia." *

This argument, drawn from the alleged Greek instruments, recoils, therefore, upon the critics themselves; and the attack upon Daniel shares the fate, which, as these pages have shown, has overtaken their so-called science everywhere besides.

La Divination chez les Chaldéens. p. 190.

THE NEW TESTAMENT HISTORY.

CHAPTER I.

THE ATTACK UPON THE NEW TESTAMENT.

A NUMBER of years ago it was firmly believed that the final battle for the New Testament Books, and for the great facts on which the faith of the Christian Church rests, had been fought and won for the believer. It was confidently affirmed that these would never again be called in question ; and we were consoled, amidst the strife which goes on around us to-day over the Old Testament, by the assurance that the citadel of the faith was safe, no matter what conclusion may be finally reached regarding the Old Testament.

There were many who were clear-sighted enough to appraise these assurances at their proper value. They saw that the attack upon the Old Testament was an indirect, but nevertheless deadly, attack upon the New Testament ; and that those who were admitting the enemy within the fortifications had, in that very act, practically surrendered the citadel. When men throw away the belief that the words of the Old Testament are the words of God as an exploded theory, how can they accept as Divine the teaching of the New Testament, which is based upon that very " exploded theory" ? In condemning that view of the Old Testament as a superstition unworthy of the twentieth century, they have condemned our

Lord and His Apostles : they have not only broken with the Old Testament ; they have also broken with the Christian faith.

This is being recognised with two-fold results. It has led to a gratifying pause on the part of many. But there has also been a further " advance " on the part of others. These cling to their former conclusions, and they are now engaged in finding accommodation for their inevitable results. The attack upon the New Testament has consequently been begun by our home critics.

There are circumstances which make this attack peculiarly difficult. In the case of the Old Testament, by denying the Mosaic origin of the Law and the antiquity of the Psalms, the critics have cleared a space of about ten centuries. Room enough can be found there for the growth of any number of legends. But the quotations from the New Testament, which are found in Christian authors, and the undoubted antiquity and early triumphs of the Christian Church, prevent the employment of similar tactics here. Nevertheless the attempt must be made, or rationalism will have to confess itself a failure. It is true that they admit that the former method cannot here be applied to the same extent. But, if the critics cannot now have a clear space of eight hundred or a thousand years, they may try to obtain at least a century. What may not be done in one hundred years! There is space enough there for hopes to translate themselves into supposed facts; for highly coloured rhetoric to be accepted as sober history, and to be furnished with additional details; for the development of doctrines; and for the growth of legend and myth.

The work of spreading these new ideas is proceeding with the old subtlety and industry. The alleged inconsistencies and contradictions of the Gospels are set forth as if they were new discoveries. No hint is given of the existence of explanations long known to all students of the Bible, and an impression is designedly created that these old infidel arguments are unanswerable. This is done, as I have said, designedly; for only thus can the belief be dispelled that we have in the New Testament God's own witness to the truth of our religion. Fallible documents cannot be Divine. They cannot be inspired by the Spirit of God. Histories hopelessly at variance with each other can only be merely human accounts, giving us the impressions of the men who wrote them, and conveying to us, not a relation of absolute facts, but, at the very most, merely a statement of what the writers honestly believed to be facts.

When we are once deftly landed in these conclusions, the rest of the work is comparatively easy. As the old adage has it, "It is human to err;" and when faith finds in its hands only human documents, it is paralysed. Its former confidence and resistance are gone; and its new masters can lead it whither they will. It is now a small matter to give up the early dates of the Gospels, and to remove these accounts of our Lord's life down to the second century. And

S

so the field is cleared for the play of the critical imagination. We are already familiar with the expression, found in the unctuous eulogiums of departed Unitarian professors, of "getting behind the Gospels." Seeing that these Gospels cannot any longer be depended upon for making us acquainted with the realities of the time with which they deal, we must, of course, welcome the man endowed with critical insight and with "historical imagination" to bring us face to face with that vanished past, and to show us the men and the things as they really were.

In this way it is hoped that the Incarnation and the Resurrection, the miracles of Jesus, the Atonement, the Imputed Righteousness of Christ, and everything which makes Christianity anything more than a philosophy will be left behind us. But there are difficulties in the way. There are testimonies outside of the New Testament writings, which the critics either forget or wrestle with in vain. Then recent research has here also been laying its tribute at the feet of the Bible; and alleged errors have been changed into proofs of historical accuracy. To a rapid survey of all these I have now to ask the reader's attention.

CHAPTER II.

The Church's Existence a Testimony to the Truth of Christianity.

ONE result of the discussions of the last century is that the great antiquity of the Christian religion, if not fully admitted, is now seldom questioned. It may prove helpful, however, to note the powerful array of facts which has compelled this acquiescence.

The persecutions of the Christians by the Roman Emperors came to an end in the year 313 A.D. In that year Constantine became master of the Empire. In him Christianity virtually took its seat upon the throne of the Cæsars. After its long wrestling with the princes of this world, the victor's wreath was placed upon the brow of the Church whose weapons were not carnal, but which, nevertheless, proved mighty to the pulling down of the strongholds of the earth's hoary idolatries. What, then, is the Church which thus wins its triumph at the commencement of the fourth century? Is its creed the creed of to-day? Are its sacred Books the sacred Books of to-day, neither more nor fewer? When we have passed through these fifteen hundred years which intervene, and have taken our stand by the Church which steps out of that sea of suffering and blood, is it one with us in every Christian conviction? Or has the

Church since then developed its doctrines and changed its sacred Books?

This is a question which is easily and satisfactorily answered. Gibbon, in writing his history of *The Decline and Fall of the Roman Empire,* found that, with Constantine and his successors, the Empire entered upon a new phase, and that, in order to explain it, he was compelled to insert at this point a very different history. In other words, sceptic though he was, he was forced to sketch the story of Christianity. He has done this with a thinly-veiled sneer, which, however, he frequently forgets to wear as his eloquent pen describes the novel features of the new faith. His admissions are of permanent value, for no one can either accuse Gibbon of ignorance, or suspect him of partiality for the Christian faith. He thus commences his celebrated fifteenth chapter:—

"A candid but rational inquiry into the progress and establishment of Christianity may be considered as a very essential part of the history of the Roman Empire. While that great body was invaded by open violence, or undermined by slow decay, a pure and humble religion gently insinuated itself into the minds of men, grew up in silence and obscurity, derived new vigour from opposition, and finally erected the triumphant banner of the cross on the ruins of the Capitol. Nor was the influence of Christianity confined to the period, or to the limits, of the Roman Empire. After a revolution of thirteen or fourteen centuries, that religion is still professed by the nations of Europe, the most distinguished portion of human kind in arts and

learning, as well as in arms. By the industry and
zeal of the Europeans it has been widely diffused
to the most distant shores of Asia and Africa; and,
by the means of their colonies, has been firmly
established from Canada to Chili, in a world unknown to the ancients."

But is this Christianity the Christianity of to-day?
Does it possess the Old Testament and the New?
And, if it possesses them, does it venerate, and trust,
and treasure them as we and our fathers have done?
In his endeavour to account for the triumph of the
Christian faith, Gibbon mentions, for one thing, its
superiority to Judaism. He says :—

"Christianity offered itself to the world armed
with the strength of the Mosaic law, and delivered
from the weight of its fetters. An exclusive zeal
for the truth of religion, and the unity of God,
was as carefully inculcated in the new as in the
ancient system; and whatever was now revealed to
mankind concerning the nature and design of the
Supreme Being was fitted to increase their reverence for that mysterious doctrine. The Divine
authority of Moses and the prophets was admitted,
and even established, as the firmest basis of
Christianity. From the beginning of the world an
uninterrupted series of predictions had announced
and prepared for the long-expected coming of the
Messiah, who, in compliance with the gross apprehensions of the Jews, had been more frequently
represented under the character of a king and
conqueror, than under that of a prophet, a martyr,
and the Son of God. By His expiatory sacrifice

the imperfect sacrifices of the temple were at once consummated and abolished. The ceremonial law, which consisted only of types and figures, was succeeded by a pure and spiritual worship, equally adapted to all climates, as well as to every condition of mankind ; and for the initiation of blood was substituted a more harmless initiation of water. The promise of Divine favour, instead of being partially confined to the posterity of Abraham, was universally proposed to the freeman and the slave, to the Greek and to the barbarian, to the Jew and to the Gentile. Every privilege that could raise the proselyte from earth to heaven, that could exalt his devotion, secure his happiness, or even gratify that secret pride, which, under the semblance of devotion, insinuates itself into the human heart, was still reserved for the members of the Christian Church ; but at the same time all mankind was permitted, and even solicited, to accept the glorious distinction, which was not only proffered as a favour, but imposed as an obligation. It became the most sacred duty of a new convert to diffuse among his friends and relations the inestimable blessings which he had received, and to warn them against a refusal that would be severely punished as a criminal disobedience to the will of a benevolent but all-powerful Deity."

It will be clear to everyone that the Church of to-day is in every important respect the Church of the fourth and the third centuries of our era. All the doctrines of the Christian Church are already there, and the great facts of the gospel story are as fully known and rejoiced in as they are now. Let us now pass over other two centuries. About the year 125 of our era, an "apology" for Christianity was presented to the Emperor Hadrian by an Athenian philosopher, named Aristides. It was, along with a similar work by a writer named Quadratus, the earliest of those famous writings which bore this title, and which were laid from time to time before the Emperors to enlighten them concerning the new faith, exposed to persecution both from prince and people. Eusebius speaks of both productions. To Hadrian, he says: " Quadratus addressed a discourse as an apology for the religion that we profess; because certain malicious persons attempted to harass our brethren. The work is still in the hands of some of the brethren, as also in our own, from which any one may see evident proof, both of the understanding of the man, and of his apostolic faith. This writer shows the antiquity of the age in which he lived in these passages: ' The deeds of our Saviour,' he says, ' were always before you, for they were true miracles; those that were healed, those that were raised from the dead, who were seen, not only when healed and when raised, but were always present. They remained living a long time, not only whilst our Lord was on earth, but likewise when He had left the earth. So that some of them have also lived to our own times.' Such was Quadratus. Aristides also, a man faithfully devoted to the religion we profess, like Quadratus, has left to posterity a defence of the faith addressed to Hadrian. This work is also preserved by a great number even to the present day." *

Both these works had long disappeared. The apology of Quadratus has not yet been discovered; but Professor R. Harris found a translation of the Apology of Aristides among the manuscripts in one of the libraries of the Convent of St. Catherine at Mount Sinai. From this, and also from another document which contains the Apology, we learn that the great facts of the gospel history were known to Aristides, and that " the writings," plainly the New Testament Books, had been read by Aristides. Speaking of Jesus, he informs the Emperor that " it is said that God came down from heaven, and from a Hebrew virgin took and clad Himself with flesh; and in a daughter of man there dwelt the Son of God." He also states that "He was pierced by the Jews; that He died and was buried; that the third day He rose again; and that He ascended into heaven." The hope of the Christian Church is also presented in the following beautiful statement : "And they labour to become righteous as those that expect to see their Messiah, and receive from Him the promises made to them with great glory. But their sayings and their ordinances, O King, and the glory of their service, and the expectation of their recompense of reward according to the doing of each one of them, which they expect in another world, thou art able to know from these writings."

The following references to eternal judgment and

---

* *Ecclesiastical History*, B. IV., Ch. 3.

the nature of the New Testament Scriptures are also wholly in accord with the teaching of later times. " If they see," he says, " that one of their number has died in his iniquity or in his sins, over this one they weep bitterly and sigh, as over one who is about to go to punishment." " Let all those, then," he adds, in another place, " approach to the gateway of light, who do not know God, and let them receive incorruptible words, those which are so always and from eternity; let them, therefore, anticipate the dread judgment which is to come by Jesus the Messiah upon the whole race of men." He also appeals to " their writings " as containing all these and other things which he names as believed and taught by the Christians. He says : "And truly this is a new people, and there is something Divine mingled with it. Take now their writings and read in them ; and lo ! ye will find that not of myself have I brought these things forward, nor as their advocate have I said them, but as I have read in their writings these things I firmly believe, and those things which are to come." * He mentions also, among other matters, that Jesus had twelve disciples, who, after His resurrection, " went forth into the known parts of the world and taught concernng His greatness with all humility and sobriety."

There are many other testimonies in Justin Martyr, Irenæus, and the Christian Fathers, which the want of space prevents my quoting. But there is evidence in existence of still greater importance,

* Helen B. Harris, *The Newly Recovered Apology of Aristides*, pp. 29-44.

and to this we shall now turn in the following chapter.

CHAPTER III.

ANCIENT HEATHEN TESTIMONIES TO THE FACTS OF THE GOSPEL.

THE testimonies, of which some specimens were given in the preceding chapter, are of inestimable value. They prove that the great facts of the Gospel were preached in the first century just as they have been handed down to ourselves. They have not been evolved : they have not been modified. But we are now to listen to the testimony of witnesses whose evidence is of even greater moment. I refer to those heathen testimonies, so familiar to scholars, but which even they require to be reminded of. These are irreconcilable with any theory of the mythical origin, or the gradual development, of the great doctrines of the Christian faith.

So numerous and varied are these testimonies that it is necessary to make a small selection here also. During the third century, Christianity, which had spread over the whole empire, and which was daily adding to its triumphs, presented one of the hardest problems with which the heathen Emperors had to deal. Their persecutions of the Christians make too full an admission both of the existence and of the beliefs of the Christian Church to permit any scope to critical theories. Let us begin with the closing years of the second century; we shall then proceed upward as high as this external evidence takes us.

About the year 180, Galen, the great physician, wrote his celebrated medical treatises. He was a native of Pergamos, and, consequently, wrote in Greek. He has two references both to Moses and Christ as teachers. These references, it will be seen, are of a very peculiar kind. He alludes to them as claiming to speak with Divine authority, and as the heads of two schools, equally well-known to all men in the end of the second century as composed of those who received with implicit faith and unquestioning obedience the words of their Founders. The first of these references is found in a passage in which " he blames Achigenes for not giving a demonstration, nor so much as a probable reason, of some things advanced by him. So that," says he, "we seem rather to be in a school of Moses, or Christ, where we must receive laws without any reason assigned, and that in a point where demonstration ought not by any means to be omitted." Here, the reader will note, it is plainly implied that Christ has given laws; and that these laws are received as unquestioningly by the Christians as the laws of Moses were received by the Jews. The second reference is similar. "It is easier," he says, "to convince the disciples of Moses and Christ, than physicians and philosophers, who are addicted to particular sects." * Here the

---

* *Lardner's Works*, vol. vii., pp. 300, 301.

fidelity of Jews and of Christians is referred to as notorious in Galen's day.

In Galen we see how learning could fling its taunts at the new faith ; but other writings have come down to us from the same period which show how the Church was then assailed with all the shafts of wit and bitter raillery. Lucian, a native of Samosata in Syria and an official of the Empire, lived and wrote somewhat earlier than Galen—about 170 A.D. In a letter to a friend, Lucian gives an account of a philosopher named Peregrinus, or Proteus. He was obliged, through his crimes, to abandon his home; and he then, says Lucian,

" learned the wonderful doctrine of the Christians by conversing with their priests and scribes near Palestine. . . They, therefore, still worship that great man who was crucified in Palestine, because He introduced into the world this new religion. For this reason Proteus was taken up and put into prison; which very thing was of no small service to him afterwards for giving reputation to his impostures, and gratifying his vanity. The Christians were much grieved for his imprisonment, and tried all ways to procure his liberty. Not being able to effect that, they did him all sorts of kind offices, and that not in a careless manner, but with the greatest assiduity ; for even betimes in the morning there would be at the prison old women— some widows—and also little orphan children : and some of the chief of their men, by corrupting the keepers, would get into the prison, and stay the whole night there with him ; there they had a good supper together, and their sacred discourses. And this excellent Peregrinus (for so he was still called) was thought by them to be an extraordinary person, no less than another Socrates; even from the cities of Asia some Christians came to him by an order of the body, to relieve, encourage, and comfort him. For it is incredible what expedition they use when any of their friends are known to be in trouble. In a word, they spare nothing upon such an occasion; and Peregrinus's chain brought him in a good sum of money from them; for these miserable men have no doubt but they shall be immortal, and live for ever; therefore, they contemn death, and many surrender themselves to suffering. Moreover, their first lawgiver has taught them that they are all brethren, when once they have turned and renounced the gods of the Greeks, and worship that master of theirs who was crucified, and engage to live according to His laws."*

Let it be remembered that Peregrinus died about 165 A.D., and that these things happened in that philosopher's youth or early manhood. He was an old man when he died. We are consequently taken back here to a period not later than 130 A.D. At that time Christ the Crucified was the object of the adoration of the Christian Church. His Laws were well known and were lovingly obeyed. And among these Laws were injunctions separating from all idolatry and commanding love and self-denying service toward the brethren. The Christians were also inspired by the most vivid hopes of a glorious future, and they were ready to endure everything rather than surrender these hopes. In one word, we

---

* Pages 279, 280.

are here, some thirty years after the death of the
Apostle John, confronted with a Church which is
identical with that of the Acts and of the Epistles.
It will be felt that those intervening years allow no
space for the transformations of evolution; and the
conclusion is inevitable that the Church of Peregrinus
was merely a continuation, and not a development,
of that of the Apostle John.

But we are able to go still farther back, and to
confirm this conclusion by the testimony of additional
facts.   Hadrian was born in the year 76 A.D., became
Emperor of Rome in 117, and died in 138.   When
he became Emperor in 117 A.D. (and before that
time, as we shall see immediately) Christianity had
spread so largely over the Roman Empire that the
treatment which should be accorded to it was a
problem which the Government was compelled to
have continually before it.   This is a fact of the
greatest importance.   For our religion, as we shall
see, was launched with all the characteristics which
it afterwards retained, so that no place is left for the
operation of forces to develop the doctrines of the
Atonement and the Deity of Christ, of the Trinity,
or of any of the other distinguishing features of the
Christian faith.

I pass over the rescript which this Emperor sent
to the proconsul of Asia enjoining that Christians were
not to be proceeded against, merely because their
punishment was demanded by popular clamour, but
that proceedings should be taken against them in the
ordinary legal fashion.   There is a letter of Adrian's

extant which is preserved by the historian Vopiscus, who wrote about 300 A.D. The letter is addressed to the husband of the Emperor's sister. The following is the extract from Vopiscus:

"The Egyptians, as you well know, are vain, fond of innovations, men of all characters. For there are among them Christians and Samaritans, and such as take a prodigious liberty in censuring the present times. That none of the Egyptians may be offended with me, I shall produce a letter of Adrian, taken from the books of Phlegon, his freed-man, in which the character of the Egyptians is clearly represented. 'Adrian Augustus to the consul Servianus wisheth health. I have found Egypt, my dear Servianus, which you commended to me, all over fickle and inconstant, and continually shaken by the slightest reports of fame. The worshippers of Serapis are Christians, and they are devoted to Serapis who call themselves Christ's bishops. There is no ruler of the Jewish Synagogue, no Samaritan, no presbyter of the Christians, no mathematician, no soothsayer, no anointer: even the patriarch, if he should come to Egypt, would be required by some to worship Serapis; by others Christ. A seditious and turbulent sort of men. However, the city is rich and populous. Nor are any idle. Some are employed in making glass, others paper, others in weaving linen. They have one God—Him the Christians, Him the Jews, Him all the Gentile people, worship.'" *

The purport of the Emperor's satire is evident. To him all this division, and zeal, and turmoil is simply

---

* Page 98.

"much ado about nothing." Without knowing it, they all alike worshipped the same God ! This would appear to be the meaning also of the statement that the worshippers of Serapis were Christians, and that even Christ's bishops worshipped Serapis. But that there was open and eager antagonism between them is plain from what is added : " Even the patriarch, if he should come to Egypt, would be required by some to worship Serapis, by others Christ." The letter was written in 134 A.D. ; so that some thirty years after the death of the Apostle John, Christianity was not only spread abroad in Asia, but had also attained such proportions in Egypt that in the capital of the country it formed a party strong enough to cope with the followers of the national idolatry.

The philosopher, Epictetus, who was preceptor to Arrian (to whose celebrated pen we owe the report of the sayings of his master) in 103 A.D., has a reference to the firmness displayed by the Christians in the midst of persecution. He speaks of them as " Galilæans," a name applied to them long afterwards by the Emperor Julian. " Speaking of intrepidity or fearlessness," writes Lardner, " and particularly in regard to a tyrant, surrounded by his guards and officers," Epictetus " says : ' Is it possible that a man may arrive at this temper, and become indifferent to those things from madness, or from habit, as the Galilæans, and yet that no one should be able to know by reason and demonstration that God made all things in the world ?' " *

* Pages 88, 89.

Pliny the Younger was born in 61 A.D., and entered into public life at the age of nineteen. He went to Bithynia as proconsul in 103 A.D., and wrote the following letter from that province to the Emperor Trajan in the following year, 104. The letter is as follows:

"Pliny to the Emperor Trajan wisheth health and happiness.

"It is my constant custom, Sir, to refer myself to you in all matters concerning which I have any doubt. For who can better direct me where I hesitate, or instruct me where I am ignorant? I have never been present at any trials of Christians: so that I know not well what is the subject matter of punishment, or of inquiry, or what strictness ought to be used in either. Nor have I been a little perplexed to determine whether any difference ought to be made on account of age, or whether the young and tender, and the full-grown and robust ought to be treated all alike: whether repentance should entitle to pardon, or whether all who have once been Christians ought to be punished, though they are now no longer so: whether the name itself, although no crimes be detected, or crimes only belonging to the name, ought to be punished. Concerning all these things I am in doubt.

"In the meantime I have taken this course with all who have been brought before me, and have been accused as Christians. I have put the question to them whether they were Christians. Upon their confessing to me that they were, I repeated the question a second and a third time, threatening also

T

to punish them with death. Such as still persisted,
I ordered away to be punished ; for it was no matter
of doubt with me, whatever might be the nature of
their opinion, that contumacy, and inflexible ob-
stinacy, ought to be punished. There were others of
the same infatuation, whom, because they are Roman
citizens, I have noted down to be sent to the city.

" In a short time, the crime spreading itself, even
whilst under persecution, as is usual in such cases,
divers sort of people came in my way. An information was presented to me, without mentioning the
author, containing the names of many persons, who
upon examination denied that they were Christians,
or had ever been so : who repeated after me an in-
vocation of the gods, and with wine and frankincense
made supplication to your image, which for that
purpose I have caused to be brought and set before
them, together with the statues of the deities.
Moreover, they reviled the name of Christ. None
of which things, as is said, those who are really
Christians, can by any means be compelled to do.
Those, therefore, I thought proper to discharge.

" Others were named by an informer, who at first
confessed themselves Christians, and afterwards
denied it. The rest said they had been Christians,
but had left them ; some three years ago, some
longer, and one, or more, above twenty years. They
all worshipped your image, and the statues of the
gods : these also reviled Christ. They affirmed that
the whole of their fault, or error, lay in this, that
they were wont to meet on a stated day before it
was light, and sing among themselves alternately a
hymn to Christ as a god, and bind themselves by an

oath, not to the commission of any wickedness, but not to be guilty of theft, or robbery, or adultery, never to falsify their word, nor to deny a pledge committed to them when called upon to return it. When these things were performed, it was their custom to separate, and then to come together again to a meal, which they ate in common, without any disorder : but this they had forborne since the publication of my edict, by which, according to your commands, I prohibited assemblies.

"After receiving this account I judged it the more necessary to examine, and that by torture, two maid-servants, who were called ministers. But I have discovered nothing, besides a bad and excessive superstition.

"Suspending therefore all judicial proceedings, I have recourse to you for advice : for it has appeared unto me a matter highly deserving consideration, especially upon account of the great number of persons who are in danger of suffering. For many of all ages, and every rank, of both sexes likewise, are accused, and will be accused. Nor has the contagion of this superstition seized cities only, but the lesser towns also, and the open country. Nevertheless it seems to me that it may be restrained and corrected. It is certain that the temples, which were almost forsaken, begin to be more frequented. And the sacred solemnities, after a long intermission, are revived. Victims likewise are everywhere bought up, whereas for some time there were few purchasers. Whence it is easy to imagine what numbers of men might be reclaimed if pardon were granted to those who shall repent."

To this the Emperor sent the following reply:

"Trajan to Pliny wisheth health and happiness.

"You have taken the right method, my Pliny, in your proceedings with those who have been brought before you as Christians; for it is impossible to establish any one rule that shall hold universally. They are not to be sought for. If any are brought before you, and are convicted, they ought to be punished. However, he that denies his being a Christian, and makes it evident in fact, that is, by supplicating to our gods, though he be suspected to have been so formerly, let him be pardoned upon repentance. But in no case of any crime whatever may a bill of information be received without being signed by him who presents it: for that would be a dangerous precedent, and unworthy of my government." *

Here, then, in the year 103, when Pliny entered upon his proconsulate, Christianity had made such progress that the temples had been "almost forsaken." It had seized not "cities only, but the lesser towns also, and the open country." And this was not a recent irruption of what Pliny calls "this superstition." It had been the condition of the province for a considerable time; for he says that "the sacred solemnities, *after a long intermission,* are revived." Paul had traversed these very regions some fifty years before, and here were the fruits of his labours! The seed sown by apostolic hands had indeed fallen upon fruitful soil; and now, when Rome contemplates crushing the new faith, its statesmen

---

are appalled at the task. "For many," says Pliny, "of all ages, and of every rank, of both sexes likewise, are accused, and will be accused."

It will be noticed also that what is revealed by confession and torture presents the very features of the Church which we behold in the Acts and in the Epistles. There is the same beautiful simplicity; the same trust in Jesus, the Divine Saviour; the same readiness to follow in His steps even unto death; the same zeal for holy living. The mention of the "two maid-servants which were called ministers," inevitably reminds us also of "Phœbe our sister, which is a servant (or minister) of the Church which is at Cenchrea" (Romans xvi.1). Here were still found, therefore, the love of the brotherhood and the simple organisation of the Apostolic time.

But, Providentially, we are enabled to pass up even into the Apostolic times, and to see how the fruits of Apostolic toil appear to the eyes of heathen onlookers. Shortly after Paul had ended the two years' residence which formed his first sojourn at Rome—indeed, according to the received reckoning, twelve months after, one of the most memorable scenes in ancient history suddenly opens before us. Rome is filled with terror. A fearful conflagration laid a great part of the city in ashes. Nero, who had almost completed the round of possible crimes, was popularly believed to have added this to the long list. To save the imperial honour, an attempt was made to throw the blame upon the Christians. The

Roman historian, Tacitus, tells the story. After describing the fire, and Nero's orders for the rebuilding and beautifying of the city, he continues :

" But neither all human help, nor the liberality of the Emperor, nor all the atonements presented to the gods, availed to abate the infamy he lay under of having ordered the city to be set on fire. To suppress therefore this common rumour, Nero procured others to be accused, and inflicted exquisite punishment upon those people who were in abhor- rence for their crimes, and were commonly known by the name of Christians. They had their denom- ination from Christus, who in the reign of Tiberius was put to death as a criminal by the procurator, Pontius Pilate. This pernicious superstition, though checked for a while, broke out again, and spread, not only over Judæa, the source of this evil, but reached the city also; whither flow from all quarters all things vile and shameful, and where they find shelter and encouragement. At first they were only apprehended who confessed themselves of that sect ; afterwards a vast multitude discovered by them : all which were condemned, not so much for the crime of burning the city, as for their enmity to mankind. Their executions were so contrived as to expose them to derision and contempt. Some were covered over with skins of wild beasts, and torn to pieces by dogs ; some were crucified ; others, having been daubed over with combustible materials, were set up as lights in the night time, and thus burned to death. Nero made use of his own gardens as a theatre upon this occasion, and also exhibited the diversions of the Circus, sometimes standing in the crowd as a spectator, in the habit of a charioteer, at other times driving a chariot himself : till at length these men, though really criminal and deserving exemplary punishment, began to be com- miserated as people who were destroyed, not out of a regard to the public welfare, but only to gratify the cruelty of one man." *

The importance of this testimony, though full of the learned prejudices of the time (which we are well able to understand when we recall the opposition of the Chinese literati to Christianity in our own day), cannot be overestimated. We gather nothing from it as to the character, or the beliefs, of the apostolic Church, except what we mark of the faith of the believers in Jesus ; of their heroic endurance ; and of their open and uncompromising antagonism to idola- try, which proclaimed them the enemies of the gods, and, consequently, the most wicked and abandoned of mankind. But this witness to the immense numbers of Christians in Rome—"a vast multitude," says the historian—proves that the gospel was preached in the places and at the times recorded in the New Testament. It confirms also that record of the marvellous results achieved by those who "went forth, and preached every where, the Lord working with them, and confirming the word with signs following " (Mark xvi. 20). The record there- fore is history, and we who receive its testimony are not following the " cunningly-devised fables " which

* Volume vi., pp. 628, 629.

the new criticism would persuade us that it is. These heathen testimonies are sufficient in themselves to convince us that the "cunningly-devised fables" are the new theories, and not the old Books.

<hr />

CHAPTER IV.

WHEN WERE OUR GOSPELS WRITTEN?
EXTERNAL TESTIMONY.

<hr />

IT will be seen that the reply to the above question is vitally connected with the greater question which is behind it. Is our faith founded upon fact, or upon fiction? Have we testimony to the record of our Lord's sayings, and to the facts of His life, which no sane and honest man will question? In other words, Have we in the four Gospels witness belonging to the very time—a witness also Divinely and graciously given; or have we mere late collections of floating traditions, strung together by men who worked them up to bear out their preconceived notions and personal fancies or enthusiastic dreams?

I shall not attempt to expound, or even to chronicle, the various theories which have been advanced to deprive the New Testament, not only of authority, but of truth. It is enough for us to note that the element of time is vital to them all. If the Gospels were *not* of late origin; if they were written by men who had known the Lord, and who were

numbered, some of them among the twelve who com-
panied with Him, and all of them with those who
possessed a first-hand acquaintance with the facts ;
then the rationalistic theories are all alike brushed
aside as impossible. My present task is to show
that the conclusion that the Gospels were so
written is the only possible interpretation of the
evidence.

We have been often told that the New Testament
Books were received into the Churches by the
Councils, the first of which assembled at Nicæa by
command of the Emperor Constantine in the beginning of the fourth century. There is no foundation
for these statements. There would have been no
Councils, indeed, had there not been a Church to be
summoned to them ; and the Church existed because
it had been nurtured by the New Testament. The
Canon was never made by any assembly. The Canon
made itself. As the inspired writings were given,
they were handed to Churches in the midst of which
the writers laboured, and to which the writers were
known as inspired ministers of God's Word. Their
writings were thus certified to the more distant
Churches to which they were subsequently handed on.
There were inquiries afterwards about some of the
lesser epistles ; but these inquiries were satisfied in
the same way. Those who had received them were
able to say from whose hands they had come. The
matter for astonishment to-day is not the existence
of these inquiries, but the vast and absolute unanimity with which the Churches, scattered over the

whole known world, received the sacred deposit, and the astonishing fact that all these Books so received are now seen to be separated by a deep and impassable gulf from all the other literature of the time, whether sacred or profane.

This unanimity found a touching and impressive expression in this first Christian Council, which was summoned by the Emperor Constantine. The Four Gospels were placed upon a throne in the midst of the Assembly. These were the unchallenged Law of the Churches everywhere—the great gift which had made them what they were—the treasure which they were commissioned to give to the world around them, and to hand down to the ages which were to follow.

When did these come into the Church's possession? When did this four-fold witness assume the form which it has retained unaltered ever since? Some testimonies and facts, passed in rapid review, will give us a clear and satisfactory reply to a question which is likely enough to assume a greater urgency than those who love our country best would wish.

Lucian dedicated one of his works to Celsus, a writer who had endeavoured to stem the advance of the new religion by what seems to have been regarded as a crushing exposure of its claims. The work of Celsus lived on long after his decease; and Ambrose, a friend of Origen's, desired the great Alexandrian catechist to reply, and entreated him to leave nothing unanswered. To Origen's compliance with his friend's request we owe our very full knowledge of the work of Celsus: for it has long since passed away, and left no trace beyond what is found in Origen's refutation of it.

Celsus cannot be placed later than about 170 A.D. ; and, as he makes about eighty quotations from the New Testament Books, these must, of course, have been in existence, and must have been in existence so long as to challenge the attention of the world as the universally acknowledged source of the Christian faith. It is a remarkable fact also that there is not one reference to a single Apocryphal Gospel. This was a kind of weapon which the dexterous hand of Celsus would have used with telling effect. That he did not avail himself of the Apocryphal Gospels proves that he knew nothing of them. They were plainly inventions of a later time.

A few quotations will show that the Gospels existed in the time of Celsus as we now have them, and that no room whatever was left for " the developments," on the supposed existence of which the critical case rests. He had in his possession the Gospels of Matthew and Luke ; for he says that the composers of the genealogies of Jesus " were very extravagant in making Him descend from the first man"(Luke iii.), "and the Jewish kings " (Matthew i.) He speaks of the command against resisting injuries, and quotes from the Sermon on the Mount as narrated in Matthew. He endeavours to show the absurdity of the statement as to the impossibility of serving two masters. He says that Moses and Jesus, though both are said to have been sent from God, do not agree. " Moses," he writes, "encourages the people to get riches and to destroy their enemies. But His Son " (meaning " the Son of God ") " the Nazarean man, delivers quite contrary laws. Nor will He allow a rich man, or one that affects dominion, to have access to His Father. Nor will He allow men to take more care for food, or treasure, than the ravens ; nor to provide for clothing so much as the lilies; and to him that has smitten once He directs to offer, that he may smite again." There seem also to be distinct references to John's Gospel. Origen says : "He pretends that Christians argue miserably when they say that the Son of God is the Word Himself" (see John i.) He quotes from I. Corinthians iii. 19, that "wisdom in men is foolishness with God." He has an evident reference also to I. Corinthians viii. 4-11, when he asks, " If those idols are nothing, what harm can there be to partake in their feasts ?" He quotes Galatians vi. 14 in the following words : "Notwithstanding the many divisions and contentions which are among them, you may hear them all saying : 'The world is crucified unto me, and I unto the world.'" There is a reference to the famous passage about " the spirits in prison " in I. Peter iii. 19, 20, in the following : " Surely you will not say that when He could not persuade those that were here, He went to Hades to persuade those who are there?" He makes similar reference to I. John i. 1, when he writes that Christians " expect to see God with the eyes of the body, and to hear His voice with our ears, and to handle Him with our sensible hands."

From these and many other passages which might be quoted, it is plain that Celsus, writing about 170 A.D., had the same New Testament before him which we have now.

From a multitude of other testimonies regarding the early origin and acknowledged authority of the four Gospels, I select the following. Tatian, a disciple and companion of Justin Martyr, was born in Assyria in 112, according to others 120, A.D. After travelling through many lands, and acquainting himself with the philosophies and the religious systems of the various nations, " I fell," he says, " upon certain barbaric books, too old to be compared with the learning of the Greeks, and too Divine to be put on a level with their erroneous teachings." These were the Books of the Bible. He became a convert to Christianity and a disciple of Justin Martyr, whom he accompanied to Rome; and after the martyrdom of his master he took the direction of his school. It was a constant tradition that he wrote a harmony of the four Gospels. The importance of that fact was too plain for the statement not to be contested by the rationalists. If the Gospels, including that of John, which was not written until nearly 100 A.D., were harmonised by Tatian, several facts are established which are of the first importance. All the Gospels must not only have been in existence about 150 A.D.; but they must also have been unquestioningly and universally received from the very first. They must also have become so well known by the middle of the second century that their variations had been marked, and a desire had been felt to have their combined testimony presented in one full and continuous narrative.

A fact of that kind was fatal to the theory of development, and to the growth of legends concerning Jesus. There was no room for either. The Gospels must have been the work of contemporaries of our Lord; and the fact of there being four of these would compel even the rationalistic mind to admit that this multiplied testimony carried with it the assurance that it placed us face to face with Jesus. The impression, therefore, that there ever had been such a work had to be effaced. This was the more easily done that the Harmony had apparently perished. The clearest testimonies as to its existence and nature were set aside. The author of *Supernatural Religion* concludes a long discussion with the assertion that there never had been any such harmony, and that " all that we know of " Tatian's lost work "identifies it with the Gospel according to the Hebrews,"* an apocryphal work.

An unexpected discovery has annihilated this refuge of a distressed unbelief. It was known that St. Ephraem, the celebrated Syrian Bishop who died about 378 A.D., had written a commentary on Tatian's Harmony, or Diatessaron, as the book was called. But the commentary had also disappeared. An ancient Armenian translation, however, of Ephraem's work, including this commentary, was published in 1836; yet, strange to say, the attention of the

---

* Volume li., p. 162.

learned was not attracted to the publication, and the discovery remained unknown. Professor Moesinger published a Latin translation of Ephraem's Commentary in 1876 ; but this also remained practically unknown for four years. When these works at last became known, a further, and humiliating, discovery was made. Tatian's work had not been lost at all. A Latin translation of it, found by Victor, Bishop of Capua, had existed and been known for 1,300 years. Victor, after enquiry, concluded that this was Tatian's work. But the verdict of scholarship was that the bishop had made a mistake, and his book was set aside as having no bearing upon this question. The folly of that conclusion was shown when Victor's discovery was compared with Ephraem's Commentary.

The recovery of Ephraem's Commentary might possibly have been regarded as still leaving some loophole for unbelief to wriggle through. That possibility, however, was removed in 1888. It transpired that an Arabic translation of Tatian's work lay in the Vatican Library, though little reliable information could be had concerning it. One of the scribes of the Library, named Ciasca, gave a fuller account of it in 1883, and promised that it should be published at some future time. While this project was being entertained, Antonius Morcos, Vicar Apostolic of the Catholic Coptic Church, visited Rome. On being shown the manuscript, he said that he had seen a similar copy in Egypt. This was obtained, and published in 1888 ; and the long controversy was ended. Tatian's Harmony was a harmony of the four Gospels which we now have. The Harmony begins with the opening words of John's Gospel. Then follows an extract from Luke. We find next a few verses from Matthew. These are succeeded by a further quotation from Luke, till the story of the infancy is fully told. The same plan is followed throughout. There is not one word from any apocryphal " Gospel;" and it is quite evident that neither these, nor the fictitious "Gospel to the Hebrews" existed in the time of Tatian.

Church historians differ greatly as to the year to which they assign the birth of Irenæus, the second Bishop of Lyons. Their dates are as wide apart as 97 A.D. and 140 A.D.; but there is no question whatever as to the following facts, and these are more important than the year of his birth. He was, in his boyhood, a hearer of Polycarp, Bishop of Smyrna, who, in his turn, had been a disciple of the Apostle John. Irenæus in this way links us on to the Apostolic time. The earlier part of his life was spent in diligent converse with men, who themselves had in their youth been in fellowship with those among whom the foundations of the Church had been laid. This fact gives peculiar interest and force to his testimony.

What, then, has Irenæus to say of the Gospels? Does he find them in process of evolution? Is the great collection of "sayings," which critics have imagined to be the quarry from which our Gospels were taken, just fading out of sight? Does he, or Polycarp, know anything of a struggle among a host of contending Gospels, or of the gradual extinction of the multitude and the survival of the four fittest ? Here is the reply. " We have not received," writes Irenæus, "the knowledge of the way of our salvation by any other than those by whom the gospel has been brought to us ; which gospel they first preached, and afterwards, by the will of God, committed to writing, that it might be for time to come the foundation and pillar of our faith.—For after that our Lord rose from the dead, and they [the apostles] were endued from above with the power of the Holy Ghost coming down upon them, they received a perfect knowledge of all things. They then went forth to all the ends of the earth, declaring to men the blessing of heavenly peace, having all of them, and every one alike, the gospel of God." He then mentions how by these the four Gospels were written, and proceeds to show that in the number "four" we have a Divine complete-ness, so there could neither have been more nor fewer. "Whence it is manifest," he adds, "that the Word, the former of all things, who sits upon the cherubim, and upholds all things, having appeared to men, has given us a gospel of a four-fold character, but joined in one spirit. The Gospel according to John declares his primary and glorious generation from the Father : ' In the beginning was the Word.' But the Gospel according to Luke, being of a priestly character, begins with Zacharias, the priest, offering incense to God. Matthew relates his generation, which is according to man : ' The Book of the genera-tion of Jesus Christ, the son of David, the Son of

v

Abraham.' Mark begins from the prophetic Spirit, which came down from above to men, saying: 'The beginning of the gospel of Jesus Christ, as it is written in Esaias the prophet.'"* Here, then, are the Gospels as we have them to-day, and received as the fully-inspired Word of God. It has been said by the Romanists that Protestantism exaggerated the doctrine of inspiration; and the critics hint that we who oppose them have outdone ordinary Protestants in that matter. But the Protestant Churches and ourselves are merely in line with the Apostolic Church. And there is comfort in the conviction, however much such faith may be condemned and scorned. The Church that believed in a full inspiration was the Church that triumphed. The Church needs only the same simple, unswerving faith to triumph again.

Justin Martyr, who has been mentioned already in connection with his disciple Tatian, had a history which closely resembled that of the latter. Born sometime between 89 A.D. and 100 A.D., he early engaged in the search for wisdom. After attaching himself to various philosophic schools in succession, he became acquainted with Christianity, and then cordially embraced what he calls the "only certain and useful philosophy." He is described by an ancient writer as a man not far removed from the apostles in time or in virtue. Not only does he refer to the Gospels, including that of John, but he also speaks as if these were already known outside the Churches. In a dialogue composed by him, Trypho,

---

* Lardner, vol. ii., pp. 169-171.

a Jew, is reported as saying : " I am sensible that the precepts in your Gospel, as it is called, are so great and wonderful that I think it impossible for any man to keep them. For I have been at the pains to read them." From this it is evident that the Gospels were already among the sacred Books of the Christian Church; that copies had been multiplied of them; and that they were in the hands not only of the Christians, but also of others, and this before the middle of the second century.

In reference to Justin's testimony to the other Books of the New Testament, I may refer to the quotation from 2 Peter iii. 8 in these words of his : " We have also understood that the saying, that ' a day of the Lord is as a thousand years ' belongs to this matter ;" and to the following statement regarding Revelation : "And a man from among us, by name of John, one of the apostles of Christ, in the revelation made to him, has prophesied that the believers in our Christ shall live a thousand years in Jerusalem ; and after that shall be the general, and, in a word, the eternal resurrection and judgment of all men together (Revelation xx.) The same thing, which our Lord has said : That ' they shall neither marry, nor be given in marriage, but shall be equal to the angels, and shall be the children of God, being (the children) of the resurrection ' (Luke xx. 35, 36)." It will be seen from these references how, at once, without delay or hesitation, the New Testament Scriptures took that place of loftiest eminence which they have ever since maintained.

This can be explained in only one way. The Books must have been received from the hands of recognised, unquestioned, and indeed supreme, authority.

I cite only one other witness, Ignatius, who was Bishop of the Church of Antioch in Syria—the Church from which Paul and Barnabas set out on their first missionary journey—at the close of the first century of the Christian era, and the beginning of the second. His testimony takes us, therefore, into the midst of the generation which succeeded that of Paul, of Peter, and of the rest of the Apostles, and into the last days of the Apostle John. Of his writings there are seven epistles sent to Apostolic Churches. These existed in two editions, a shorter and a longer. It seemed natural to suppose that the shorter was an abbreviated edition; but the opinion long prevailed that this was the only genuine edition, and that the longer letters were interpolated. This opinion has had to give way, however, before increasing evidence; and the genuineness of the longer epistles has been ably vindicated by Zahn in Germany, and by the late Bishop Lightfoot in our own country. I may note, in passing, the latter's explanation of how he was compelled to abandon his earlier opinion. "In revising my own exegetical notes," he says, "I found that, to maintain the priority of the Curetonian letters, I was obliged from time to time to ascribe to the supposed Ignatian forger feats of ingenuity, knowledge, intuition, skill, and self-restraint, which exceeded all bounds of probability." *

* *Apostolic Fathers*, Part II., vol. i., p. 7.

A few of the references in these epistles will show
the place which the New Testament already held at
the end of the first century and the commencement
of the second. He speaks of our Lord as " Baptized
of John, that all righteousness might be fulfilled by
Him " (see Matthew iii. 15). " These are not a plant
of the father," a reference to Matt. xv. 13 : " Every
plant which My heavenly Father hath not planted
shall be rooted up." " Yet the Spirit is not deceived,
being from God : for it knows whence it comes and
whither it goes, and reproves secret things," shows
quite as clearly acquaintance with John iii. 8 : " The
wind bloweth where it listeth, and thou hearest the
sound thereof, but canst not tell whence it cometh,
and whither it goeth." There are similar references
to Mark and Luke, to the Book of Acts, and to every
other Book in the New Testament, with the exception
of 2 Thessalonians, 2 John, and Jude, these exceptions apparently being due to the fact that Ignatius
in his extant writings had had no call to quote from
them, or to allude to them.*

Upon ground, therefore, which can not be
challenged, we have gone right up to the times of
John the Apostle, and into the midst of the generation which succeeded that which had seen and heard
Peter, and James, and Paul. And, having reached
these first days, we find the New Testament already
in the hands of the Churches. It has been accepted
without hesitation. It has been accepted as the
Word of God. These Gospels, then, were written,

---

* *Ibid.*, vol. ii., pp. 1,107-1,109.

not by late gatherers of traditions, but by eye-witnesses and ministers of the living Word. They place us face to face with the Christ. And the fact of their four-fold testimony may prove to the most sceptical that we are not confronted by merely human impressions of our Redeemer. The Evangelists are no word painters. They tell us what He said : they narrate simply and clearly what He did. We see and company with the living Christ.

CHAPTER V.

THE LANGUAGE USED IN JUDEA AND GALILEE IN THE TIME OF OUR LORD.

IN the last chapter we have weighed the external testimony to the Gospels. We have asked when these writings took their place among the world's literature, and the reply wrecks the hypothesis that the Gospel narratives are late traditions, embodying legends or beliefs rather than facts. Testimony of the most certain kind places it beyond doubt that the four Gospels, as we have them now, were in the possession of the Churches at the beginning of the second century of our era, and that they were then revered as Scripture. The Gospels had won this position within seventy years from the death of our Lord. They must have originated, therefore, in the Apostolic times, and must have come into the churches with full Apostolic sanction.

But there is another source of evidence, which is of almost equal importance with this external testimony. This is the evidence of the Books themselves. The constant tradition affirms that they were written by Jews, and written in Greek, which was to them a foreign tongue. To appreciate the force of this internal evidence it will be necessary to deal with the subject indicated by the title of this chapter—the language spoken in Judea and in Galilee in the time of our Lord.

What we may call the universal belief has been that the language of Palestine at this time was Aramean. The Jews retained their ancient tongue, the Hebrew, till the days of Jeremiah and of the captivity. Dispersed afterwards among the populations of Babylonia, they were compelled to speak the language of their new masters. Had they lived together in large numbers, and been able themselves to furnish what was necessary to meet their needs, their mother tongue might have been preserved. But this gathering together of the captives in large masses was just the kind of thing which the Babylonians were anxious to prevent. Their condition may be inferred from the message sent to them through Jeremiah : "Seek the peace of the city whither I have caused you to be carried away captives, and pray unto the Lord for it : for in the peace thereof shall ye have peace" (Jeremiah xxix. 7). Here it is plain that they were scattered throughout the cities of Babylonia. They had consequently to pick up as speedily as possible the Aramean which was spoken by their captors.

The Aramean, which is closely connected with Hebrew, existed in two dialects—the Western Aramean, which was spoken in Syria, of which Palestine was geographically a part, and the Eastern Aramean, which was spoken in Babylonia. It was the latter dialect which the Jews were forced by their circumstances to adopt, and which, after their return, though surrounded by those who spoke the Syrian dialect, they still retained.

This fact is proved by the Rabbinical literature of the Jews. But the nation was subjected to other political changes which seemed to form a foundation for questioning the undisturbed belief that Aramean was the language spoken by the Lord and His early disciples. In 332 B.C. Alexander the Great and his Greek host seized the Persian dominion. Palestine came into the possession by-and-bye of one of Alexander's generals; and the Jews were compelled by their new circumstances to become more or less acquainted with Greek, the language of the conquerors. We also know that at a later period the Romans laid their hand upon Palestine. Herod the Great was appointed Procurator of Judea by Julius Cæsar in 47 B.C.; and in the year 6 of our era the Herod dynasty was swept away, and the land was proclaimed a Roman province. This change, which brought Roman armies and Roman officials into the country again, made the Jews more or less acquainted with another tongue—the Latin. These facts were quite enough to suggest theories to modern scholars. In the year 1771 E. F. Wernsdorf published at

Wittemberg, in Germany, a treatise which proposed to prove that Latin was the language of our Lord. He was able to point to the few Latin words which appear in the Gospels. But the presence of these words proved nothing more than that the Gospels were written during the Roman occupation of Palestine. They were a mark, indeed, that the Gospels belonged to the place and time which, as the Churches have always believed, witnessed their origin. But any larger conclusion than this these Roman words refused to bear, and Wernsdorf's theory was soon forgotten.

A similar venture, however, has had a longer span of existence. Isaac Vossius, the famous Dutch scholar, whose works have won for him a reputation for love of novelty as well as for extensive erudition, ventured to maintain in 1685, more than a century before Wernsdorf's treatise appeared, that our Lord and His disciples spoke Greek. His reasoning appealed to some ; and Diodati, an Italian archæologist, and others maintained in subsequent publications the opinion of the Dutch scholar. Paulus, one of the founders of Rationalism, placed this opinion on what seemed to him a more secure basis. He admitted that the Jews in Palestine, as a rule, spoke Aramean ; but he maintained that Greek was so well known in Galilee and in Jerusalem that our Lord and His disciples were able to make use of it as often as they judged it to be necessary to do so. These views were strongly opposed by men of profound learning ; and, for scholars generally, there was an end to the question, when interest in this old controversy was revived in our own country by a book from the pen of Professor Roberts, entitled *Discussions on the Gospels*, in which he maintained the view advocated by Paulus. To this, which appeared in 1862, there were many replies; but these did not modify his views, and in 1888 he published a further work, entitled *Greek the Language of Christ and His Apostles.*

It must be admitted that the knowledge of Greek was widespread, and that it was, indeed, in a very real sense, the universal language of the time. Dr. Roberts's facts and arguments are of value in making that perfectly clear. But it is a very different matter to contend that any one, desirous of reaching the multitude in Judea and Galilee, could attain that object by using the Greek tongue. One fact seems enough to outweigh all possible arguments. The Lord's enemies were eager to press upon Him the charge of innovation. Is it possible that He could have used an alien language in His discourses, and that the Pharisees would have permitted that apparent contempt of the sacred tongue to pass unnoticed? But the language of His addresses is never mentioned, nor is there the faintest suggestion that Jesus ever changed from one language to another, or that He addressed His hearers at any time in any language but that which was their mother tongue.

It is needless to reply to Dr. Roberts's arguments. There is a stupendous array of facts which prove that his theory is an impossibility. It is quite true that coins of Herod have been found, on which the title " Ethnarch " appears in Greek. But, as Vigouroux has remarked,* British coins have Latin legends, although Latin is not the language of this country. It is also true that Josephus says that Gaza, Gadara, and Hippos were Greek cities, and were on that account separated from the government of Archelaus and added to the Province of Syria.† But this very fact plainly implies that in this peculiarity these three cities were distinct from the rest of the country, and that the cities of Archelaus's territory could not be described as Greek cities. It may also be true that there was a decided tendency among a section of the Jewish population to acquire a know-ledge of the Greek tongue. There are similar tendencies among some of the inhabitants of London to the study of German and French. But he would be a bold man who should affirm that a teacher, desiring to reach the masses of that city, would choose either French or German as the language best suited to his purpose.

We are not, however, reduced to the necessity of contesting these arguments. There are facts which, as I have said, are destructive of the theory. Josephus, a Jewish contemporary of the apostles, states distinctly that Eastern Aramean, the Hebrew of the time, was the language of the Jewish people. He says in the Preface to his *Wars of the Jews*: " I have proposed to myself, for the sake of such as live under the government of the Romans, to transcribe

---

* *Le Nouveau Testament et les Decouvertes Archæologiques Modernes*, p. 21.
† *Antiquities*, xvii., xi. 4.

those books into the Greek tongue, which I formerly composed in the language of our own country."* This is explicit enough. The language of the Jews was not Greek, or else Josephus would have been under no necessity of making a Greek translation of his work. In his description of the siege of Jerusalem by Titus, he speaks of the huge engines used by the Romans which threw enormous stones further than a quarter of a mile. The sharp-sighted Jewish watchmen used to give notice of these to the defenders on the wall shouting, says Josephus, "in their own country language, ' THE SON COMETH,' so that those who were in its way stood off, and threw themselves down upon the ground." † The phrase, "the son cometh," exercises Whiston, the English translator of Josephus, exceedingly. He labours in a note to account for it as a probable corruption of the text. But the phrase, as it stands, will appeal to every Hebrew scholar as an additional proof that Hebrew and not Greek was at this time the language of the Jews. "The son of" is constantly used for the product of anything. It was the correct Hebrew idiomatic phrase for the missile sent from the engine.

In his answer to Apion, Josephus mentions other facts which are capable only of the same interpretation. In defending the accuracy of the work, from which the above quotation is made, he shows that he had the best information regarding the events which he records. As a captive he was sent with Titus to Jerusalem, and was present throughout the siege;

---

* Preface, i. † *Wars of the Jews*, v., vii. 3.

"during which time," he says, "there was nothing done which escaped my knowledge; for what happened in the Roman camp I saw, and wrote down carefully; and what informations the deserters brought [out of the city] I was the only man who understood them." * These Jews were, therefore, unable to speak Greek, for otherwise no interpreter would have been required; and the fact, that there was no other Jewish prisoner in the Roman camp who knew enough Greek to act as interpreter between the deserters and the Romans, shows how rare it was to find a native of Palestine who understood the Greek tongue. And, further, Josephus has himself told us how limited his own acquaintance with that language was. In a very remarkable passage, in the conclusion of his antiquities, he says: " I have taken a great deal of pains to obtain the learning of the Greeks, and understand the elements of the Greek language, although I have so long accustomed myself to speak our own tongue that I cannot pronounce Greek with sufficient exactness: for our nation does not encourage those that learn the languages of many nations, and so adorn their discourses with the smoothness of their periods . . . on which account, as there have been many who have done their endeavours with great patience to obtain this learning, they have yet hardly been so many as two or three that have succeeded therein, who were immediately well rewarded for their pains." † In another of his works he indicates that in his own case he had to lament

---

* *Contra Apion.*, i. 9.   † *Antiquities*, xx., xi. 2.

more than defective pronunciation. He had written his notes of the Jewish Wars in Hebrew. "Afterward," he says, " I got leisure at Rome; and when all my materials were prepared for that work, I made use of some persons to assist me in learning the Greek tongue, and by these means I composed the history of those transactions." * The knowledge of Greek which had availed him as interpreter in the Roman camp was by no means enough to enable him to write in Greek; and so he had to prepare himself for this task by fresh studies.

And this testimony by no means stands alone. Gamaliel, at whose feet the Apostle Paul sat, and who was a contemporary of our Lord and of the Apostles, has left behind him some letters addressed to the people of Upper and Lower Galilee about fixing the day of the New Moon. These letters are written in Eastern Aramean. This settles the question as to the mother tongue of our Lord and His early disciples, who were all of Galilee. The most ancient prayers used by the Jews, apart from those in the Scripture, are in the same language. And, when we come to the New Testament itself, the testimony is the same. The Apostle Peter mentions (Acts i. 19) that the inhabitants of Jerusalem named the field, which was the scene of the suicide of Judas, "in their proper tongue, Aceldama, that is to say, The field of blood." Aceldama is composed of two Aramean words—*chakal*, field; and *demâ*, blood. We find some Greek names among those of the

* *Contra Apion.*, i. 9.

disciples and of the Jewish contemporaries of our Lord. Philip, Nicodemus, Stephen, are examples. There are also Latin names, such as Mark and Luke, which reveal the influence of the Roman masters of Palestine. But the names given by the Lord Himself are Aramean. Simon's name is changed to Kephas. Kepha is Aramean. The *s* is added to give it a Greek form; but in Greek the name was Petros— "a stone." James and John are named *Boanerges*, which means, in Aramean, "the thunderers." To the same tongue belong the titles *Rabbi* and *Rabboni* —"master," "my master"—given by the disciples to Jesus. When the Lord makes His solemn entry into Jerusalem the people hail Him with the Aramean *Hossanna*—"Save, I pray you!" In the same way the language used by our Lord and the Jews makes itself felt in the Greek of the Gospels by the introduction of Aramean words and phrases, which are simply written in Greek letters. The priest Zacharias, the aged father of John the Baptist, is told that the child must not taste "wine nor strong drink" (Luke i. 15). Here *sikera*—the word for "strong drink"— is transferred from the Aramean, *shekara* being put into Greek letters. It is the same with the names "Pharisees" and "Sadducees;" with the term *pascha*, "Passover;" *Sathanas*, "devil," whence our word "Satan;" *Messias*, "the Anointed One," "the Christ;" the word *Amen*, so often in the lips of Jesus, "in truth." We have also words and phrases in the sayings of our Lord which have been carried bodily into the Greek New Testament. We read in

the Sermon on the Mount : "Whosoever shall say to
his brother, *Raca,* shall be in danger of the council:
but whosoever shall say, Thou fool, shall be in danger
of the Gehenna of fire" (Matthew v. 22). Our
translators have preserved only one of the two words
in its Aramean form, having translated Gehenna by
"hell." But both are Aramean. *Reka* is used in the
Talmud in the sense of "empty," "stupid." Gehenna
means "the valley of Hinnom," more fully "the
valley of the son of Hinnom," which runs along the
south and west of Jerusalem. The place had been
polluted on account of the sacrifices which the Jews
had offered there to Moloch ; and it became still
more a type of the place of eternal punishment by
the practice of the time of burning there the bodies
of those who were condemned to suffer capital
punishment. *Mámmona,* "mammon," "riches;" and
Corban, "a gift," "a thing devoted," are other
examples.

Other words and phrases which have been preserved in the New Testament might be quoted; but,
in view of the facts stated above, it is clear that the
language spoken by our Lord, and which formed the
mother tongue of the apostles and evangelists, was
Aramean. The importance of this fact, in view of
present controversies, will be immediately seen.

CHAPTER VI.

THE LANGUAGES OF THE BIBLE.

BEFORE attempting to fulfil the promise made in closing the preceding chapter, it is necessary to say a word or two regarding the place of language in the Scripture. Reference has been made more than once to the symbolic use of language in Scripture; and the question why more than one language should have been used in God's revelation to men now meets us fully. We have just seen that the language of our Lord and of His disciples, in common with the rest of the nation, was Eastern Aramean. If our Lord, then, delivered His discourses in Aramean, why have not these been preserved to us in that tongue?

At first sight, this question appears to be invested with no small importance. It would have been a great matter to us to have had the very words which Jesus uttered, to have the sound of these Aramean words still ringing in our ears, and to have caught the emphasis and the shades of thought and feeling shown in the selection of the words and in the very order in which they fell from the lips of the Master. It is quite true that, if we have the Spirit's rendering of the Lord's words in the New Testament Greek, we lose nothing; and that, indeed, we may gain something by having thus the ministry of Him whose it is to take the things of Christ and show them to

W

us. But yet the question returns, why it was needful to do this in Greek. Why should this latter tongue be used to report words which were uttered, and which might have been handed on to us, in the Aramean? The inquiry recurs, when we leave the Gospels and open the Acts, the Epistles, and the Revelation. If all the writers were at home in the Aramean, why should their work have been thrown into a foreign mould? And why, above all, is even the Epistle to the Hebrew Christians written in this Greek tongue, which, as we have just seen, very few of them were able to understand? It could only have been brought before the vast majority of them by means of an interpreter; but why was not that necessity dispensed with, as it would have been had the apostle taken what was obviously the natural course, and addressed these Jews in their native tongue?

It is evident that the natural course was departed from only from some high necessity. Is it possible to say what that necessity was? Fortunately the solution of this mystery is not far to seek. It really lies upon the surface. The fact that the Old Testament is in Hebrew tells us that it was primarily for the people who spoke that language. It was given in charge to them, and was specially intended in the first place for their enlightenment. The Gentiles could receive it only as the Jew handed it on, and became its interpreter. The Jew was, therefore, first in that dispensation. He of all men was selected to be its custodian and its minister.

If the Jew, then, were to be displaced from this pre-eminence in the things of God, a change in the language of Revelation would indicate that. There had already been some significant indications of this in the Old Testament. The chief instance is the use made of the Aramean tongue, the universal Gentile language of the time, in the Book of Daniel. This has been one of the problems of the Book. Why one-half of the Book should be in an alien tongue it seemed difficult to say; but the usual notion was that the language changed when the reply of the Chaldeans to the king had to be recorded. But that solution would soon have broken down if it had been considered seriously. Why did not the Aramean stop when the speech of the Chaldeans ceased? Why is it used to give the reply of Shadrach, Meshach, and Abednego to Nebuchadnezzar (iii. 16-18), and even Daniel's address to the same king (iv. 19-27), and his words to Belshazzar (v. 17-28)? A glance at the chapters shows that they form a series of prophetic sketches of the Gentile supremacy over Israel, and the use of the Aramean, the common Gentile language of the time, is thus explained. As soon as the story of that long supremacy has been completed in the account of its judgment, the Hebrew is resumed at the commencement of chapter ix. There, in Daniel's repentance, we seem to see that of his people, the long chastised Israel. The things concerning Christ, Israel's concluding conflict, the resurrection of the saints, and Israel's full salvation are then revealed. It is in this section that we find the marvellous prediction which fixed the very year of Christ's manifestation (chapter ix.); and this is placed here, no doubt, as God's seal to the words which shall yet strengthen Israel in the throes of that supreme anguish—"the day of Jacob's trouble."

There are three other parts of the Old Testament in which the Aramean appears. These are fresh illustrations of this symbolic use of language. The Book of Ezra has to chronicle the interference of the Persian kings in the erection of the Temple at Jerusalem and in the re-appointment of the Temple service. Here the Gentile supremacy was painfully apparent, and the whole of this is in Aramean. This portion begins with the eighth verse of chapter iv. and extends to ver. 26 of chap. vii.—with one eloquent exception. The section, chapter vi. 19—vii. 11, is in Hebrew. This records the keeping of the Passover by the returned Jews, and the genealogy of Ezra and of the men who were his companions. With this the Gentile over-lord had nothing to do. A break is therefore made in the Aramean portion of the Book, and the Hebrew is for a moment resumed.

The second instance is one verse in the prophecies of Jeremiah. It is the following : " Thus shall ye say unto them, The gods that have not made the heavens and the earth, even they shall perish from the earth, and from under these heavens " (x. 11). Why this sudden and unique change should be made in the language of the prophet has exercised the minds both of Jewish and of Christian commentators. That the change has a symbolic import will hardly be doubted. Keeping

our feet upon what we have seen to be sure ground,
that the use of the Aramean indicates the time of the
Gentile supremacy over Israel, the words would bear
the meaning that, during this supremacy, the idolatries of the nations would die. And true enough they
have died. The gods of Egypt, Chaldea, and
Assyria, of Edom, Moab, and Phœnicia have long
since perished. The gods of Greece and Rome have
followed. Other idolatries have perished in our own
day, and some are slowly dying now. The gods that
have not made the heavens and the earth have passed
away, and are passing away, from the earth and from
under these heavens.

The last instance, which we are now to notice,
removes a difficulty which was felt from the earliest
times, and which has left its mark in versions and in
commentaries. I refer to the command in the second
Psalm : " Be wise now therefore, O ye kings : be
instructed ye judges of the earth. . . . . Kiss the
Son, lest He be angry, and ye perish from the way,"
&c. (verses 10-12). The root of the trouble is that
the word translated " Son " is in Aramean, and not
in Hebrew : we find *bar* instead of the Hebrew *ben*.
This is all the more striking that we find the ordinary
Hebrew word *ben* in verse 7 : " Thou art My Son ;
this day have I begotten Thee ;" but when we come
to the command, " Kiss the Son " (verse 12), the
Aramean *bar* is used. Why is this change made ?
There have been faint suggestions, but no firm reply.
Let us once more apply the key to this symbolism
which the Scripture has placed in our hands, and

an explanation is immediately forthcoming. The Aramean indicates the time of the Gentile supremacy. It is the time, too, of the Gentile Church and of the Gentiles' Christ. This is the day of mercy for the Gentile princes and the Gentile peoples. Let it not be despised or neglected ; for it will end in judgment : " Kiss the Son *(bar)*, lest He be angry, and ye perish from the way when his wrath is kindled but a little.''

Here, then, in one half of the Book of Daniel, a large section of another Book, in a single sentence, and in a word, the use of the universal Gentile tongue indicates the time of the Gentile supremacy. Now, in the time of our Lord and His apostles the universal Gentile tongue was no longer Aramean. The West had, more than three centuries before, conquered the East, and imposed a new language upon it. This was the Greek. Though the dominion of Alexander had passed to the Romans, the language remained unaltered. The Greek tongue and Greek literature were carried everywhere by the Roman armies. The prophecy, which was silently embodied, therefore, in the change then made in the language of Scripture will now be clear. It has been very strongly maintained by Tregelles and others that Matthew wrote his Gospel in Hebrew. I do not enter here into this question. It is enough to note these two things : (1) If there ever was such a Gospel, no trace of it has been found ; and (2) that it is universally acknowledged that our Greek Gospel of Matthew, known and quoted from in the earliest times, has no marks such as a translation must necessarily bear. It is an original work, and is believed even by some who contend for the supposed Hebrew Gospel, to have come also from the hand of the apostle. Certain it is, that no Hebrew copy of it was ever given to the Gentile Church; and that this and every other Book of the New Testament, even the Epistle to the Hebrew Christians, is written in Greek, the universal Gentile tongue of the time. This meant that "the times of the Gentiles" *had begun, and that they were to continue.* The Spirit of God handed the Truth over to Gentile custodians; and if the Jew was to share the blessing, he must partake of it at the Gentiles' table. The words of the Lord to the Jews were now fulfilled : " The kingdom of God shall be taken from you, and given to a nation bringing forth the fruits thereof" (Matthew xxi. 43). The founding, the unexampled triumphs, the persistency, and the vigour of the New Testament Church form, apart from the presence and the life of the Lord Jesus Himself, the most stupendous phenomenon in history. But surely this clear outlook into the future shown, not only in these words of Christ, but also in the language in which the New Testament revelation has been given, is hardly less astounding.

In closing this chapter, a word may be added as to the kind of Greek in which the New Testament was written. A warm, and, indeed, fierce, controversy was waged for nearly 200 years over the question as to whether the New Testament is, or is not, written in classical Greek. From the beginning of the seventeenth century to the middle of the eighteenth, it was strongly contended that New Testament Greek matched the writings of Plato and of the other classic authors in elegance and purity. This was an extreme opinion. But the opponents of these " purists," as they were called, were equally extreme and much less reverent. The New Testament writers, according to some, had presented us with Greek somewhat similar to an ordinary Hindoo's English, or to an ordinary Englishman's Hindustanee. Prepositions, for example, were supposed to have been used without any due regard to the fine distinctions which they express, and even without regard to their meaning.

The absurdities of this school have now been consigned to well-merited oblivion. The Greek of the New Testament has impressed scholars with confidence and reverence the more deeply it has been studied. There is no loose use of prepositions; there is no lack of grammatical arrangement. That marvellous instrument for the expression of thought has been used by the New Testament with full and clear consciousness of its capabilities; and the student of the original Scripture is instructed, impressed, and charmed by shades of thought, and by the far-reaching hints conveyed by the precision, and flexibility, and rich fulness, of the language. But it is not classical Greek; for that had long ceased to be the language of the people. It was the Greek of the time, the language of the day, the mother tongue of the then instructors of the nations, which was adopted and used by the Spirit of God. Just as the men of that day were taken and fitted for their high service, so was the universal tongue of the time chosen and fitted to be the medium through which they were to enlighten their own and after generations. Words were dropped which had become too closely associated with shades of thought which would have misrepresented the Spirit's meaning. Other words were brought into prominence. In this way a language was secured that could receive the new thought and the full truth which were to change the world. It is a language, too, which has retained them in undiminished fulness and splendour; and which will carry the water of life, still fresh, and clear, and sparkling, to the lips of men as yet unborn.

CHAPTER VII.

THE NEW TESTAMENT AUTHORSHIP—WAS IT APOSTOLIC?

THE two preceding chapters have prepared us for finding a clear reply to the above important question; and, when that is found, we shall have virtually answered another question, which is among the most urgent of those which are being asked to-day. If the whole of the New Testament belongs to the last sixty years of the first century, has there ever been such another galaxy of spiritual leaders? Each of these writers is worthy of this glorious fellowship, whose words have been light and inspiration to

all the Christian ages, but have never been matched
by any.   One such writer would have raised the
question whence he had received his endowment; but
this assembly of spiritual princes, while it emphasises
the question, also solves it.   There must have been,
as the Scripture tells us, a miraculous outpouring of
the Spirit of God.   These are only giving us, as they
themselves declare, the things which they have
received of Him.

The fact that all the Books of the New Testament
are in Greek might seem to favour the view that they
are of comparatively late origin.   It might be argued
that writers use the language with which they are
most familiar, and that the New Testament writers
must consequently be Greeks.   But when did the
Greek tongue become familiarised with Christian
ideas?   Certainly not, we might be assured, till a
generation had been reached that had grown up in the
atmosphere of Christian homes.   The inevitable conclusion would then seem to be that the Gospels could
not be much earlier than the middle of the second
century.   But all this is set aside by other considerations, which cannot be shut out of view.   The writers
had to select the language of those to whom they
addressed themselves.   A German merchant, who is
transacting business with this country, will write to
his correspondent here in English, if he is able to do
so.   The apostles and their fellow-labourers who
went to the Gentiles naturally adopted the language
which their readers understood; and the fact that all
of the New Testament writers, whether sent to the

Jews or to the Gentiles, were led to adopt this tongue, declared that the Gospel was committed to the Gentiles. The new Law was given in the language of the new people.

But an inspection of the writings takes us farther. It will tell us whether these who convey heaven's message are Greeks or Hebrews. There was good reason why the Hebrew stamp should be very deeply impressed upon genuine apostolic writings. The Hebrew language had been moulded by the Old Testament writings. Cremer, in his Preface to his *Lexicon of New Testament Greek*, says : " In fact, ' we may,' as Rothe says *(Dogmatik,* p. 238, Gotha, 1863), 'appropriately speak of *a language of the Holy Ghost.* For in the Bible it is evident that the Holy Spirit has been at work, moulding for itself a distinctly religious mode of expression out of the language of the country which it has chosen as its sphere, and transferring the linguistic elements which it found ready to hand, and even conceptions already existing, into a shape and form appropriate to itself and all its own.' We have," Cremer adds, " a very clear and striking proof of this in New Testament Greek." * When we speak, then, of the Hebrew modes of thought and speech which are so marked in New Testament Greek, let it be remembered that it is the Hebrew of the Old Testament to which reference is made. In other words, in these Hebraisms, we find in the New Testament the same " language of the Holy Ghost " which meets us in the Old Testament. On this

* First Edition, p. 5.

account our argument might easily assume a bolder front, and prove not only apostolic authorship, but also New Testament inspiration. It will be quite enough, however, if we content ourselves with the inevitable conclusion that the New Testament Scriptures came from apostolic hands.

This Hebrew tinge, which runs all through the New Testament, is fully acknowledged by all competent observers, and the fact calls now for illustration rather than for argument. The late Emmanuel Deutsch, whose authority in matters of Hebrew speech and literature is undisputed, says : " The style, the idiom, the innumerable open and latent allusions, the form and substance, in fact, of the fundamental Books of Christianity contained in the New Testament, written, as Lightfoot has it, by Jews, among Jews, for Jews, can only be properly appreciated and thoroughly understood by constant reference to the oral literature "—that is, the Hebrew oral literature—" of the period." *

To begin with, the reader of the New Testament is struck with the presence of the Hebrew words and phrases to which we have referred in what was said of the language used by our Lord. These are retained in the Gospels, and are occasionally even left without explanation. In Matthew v. 22 we read : " Whosoever shall say to his brother ' Raca,' shall be in danger of the council." What is there that is harmful or offensive in this epithet ? What does the word mean ? To these questions there is no reply in

---

the Scripture; and we have to search through the
Jewish literature, which takes us back to the times
before we find the required explanation. "The word,"
says Lightfoot, "is a Jewish nickname, and so used
in the Talmud, for a despiteful title to a despised
man; as 'Our Rabbins show a thing done with a
religious man that was praying in the highway: by
comes a great man, and gives him the time of day:
but he saluted him not again: he stayed for him, till
he had finished his prayer: after he had done his
prayer he said to him, "Reka," is it not written in
your Law, that ye shall take heed to yourselves? Had
I struck off thy head with my sword, who should have
required thy blood,' &c. And so goes the angry man
on. Irenæus hath a phrase, nigh to the signification
of this word; '*qui expuit crebrum,*' 'a man that hath
no brains:' and so 'Raka' signifies a man empty,
whether of understanding or goodness: so the Greek
word *kenos* is frequently taken." *

There is another word which has claimed a place
in our own language. The word *Amen* frequently
occurs, and specially in the solemn "verily, verily
(amen, amen) I say unto you" of our Saviour. He
is Himself also named "The Amen." † This is a
word which, it now appears, Abraham carried away
with him from Babylonia. It concludes the ancient
incantations and hymns of Chaldea, just as it ends
our prayers to-day. But it was from the Jews
that it came into the New Testament and into the
worship of the Christian Church. Its use is frequent

---

* *Works*, vol. iv., pp. 27, 28.   † Revelation iii. 14.

in the Old Testament. In the arrangements made for the rehearsal of the Law in Palestine (Deut. xxvii.) it is enjoined that "all the people shall say Amen." The use of the word is still more frequent in the New Testament, into which this Hebrew word is carried without translation. It is simply put into Greek letters, just as our Version has put it into English letters.

To these may be added many others which have been carried over into the New Testament almost always without explanation. The reader will recall the phrase "the mammon of unrighteousness." The word *mammon*, meaning "property," or "wealth," is a common one in the Aramean, or later Hebrew, of the Jews. In 1 Samuel viii. 3 we are told that Samuel's "sons walked not in his ways, but turned aside after lucre, and took bribes, and perverted judgment." The Jewish, or Chaldaic, translation, called the *Targum*, renders this "turned after false *mammōn*." In Isaiah xxxiii. 15, for "he that despiseth the gain of oppressions," the Targum has: "and separates himself from the mammōn of iniquity." It was also used as a legal term. Maimonides has a treatise regarding damage done to another's property. The word which is there used for "property," or "estate," is *mammōn*."

Gehenna, "the valley of Himmon," a term used for the place of everlasting punishment, and Beelzebub, "the prince of the devils," are other examples. The phrase *maran-atha*, "the Lord cometh," *Rabbi* and *Rabboni*, "master," have been already mentioned.

But the presence of these words is merely one symptom of a widely prevalent element in New Testament Greek. The New Testament language is formed to a considerable extent upon Old Testament lines. This is quite in keeping with the fact that these two Books are the continuous revelation of the Spirit of God; but what we have now to notice is that this characteristic is there. In the Old Testament, for the term "Israelites," we find the phrase, "the children of Israel." The Ammonites are "the children of Ammon." Men are "the children of men." The Levites are "the children of Levi;" the Ephraimites "the children of Joseph." The inhabitants of Jerusalem are "the sons and the daughters of Jerusalem." We read of "children of Belial." Eli's sons are described as "sons of Belial" (I. Samuel ii. 12). The word *Belial* is composed of two words, which mean "without profit." It would thus have the root meaning of "unprofitableness;" but it is used in the Old Testament as having a much stronger sense. It occurs in the sense of "wickedness" and also of "destruction." Now, this idiom, which represents a class as the children or the sons of that by which the class is distinguished, appears very frequently in the New Testament. It will be enough to mention the following phrases: "The children of this world" (Luke xx. 34); "the children of the resurrection" (verse 36); "the son of peace" (Luke x. 6); "children of light" (Ephesians v. 8); "the child of hell" (Matthew xxiii. 15); "the son of perdition" (John xvii. 12); "the children of wrath;"

"cursed children," literally, children of "cursing" or "punishment" (II. Peter ii. 14).

Other phrases were still more strange to Greek readers. The word *opheilēma*, "debt," is used in the sense of "sin:" "and forgive us our debts as we forgive our debtors" (Matthew vi. 12). We find in the Old Testament that the word "cup" is figuratively used of a portion assigned to any one by God. "Upon the wicked He shall rain snares, fire and brimstone, and a horrible tempest : this shall be the portion of their cup" (Psalm xi. 6); "The Lord is the portion of mine inheritance and my cup" (Psalm xvi. 5); "For in the hand of the Lord there is a cup, and the wine is red; it is full of mixture; and he poureth out of the same : but the dregs thereof, all the wicked of the earth shall wring them out and drink them" (Psalm lxxv. 8); "the dregs of the cup of my fury" (Isa. li. 17); "I will give her cup into her hand" (Ezekiel xxiii. 31); "Thou shalt drink of thy sister's cup" (ver. 32). The same figure meets us in the New Testament. The Lord asks the two disciples: "Are ye able to drink of the cup that I shall drink of?" (Matthew xx. 22). He asks again: "The cup which My Father hath given Me, shall I not drink it?" (John xviii. 11). Similar phrases will be remembered : "Ye cannot drink the cup of the Lord and the cup of devils" (I. Cor. x. 21); "If any man worship the beast and his image, and receive his mark in his forehead, or in his hand, the same shall drink of the wine of the wrath of God, which is poured out without mixture into the cup of his indignation" (Rev. xiv. 9, 10).

Another common Hebrew phrase is "the edge," literally, "the mouth," of the sword. This is the usual
phrase for destroying with the sword from Genesis to
Jeremiah. "Simeon and Levi slew Hamor and Shechem
his son with the mouth of the sword " (Gen. xxxiv.26).
The Israelites smote Ai "with the mouth of the
sword" (Joshua viii. 24). The very same phrase,
notwithstanding its peculiarity, appears in the New
Testament. We read in Luke xxi. 24: "They shall
fall by the edge *(stoma,* 'the mouth') of the sword;"
and in Hebrews xi. 33, 34 : "Who through faith . . .
escaped the edge *(stoma,* 'the mouth') of the sword."
This is but one instance of a number of words
similarly used. In Hebrew, the body is called *basar,*
"flesh." The Greek word for body is *sōma.* But the
New Testament writers, with the exception of Luke,
and Paul, and some passages in Matthew, use the
Greek *sarx,* "flesh," for the living body, and *sōma* for
the body when life has departed from it. The only
other constituent of "the natural man," according to
the Old Testament, is *nephesh,* the "soul." "The soul,"
in Greek, *pyschē,* is used in Hebrew where we should
employ the terms "life" and "mind." In Gen. ix. 5,
"the blood of your lives" is, literally, "the blood of
your souls." "Escape for thy life," said to Lot, is
"escape for thy soul" (xix. 17). The word to Moses:
"All the men are dead who sought thy life" is, "who
sought thy soul" (Exodus iv. 19). The command in
Numbers xxxv. 31 : "Take no satisfaction for the life
of a murderer," speaks of "the soul of a murderer."
This has been carried also into the New Testament.

X

We read in Matthew ii. 20: "They are dead who sought the young child's life (soul);" "Take no thought for your life (soul)" (vi. 25); "He that findeth his life (soul) shall lose it, and he that loseth his life (soul) for My sake shall find it" (x. 39); "Is it lawful to save life (soul) or to destroy it?" (Luke vi. 9). Paul says: "Sirs, I perceive that this voyage will be with hurt and much damage, not only of the lading and ship, but also of our lives (souls)" (Acts xxvii. 10); and in Revelation xii. 11 we read of those who "loved not their lives (souls) unto the death."

The same strange use of "soul" in the sense of "mind" is found in both parts of the Scripture. Abraham says: "If it be your mind (soul) that I should bury my dead out of my sight" (Gen. xxiii. 8); and in 2 Kings ix. 15 Jehu said: "If it be your minds (souls), then let none go forth nor escape out of the city to tell it in Jezreel." One instance of this use occurs, for example, in Acts xiv. 2, in the writing of Luke, who has been regarded as the most classical of all the New Testament writers: "But the unbelieving Jews stirred up the Gentiles, and made their minds (souls) evil affected against the brethren."

Another use of the Hebrew word *nephesh*, "soul," is more peculiar still. It is used instead of the personal pronouns. Where we should use "I" or "me," "he" or "him," "she" or "her," &c., the Hebrew frequently employs *nephesh*. Abraham, for example, entreating Sarah to say she is his sister, adds: "My soul shall live because of thee," instead of simply

saying, " I shall live because of thee." In like manner
the Psalmist says : " My soul shall make her boast in
the Lord " (xxxiv. 2) ; " Our soul waiteth for the
Lord " (xxxiii. 20) ; the Messiah " shall save the souls
of the needy" (lxxii. 13) ; " He spared not their soul
from death " (lxxviii. 50). This use of the word,
strange though it is, is carried into the New Testament Scripture, and the Greek *pyschī* is employed in
the same way. " Mary said, My soul doth magnify the
Lord " (Luke i. 46). Our Lord exclaimed : " Now is
My soul troubled ; and what shall I say ? " (John xii.
27). Even Luke thus sums up the first-fruits of the
gospel-preaching : " The same day there were added
unto them about three thousand souls," meaning
persons. Paul, who has been credited with almost
equal erudition and facility in Greek composition,
writes : " Let every soul be subject unto the higher
powers " (Romans xiii. 1), where the phrase is used
in the same Jewish way for " everyone." Peter,
speaking of the salvation of Noah and his house,
tells us that " eight souls were saved " (1 Peter iii.
20), meaning eight persons.

Those peculiarities which we have now noticed
lie upon the surface. But the Jewish element in the
Books of the New Testament goes deeper; it is
woven into their texture; it is part of their very
essence. God has unified His Church in this way.
If the Gentile has taken the place of the Jew, he has
been led up to it, and been brought into it, and been
established in it, by the rich, and patient, and Christ-
like ministry of the Jew. And this fact God intended

should be apparent till earth's latest day. Greek is a
language of long sentences and of musical cadences.
Hebrew is simple, brief, direct, and clear. The New
Testament is Greek as to language, and is utterly
correct in its use of the marvellous facilities of that
tongue for precise expression ; but it is, at the same
time, Hebrew as to style. With the exception of
one or two phrases in Revelation of an evidently
symbolical character, the language is never ungram-
matical or rude ; but the mind is Hebrew. The same
fact is equally impressed upon us when we note the
differences of the two languages in regard to philosophical and abstract terms. Greek is the most perfect
instrument which the world has produced to express
and record the researches and the triumphs of
philosophy. It is plentifully supplied with abstract
terms, and it lends itself admirably to the adventurous
pursuit of clear comprehension in the realm of
abstract, or "pure," thought. It is the language of
the philosophers and of the thinkers. Dean Milman
speaks of "the exquisite distinctness and subtlety of
the Greek language," and of "the anatomical precision of philosophic Greek." * The Hebrew, on the
other hand, deals with things rather than with
abstractions. It is the language of the people—of
those whom we may call the observant many—rather
than of the severely reflective few. It brings us back
to fact, to nature, to things as they are. It is the
language of restful faith, accepting things revealed,
and not of speculative restlessness, ever seeking to get

* *History of Christianity*, vol. ii., p. 352.

beneath or behind them, and so frequently missing them altogether. The Greeks shone as thinkers but not as saints. And we have to thank God that Hebrew thought is the thought of His entire Revelation. It is the vehicle of the New Testament as well as of the Old. Writing Greek correctly and powerfully, the New Testament writers retain the simplicity, the direct contact with things, and the restfulness in fact, which the Greek left largely behind him, but which the Hebrew never abandoned.

And now the conclusion, to which this long investigation leads, may be stated in a sentence or two. If the New Testament, while written in Greek, is Hebrew to the core, this must be because it is the Apostolic Book which it claims to be. For what is necessarily implied in this utterly Jewish character of all the New Testament Books? We are told that the first preachers of the Gospel were Jews. The Hebrew "disciples went forth and preached everywhere, the Lord working with them, and confirming the word with signs following" (Mark xvi. 20). We are also told that the nucleus of the first Christian assemblies was largely Jewish. The Apostles began at the synagogues, and the converts who were gathered together were made, in the first instance, from their own countrymen, from the Gentile prose-lytes who were united to them, and from the Gentile seekers after God who frequented the Jewish syna-gogues. When we bear in mind that these were the original converts; that they were to be the teachers of all who should be afterwards gathered ; and that for

them the New Testament Books were first of all
intended ; we understand why this Hebrew character
of the New Testament would have been unavoidable,
even if it had not been designed.　These Books were
" written," as Lightfoot has said, in words already
quoted, " by Jews, for Jews, and among Jews."　Now,
when was that possible ?　The only admissable reply
is—*in the apostolic age;* and further, in the very
commencement of it, and at the very time when the
Church has always believed that the New Testament
was written.

This Jewish mould could not be imitated.　No
Greek writer in the second century of the Christian
era, when the Greeks had crowded into the Churches,
and when the nationality of the early Church had
been completely changed, could have resuscitated the
Hebrew style ; and even if he had been able to
resuscitate it, it would have been utterly unsuitable
for the new congregations.　This conclusion is in
perfect harmony, as we have seen, with the testimonies which show that the New Testament writings
were already in existence at the beginning of the
second century.　It is also powerfully supported by
the contents of the Gospels.　These set before us the
personages, the customs—religious, political, and
social—in a word, the manifold life, of Judæa and
of Galilee in the very time of our Lord.　All those
customs ceased, all that life was swept away, forty
years after His death.　When thirty or fifty years
more had passed away, the whole was forgotten.　No
writer of even the beginning of the second century

could have painted that past, and no amount of
genius could have made the readers of his book live
and move among it. But all is embalmed, or rather is
enshrined, with all the freshness, and the vigour, and
the rich hues, of actual life, in the Gospels. We may
call these Books, indeed, an unconscious picture of
the time, as all contemporary writing is an unconscious picture of its time. But to present that
picture the writers must have been of the time.
That conclusion is inevitable in every case of the
kind. It is impossible to escape it in view of the
language and the contents of the Gospels.

THE FOUR GOSPELS.

CHAPTER I.

WHENCE HAVE OUR GOSPELS COME?

THIS question is confessedly the hardest of all those with which modern "criticism" has concerned itself. It is assumed, as a matter of course, that these four Gospels have come into existence just as other books have come into existence—in a purely natural fashion. That is the assumption which is now made with regard to every Book in the Bible. Some of the critics boldly avow that this is not only their own conviction, but also the conviction which they hope to plant in the breasts of posterity. For them the supernatural has no existence, and belief in inspiration is regarded as merely a long enduring superstition. There are critics, on the other hand, who speak as if we must continue to believe in some kind of inspiration. The Bible, according to them, is not quite as other books. They speak of its having no peer in the world's literature. But, when we ask them what they mean by inspiration, and press them to say whether they admit a real Divine authorship of the Bible, they reply with the vaguest generalities. They carefully dissociate themselves from the current beliefs, and they make it painfully evident that the goal to which they are drifting is the openly avowed unbelief of the "advanced," who are really the only logical, "critics."

But, when the inspiration of the Gospels has been cast away, the difficulties of the critics begin. Much has been said of "the variations" in the Gospels, and of their alleged inconsistencies, discrepancies, and contradictions. Of these we shall have something to say immediately; but they do not form by any means the chief trouble in the Gospel problem. For, strange to say, it is the striking agreements of the Gospels beneath which all the theories of the critics labour most heavily. "Few are aware," writes Dr. E. A. Abbott, "of the very small extent to which independent narrators of the same events use the same words. A comparison of a few specimens of independent narratives . . would show that the narratives often contain scarcely two or three consecutive words in common, and rarely or never a whole clause of five or six words. The same statement applies to narratives of discourses of any length reported from memory, and not from notes taken at the moment. Now, it is well known that in many parts of the first three Gospels the same words and phrases are curiously interlaced, in such a way as to suggest that the writers have borrowed either from each other or from some common source."*

What these agreements mean will be apparent by-and-bye. Meanwhile, let us glance at the replies which have been given to our question. In his

---

* *The Encyclopædia Britannica*, Art. *Gospels*.

Introduction to his *Life of Jesus*, Renan maintains that Matthew and Mark were the original Gospels. Luke's came into existence afterwards, he says; and John's, as we all admit, was the last of the four. "These two works, entitled Mark and Mathew," he writes, "remained for a long time in a loose state, if I may so speak, and were susceptible of additions. On this point we have an excellent witness, who lived in the first half of the second century. This was Papias, bishop of Hierapolis, a grave man, a traditionist, who was busy all his life in collecting what was known by any one of Jesus. After declaring that in such cases he preferred oral tradition to books, Papias mentions two accounts of the acts and words of Christ. First a writing of Mark, the interpreter of the Apostle Peter, a short, incomplete composition, without chronological order, including narratives and discourses, composed from the information and recollections of the Apostle Peter; second, a collection of sayings *(logia)* written in Hebrew by Matthew, which everybody has translated as he listed. Certain it is that these two descriptions accord pretty well with the general tenor of the two books called the Gospel according to Matthew and the Gospel according to Mark—the former characterised by its long discourses; the second, above all, by anecdote, and being much more exact than the other in minor details—brief even to dryness, the discourses few in number and indifferently composed."

These two, Renan attempts to show were much changed. They were not looked upon as Scripture. They were regarded as collected memoranda of the

Lord Jesus, which each one felt himself at perfect
liberty to add to as he was able. He says:—

"That which appears the most probable is that we
have not the original compilation of either Matthew or
Mark, that the two first Gospels as we have them are
adaptations in which each sought to fill up the lacunes
of one text from the other. In fact, each was desirous
of possessing a complete copy. He, whose copy contained discourses only, filled it out with narratives, and
contrariwise. It is in this way that 'The Gospel
according to Matthew' is found to have appropriated
all the ancedotes of Mark, and that 'The Gospel
according to Mark' contains to-day many of the
details which come from the *Logia* of Matthew.
Each, moreover, imbibed largely of the oral tradition
which floated around him."

This theory, which is worked out with such confidence, shows a strange blindness to one of the most
obvious of conclusions. If these original Gospels
had been pieced out in this fashion, their individuality would have been completely lost. If what had
been peculiar to Matthew had been inserted in the
original Mark, and what had been peculiar to Mark was
inserted in the original Matthew, the inevitable result
would have been one comprehensive Gospel, and not
two separate and distinct Gospels. Every borrowed
addition would have diminished the distinctions
which originally separated Matthew and Mark; and
when the borrowing was completed, the distinction
would have utterly disappeared. What a light it
sheds upon the worth of those theories that so

thoroughly obvious a conclusion as that should not
have occurred to one of the foremost literary men of
his time! But there is something behind, which is
more astounding still. The one thing, on account of
which we are expected to yield up our convictions
and to accept the critical theories, is the extensive
and accurate scholarship of these men, and their deep
and unwearied research. We cannot follow their
methods, for these, it is intimated, are high and out
of sight of ordinary mortals such as we are; and we
dare not question their fitness for this great task, on
pain of having ourselves written down as arrogant
and presumptuous fools. All that we are now expected to do is to gather together "the ascertained
results of the higher criticism."

But there is a fatal flaw in the above argument, and
it is of such a nature that our confidence in these
self-appointed guides is profoundly shaken. Renan,
it will be observed, speaks of the *Logia* of Matthew.
This *Logia* has been a word to charm with. By Renan
and all the rest it is taken—without any argument,
and without the slightest apparent suspicion that
any argument was needed—in the sense of "sayings."
It is then argued that these "Sayings of our Lord"
cannot be our "Gospel of Matthew," seeing that this
contains narratives as well as "sayings," or discourses.
The Greek word *logia* is here confounded with
another Greek word *logoi*—an astounding blunder.
Logoi, indeed, means "sayings" or "discourses"; but
logia means something entirely different. *Logion* has
the sense of *oraculum divinum*, "a Divine oracle," and

the plural, *logia*, means "oracles." Thus Stephen says (Acts vii. 38) of Moses that it was he "who received the living oracles to give unto us." The word in the original, here rendered "oracles," is *logia*; and it refers to the entire Law given on Mount Sinai. When Paul asks (Romans iii. 1): "What advantage, then, hath the Jew?" and replies (ver. 2): "Much every way. . . chiefly, because that unto them were committed the oracles of God." The word in the original, which is here rendered "oracles," is *logia*. It applies to the entire collection of the sacred Books committed to Israel; and it covers prophecy and history. The word occurs in two other places in the New Testament. In Hebrew v. 12 it is applied to the Scriptures: "Ye have need that one teach you again which be the first principles of the oracles *(logia)* of God." The only other passage is 1 Peter iv. 11: "If any man speak, let him speak as the oracles *(logia)* of God."

"Thus we find," writes Dr. Salmon, "that in the New Testament, *logia* has its classical meaning 'oracles,' and is applied to the inspired utterances of God in His Holy Scriptures. This is also the meaning the word bears in the Apostolic Fathers and in other Jewish writers. Philo quotes as a *logion*, an oracle of God, the *narrative* in Genesis iv. 15: 'The Lord set a mark upon Cain, lest any finding him should kill him'; and as another oracle the words, Deut. x. 9: 'The Lord is his inheritance.' The quotations from later writers, who used the word *logia* generally as inspired books, are too abundant to be cited."* The

* *Introduction to the New Testament*, p. 118.

logia by Matthew, spoken of by Papias, could have
been no other than the Divine oracles which were
given through him to the Church. In other words, it
was Matthew's Gospel.

The theory is, on other grounds, inadmissable.
Papias lived in the first half of the second century. If
the Four Gospels had been formed from these alleged
"discourses," they could not have been in existence
till about the end of the second century. But, as we
have seen, they were already in the possession of the
Churches about the close of the first century, and
they were then four in number, neither more nor fewer.
Another greatly favoured solution of the question as
to the origin of our Four Gospels has been the theory
of an "oral tradition." It is said that the Apostles,
in instructing the Churches regarding the life of our
Lord, naturally came by-and-bye to follow a stereo-
typed form. These instructions were the quarry, it
is said, from which the Evangelists drew the materials
for the four Gospels which we now possess. This,
we have been told, quite accounts for those strange
agreements in words and phrases which have perplexed the theorists. But this "oral tradition," writes
Rev. Ezra P. Gould, "must have been in Aramaic,
the language of Palestine, while these resemblances
are in Greek Gospels, and *verbal resemblances disappear
in translation.*" * The italics are Mr. Gould's.

The striking peculiarity of these verbal agreements,
in which the Gospel accounts agree often phrase for
phrase, and word for word, and this last sometimes,

---

* *The International Critical Commentary. St. Mark*, p. 10.

too, where the words are unusual, thus entirely disposes of the imaginary Oral Gospel. And yet, with
a kind of infatuation, writers cling to the natural
origin of the Gospels. The same writer, who is quoted
above, says, after noticing that sometimes the same
rare Greek word appears in two or more of the
Gospels, and in the same unusual sense: "These
verbal resemblances can be explained only by the
interdependance of the *written accounts*. Either the
Gospels are drawn from each other, or from some
common written source."* But why? Is the explanation not at least equally good that they have come
from ONE MIND, by which the account was varied
when the distinct purpose of each Gospel called for
variation, and by which the similarity was preserved
when no variation was called for? But this notion is
apparently one not to be entertained. There are six
possible theories, if we suppose that the three first
Gospels were copied from each other. The figure (1)
denotes the supposed original Gospel, (2) that which
was first copied from it, (3) that which was copied
from the other two.

Theory   I. (1) Matthew; (2) Mark; (3) Luke.
  „   II. (1) Matthew; (2) Luke; (3) Mark.
  „   III. (1) Mark; (2) Matthew; (3) Luke.
  „   IV. (1) Mark; (2) Luke; (3) Matthew.
  „   V. (1) Luke; (2) Matthew; (3) Mark.
  „   VI. (1) Luke; (2) Mark; (3) Matthew.

Let the reader run his eye down these columns,
and he will encounter the best "ascertained result of

---

* *Ibid.*, p. 11.

the higher criticism," and an unquestioned demonstration of its unreliableness. The order of the
Gospels, running down the first column is Matthew,
Mark, Luke. In the second column we find also the
same three—Mark, Luke, Matthew. In the third
column the order is changed again, but all the
Gospels are there also—Luke, Mark, Matthew. In
other words, criticism tells us (1) that each of the
three was the original Gospel; (2) that each of the
three was derived from another; and (3) that each of
the three was derived from the two others! It does
not, therefore, surprise us to learn that all these six
theories have been tried, and that none of them is
accepted as satisfactory. Gould finds refuge in the
theory, which is advocated by Renan, making the
same absurd mistake that *logia* means "sayings" or
"discourses." As we have seen, Papias, by the word
Logia, indicated that Matthew's Gospel was already
received as "the oracles of God"; and was, therefore,
not a thing to be cut and carved. With this disappears
the supposed "written sources" of the Gospels, and
criticism stands before us with empty hands confessing that none of its theories will stand the test of
facts. The only theory besides these and that of the
Oral Gospel is that there was an original written
Gospel in Greek—a *Protevangelium*—a first Gospel.
"A closer examination of the synoptic Gospels,"
writes Bishop Westcott, "showed the inadequacy of
this supposition to explain the phenomena which they
present, and the historical difficulties which it involved
were even greater than those of the 'supplemental'

hypothesis," that is, that the Gospels were derived from each other. He adds: "The loss of a Greek Protevangelium necessarily appeared inconceivable." * The theory of an Aramaic written original, like that of an Aramaic oral Gospel, goes to pieces on those strange verbal agreements of the Gospels.

Every suggestion of the rationalistic fancy has been tried and has been found wanting. The problem of the origin of the Gospels is the heaviest which criticism has had to encounter, and the solutions which are accepted, are accepted not because they are satisfactory, but solely because no better account of the human origin of the Gospels is available. But there is a solution as simple as it is satisfying. It lifts our eyes, however, away from man to God. We now turn to it.

CHAPTER II.

THE PROBLEM SOLVED.

FORTUNATELY, when scholarship, having done all it can, confesses that it must leave us in the darkness still, the Scripture comes to our assistance. The light we need is found in the Gospels themselves. Luke has told us how his Gospel originated, and has given us a description of the state of things which the first of the Gospels displaced.

---

* Introduction to the Study of the Gospels, p. 184.

Y

Here are the well-known words as they appear in the Authorised and the Revised Versions :—

AUTHORISED.	REVISED.
" Forasmuch as many have taken in hand to set forth a declaration of those things which are most surely believed among us, even as they delivered them to us, who from the beginning were eyewitnesses, and ministers of the word ; it seemed good to me also, having had perfect understanding of all things from the very first, to write unto thee in order, most excellent Theophilus, that thou mightest know the certainty of those things, wherein thou hast been instructed " (Luke i. 1-3).	" Forasmuch as many have taken in hand to draw up a narrative concerning those matters which have been fulfilled among us, even as they delivered them unto us, who from the beginning were eyewitnesses and ministers of the word, it seemed good to me also, having traced the course of all things accurately from the first, to write unto thee in order, most excellent Theophilus ; that thou mightest know the certainty concerning the things wherein thou wast instructed " (Luke i. 1-3).

I may say at the outset that the differences between the two versions of this passage are not due to any difference in the Greek text. The Greek text adopted by the Revisers is in this instance identical with that from which the Authorised Version was made. The differences are, therefore, due to translation alone, and will be dealt with as we proceed. Our chief concern is to see what it is that Luke here conveys to us. The first thing which we learn is that there were numerous Gospels already in possession of the Churches when that of Luke was added to the number. " Many," he tells us, " had taken in hand to set forth in order a declaration of those things which are most surely believed among us." The Revised has "to draw up a narrative " instead of "to set forth in order a declaration." This leaves out the important feature that the narratives were well-ordered accounts, which the older translators loyally retain in the words " to set forth in order." These Gospels were, therefore, well arranged. They placed the incidents of our Lord's life and His words in their true historical connection. The Evangelist describes what these things were in a most important phrase which again is variously rendered, though the Greek words are absolutely the same. The Revisers say, "which have been fulfilled among us," instead of " which are most surely believed among us." That idea, in itself, is helpful. The birth and the character of our Lord had been predicted. So also had been the incidents in His life, His death, and His resurrection. And now all had been fulfilled before the eyes of the generation to which Luke, Theophilus, and the others whom he addresses belong. But, while that translation gives a perfectly intelligible sense, we have to make sure that it is the sense of the words. The word *plerophoria* means, not " fulfilment," but " full assurance," in the four passages in which it occurs in the New Testament. In Colossians ii. 2, we read of " the riches of the *full assurance* of understanding." In 1 Thessalonians i. 5, the Apostle reminds the believers that the Gospel came to them " in much *assurance.*" In Hebrews vi. 11, he writes : " We desire that every one of you do show the same diligence to the *full assurance* of hope unto the end ; " and in x. 22, he entreats : " Let us draw near with a true heart in *full assurance* of faith." The verb *plerophoreo* is used in Romans iv. 21, and xiv. 5, in the

sense of being "fully persuaded." These passages
indicate that the makers of the Authorised Version
were diligent students of the Greek Testament, and
Alford (see Commentary) says : " The more likely
rendering is that of the English Version, ' Certainly
believed.'" The reader will, therefore, do well to
keep, here at least, to the Authorised Version. The
Evangelist tells us that the things, which those first,
and merely human, Gospels contained, were those
facts concerning the Lord Jesus which have been the
foundation of the Christian Church in every age, and
that they had set them forth in orderly fashion.

A moment's reflection will show us how natural
it was that this crowd of Gospels should have come
into existence. It was a literary age. Readers and
writers were everywhere. Shorthand had become
fashionable and was extensively practised, so that a
speaker's words were able to be taken down while he
was addressing an audience. It was natural that the
Christian communities, scattered everywhere, should
desire to preserve the communications made to them
by the Apostles and the Apostolic men who told
them what the Saviour had said, and done, and
suffered. Here, then, were the means of continuing
this precious ministry among them, when the visit had
come to an end. Many had, therefore, taken in hand
to set forth in order an account of those things which
the Christians everywhere had accepted with full
belief, and which they desired to comprehend still
more fully.

But of what sort were these narratives ? Were

they accurate and reliable? We naturally assume
that an affirmative answer could not be given to that
question; for why, then, should they have been displaced if they were accurate? But we now learn
that this was not the reason for their being set aside.
On the contrary, Luke awards them very high praise.
These things, the facts on which the faith of the
Christian Church rested, were written down in those
Gospels, says Luke, "even as they delivered them to
us, who from the beginning were eyewitnesses and
ministers of the Word." This means that the writers
had striven after accuracy, and that they had succeeded. They had been careful to mis-state nothing,
and to put nothing out of its original connection; and
these first documents were accordingly, in matter,
form, and origin, such as those theories of to-day which
place our four Gospels highest, represent these to be.
They were accurate, but yet merely human, documents.

But God who sent His Son was not to leave the
perpetuation of that life and ministry of His to unaided
men, though naturally the ablest and the best inten-
tioned. Luke will now make this plain to us. Notice
the modesty with which he enters the field. He takes
his place among those writers as a fellow-labourer,
who makes full admission of the value of services
which had had their place, though they are now to
give way to God's better gift. "It seemed good to
me also to write unto thee in order, most excellent
Theophilus," he says. But why does he intrude?
Is he bringing to Theophilus ("lover of God") anything different from what Theophilus has yet had?

This he at once proceeds to explain. But here we have again to weigh the words and to scan our translations. "Having had perfect understanding of all things," says the Authorised Version. The Revised Version runs: "Having traced the course of all things accurately." Now, even with the Revised translation of the words we should experience no small difficulty. Where is the modesty that but a moment before shone out in those words: "It seemed good to me also to write"? Here is a man whom nobody is able to correct! The others have been indebted to the Apostles, but he seems to have gone beyond even them! He himself has traced the course of all things. Nothing has escaped him. No new thing can be brought to his notice, and there is nothing of which his knowledge can be increased!

But here again we have to prefer the older version. *Parakoloutheō* does mean to follow, but in the sense of accompanying. It is also used in the sense of "knowing fully," no doubt with a hint of companionship. In this sense we find the word in 2 Tim. iii. 10, where the Apostle writes: "But thou hast *fully known* my doctrine, manner of life, purpose, faith, long-suffering, charity, patience." Timothy had not investigated, he had not searched out these things. He had fully known them, because he had been brought into contact with them. This sense of the word is accentuated by the addition of *akribōs*, "accurately," which Luke here uses. Now, in what company had Luke known these things with accuracy? Not in the Master's earthly progress; for there is no intimation that he was of the twelve, or that he was ever associated with them. But there was "Another Comforter" whom the Master had promised to send, and who, He said, should lead those who were to make Him known, "into ALL truth." Imagine for a moment that Luke had been so led by the Spirit of God, and led into all the truth concerning the life of Jesus, should we not understand at once his use of this word *parakoloutheō* with its hint of companionship? And would it not be perfectly plain that this high claim has no boastfulness in it, and is full only of praise to God?

This is more clearly explained when we come to the next word *anōthen* translated in the Authorised, "from the very first;" and in the Revised, "from the first." It will be noticed that when the Evangelist in verse 2 has to say "from the first" or "from the beginning," he used a plain Greek phrase to convey that meaning—*ap' archēs*. But here he employs a different term, which is frequently used in the New Testament with the meaning of "from on high," "from heaven," "from above." Lightfoot says: * "'It seemed good to me also, having had perfect understanding of all things *from above*.' For so *Anōthen* be best translated. . . . . . And thus taken, it sheweth Luke's inspiration from heaven, and standeth in opposition to the many gospels mentioned, verse 1; which were written from the mouths and dictation of men, verse 2; but his intelligence for what he writeth was 'from above.'"

---

* *Works* (edition by Pitman), vol. iv., pp. 114, 115.

The word refers to what is "upper" or "higher." In Matthew xxvii. 51, we read that "the veil of the temple was rent in twain from THE TOP *(anōthen)* to the bottom." There *anōthen* indicates what was above, the upper part. The word also appears in this very connection in Mark xv. 38. It occurs five times in the Gospel of John. In the third chapter there is a very regrettable mistranslation, which has added a deeper shade to the mystery of regeneration. In verse 3, our Lord says : "Verily, verily, I say unto thee, Except a man be born AGAIN *(anōthen)*, he cannot see the kingdom of God "; and in verse 7 : "Marvel not that I said unto thee, Ye must be born AGAIN *(anōthen)*." The Revised Version has not improved matters by displacing "again" and substituting "anew," which has neither literality nor sense to commend it. A man might be born a hundred times again and anew, and yet not see the kingdom of God. What is needed is not merely a being re-born, but a being re-born with a higher life—a life which is of, and for, the kingdom of God. And all this is sharply defined by *anōthen*, when taken in its literal sense of "from above." The statements: "Except a man be born from above, he cannot see the kingdom of God"; "Ye must be born from above" require no comment. It is simply the misunderstanding of Nicodemus, who talks about a man's being born "a second time," that has perpetuated itself in these unfortunate renderings.

In the same chapter, verse 31, the context has compelled the literal rendering to be adopted : "He that cometh FROM ABOVE *(anōthen)* is above all. He that is of the earth is earthly, and speaketh of the earth : he that cometh from heaven is above all." It will be noticed that *anōthen* is here explained by our Lord to be used in the sense of " from heaven." In xix. 11 the word is clearly used in the same sense. Our Lord replies to Pilate : " Thou couldest have no power at all against Me, except it were given thee FROM ABOVE *(anōthen)*." In verse 23 it is used in a different connection but with the same meaning of " above." It occurs in the plural, *ek tōn anōthen*, "woven *from the top*," " *from the upper parts*." The only clear instance of its use in the sense of " from the beginning " occurs in Acts xxvi. 5, where the apostle refers to those who knew him " from the beginning " *(anōthen)*. Similarly in Galatians iv. 9 we meet with it in a sense which seems to be best translated by " anew." The passage is one of some difficulty. " But now," says the Apostle, " after ye have known God, or rather are known of God, how turn ye again to the weak and beggarly elements, whereunto ye desire AGAIN to be in bondage ? " The Revised renders : " over again." The words in the original are *palin anōthen*. *Palin* means " again "; but to this is added *anōthen*. Bishop Ellicot seems to give the correct explanation. He says the Galatians had been slaves to the elements as heathen, but now they wished to commence a career as Jews. *Palin*, " again," points to the repetition : *anōthen* points to the new career beginning as it were from the top, and proceeding onwards. The root meaning of *anōthen* is preserved in both instances. But the remaining instances of the use of the word bring us back to its ordinary New Testament signification. These consist of three passages in the Epistle of James. " Every good gift," we read, "and every perfect gift is FROM ABOVE *(anōthen)*, and cometh down from the Father of lights, with whom is no variableness, neither shadow of turning " (i. 17). Here *anōthen* is used as equivalent to "from heaven," or to our own phrase "from on high." The others are as follows: " This wisdom descendeth not from above *(anōthen)*, but is earthly, sensual, devilish" (iii. 15) ; " But the wisdom that is FROM ABOVE *(anōthen)* is first pure, then peaceable," etc. (iii. 17). That this was the sense in which *anōthen* was anciently understood in these words of Luke seems to be indicated in the words of Irenæus. "For after our Lord," he writes, " rose from the dead, and they "—the Apostles—" were endued *from above*, with the power of the Holy Ghost coming down upon them, they received a perfect knowledge of all things."* The reference to Luke's introduction appears to be unmistakable; and it is equally clear that "from above " is the sense which in the time of Irenæus was given to *anōthen* in verse 3. The Evangelist was " endued from above, with the power of the Holy Ghost coming down upon " him.

The force of the words will now be felt. Luke comes with an equipment which enables him to give to the Churches what none of those willing helpers has been able to bestow. He makes no use of these

---

* Adv. Hær., iii. 1.

abundant documents. This work of his is no new and complete edition of the pre-existing Gospels. Nor does he refer to his companionship with Paul or to his acquaintance with others of the Apostolic band as indicating his fitness for the task. He has "had perfect understanding of all things from above." And note now what he promises to his readers. He writes to Theophilus "in order that thou mayest know the certainty of those things wherein thou hast been instructed" (verse 4). He does not write to give Theophilus information. Theophilus has had that already: he has "been instructed" in these things. But that information, which has quenched one thirst, has created another. Theophilus wants to know whether these things are sure. He is stepping out from the faith of his fathers: he is abandoning the old beliefs and the old pathways. Are his feet upon eternal verities? Luke brings him the assurance which he seeks. He writes in order that he may know "the certainty" of those things most assuredly believed in the Christian Church and already imparted to Theophilus. But what is it that enables this Gospel to make a man not merely know these things, but to be assured of their certainty? The other merely human Gospels contained the words which faithful reporters had taken down from the lips of the Apostles. There was man's testimony to what the Apostles had said. But Luke brings something better. He conveys to Theophilus the words of the Spirit. This is the Divine testimony. In this light we can now see the intention and force of every word in Luke's preface. The Evangelist has had "full" and "accurate understanding" "of all things" "from above," "that thou mayest know the certainty of those things wherein thou hast been instructed."

Theophilus, with the entire Christian Church, received this Gospel, and afterwards the other three as God's direct gifts. These were "the Divine Oracles," conveying not only information, but also absolute assurance. The perfectly honest, well informed, and helpful, but merely human, documents ceased to be consulted, and speedily passed away leaving no trace. From the commencement of the second century the Churches know these four Gospels, and these four only. Is it possible for us to make sure of their claims? Are we able still to clearly discern their Divine origin and so "to know the certainty of those things" wherein we have been instructed? The following chapters will attempt to furnish a reply.

CHAPTER III.

WHY HAVE WE FOUR GOSPELS?

A REFERENCE to the preceding chapter will show that it is impossible to give to the above question what may seem to some the only rational reply. "There is no reason for astonishment," it may be said, "in our having four Gospels; the marvel is that we have not had more. The Life of

Christ must have been a tempting theme, and many must have tried to set forth what was known regarding Him."

We have just seen that this was exactly what had occurred, and that many had "taken in hand to set forth in order a declaration of those things which are most surely believed among us" (Luke i. 1). But we have also seen that these narratives had been set aside, not because they were inaccurate, but because, being merely human accounts, they could not convey in that terseness and livingness, in that vivid portraiture, and that inimitable touch of the Divine Spirit the certainty for which men yearned then, and for which men yearn still. The Scripture could not be silent about Jesus. And, since these well-meant attempts, however successful, had in their very essence human limitations, which would have become more and more apparent as the ages rolled on, they could not be bound up with that " Word of God which liveth and abideth for ever." The Spirit of God had, therefore, to lead forth specially endowed men to be His instruments in this service for humanity.

Here, then, is our problem. The Gospels are the Spirit's gift. But, if these are, as we know them to be, God's work, why have we four Gospels and not merely one ? When the first Gospel was given, why was a second necessary, and then a third, and even a fourth ? We can understand man forgetting and omitting, or forming some narrow plan which was found to be too contracted to admit everything.

We can understand how in this way more than one Gospel would have to be written; but how could such repetition be necessary with God, whose work is never marred by limitations? He could forget nothing, nor could He be constrained to omit through having based His work on too contracted a plan. Why, then, should there be four Gospels instead of one?

A moment's reflection will show that the suppositions which we have just named are not exhaustive. There may be other reasons for repetition. There are three accounts, for example, of Paul's conversion; and these are all contained in a single Book—that of Acts. We have first of all the record of the event in the ninth chapter. This is necessary, for the Evangelist has to explain how the persecutor becomes an Apostle. But Paul himself tells the story twice, when defending himself first before the Jews in the Temple (xxii. 1-21), and afterwards before Agrippa and Festus (xxvi. 1-29). Together with substantial agreement, there are significant differences in the three accounts. The first is in every respect suitable as an introduction to that unexampled career of zeal and self-sacrifice. This is specially apparent in these words of the Lord to Ananias: " Go thy way ; for he is a chosen vessel unto Me, to bear My name before the Gentiles, and kings, and the children of Israel. For I will show him how great things he must suffer for My name's sake " (ix. 15, 16).

In each of the accounts given by Paul himself we

notice its adaptation to the environment. To the Jews bent upon his destruction he explains: "I am a Jew, born in Tarsus of Cilicia, yet brought up in this city at the feet of Gamaliel, and taught according to the perfect manner of the law of the fathers, and was zealous towards God, as ye all are this day. And I persecuted this way unto the death, binding and delivering into prisons both men and women" (xxii. 3, 4). When he comes to the intervention of Ananias, he also is introduced in a manner calculated to win the regard of the assembly: "One Ananias, a devout man according to the law, having a good report of all the Jews that dwelt there" (verse 12). The next thing which the Apostle records, after the healing of his blindness and his baptism, is his coming again to Jerusalem and his praying in the Temple (verse 17). So thoroughly does Paul keep in touch with his audience that it is only when he is compelled to mention the Divine command to go to the Gentiles that the spell is broken, and that the rage of the crowd is once more let loose.

We notice a like adaptation in the account given at the Roman tribunal. He addresses himself specially to King Agrippa, a Jew, but closely associated in this matter with the Gentile Governor. It will be noted how he meets the scepticism with which the cultured Romans of the period and their Jewish associates were infected. The Apostle is about to speak of the risen Christ, and the tribunal is startled by the question: "Why should it be thought a thing incredible with you, that God should raise the dead?" (verse 8). In neither of the other two accounts is this emphasised as it is here. And the reason for its presence here is evident. The command of the risen Saviour is Paul's justification; but that will go for nothing unless he speaks to faith. It will be observed, too, how fully the command is set forth. Details are mentioned which explain the confidence with which he stands before them, and which make it evident how impossible it is that a mission such as his could be laid aside. "Rise," said the living Saviour, "and stand upon thy feet: for I have appeared unto thee for this purpose, to make thee a minister and a witness both of these things which thou hast seen, and of those things in the which I will appear unto thee; delivering thee from the people, and from the Gentiles, unto whom now I send thee, to open their eyes, and to turn them from darkness to light, and from the power of Satan unto God, that they may receive forgiveness of sins, and inheritance among them who are sanctified by faith that is in Me" (verses 16-18).

Here, then, is a repetition which has distinctly enriched us. The repetition has also been recorded with intention. Instead of merely telling us that Paul gave an account of his conversion, Luke was led to record the words spoken on each occasion. Is it possible, then, that the Life of our Lord has been thrice re-told that we might see it *from four points of view?* That is a suggestion which will inevitably occur to any careful reader of the Book of Acts.

But we meet a still closer parallel when we turn to the Old Testament. There, as everyone knows, the Books of Chronicles repeat the history of Israel previously recorded in the Books of Samuel and of Kings. And that this is not done merely to import additional matter into the Scripture history is abundantly evident. It cannot be denied, indeed, that we do find much in Chronicles which is narrated nowhere besides. In that respect the Chronicles bear the same relation to the earlier Books that John does to the earlier Gospels. The abundance and importance of the new matter in each of these later works have formed standing problems for sacred scholarship. But 1st and 2nd Chronicles are books, and are not merely supplements to pre-existing books. The former commences with a genealogy which takes us back to the Creation. The opening words are: "Adam, Sheth, Enosh" (1 Chronicles i. 1). The line is continued through Shem and Abraham, Isaac and Jacob. The first nine chapters are taken up with these genealogies. The history proper begins with a brief notice of Saul's last conflict with the Philistines and of the death of himself and of his sons. The election of David by the assembled tribes at Hebron is then recorded, and the history becomes the story of David and of his successors until the captivity.

The Books of Chronicles are, therefore, a complete history; but they are not a mere repetition of those of Samuel and Kings. What, then, is their purpose? What this is becomes at once apparent when we

Z

compare them with the preceding historical Books.
2 Kings concludes with the captivity. The last
chapter tells of the final blow under which the
Jewish kingdom fell, of the plundering and burning
of the Temple, the burning of the houses of Jerusalem, and the breaking down of its walls. It concludes with one glimpse of mercy in that terrible
overthrow. Jehoiachim is taken from prison in the
thirty-seventh year of his captivity by Evil-Merodach,
who "spake kindly to him, and set his throne above
the thrones of the kings who were with him in
Babylon" (v. 28). It was a Book for the Captivity.
It explained why the Divine hand had fallen in so
heavy a fashion, first upon the ten tribes, and then
upon the two.

We have only to turn to the concluding words of
2 Chronicles to note that its stand-point is different.
There the last words tell of the Edict of Cyrus
terminating the captivity and announcing the
restoration of the Temple. These last Books were
written, therefore, for the Return. The story of the
past is re-told for the purpose of explaining not only
why the heavy chastisement had fallen, but also
where it was that the fathers had begun to stray
from the way of prosperity. One characteristic of
the Book, which every reader will readily recall, and
which the higher criticism has fatally misread, finds
an immediate explanation here. In Samuel and
Kings the emphasis is laid upon Israel's idolatry.
Now, when Israel was returning, this was less
necessary. The tendency to idolatry had received

its death-blow in the marvellous fulfilments of
Scripture prophecy which the banished people had
witnessed. But it was now necessary that they
should be led back to their long neglected duty in
regard to the Temple worship and the faith which
Jehovah demanded from His chosen people. The
setting forth of these is visible on almost every page
of Chronicles.

The consideration of these examples gives weight
to the suggestion that the Four-fold Gospel has a
distinct four-fold purpose. It is true that the very
repetition of the Redeemer's story has always called
the attention of the Christian Church in every age to
one great fact. Christ is the centre of Revelation.
The Old Testament points on to Him ; the New Testament points back to Him. Without Christ the New
Testament would not have existed. Without Christ
the Old Testament would have remained an un-
fulfilled prediction. Apart from Christ neither can
satisfy ; each helps us only as it takes the things of
Christ and shows them to us. The four-fold Gospel
has always impressed that cardinal fact upon the
continuous reader and expositor of the Scriptures.
We open the New Testament, and we are told of
the parentage and birth of the Messiah; of His
childhood, His entrance upon His great life-work,
His sufferings, His death, His resurrection, and the
command given to the disciples to go forth and make
disciples of all nations. The reader naturally
expects, as he turns to the next Book, to be told
now of the fulfilling of that command and of the

preaching of the Gospel among the Gentiles. But no! he begins anew the story of Jesus! When this happens a second and a third time, who does not hear the cry: " This is My beloved Son; hear ye Him"? And when, as we shall now see, each of these memoirs of the Lord Jesus bears upon it the stamp of its Divine origin, since it is manifestly part of a plan which God alone can have arranged, that testimony will be graven still more deeply on heart and memory.

CHAPTER IV.

THE DIFFERENCES BETWEEN THE GOSPELS.

THE problem raised by the four Gospels, viewed on whatever side it may for the moment be looked at, is the highest with which criticism has ever undertaken to deal. We have seen something of this when considering the agreements of the Gospels. These at first sight seemed to give the critic the key to the mystery of their origin which he was in search of. For what does verbal agreement between two documents indicate, if not that one has copied from the other, or that both have drawn their matter from a common source? But this, which seemed at first the simplest and most triumphant of all solutions, has in this case utterly failed. Every conceivable form of the hypothesis has, as we have seen, been tried, with the result that criticism is now in despair.

It has fared similarly with the study of the differences of the Gospels. The passages peculiar to each
Gospel have been carefully marked. The very
slightest alterations in phrases common to two or
more Gospels have been recorded.* But on this side
also the task of explaining how the Books came.into
existence as merely human documents grows huger
with prolonged study. There is an explanation in
which both the agreements and the differences find
an immediate place. It is that the Books are the
work of really one Author, and that each Book is
serving a distinct purpose. With that key the problem
is solved at once. The agreements are explained by
the oneness of authorship: the differences are also
explained by the differences in purpose. But this
explanation, seeing that it involves the Supernatural,
is the last which criticism will admit. And yet, with
increasing study, the facts are seen to be pointing
towards it in a very definite fashion.

After commenting upon the additions common to
Matthew and Mark, Dr. Abbott says, in the article
already referred to : " In considering these passages
it is natural to ask whether any reason (besides
ignorance of them) can be alleged why Luke should
have omitted them. It is scarcely possible to fail to
see design in some of these omissions." After dis-
cussing somewhat elaborately these omissions in
Luke, he adds : " The above explanation of Luke's
omissions may only partially commend itself to the
reader ; but few will fail to see that there is at least

---

* See, for example, the Article " Gospels," in *The Encyclopædia Britannica.*

some method and motive in most of them." * We encounter the representative of a very different school when we turn from Dr. Abbott to the late Bishop Westcott. He finds these differences to be so constant and all pervading, that they are seen quite as clearly in minute differences as in the additions which are peculiar to each Gospel. In concluding a study of the accounts given in the four Gospels of the Resurrection of our Lord, he writes: "However incomplete the comparison between parallel evangelic narratives which has been made . . may be in some of its details, it seems impossible not to feel that it throws a striking light upon the individuality, the independence, and the inspiration of the Gospels. A more complete examination, which should take account of every shade of difference, such as could only be apprehended by personal study, would fill up an outline which is too plain to be easily mistaken. The characteristic traits which have been noticed appear in the records of a series of incidents which have been selected for their intrinsic importance and not arbitrarily. They are so subtle that no one can attribute them to design; and yet so important that they convey their peculiar effect to the narratives. Without any constant uniformity, they converge towards one point ; and even when their connection is least apparent, they present a general impression of a definite law to which they are subject. Diversity of detail is seen to exist without contrariety ; and the exhibition of a spiritual purpose with the preservation of literal accuracy." Notwith-

---

Encylopædia Britannica, vol. x., pp. 795, 796.

standing his apparent dread of any high doctrine of inspiration, he concludes the chapter with these words: "Nothing less than the constant presence of the Holy Spirit, if we can in any way apprehend the method of His working, could preserve perfect truthfulness with remarkable variations; a perfect plan with childly simplicity; an unbroken spiritual concord in independent histories." *

There is a remarkable three-fold portrait of Cardinal Richelieu in our National Gallery. It consists of a full-face portrait and one of each side-face. To catch a glance of the picture is to be instantly drawn to it; and once there, we are compelled to study it with deep, and indeed eager, interest. These three portraits, so much alike that none of them could have belonged to any other man than this, and yet with such subtle differences, enable us, if not to read the man, to understand something of the manifoldness of his character. Bishop Wetscott mentions another painting of this kind which supplies us with a still closer analogy to our four-fold Gospel. Vandyke prepared such another three-fold portrait of Charles I. for the sculptor, that his chisel might fashion an absolutely faithful likeness of the king. It took these three portraits to enable him to accomplish the work. The minute differences and the striking agreements in them were alike required. Not even the faintest difference could have been missed without corresponding loss. We desire to know Christ, to have His image carved, so to say, and set on high among the multitude of other images which fill the chambers of our memory. Or rather, to drop a somewhat unsatisfactory figure, we desire His presence in our heart—the presence, not of the Christ of our own imagination or of any man's fancy, but the Christ of reality, our living, reigning, all-pitying, ever-near, and almighty, Redeemer. And here is the four-fold picture, through the study of which the soul will receive the impress, and retain the image, of the Christ. The agreements and the differences, from the most marked to the faintest of them, are all necessary. As these attract and hold our attention, they will fulfil their mission, and we shall know Him, and through Him the Father whom He reveals, and whom to know is life eternal.

CHAPTER V.

MATTHEW, THE GOSPEL OF THE KING.

——

MY aim in these rapid indications of the purpose of each Gospel will be apparent to the reader. Should I be permitted to complete my series of small volumes on "The Books of the Bible," a fuller treatment of this subject will be found there. My object, meanwhile, is to show the existence and the nature of a clear, distinct, and all-pervading purpose in each Gospel.

The aspect of Christ which is to be set forth in

the first Gospel is revealed in its opening words : "The Book of the generation of Jesus Christ, the son of David, the son of Abraham." The genealogy, beginning with Abraham and ending with Joseph and Mary, is given in verses 2-16. Here, in verse 1, the entire genealogy is summarised—Jesus is "the son of David, the son of Abraham." When these two fathers are named, we know the destiny of Him of whom this Gospel is to speak. When we are asked what these names cover, we remember the covenant that was given with each. To Abraham the promise was given that in his seed all the nations of the earth should be blessed (Genesis xxii. 18). This, then, is the Redeemer of the nations, the Gentiles' Christ. But there was also another and later covenant—the covenant with David ; for "God had sworn with an oath to him, that of the fruit of his loins according to the flesh he would raise up Christ to sit upon his throne" (Acts ii. 30). Here we have the regal claims of Jesus. He is Israel's monarch, the King of kings and Lord of lords.

There, then, is the reason why the hand is stretched across the ages, and why these two names are chosen and set apart from all the others. But let us now note another thing. The names are not in their chronological order, which is observed in all the verses which follow. There the names are marshalled in the order of time. Here, however, that order is reversed. David is placed first, Abraham second. One is led to ask whether this means that Christ will be first manifested as King

before the promise to Abraham can be accomplished
in all its fulness, and before all nations of the earth
shall be blessed in Him.   But, whatever may be said
as to this, it seems clear that it is the heir of David,
the anointed King set over Zion (Psalm ii.), of whom
Matthew is to speak.   Another significant hint to
the same effect is given in verse 6.   Here the word
" King " (" Jesse begat David, the King ") appears
for the first and the only time.   The fourteen names
which follow are also names of kings, but not one of
them is so designated.   The words "David the
King " are plainly a comment upon these : " The son
of David."   This is the man after God's own heart,
who will shepherd His people Israel.   This purpose
explains also why Joseph's genealogy life is followed
by Matthew.   Joseph's was the elder and regal branch
of the Davidic race.   He was the legal heir to the
vanished dominion ; and his right descended to
Jesus, who by Joseph's acceptance and adoption of
Him took the place and the rights of the eldest son.

But there is no necessity for urging these interpretations of the hints found in the opening words of
the Gospel : for the same purpose reveals itself everywhere in Matthew.   Only two of the Gospels,
Matthew and Luke, relate incidents of the infancy of
Jesus ; but the incidents related by each Gospel are
entirely different.   Those in Luke will engage our
attention later ; but it is clearly the intention of
Matthew to speak here also of the King.   He tells us
of the coming of the wise men from the East to
Jerusalem.   We know that the whole world was

expecting at this very time the advent of One in whose hand, it was said, the destinies of the nations were to lie. Those men, by some means, had got to know, not only the country, but also the time, of his birth. They had, in addition, been confirmed in their conclusions by some marvellous astronomical phenomenon. They had "seen His star in the East." And now they seek the famous city of Jerusalem, and alarm Herod and "all Jerusalem with him" with their inquiry: "Where is He that is born King of the Jews" (ii. 2)? It will be seen that, if this is the Gospel of the King, nothing could be more fitting than that this incident should be recorded here. It was equally appropriate that Matthew should tell how the then usurper of David's sovereignty sought to slay the heir. It is only in Matthew that we find any account of Herod's attempt or of the Magi's visit.

In the account of the Temptation, narrated at length only in the same two Gospels, there is a striking difference between Matthew and Luke. What is the second temptation in the latter Gospel is the third in Matthew. It seems clear that Luke places the events in their chronological order. Our Lord is driven into the wilderness by the Spirit. The first temptation occurs when He is probably surrounded by the stones of that desert, which, as travellers have stated, are by their shape peculiarly suggestive of loaves of bread. Why, asks the tempter, not turn them into the bread which they so much resemble? A word will do it. But to speak that word would break the dependence of Jesus upon the

Father's care, and so the tempter is repelled. That scene has passed near the mountain foot ; and it is plainly in the natural order of the events that the mountain should be ascended now, and then, when the tempter has been foiled a second time, that the Lord should leave the wilderness, and that the assaults should terminate in the Temple with the attempt to lead Him to make a public display of the absolute trust in God, from which He had twice refused to swerve.

That is the order of Luke. The purpose of the third Gospel did not lead him to change the order in any way. But it is not the order of Matthew. The temptation on the mountain-top is placed last. In this way emphasis is thrown upon it. It is made the Lord's crowning victory. There are also significant variations in the two accounts. Matthew alone tells us that the mountain was " exceeding " high, that from thence the devil showed our Lord, not only all the kingdoms of the world, but also "the glory of them ; " and that, when the temptations were ended, "Angels came and ministered unto Him." Now, why should the first Gospel have thrown such emphasis upon this special lure which was spread in the way of the Son of Man ? Its purpose affords a simple and satisfactory reply. Our Lord is the world's King. Satan has usurped the sovereignty, and is able to delay the Heir's entrance upon His rightful possession. He will use this temporary power to enthral the Deliverer as he has already enthralled those whom Jesus comes to save. We

know how terrible has been the pathway of the
Nazarene, and how long His waiting. Satan first
shows Him the extent and glory of His destined
possession. With that scene spread under His eye,
the Lord is told that there is no call for delay or for
suffering. Calvary can be escaped, and also these long
centuries of waiting for a sighing and suffering
Church. All that is needed is a slight compromise.
Let this front attack upon every form of evil be
stopped. Let the high claim to have *everything* sub-
ordinated to God's will be lowered. Let it be enough
that there is submission in regard to some things, and
the hope that everything else will follow in due time.
In plain language, let it be acknowledged that
Satan's power is too firmly established to be at once
overthrown, and his opposition will cease. The
devil will come with his principalities and powers to
hail the Christ. It was a bigger temptation than we
can imagine. The Church has fallen before it in every
land, and almost in every age. But in this long
enduring war the Master's cry rings out ever and
again : "Get thee hence, Satan; for it is written,
Thou shalt worship the Lord thy God, and Him only
shalt thou serve" (iv. 10). It was fitting that the
readers of "the Gospel of the King," in perusing the
story of His temptation, should carry away this as its
last word.

As one of the slighter variations, Matthew's
account of our Lord's Baptism might have been
noticed (iii. 13-17). To Matthew alone do we owe
the knowledge that, when our Lord presented Him-

self for baptism, "John forbad Him, saying, I have need to be baptised of Thee, and comest Thou to me? And Jesus answering said unto him, Suffer it to be so now; for thus it becometh us to fulfil all righteousness." It was fitting that the royal condescension of Jesus should find its record in the Gospel of the King. But, coming now to the three chapters from the 5th to the 7th, we find that this purpose, so to say, is written larger. Here only do we read in its fulness the Law of the new Kingdom; and here only is the royalty of the new Lawgiver disclosed. There are claims here which cannot be sustained unless we recognise in Jesus a possessor of Divine glory. "Think not," He says, "that I am come to destroy the Law or the Prophets. I am not come to destroy, but to fulfil" (v. 17). It is inconceivable that even the most richly inspired man could use such words. To whom could the idea have suggested itself that any mere man had come to destroy the Law and the Prophets? Who could destroy God's Word? Who could take from the world, or snatch from God's Church, the holy oracles? And who, on the other hand, could declare that *He* came to fulfil them? These questions repeat themselves again and again as we read those chapters. Who is this that says: "Ye have heard that it was said by them of old time. . . . but I say unto you" (verses 21, 22)? The answer to all is found in the concluding words which disclose Jesus as He whose decree will fix our eternal fate. He is our Lord and King. "Many will say unto Me in that day, Lord,

Lord, have we not prophesied in Thy name? and in Thy name cast out devils? and in Thy name done many marvellous works? And then will I profess unto them, I never knew you: depart from Me, ye that work iniquity " (vii. 22, 23).

The Sermon on the Mount, which sets forth the King as Lawgiver, is followed by the 8th and 9th chapters, which reveal the King in His deeds. These contain what has been happily called "a procession of miracles." The regal claims of Jesus are thus presented both in His words and in His works. The parables in the thirteenth chapter are arranged in a series, commencing with the preaching of the Gospel among the nations and closing with their final judgment. The suggestion is a very natural one that the five parables, which stand between those of the sower and of the drag-net, supply the intervening chapters of the history of this time of waiting, the era of grace and of Gospel-service. A full considera-tion of these parables will show the value of the suggestion. The second parable—that of the tares—presents in one vivid picture the struggle of the Church immediately after the Apostolic age with the heresies, which, like the deadly arms of the octopus, sought to seize it and to drain its life-blood. The mustard seed tells of the ecclesiastical establishments, the founding of which marked the Church's victorious era, when the slender shoot sprang up and became a great tree, affording for the great of the earth (who had opposed the sowing of it in the lands) lofty resting-places. The woman with " the three measures of meal " (truth concerning the Father, truth concerning the Son, truth concerning the Spirit—the contents of God's completed Revelation), preparing food for the household, but, fearing lest the unleavened bread of the kingdom may prove unpalatable, adding a little leaven and changing thereby the character of the whole—that is a feature which we are unfortunately only too well able to recognise. The Greek and the Roman Churches, and the later Patristic Church from which they both sprang, had and have all the truths which we possess to-day. But priest-craft has changed the whole. The simplicity of the Gospel has gone. The Church and the priest have been substituted for Christ, and the sacraments for His salvation. But I need not follow the story further. It is sufficient to remark that we have in those parables of Matthew what we fail to find in any of the other Gospels—the story of the Lord's Kingdom.

The aim of this Gospel is seen very markedly in other parables. Both Luke and Matthew contain the parable of the supper, but with remarkable differences. The former speaks of "a certain man " who "made a great supper and bade many" (Luke xiv. 16). But in Matthew it runs: "The kingdom of heaven is like unto a certain king, who made a marriage for his son, and sent forth his servants to call them that were bidden to the wedding" (xxii. 2, 3). In Matthew alone also do we find the continuation of the parable in which "the King comes in to see the guests," and "saw there a man who had not on a wedding garment" (verses 11-14). That again carries to its completion this setting of the story of the Lord's Kingdom.

The same feature is specially apparent in the words concerning the final judgment which conclude Matthew's account of our Lord's public ministry (xxv. 31-46). "When the Son of Man shall come in His glory, and all the holy angels with Him, He shall sit upon the throne of His glory: and before Him shall be gathered all nations: and He shall separate them one from another, as a shepherd divideth his sheep from the goats . . . Then shall THE KING say to them on His right hand. . . And THE KING shall answer and say unto them." etc. Here the aspect of Christ set forth in this Gospel is plainly declared. It is equally, though not so plainly, set forth in Matthew's version of the title placed over the cross. "THIS IS JESUS THE KING OF THE JEWS." Similarly we have Christ's majesty proclaimed in the incident preserved here of the Resurrection history. It is only in the first Gospel that we read of the "great earthquake," and of the manifestation of the angel of the Lord whose countenance was like lightning and for fear of whom "the keepers did shake, and became as dead men" (xxviii. 2-4).

The Gospel of Matthew ends with a word which might have disclosed its purpose from the first. Besides the appearing of Jesus to the women at the sepulchre on the morning of the Resurrection, the only other incident of those forty days which Matthew records is contained in the last four verses of the

Gospel. These tell of His appearing to the entire body of the early Church, the more than "five hundred brethren" (1 Cor. xv. 6) who were gathered upon one of the mountains of Galilee. Here the Lord disclosed Himself as the Divinely-appointed King. "And Jesus came and spoke unto them, saying, ALL POWER IS GIVEN UNTO ME IN HEAVEN AND IN EARTH. Go ye therefore, and teach all nations, baptising them in the name of the Father, and of the Son, and of the Holy Ghost: teaching them to observe ALL THINGS WHAT-SOEVER I HAVE COMMANDED YOU: and, lo, I AM WITH YOU ALWAY, even unto the end of the world. Amen." These words, with which the first Gospel concludes, make answer to its first words—"the Son of David, the Son of Abraham." He, in whom all nations are to be blessed, is the world's King. Those whom He sends forth are not merely to "teach" (as our Version has it) but to "make disciples of all nations." The nations are to be brought to trust and obey Him into whose hands "all authority in heaven and in earth" is committed.

Want of space prevents any further tracing of the never-forgotten purpose of this Gospel; but what we have noted is enough to show that this purpose is to set forth Jesus as the King, whom God, despite the world's rejection, hath set upon His holy hill of Zion.

CHAPTER VI.

THE PURPOSE OF THE GOSPEL OF MARK.

THE recognition of the purposes of the Gospels is a new feature in New Testament exposition and criticism. In Bishop Westcott's *Introduction to the Study of the Gospels*, which was first published in 1860, there is a clear perception of the distinct purposes of the first and of the third Gospels. Matthew's he sees to be everywhere the Gospel of the King, and Luke's that of the Saviour. But one is disappointed in his treatment of Mark. In this Gospel he can only see "the vividness of its details, and not the subordination of its parts to the working out of any one idea." And yet, strange to say, the very next words clearly indicate the working out of one idea. "The narrative," he says, "does not, indeed, vary considerably in its contents from the other Synoptic Gospels, and offers several broad divisions which mark successive stages *in the work of Christ.*" *

From this it would seem that the second Gospel has the intention of dealing with Christ as the Worker. To this Dr. Westcott does full justice in another passage. "The smaller variations in the narrative" (that is, of Mark) he writes, "offer several features of interest in addition to those which

* Page 342.

have been already noticed. One of these characterises the whole Gospel. St. Mark, more than any
other Evangelist, records the effect which was produced on others by the Lord's working. Just as he
follows out the details of the acts themselves, he
mentions the immediate and wider results which
they produced. From the beginning to the end he
tells us of the wonder and amazement and fear with
which men listened to the teaching of Christ.
Everywhere multitudes crowd to hear Him, as well
as to receive His blessings. When he was in a
house, *the whole city was gathered to the door*, and even
then the crowd could find no room. So great at
times was the excitement, that He *could no longer
openly enter into the city;* and it is said twice, that *as
many came and went He could not even eat*, so that He
seemed to His kindred *to be beside Himself.* Those
who were healed, in spite of His injunctions, proclaimed abroad the tidings of His power. And in
His retirement, *men from all the cities ran together on
foot* to see Him; and *wherever He went, into villages,
or cities, or country, they placed their sick* before Him;
and *as many as touched Him were made whole.*" *

But those were early days for this new reading of
the Gospels—a reading of them which, as other
light upon the Scripture, sprang from the studies of
believing men, and not from the theories of criticism.
Since the first publication of the late Bishop's book,
the purpose of Mark has become increasingly clear,
and may now be said to have taken its place in

* Pages 347, 348.

Exposition. A recent writer, Ezra P. Gould, says:
" Mark has a way of his own of handling his material.
Whatever may be his reason, the fact is that he dwells
on the active life of our Lord, the period from the
beginning of the Galilæan ministry to the close of
His natural life. The introduction to this career,
including the ministry of John the Baptist, the
baptism and the temptation, he narrates with
characteristic brevity. But it is not brevity for the
sake of brevity ; it comes from a careful exclusion of
everything not bearing directly upon his purpose. . .
All of these things have a value of their own, but
they are evidently regarded by the writer as introductory to his theme, the active ministry of Jesus,
and abbreviated accordingly."[*]

The peculiarity of the second Gospel is that, while
the amount of matter peculiar to itself is so very
small, its special purpose should, nevertheless, be so
distinct. This is accomplished by the very feature
which has been such a stumbling block to many—the
variations in the accounts of what our Lord said and
did. From its first word to its last, Mark's is THE
GOSPEL OF SERVICE. It opens with the statement of
its title : " The beginning of the Gospel of Jesus
Christ, the Son of God " (i. 1). It is quite natural
for a present-day reader to think that the Evangelist,
in speaking of " the gospel of Jesus Christ," means
his own book—the Gospel of Mark. But in that
case, why should he tell us that this was the
beginning of his Gospel ? Where should we look for

---

the beginning of a book but at the commencement ?
And what could any writer mean by informing us
that his opening words were his first words ?
Besides this, the word gospel (in Greek, *euangelion*)
was never used to denote one of the four lives, or
memoirs, of our Lord till well on in the second
century of our era. *Euangelion* is used in two senses
in the New Testament ; first, in its usual sense of
" glad tidings ; " and secondly, in that of the work of
declaring these glad tidings. We find it in the latter
sense, for instance, in 1 Corinthians ix. 14: " Even
so hath the Lord ordained that they who preach the
gospel should live of the gospel," that is, should be
supported by their gospel service.

But, fortunately, we find the exact phrase, which
we meet in Mark's opening words, in Philippians
iv. 15: " Now ye Philippians know also, that in *the
beginning of the gospel*, when I departed from Mace-
donia, no Church communicated with me as to
giving and receiving, but ye only." Here, " the beginning of the gospel " is plainly the beginning of
the gospel work, the service of declaring the good
tidings of God's grace in Christ. Mark has, therefore, at the very outset, placed us at the right standpoint for viewing Him whose story he is about to
tell. This book is to set forth the beginning of the
gospel-service, and so to display the example which
The Great Worker in the gospel-field has left for all
who follow Him in this service.

Quite in keeping with this, nothing is told us here
of our Lord's infancy. A short account of the work

of John the Baptist (consisting of six verses) is pre-
faced by two quotations from the prophets explaining
what John's appearance signified.   He was the
forerunner of the Messiah.   The Lord's baptism,
temptation, and entrance upon His work in Galilee
pass before us in like vividness and brevity.   But,
brief as this preliminary notice is, the purpose of the
Gospel is not forgotten.   Mark sets forth the subjection of Jesus.   Matthew and Luke tell us that Jesus
was " led " of the Spirit into the wilderness ; but
Mark's words are : " The Spirit driveth Him into the
wilderness " (i. 12).   It is from him, too, that we
learn that the temptation, which culminated in the
final three-fold attack, continued throughout the
whole of the forty days, and that the Lord " was
with the wild beasts."

The special mission of the Gospel is clearly seen,
too, in the four parables of the 4th chapter.   These
correspond to the seven parables in Matthew xiii.
The latter paint the story of the kingdom ; the
former describe as plainly the work by which the way
for the establishment of the kingdom is prepared.
The first parable in both Gospels is the same—that
of the sower.   In the next parable, however, the
second Gospel follows its own line.   It is that of the
lamp or candle.   A lighted lamp is not brought into
a room to be hid away.   It is not covered with a
bushel, nor put under a bed.   It is set on a lamp-stand
so that it may give light to all.   And so the light,
which is kindled in us, is meant for the service of
light-giving.   The third parable is that of the seed

growing secretly—one of special encouragement for the sowers of the Word: " So is the kingdom of God, as if a man should cast seed into the ground; and should sleep, and rise night and day, and the seed should spring and grow up, he knoweth not how. For the earth bringeth forth fruit of herself; first the blade, then the ear, after that the full corn in the ear. But when the fruit is brought forth, immediately he putteth in the sickle, because the harvest is come " (verses 26-29). Wickliffe, Luther, Knox, Wesley, Whitfield, Haldane, Spurgeon, and many another dropped the gospel-seed in the heart of man. It entered where they could not follow it and could not tend it. But it brought forth according to its kind. The last of the four is the parable of the mustard seed. The lowly gospel-service of apostle and of evangelist will issue in a huge organisation. And the danger, which will mark the Church's last experiences in this dispensation seems to be indicated by the incident with which the chapter concludes—the peril on the lake which the Lord ends by rebuking the wind and saying to the sea, " Peace, be still : and the wind ceased and there was a great calm " (verses 30-41).

Another parable, which we find in Mark only, discloses the same design. It is a parable of the Return, but wholly different from those in Matthew. " For the Son of Man is as a man taking a far journey, who left his house, and gave authority to his servants, and to every man his work, and commanded the porter to watch. Watch ye therefore ; for ye know not when the Master of the house cometh, at even, or at midnight, or at the cock-crowing, or in the morning : lest coming suddenly he find you sleeping. And what I say unto you, I say unto all, Watch " (xiii. 34-37). Here the Gospel of Service plainly discloses its mission.

A verse which precedes these has always presented a difficulty which would have largely disappeared, had the purpose of the Gospel been seen. " But of that day and that hour knoweth no man, no, not the angels which are in heaven, neither the Son, but the Father " (xiii. 32). It is only in the Gospel of the Servant that we find these words: " neither the Son." They form no denial of our Lord's Deity. This is, indeed, plainly indicated. Though *men* do not know the day and the hour of the Son of Man's coming, it might, naturally enough, be supposed that these would not be hid from the angels who behold God's face. But, we are told, they also are ignorant of them. And, then, the Scripture ascends yet higher, and adds: " neither the Son." The Son is therefore not included among the earthly or the heavenly creation. In other words, He is uncreated and Divine. But, since He is Divine, and therefore omniscient, how can we understand the words ? Only in the sense of a voluntary subjection. The fixing of the Day and the Hour He leaves in the Father's hands. In that matter the Lord had humbled Himself, and perhaps humbles Himself even now. He sits upon the right hand of the Majesty on high, expecting.

The same purpose is revealed in the remarkable omission of the title "Lord" as applied to the Saviour. This is never once applied to Jesus in the genuine text of Mark till after the Resurrection (see xvi. 19, 20). In ix. 24 of the Authorised Version it is found, but this is one of the very rare examples in which the received text is wanting in accuracy. A comparison of the manuscripts places it beyond all doubt that the word "Lord" in this place does not belong to the Gospel as it left the hands of the Evangelist.

The purpose is shown also in various characteristics of our Lord's service, for our knowledge of which we are indebted to this Gospel. It shows His zeal. It has all along been noted how frequently the word *eutheōs* (rendered, "straightway," "forthwith," etc.) appears in Mark. This has been mistakenly set down as one of the Evangelist's own characteristics. It was the characteristic of the Master in His consuming zeal. Mr. Jukes* says the word appears eighty times in all in the whole of the New Testament, and forty of these instances are found in the sixteen chapters of this Gospel. Similarly in this Gospel we find special information on the Lord's *methods* of service, the things which marked His dealing with men. No man can take up Christ's work with any hope of success if he has not Christ's spirit. The three first Evangelists tell us of the Young Ruler's interview with Jesus, but in Mark only do we read that "Jesus, beholding him, loved him" (Mark x. 21).

---

* *Differences of the Four Gospels*, p. 73, note.

Nor was there haste in the Lord's dealing with those whom He healed. He patiently led them into fuller blessing. He waited to be gracious. We have two remarkable instances of this which are peculiar to Mark. One is the healing of " one that was deaf, and had an impediment in his speech " (vii. 32). A word would have healed him. But our Lord " took him aside from the multitude " (vii. 32-35). In this way Jesus drew the man to Himself. The man's attention was fixed upon his healer. Then, we read, Jesus " put His fingers into his ears, and He spit, and touched his tongue ; and looking up to heaven, he sighed, and saith unto him, Ephphatha, that is, Be opened." Here faith was stimulated and directed. The placing of the fingers in the ears intimated that Jesus was about to remove that trouble. The touching of the hampered tongue with saliva (a common medical agent of the time) excited a similar expectation with regard to the removal of the impediment in the man's speech. The look heavenward and the sigh of compassionate prayer turned the man's soul, now full of expectation, to God. Here the Servant of Jehovah was bearing the man's whole burden, and meeting the need of the soul as well as the need of the body.

An incident of the same kind, which is also peculiar to Mark, meets us in the following chapter (viii. 22-26) ; " And He cometh to Bethsaida ; and they bring a blind man unto Him, and besought Him to touch him. And He took the blind man by the hand, and led him out of the town ; and when He had spit on his eyes, and put His hands upon him, He asked him if he saw ought. And he looked up, and said, I see men as trees walking. After that He put His hands again upon his eyes, and made him look up: and he was restored, and saw every man clearly." Here also the Lord might have spoken a word and passed on. But He leads the man apart so that they two are alone together. He then gives an intimation that He is addressing Himself to the removal of the man's blindness, and thus excites his faith. He might also have made the cure perfect at the first. But the man's faith, having a foothold in the partial cure, will now be able to mount higher. It is well to note that in both these cases the men are brought to Jesus by friends or relatives. So far as we are informed, they themselves ask for nothing. This taking hold of them, leading them aside, He Himself taking the place of friend and brother, and begetting faith in souls perhaps too dull, too despairing, or too timid, shows how fully Jesus meets our need. The record is full of encouragement for all who can bring some needy ones to the Healer in prayer only.

This fulness of service receives a further illustration in the Lord's dealing with the father who brought his possessed son first to the disciples and then to their Master (ix. 14-27). To Mark alone we owe the account of the Lord's conversation with the father. The man must have had some expectation of help when he set out to find the Prophet of Nazareth. But his faith must have suffered sorely when he witnessed the failure of the disciples. Our Lord first leads the man to state the case to Him. " And He asked his father, How long is it ago since this came unto him ? And he said, Of a child. And ofttimes it hath cast him into the fire, and into the waters, to destroy him : but if Thou canst do any thing, have compassion on us, and help us. Jesus said unto him, If thou canst believe, all things are possible to him that believeth. And straightway the father cried out, and said with tears, Lord, I believe; help Thou mine unbelief. When Jesus saw that the people came running together, He rebuked the foul spirit." Here it is plainly implied that our Lord had brought the father and the child away from the multitude ; and, in this case also, taking measures to be alone with the man, He awoke the faith which wrestled with unbelief.

It also belonged to this picture of service that Mark should show us the unbelief with which the Lord had to bear and to strive. He alone explains to us the overwhelming astonishment of the disciples when the Lord came to them walking upon the sea. "And He went up unto them into the ship; and the wind ceased : and they were sore amazed in themselves beyond measure, and wondered. For they considered not the miracle of the loaves : *for their heart was hardened* " (vi. 51, 52). From him only do we learn the apparently invincible unbelief of the eleven with regard to the resurrection of Jesus. " Now when Jesus was risen early the first day of the week, He appeared first to Mary Magdalene, out of whom He had cast seven devils. And she went and told them that had been with Him, as they mourned and wept. And they, when they had heard that He was alive, and had been seen of her, believed not." The two disciples from Emmaus came with their wondrous tidings; but "neither believed they them" (xvi. 9-13). It was only the presence of Jesus Himself that could convince them that the resurrection was a fact. It was needful that all this should be disclosed in the Gospel of Service. It is thus that even stubborn unbelief and hearts hardened must be borne with. For from such may, nevertheless, spring the chiefest of the servants of God.

It is a striking fact that the discernment of this purpose of the second Gospel should enable even the ordinary reader to decide a great critical controversy. The fact of the controversy has been forced upon the attention of the general public by the Revised Version. There the last twelve verses of the Gospel are separated from the rest of the Book, and the separation is accounted for by the following note in the margin :

" The two oldest Greek manuscripts, and some other authorities, omit from verse 9 to the end. Some other authorities have a different ending to the Gospel."

The controversy raised by that note I can only notice very briefly. It has resulted in a full justification of the position given to the verses in the Authorised Version, and in damaging very seriously the reputation for exact and painstaking scholarship of the authors of the Revised Version. This note, as is also the case with other marginal notes of theirs, is misleading. Dean Burgon, in a volume on the last twelve verses of Mark, has swept away a host of misconceptions which, through one influence and another, had been collecting in the minds of scholars regarding this question. Scrivener, one of our very highest authorities on the text of the Greek New Testament, says in reference to these verses:

"In vol. i., chap. i., we engaged to defend the authenticity of this long and important passage, and that without the slightest misgiving (p. 7). Dean Burgon's brilliant monograph, 'The Last Twelve Verses of the Gospel according to St. Mark vindicated against recent objectors and established' (Oxford and London, 1871), has thrown a stream of light upon the controversy, nor does the joyous tone of his book mis-become one who is conscious of having triumphantly maintained a cause which is very precious to him. We may fairly say that his conclusions have in no essential point been shaken by the elaborate and very able counter-plea of Dr. Hort (Notes, pp. 28-51). This whole paragraph is set apart by itself in the critical editions of Tischendorf and Tregelles. Besides this, it is placed within double brackets by Westcott and Hort, and followed by the wretched supplement derived from Codex L., annexed as an alternative reading."*

The case for the omission of the verses rests largely on the two manuscripts B (the Vatican) and Aleph (the Sinaitic), the "Sceptical Character" of

---

* *A Plain Introduction to the Criticism of the New Testament* (Fourth Edition), vol. ii., p. 337.

which is specially marked. They show a close connection in similar omissions from the Gospels. Passages are omitted relating to the Divinity of our Lord, as well as to Everlasting Punishment.* They were written in a bad time—that of the Arian lapse. But Dean Burgon has shown how impossible it was for the Vatican MS. to suppress the testimony to the genuineness of these last twelve verses. *A blank space is left for them in the manuscript*—the only blank space, indeed, which it contains. This proves that *the verses were in the earlier manuscript* from which the Vatican was copied. A close scrutiny of the other MS., the Sinaitic, has revealed a still more damaging fact.† Two pages of the original MS. have been taken out and two others inserted, apparently by the writer of the Vatican MS. These contain the close of Mark and the beginning of Luke. *The pages were evidently re-written for the purpose of excluding these twelve verses.* There are six columns out of the eight on these two pages devoted to Mark ; but "these are so spread out," says Mr. Miller, "that they contain less matter than they ought." It seems, notwithstanding this wider writing, that the omission of the twelve verses left a larger space than had been anticipated just as the writer was approaching the end of his task, and the fifth column "is so arranged as to contain only about five-sixths of the normal quantity of matter." He also filled up the last line with ornamentation lest any

---

* See *The Traditional Test of the Holy Gospels,* Burgon and Miller, pp. 287-291.
† *Ibid.,* pp. 298-307.

one should afterwards indicate that there had been anything further to add.

The testimony for the genuineness of the verses is otherwise overwhelming. But why should any attempt have been made to omit them, or to alter them? The exposure of the persistent unbelief of the Apostles in the Lord's resurrection seems to have been one reason. When these manuscripts were written, in the fourth or fifth centuries, priestly pretensions were advancing by leaps and bounds. It was exceedingly inconvenient to remind the people at such a time that even the Apostles had been but dull, stubborn, incredulous, men. The whole class suffered in the humiliation of those on whose greatness they founded their pretensions. There was very probably also an additional reason for the suppression of the verses, which would tell powerfully upon a daring and un-scrupulous man. Multitudes were now pouring into the Churches. Among these were some of the sharpest intellects which any age has seen. What an instrument for evil might not these make out of those 17th and 18th verses: "And these signs shall follow them that believe; In My name shall they cast out devils; they shall speak with new tongues; they shall take up serpents; and if they drink any deadly thing, it shall not hurt them; they shall lay hands on the sick, and they shall recover?" Would the words hold good? Here seemed to be a short and easy method of disposing of the claims of the Redeemer. Let the Christians exhibit the powers which He declared should be given them. Let them take up deadly serpents. Let them drain the hemlock cup, and show that, though it killed Socrates, it will not kill them. If they fail, or decline the contest, then one of two things will be clear. Either they are not believers; or their Master was a deceiver.

It seemed, no doubt, wiser to avoid placing such a weapon in the hands of a foe; and the passage was accordingly suppressed—probably only in some manuscripts intended for public reading. But there was a simple and conclusive answer to any caviller. These signs *had* followed them that believed. We have evidence from a Jewish source that the early Christians were armed with power to heal others even who had been bitten by serpents. These gifts had been heaven's testimony to the early converts. The gifts of the Spirit were conferred upon the early believers by the laying on of the hands of the Apostles. But, when the Apostles had passed away, this sign, intended only for the introduction of Christianity, began to be withdrawn. No more of these miraculous powers could be bestowed, and they ceased with the death of those who had received them. But cowardice finds its readiest refuge in dishonesty. The suppression of the passage seemed an easier way out of the difficulty than an explanation.

But the student of the Gospels has a text in his hands whereby the genuineness of the last verses can be thoroughly tested. We have seen that this Gospel never forgets, either in great or in small matters, its mission. It is throughout the Gospel of Service.

Is that also the mission of these verses? We have just seen how they alone show us the obstinate unbelief of the very Apostles, and how Jesus bore with them, and overcame their unbelief by "many infallible proofs" (Acts i. 3). There is hope there, and direction for the servant of God in many a dark hour. That is the subject of the first six verses (9-14), so that these are stamped distinctly with the hall-mark of this Gospel. The next two verses ring with the urgency of the service : "And He said unto them, Go ye into all the world"—there is not a corner of it to be left unvisited—"and preach the gospel TO EVERY CREATURE "—none are to be left out because their fellows may have ceased to regard them as men—"every creature," Greek, barbarian, Scythian, bond and free, male and female, are to have the gospel preached to them. " He that believeth and is baptised "—that believeth and confesseth his new faith, showing himself not ashamed of his new Master—"shall be saved. He that believeth not shall be damned." Could words have emphasised more the urgency, or the awful solemnity, of this world-wide mission?

We have looked just now at the two verses which follow these (17, 18). They also ring with the urgency of the work. " Go forth fearlessly," they seem to say ; " God will seal your work and make it manifest as His to all men." "And these signs shall follow them that believe. In My name shall they cast out devils ; they shall speak with new tongues ; they shall take up serpents ; and if they drink any deadly thing it shall not hurt them; they shall lay hands on the sick and they shall recover." And now the last two verses (19, 20) take their place as the conclusion of the Gospel, in such a way as to show, not their genuineness only, but also their Divine inspiration. The reader will recall the first words of the Book— " the beginning of the gospel of Jesus Christ, the Son of God." Here is THE CONTINUATION of the gospel service. It may be said that we have taken up the work of the Lord Jesus, and are following in His steps. But the truth is greater than that. The Lord is still carrying on the work, and we are co-operating with Him. "So then, after the Lord had spoken unto them, He was received up into heaven, and sat on the right hand of God. And they went forth and preached everywhere, THE LORD WORKING WITH THEM, and confirming the Word with signs following." The last words of this Gospel, therefore, make answer to the first, and form a completion of the Book such as shows that its special purpose was clearly grasped from the very outset. No one detected that purpose for long ages. There was some vague sense of its existence, but no clear discernment. It is only in the nineteenth century of our era that it has been seen with any clearness. Who, then, saw it in the beginning, and moulded these last verses so as to continue and complete it? That question leads us far past that of the genuineness of the last twelve verses. It brings us face to face with the Divine inspiration of these verses and of the entire Book.

CHAPTER VII.

THE GOSPEL OF LUKE—THE GOSPEL OF THE SAVIOUR.

THE third Gospel is broadly marked by an equally distinct purpose. " The great means of conversion to Christianity," says Godet, " amongst pagan populations was the proclamation of Jesus as the Saviour of humanity. The work of redemption wrought out by Him in favour of all men, and offered gratuitously and without the condition of works of the Law to the faith of each individual: such was, in this new medium, the power by which the Gospel laid hold of hearts. And it is precisely this which forms the characteristic feature in the narrative of St. Luke."[*]

This was clearly recognised some years before by others, among whom an honoured place must be given to Bishop Westcott. In his marginal summary, we find: "St. Luke. Christ the Saviour."[†] A minute analysis of Luke's introduction to the Gospel would disclose the purpose there. It is quite enough, however, to direct attention to what is told us by Luke of the birth and infancy of Jesus. The first announcement of the Lord's advent is given by the angel to shepherds "abiding in the field, keeping

---

[*] *Commentary on St. John's Gospel*, vol. i., p. 2.
[†] *Introduction to the Study of the Four Gospels*, p. 349.

watch over their flocks by night" (ii. 8). But why were these men selected for this high honour? What were they, or what had they done, that heaven's ambassador should be sent with the tidings to *them?* Why was not the announcement made to the chief priests and the elders of the people? Or, if not to these, why not to Simeon and Anna, or to other waiters for the salvation of Israel? The reply is startling. These men were outcasts. The ordinary idea is that the shepherd's occupation was one of the most honourable in Israel. It is questionable whether this was so at any time. It does not appear, at least, to have been the case in David's time. When the Divine expostulation was carried to him, the king was reminded that God had taken him from the sheep-cotes—evidently, therefore, a base occupation—and placed him upon the throne of Israel. There is no question, however, as to the status of the shepherd in the days of our Lord. "Among the Jews," says Godet, "the occupation of keepers of sheep was held in a sort of contempt. According to the treatise *Sanhedrin,* they were not to be admitted as witnesses ; and according to the treatise *Aboda Zara,* succour must not be given to shepherds and heathen." * The shepherd was to the Jew "as a heathen man and a publican." It was, then, to these, the Pariahs of Judaism, the outcasts of Israel, that the news was borne by the Angel of the Lord with heaven's glory.

This will enable us to understand the significance

---

* *Commentary on Luke,* vol. i., p. 130.

of some things in the context. Note the sign which is given to the shepherds that this is *their* Christ. "And the angel said unto them, Fear not: for, behold, I bring you good tidings of great joy, which shall be to all people. For unto you is born this day in the city of David a Saviour, who is Christ the Lord. And this shall be a sign unto you ; Ye shall find the babe wrapped in swaddling clothes, lying in a manger " (verses 10-12). Now there was nothing of a special, not to say of a peculiar, kind in the babe's being wrapped in swaddling clothes. But it nevertheless emphasises the peculiarity of that which formed the sign. There was no lack of care in regard to the child. There had been no want of foresight, or of diligent and affectionate provision. The swaddling clothes had been prepared and were at hand. This, however, was the peculiarity that, notwithstanding all this tender care, the child should be cradled in a manger.

But the providing of that manger-bed for the infant Christ was the token of a higher care than that of Joseph's and Mary's. God was to have guests that night, and preparations had to be made for them. Therefore it was that Joseph and Mary could find no room in the inn. For, had the Christ been laid in one of its chambers, these outcasts, the shepherds, would not have felt themselves at home there. But, not knowing why the hardship befell them, the weary travellers take up their abode in the stable ; and there these men are indeed at home. The Christ has entered into, and taken up His dwell-

ing in, what we may call their own peculiar territory.
He is cradled in the manger which, perhaps, they
have often filled with fodder for their cattle. This
was indeed a sign that unto *them* was born that day
"a Saviour who is Christ the Lord." The place
where His infant head first rested proclaimed that
He is the Saviour of the outcast.

The record of the incidents in the Temple keep
steadily in line with this same purpose of setting
forth Jesus as the Saviour. Simeon took up the
child " in his arms, and blessed God, and said, Lord
now lettest Thou Thy servant depart in peace,
according to Thy word : for mine eyes have seen
THY SALVATION, which Thou hast prepared before
the face of all people ; a light to lighten the
Gentiles, and the glory of Thy people Israel "
(ii. 28, 32). And so Anna, " coming in that instant,
gave thanks likewise unto the Lord, and spake of
Him to all them that looked FOR REDEMPTION in
Jerusalem " (verse 38).

It is unnecessary to enter into the long-enduring
controversy regarding the genealogies of our Lord
contained in Matthew and Luke. The form of the
two genealogies is different. Matthew's runs thus :
" Abraham begat Isaac, and Isaac begat Jacob."
It is also a descending line. Luke's is an ascending
one, and our Lord is apparently the subject of each
sentence. When we read : " who was the son of
Heli, who was the son of Matthat, who was the son
of Levi," etc., it is our Lord who is in each case
represented as the offspring of each of these ascend-

ing links. It is in this way that we have to understand the last statement in the series—" Who was
the Son of God " (verse 38). It was not Adam who
was God's Son; for to him that epithet is never
applied. It is Jesus, who, by that title, is distinguished from us and not bound up with us. All
this, I may add, is more evident in the original
than in our version. The former runs literally :
" Who was the son of . . . . Heli, of Matthat,
of Levi, of Melchi . . . . . of Seth, of Adam, of
God."

When we ask whose genealogy this is, a bit of old
Jewish hate supplies the answer. It is the genealogy
of Jesus *through Mary*, and it thus gives us the
natural descent of our Lord. " There is a discourse,"
says old Dr. Lightfoot, " of a certain person, who, in
his sleep, saw the punishment of the damned.
Amongst the rest *chama Miriam, bath Eli betzelim ;*
which I would render thus, but shall willingly stand
corrected if under a mistake :* ' He saw Mary the
daughter of Heli amongst the shades. R. Lazar
ben Josah saith . . . . That she hung by the glan-
dules of her breasts. R. Josah bar Haninah saith . . .
That the great bar of hell's gate hung at her ear.'
If this be the true rendering of the words—which I
have reason to believe it is—then thus far, at least, it
agrees with our evangelist, that Mary was the daughter of Heli ; and questionless all the rest is added in
reproach of the blessed Virgin, the mother of our

---

* There can be no doubt in regard to the translation. *Chama* is Aramean,
meaning " He contemplated." The rest is Biblical Hebrew.

Lord ; whom they often vilify elsewhere under the name of ' Sardah.' " *

The bitterness through which the Lord and His people have had to pass is painfully apparent in these representations. The bitterness has, unfortunately, not been manifested by the Jews only. Blasphemies, quite as malignant and as frightful, could be culled from the writings of leaders in literature and in politics who owed the things they valued most to the religion which they tried to crush. But we have to thank God for the preservation of the words which we have just quoted ; for, as has been already said, they settle this vexed question. " It is remarkable," writes Godet, " that, in the Talmud, Mary the mother of Jesus is called *the daughter of Heli* (Chagig. 77. 4). From whence have Jewish scholars derived this information ? If from the text of Luke, this proves that they understood it as we do ; if they received it from tradition, it confirms the truth of the genealogical document Luke made use of." †

The Jews must either have taken the genealogy in Luke as that of Mary, or they must have known from independent sources that Mary was the daughter of Heli. In either case, this information assures us that Luke gives us the natural descent of Jesus. I need hardly point out how fitting it was that the Gospel of the Saviour should thus present Him as " the seed of the woman," and that the genealogy should close with reminding us that He is the Son

---

" *Works* (8vo), XII., 53.   † *Commentary on Luke*, vol. i., p. 202.

of God as well as the son of Adam, and therefore
" mighty to save."

Luke abounds with parables and incidents peculiar
to it, and which are plainly selected because they
reveal Jesus as the Saviour. It is only here that we
are told of what our Lord read and said in the
Synagogue at Nazareth : "And He came to Nazareth,
where He had been brought up : and, as His custom
was, He went into the synagogue on the Sabbath
day, and stood up for to read. And there was
delivered unto Him the book of the Prophet Esaias.
And when He had opened the book, He found the
place where it was written, The Spirit of the Lord is
upon Me, because He hath anointed Me to preach the
Gospel to the poor ; He hath sent Me to heal the
brokenhearted, to preach deliverance to the captives,
and recovering of sight to the blind, to set at liberty
them that are bruised, to preach the acceptable year
of the Lord . . . And He began to say unto them,
This day is this Scripture fulfilled in your ears. And
all bare Him witness, and wondered at the gracious
words which proceeded out of His mouth " (iv. 16-22).
This is the programme of the ministry of mercy then
begun and since continued. That it should have
been reserved to the third Gospel to give it to the
Church and the world is another indication of the
purpose which this Gospel serves.

In the seventh chapter we have two other incidents,
for our knowledge of which we are indebted to this
Gospel. The first is the restoring to life of the
widow's son at Nain. Our Lord and the multitude

which followed Him were drawing near to the city-
gate, when a procession of mourners was seen to
issue from it on its way to the burying place outside
the city walls. The two processions met—the one
of death, the other of life. " Now when He came
nigh to the gate of the city, behold, there was a dead
man carried out, the only son of his mother, and
she was a widow : and much people of the city was
with her. And when the Lord saw her, He had
compassion on her, and said unto her, Weep not.
And He came and touched the bier (and they that
bare him stood still). And He said, Young man, I
say unto thee, Arise. And he that was dead sat up,
and began to speak. And He delivered him to his
mother " (vii. 12-15). It will be noted how striking
a revelation we have here both of the infinite compassion and of the infinite power of the Saviour.

The next shows us to what depths the mercy of
Jesus can stoop to save, and to what heights the
rescued are raised. The beginning of the story has
not been told us. We read that "a woman in the
city who was a sinner " desired to anoint the Lord ;
but we are not told why she wished to pay Him this
tribute. Probably, while standing listening in the
crowd, the message had touched her. She saw her
sin ; but she had also heard and believed the message
of mercy. And now, when she hears that He has
entered the Pharisee's house, and will be his guest
for some short time, the question seems to have
flashed upon her—Can *she* do nothing to honour
Him who has brought her to God and peace ? She

remembers the alabaster box of ointment, bought for her adorning in days of shame. She will take that and anoint Him with it. The box is seized and she hastens upon the errand. She has entered the chamber, scanned the guests, and marked where the Lord is reclining. According to the custom of the place and time, He is resting upon a couch, His head at the table round which the other guests are in like manner gathered, and His feet towards the advancing penitent. She has come so far, but can go no farther. A sudden thought has slain her purpose. Who is she, that she should dare to approach this holy servant of God? Her sins take hold upon her, and, as she stands by the feet of Him to whom she would fain show her affection, but whom she dare not profane with her touch, a heavy tear rolls down her cheek and falls upon the Prophet's feet. She stoops down to brush the defiling drop away. But the flood-gates of her sorrow and of her love are opened. The tears rain down. She wipes them away with her hair, and kisses the feet that brought her the message of the all-pardoning love. And then, in her utter lowliness, she pours upon His feet the ointment which she had at first intended for His head. And through all this, although the woman and her deed are the centre of universal observation, the Lord surrenders Himself to her. Had a muscle of those feet moved, the woman would swiftly have read the indication of aversion. I need not retell the story, or remind the reader of the parable of the two debtors in which the Pharisee was judged and the woman honoured. It is enough to note that all this was reserved for Luke to tell. It had its place in the Gospel of the Saviour (vii. 36-50).

Similarly it is in the third Gospel only that we find the parable of the Good Samaritan (x. 30-37), who went to the plundered, wounded, helpless, and hopeless man whom Priest and Levite had passed by, and "had compassion on him, and went to him, and bound up his wounds, pouring in oil and wine, and set him on his own beast, and brought him to an inn and took care of him." Luke and John both give us glimpses of the home at Bethany. But it is Luke only who tells us that Martha was in danger of neglecting the great salvation, and that Mary "sat at Jesus' feet and heard His word" (verse 39). In the parable of the Great Supper, recorded by Matthew and Luke, the latter alone gives us those excuses of the invited guests which have furnished shafts for so many gospel arrows. To him also we are indebted for the information that the servants were sent forth a second time to gather in the needy that the festal halls might be furnished with guests. I place the two accounts side by side:

MATTHEW.	LUKE.
"Go ye therefore into the highways, and as many as ye shall find, bid to the marriage. So those servants went out into the highways, and gathered together as many	"Go out quickly into the streets and lanes of the city, and bring in hither the poor, and the maimed, and the halt, and the blind. And the servant said, Lord, it is done

MATTHEW.	LUKE.
as they found, both bad and good, and the wedding was furnished with guests " (xxii. 9, 10).	as Thou hast commanded, and yet there is room. And the Lord said unto the servant, Go out into the highways and the hedges, and compel them to come in, that My house may be filled" (xiv. 21-23).

That, "And yet there is room," has been the gospel motto through all the ages. The Gospel of the Saviour discloses itself equally in the description of those whom the Maker of the Feast invites. Every word in that description is a seed of hope; for every word speaks of need, and not one of worthiness.

The purpose of the third Gospel shines out in special splendour in the 15th chapter. The first of these marvellous parables contained in the chapter, that of "the ninety and nine," occurs also in Matthew (xviii. 12); but the ending of the parable is peculiar to Luke. Both evangelists tell of the Shepherd's leaving the ninety and nine in the wilderness, and of his seeking until he finds the one that was lost. Luke alone adds: "And when he hath found it, he layeth it on his shoulders, rejoicing. And when he cometh home, he calleth together his friends and neighbours, saying unto them, Rejoice with me; for I have found my sheep which was lost" (xv. 5, 6). The same purpose is manifest in the grouping with this the parables of the lost piece of silver and of the lost son. It is still more conspicuous in the details.

To refer only to the last of the three, we have there what is perhaps the most touching of all the Scripture representations of God's delight in the receiving of him who turneth from the error of his way. There is also a fulness in the representation which has not always been marked. It has not seldom been objected that it shows us God's pardoning and receiving without any atonement. In other words, that we have here remission of sins without shedding of blood. The usual answer to this has been that everything cannot be got into a parable. But the great doctrine of the Gospel has been there from the first. The sinner has to enter with a glory that is not his. At the door of the father's house he is arrayed that he may worthily enter in. A ring, which he has not purchased, is put on his hand; and shoes, which he has not toiled for, are put on his feet; so that wherever the eye may rest upon him it will meet the marks of worthiness. But, above all, "the best robe" is brought forth and put upon him. What is that? There is no better in all the Father's house than it. It is *the best* robe. Interpret it as the imputed righteousness of Christ, and you have an explanation. Apart from that, there is none. Nor is there anywhere in Scripture a more beautiful and touching presentation of the gospel to the Pharisee than is found in the Father's reply to the angry elder brother, who feels within him not a spark of heaven's joy over a pardoned, accepted, and restored sinner: and experiences only annoyance and scorn at the jubilation over his return. He has been trying all his life to make himself worthy of approach to God. He has kept himself from the sinful throng, that he might not be shut out from the heavenly glory. And now he is told how he also may feel at once his unworthiness and the Divine mercy. " Son, thou art ever with me, and all that I have is thine." Fellowship with God, and the fulness of the eternal glory are his now if he will only have them. He knows himself unworthy, otherwise his painful striving would have ceased to have had the motive which has hitherto inspired it—his desire to achieve acceptance. Let him receive these now, and he will stand by the reclaimed sinner's side. He will rejoice in a salvation which he did not purchase, and love will lead into a service such as fear never knew.

Little requires to be added to prove Luke to be the Gospel of the Saviour. But the reader of this Gospel finds that purpose cropping up everywhere. It is only in Luke that we are told how, in that last journey of Jesus to Jerusalem, "when He was come near, He beheld the city and wept over it, saying, If thou hadst known, even thou, at least in this thy day, the things which belong to thy peace! but now they are hid from thine eyes " (xix. 41, 42). It was fitting also that Luke should alone tell us of the bloody sweat in Gethsemane (xxii. 44) ; of the Lord showing mercy even in His agony to the dying thief, and gathering from the very cross this first-fruit of His sufferings; and of that walk to Emmaus in which the Risen Lord, the Great Shepherd and Bishop of our souls, went after two straying disciples and sent them back on joyous feet to Jerusalem and the Upper Room (xxiv. 13-35). The Gospel fitly concludes with the Lord's ascension. "And He led them out as far as to Bethany, and He lifted up His hands, and blessed them. And it came to pass, while He blessed them, He was parted from them, and carried up into heaven." That is this Gospel's last glimpse of Jesus, and in it we behold the Saviour.

CHAPTER VIII.

The Gospel of John—the Gospel of the Friend.

THE fourth Gospel has presented one of the most formidable problems to New Testament criticism. It has, consequently, commanded special attention, and everyone has been compelled either to adopt or to find an opinion as to the purpose with which it was written. It confessedly came into existence long after the three first Gospels were in circulation. It is therefore taken for granted that its object could not be merely to make known the facts of our Lord's life. These were already known; and, if John re-tells the story, it must be to show the Redeemer in some fresh aspect.

The notion, which was early suggested, that the fourth Gospel was intended to be a supplement to the other three, is now abandoned. The Gospel shows no sign of being a supplement. It is a Book, telling the story of the Lord Jesus in a perfectly orderly way, commencing, after a word on His eternal glory, with John the Baptist's testimony to Him, and ending with His death and resurrection. But this leaves the question still in front of us as to why the fourth Gospel was written. Renan denotes an appendix to his " *Life of Jesus* " to a discussion of the fourth Gospel and its aim. " The author," he writes, " has a theology ; . . . he wishes to prove a thesis, to wit, that Jesus is the Divine *logos*." And the explanation which this suggests to him is very simple and, to unbelief like his, entirely natural. It was at first expected, he says, that the Lord would immediately return again. But, when the end of the first century was nearly reached, that hope was dead. Something, then, had to be done to keep the Christian Church together ; and so the new doctrine was promulgated by the fourth Gospel that Jesus was Divine. The theory, is open, however, to two somewhat important objections. The hope of the Lord's return did *not* die at the end of the first century. History proves that it was the mightiest element in the all-powerful Christian faith down to the fourth century. It lives even now. The other objection is equally fatal to Renan's theory. The doctrine of our Lord's Divinity did not require to be invented at the end of the first century. It had been the Church's belief from the commencement.

The general opinion is that this Gospel sets Jesus forth as the Son of God, and that it is intent upon showing us His glory. This is naturally suggested

by the opening words; but a study of the entire
Gospel leaves us dissatisfied with this account of it.
The glory of Christ is undoubtedly set forth in John; •
but this, I believe, comes in in the carrying out of
another purpose. The key-note of the Gospel is
heard clearly in the Lord's manifestation of Himself
in Chapter xiii. It sets forth Jesus, indeed, as the
Son of God; but it also does more. It discloses to
me " The Son of God who loved me and gave Himself for me." It is the Gospel of the Friend. When
we see it in this light, the greatest problem of the
Gospel is solved at once. This is the striking difference between it and the rest. John had to take us
into quite different scenes to show us the Lord in this
aspect. The others reveal Jesus to us in His dealing
with the multitudes. With them we accompany the
Lord in His marvellous ministry. With John, on the
other hand, we leave the multitudes and pass within.
We are now with the Lord in the inner circle.

This reading of the Gospel will justify itself as we
proceed. We first of all inquire what is meant by
the apparently mysterious naming of Christ as " the
Word." That is a question which everyone has
asked who has read these opening words: " In the
beginning was the Word; and the Word was with
God; and the Word was God." There have been
still more mysterious replies to that question, and
some theories wanting alike in helpfulness to the
reader and in honour to the Scripture. It has been
said that John was indebted to Philo, an Alexandrian
Jew, who wrote during the first century. But this

supposed explanation is now discarded. When we search the Scripture itself we find an answer. The name is applied to Jesus in the Gospel of Luke, and, strangely enough, in the introduction also to his Gospel. He says that many had taken in hand to publish orderly accounts of "those things which are most surely believed among us even as they delivered them unto us who from the beginning were eye-witnesses and ministers of the Word" (i. 1, 2). Here, plainly, our Lord is meant. It was a person, and not a message, whom the apostles are said to have beheld from the beginning.

The name is twice again applied to the Lord by John. Before looking at these other instances let us try to gather what it means in the third and fourth Gospels. I do not think that we exhaust the significance of the name when we say that, as our word expresses our thought, so Christ manifested has revealed the mind and will of God. All that is true. Jesus is the Revealer of the Father. But this name of the Redeemer seems to carry us farther. Where shall I, who cannot company with Christ as the Apostles did, now find Him? How shall I sit like Mary at His feet and hear His speech? This name supplies the answer. It identifies Jesus with the Scripture, and tells us, in effect, that we shall find Him in the Bible. The Lord's revealing work was not confined to His earthly ministry. It was illustrated by it. This is the mystery that touches us with its marvellous love and infinite condescension. The Lord meets us, communes with us, imparts

Himself to us, in this Book. He is its Alpha and Omega, its first letter and its last.

The two other passages shows how well this interpretation applies. In the opening of his first Epistle the Evangelist writes : " That which was from the beginning, which we have heard, which we have seen with our eyes, which we have looked upon, and our hands have handled, of the Word of life . . . . . declare we unto you, that ye also may have fellowship with us." But how are we to have this fellowship ? The Apostle, or rather the Scripture, assumes that the attaining of this fellowship is certain and easy. And it is both. As the Lord, in His humanity, submitted Himself to be heard and seen and looked upon and handled, so He submits Himself now in the Scripture. The other passage is Rev. xix. 13. The Lord is seen coming from heaven to judge the world: " And He was clothed with a vesture dipped in blood : and His name is called The Word of God." Coming to fulfil the Scripture, He shows His identity with it. It is His name.

That the Lord should be so called, in the very opening of this Gospel, is, therefore, quite in keeping with the purpose which I believe it serves. The Lord desires our fellowship ; and here He has made a place for our communing. It is He we meet with in the Scripture. It is *His* gracious welcome we encounter. It is the place and the brightness which He provides that we here rest in. But we must leave this enticing theme and note the broader features which reveal the purpose of the Gospel.

We may remark, however, that the whole of the introduction has this as its key-note. Jesus is the Creator. And, as He meets the need of all life that He has made, so He meets the need of man. He does this last by giving Himself, and becoming each man's greatest, nearest Friend. He is the Life and Light of men (verse 4).

One distinguishing feature of this Gospel is its personal interviews with Christ. Chapter i. shows that it was in this way that the Apostles were gathered and the Church was founded. It was in the friendship of Jesus that these living stones were laid into the foundation and the walls of the Church of God. Here is the beginning of the story. "Again the next day after John stood, and two of his disciples; and looking upon Jesus as He walked, he saith, Behold the Lamb of God! And the two disciples heard him speak, and they followed Jesus. Then Jesus turned, and saw them following, and saith unto them, What seek ye? They said unto Him, Rabbi, (which is to say, being interpreted, Master,) where dwellest Thou? He saith unto them, Come and see." It was the commencement of a fellowship that changed everything for them. They immediately began—their hearts were so fired—to bring others to Him. But each was brought to Jesus in his own fashion. Each was made to rest, not on the testimony of another, but on his own acquaintance with Jesus. A link was fashioned direct between the man and Christ. He came as near to Christ—he had as large a place in Christ's fellowship—as any other.

The 2nd chapter tells of the marriage at Cana. Here we meet an incident which has perplexed many, and which is only understood fully when we look at the Lord from the standpoint of the fourth Gospel. The Lord has gone down to Nazareth, and is met there by an invitation to a marriage at Cana. His disciples, who have accompanied Him, are also invited. His mother seems to have set out previously. The invitation had been accepted, and the Lord and His disciples had been there apparently for some time, when a thoroughly disquieting discovery was made by those on whom rested the burden of hospitality. The wine was done! It throws a pleasing light upon the character of Mary to find that she at once makes this burden her own. It is impossible to suppose that she expected the Lord to work a miracle. Hitherto He had worked none; for this, we are distinctly told, was the "beginning of miracles." Nor does she give any indication of such an expectation. In those past years, in her straitened circumstances, she has experienced many a like difficulty; and apparently she has been in the habit of consulting Jesus. She has never done so without receiving some helpful suggestion or some active assistance. She comes to Him now with a faith that rests calmly upon her past experience. He will find a way to save her friends from shame; and so, thinking that He will require the aid of the servants in bringing the needed help, she directs them to wait upon Him, and "whatever He saith unto you," she says, "do it."

But a word has been spoken to Mary which she has hid in her heart and carried away with her. When she made known this trouble to Jesus and said, "They have no wine," the Lord replied: "Woman, what have I to do with thee? Mine hour is not yet come" (verses 3, 4). That is, literally, "What is there to Me and to thee?" In other words, "What have we in common?" Mary has, so to say, suggested a co-partnery in helping and blessing. Has she any notion with whom it is she would enter into such an association? She has been acting hitherto, she is thinking and speaking now, as if Jesus were wholly and altogether her son, as if she and He were of one nature, and stood upon the same level. That delusion must perish if Mary is not to miss the blessing. She must know herself a sinner, and her son as the Saviour. Hence, therefore, this sword-thrust into the very heart of her self-complacency: "Woman, what is there in common to Me and thee?" Around that memory will spring up many another. But why should this scene be found only in this Gospel? When we mark in it Jesus the Friend of the soul, its Sun, its Life, we find the answer.

I have already spoken of the Lord's revealing Himself to individuals as a marked feature of this Gospel. Closely connected with this are the protracted interviews in which Jesus comes closer and closer to the soul. In the third chapter we have the interview with Nicodemus; in the fourth chapter, the equally prolonged conversation at Jacob's well with the woman at Sychar; in the fifth, the finding of the paralytic at the Pool of Bethesda; in the eighth chapter, the dealing with the adulteress; in the ninth chapter, with the man born blind whose eyes the Lord had opened, and whom the Jews had cast out of the synagogue; in the eleventh chapter, with Mary and Martha on the way to the grave of Lazarus; in the thirteenth chapter, with Peter in the Upper Room; in the fourteenth, with Thomas and with Philip; in the eighteenth, with Pilate; in the twentieth, with Mary Magdalene and with Thomas; and in the twenty-first, with Peter and John. In all of these we find the Lord disclosed as the Friend of the soul.

This close relationship of each to the Saviour finds abundant illustration in the figures of the fourth Gospel. Here only is He set before us as the Bridegroom (iii. 25-29). John's disciples have carried to their master the tidings of the vast popularity of the new Prophet. "All men," said they, "come to Him." John replied: "He that hath the Bride is the Bridegroom: but the friend of the Bridegroom, who standeth and heareth Him, rejoiceth greatly because of the Bridegroom's voice: this my joy therefore is fulfilled." Here Jesus is more than the *friend* of the believer: He is the Bridegroom of the Church. There are other figures of this relationship which show how the Lord and the believer exist for each other, and which are to be found in this Gospel only. Take, for example, the marvellous parable of the vine (xv. 1-6). We, in believing, are planted in Christ. We are one with Him. His life flows into us and is manifested in our thought, and speech, and action, just as the life of the vine flows into its branches and is manifested in leaf, and blossom, and fruit. Even to the carnal and unresponsive multitude that filled the synagogue at Capernaum, our Lord unfolded and dwelt upon this mystery. He is the Bread which we must eat, and without which we die. It was of this, He told them, that the heavenly food provided for their fathers in the wilderness prophesied. " I am that bread of life. Your fathers did eat manna in the wilderness, and are dead. This is the bread which cometh down from heaven, that a man may eat thereof, and not die. I am the living bread which came down from heaven. If any man eat of this bread, he shall live for ever : and the bread that I will give is My flesh, which I will give for the life of the world " (vi. 48-51). And when they "strove among themselves, saying, How can this man give us His flesh to eat ?" the Lord took up their own statement and pressed this truth home upon them. "Then Jesus said unto them, Verily, verily, I say unto you, Except ye eat the flesh of the Son of Man, and drink His blood, ye have no life in you. Whoso eateth My flesh, and drinketh My blood, hath eternal life ; and I will raise him up at the last day. For My flesh is meat indeed, and My blood is drink indeed. He that eateth My flesh, and drinketh My blood, dwelleth in Me, and I in him. As the living Father hath sent Me, and I live by the Father : so he that eateth Me, even he shall live by Me " (verses 53-57). All this was pressed home upon His disciples, and is now

pressed home upon us, in the words with which He
explained away their difficulty : " It is the Spirit that
quickeneth ; the flesh profiteth nothing : the words
that I speak unto you, they are spirit, and they are
life " (verse 63).

I cannot here make any attempt to unfold this
mystery. Though it is still pressed upon the
multitudes in the synagogues, it is to be feared that
it is not yet grasped by them all.   I ask the reader
merely to note that it is in this Gospel alone that
this vitally close relationship between the believer
and his Lord is explained and enforced.   The next
chapter presents it again in another figure.   " In the
last day, that great day, of the feast, Jesus stood and
cried, saying, If any man thirst, let him come unto
Me, and drink.   He that believeth on Me, as the
Scripture hath said, out of his belly shall flow rivers
of living water. (But this spake He of the Spirit,
which they that believe on Him should receive : for
the Holy Ghost was not yet given ; because that
Jesus was not yet glorified) " (vii. 37-39).   It comes
before us again in the parables of the door of the
sheepfold ; and of the Good Shepherd.   " I am the
door : by Me if any man enter in, he shall be saved,
and shall go in and out, and find pasture. . . . I am
the Good Shepherd : the Good Shepherd giveth His
life for the sheep. . . I am the Good Shepherd, and
know My sheep, and am known of Mine " (x. 9-14).
These representations of the close and abiding relation
between the believer and the Saviour are also to be
found in the fourth Gospel only.

CHAPTER IX.

THE PURPOSE OF JOHN'S GOSPEL
(Concluded).

———

U NFAMILIAR though the reading of the fourth Gospel may be, which is suggested in the preceding chapter, it will be found to approve itself upon reflection. It alone accounts fully for the special glories of this Gospel. Everyone will recall the Home of Bethany. Luke has shown us (x. 38-42) how the Lord's visits were prized. But it was left to John to write : " Now Jesus loved Martha, and her sister, and Lazarus " (xi. 5). We mark the same distinction in the account of the communing between the Lord and the disciples in the upper room, on that last night of the Lord's earthly life. This is fitly introduced by the words : " Having loved His own who were in the world, He loved them to the uttermost " (xiii. 1). It is in that communing, too, that we find these words, which might fitly be taken as a motto for the fourth Gospel : "Greater love hath no man than this, that a man lay down his life for his friends. YE ARE MY FRIENDS, if ye do whatsoever I command you. Henceforth I call you not servants ; for the servant knoweth not what his lord doeth : but I have called you FRIENDS ; for all things that I have heard of My Father I have made known unto you " (xv. 13-15).

We see the same purpose in a subtle change which is made in the name of the Apostle. Up till that last ̈night, John's personality is kept out of sight. When he has to be mentioned he is "another disciple" and "that other disciple" (xviii. 15, 16). But he has just before been hinted at under a description which has gone home to the hearts of Bible-readers for eighteen centuries. "Now there was leaning on Jesus' bosom," he writes, "one of His disciples, whom Jesus loved" (xiii. 23). This name is evidently taken by John in the record of this incident of the crucifixion, which he alone records: "When Jesus therefore saw His mother, and the disciple standing by, whom He loved" (xix. 26). I have said this is evidently John, for he immediately afterwards speaks of himself as a close spectator of these last moments in the earthly life of Jesus: "And he that saw it bare record, and his record is true: and he knoweth that he saith true, that ye might believe" (verse 35). Three times is John so named in the two concluding chapters of the Gospel. What does the new name mean? What has led to its adoption? It seems to me to point to the purpose of the Gospel. The Lord manifested His love—that love to the uttermost—in that last communing. John believed the testimony, and by faith took up and rejoiced in this new portion. This is the name by which to his latest day he desires to think of himself. It is not egotism: it is the overwhelming recognition of Divine affection. The publican's sin was so vast, so infinite, that he could only speak of himself as

" the sinner." And to John the revelation has come of how much he is to Jesus ; how the Lord, if I may so speak, has particularised him. He is all the world to Jesus. He has grasped the central one of those amazing antitheses of the Divine nature. God loves all. Yes, but He also loves each as fully as if no other existed. The love of Christ is limitless to each, and John has grasped this truth. The writer of "the Gospel of the Friend " has become an example to us. He himself has tasted the cup which he holds to our lips. He is " the disciple whom Jesus loved." There is a world of peace, and glory, and wonder there out of which he cannot pass. It is a fitting name for him who was to set forth Jesus as THE FRIEND of the believer.

Two further illustrations of this purpose must suffice. The first of these is found in the Lord's dealing with Simon Peter. He has fallen ; and the shame of his sin comes between him and perfect confidence. But without that confidence this man's work, for which the world waits, will never be done. Therefore the three-fold question : " Simon, son of Jonas, lovest thou Me ? " and after each reply, the apportionment of service (xx. 15-17). In the knowledge of that love which entreats our love lies the yoke of all true service for God and man. The knowledge of Christ the Friend of the Soul, " The Son of God, who loved me and gave Himself for me " is the one effectual consecration to all apostleship and service.

The other illustration of this Gospel's purpose to

which I refer is found in those last words which
have been to some a stumbling-block, but to multitudes a touching reminder of the infinite fulness of
that ministry which has changed the world : "And
there are also many other things which Jesus did,
the which, if they should be written every one, I
suppose that even the world itself could not contain
the books that should be written" (xxi. 25). "The
which," in the original *'osa*, indicates how large the
number is of those things which are omitted. But
this is plainly stated also in those words which tell
us that if these "should be written every one, I suppose that the world itself could not contain the
books that should be written." The number of the
things that are not recorded in the Gospel are therefore out of all proportion to that of the things which
have found a place in it. It need not surprise us
that this has been set down as an enormous exaggeration. Suppose, it has been argued, that we confine
ourselves to a single town. Let us imagine that
every house in a single street is filled with the books ;
and that we then proceed to pile them up outside in
the street itself. Would it be possible to find matter
for all these books even in the busy ministry of
Jesus ? And then to imagine all the streets of the
town filled in similar fashion ; and all the towns and
villages and cities of the kingdom ; and all its roads,
and forests, and hills, and mountains, and fields, and
meadows ; and then all the countries of the world to
be similarly supplied with books after that—is it to
be supposed that these words which close the Gospel

were ever weighed by the writer of them, or that he could have paused for a moment to consider their meaning?

Such is the unbelieving objection. It has weighed even with many expositors. " The meaning of this hyperbole," says Godet, " which, taken literally, would be ridiculous, even attenuated as it is by the word *I think*, is evidently this : the infinite cannot be completely contained within the compass of the finite," etc. " This is, indeed, extravagantly spoken," says Luthardt. These samples may suffice. There can be little doubt, also, that the readiness with which expositors have welcomed the suggestion, that the two last verses are not from the hand of the Apostle, is due to this cause. One writer, Hoelemann, has indicated that we have here a larger outlook. He believes that the words " embrace the pre-terrestrial and super-terrestrial working of the Logos from the beginning of the world."* But this is mentioned by Luthardt only to be rejected. He thinks that it is a sufficient objection that the Lord is here spoken of as " Jesus "—" many other things which Jesus did "—and that this name confines our thoughts to the Lord's earthly life. But why should it do so? If the Apostle, or rather the Spirit of God by him, wished by this name to indicate that "this same Jesus," whom men have seen and known, is the Creator of the Universe, could the suggestion be better conveyed? And if this supposed hyperbole were kept in front of us until that truth dawned upon

---

* Luthardt, *The Gospel of John*, vol. iii., p. 389.

our minds, and we grasped the infiniteness of the Lord's activity and the endlessness of His beneficence and praise, would it not have served the Churches well? And, if this were the intention of the Scripture, could there have been a grander ending to the four Gospels than these last words?

It may be pointed out that the Apostle speaks of things which Jesus *did*. The reference is to deeds, and not to words and deeds. This is quite in accord with the suggestion that the Evangelist may be speaking here of things done before the incarnation. But that interpretation rests on a still surer foundation. It seems to be part of the plan of the Gospels that the last words in each make an answer to the first. We saw in Matthew how the opening sentence, which announces Jesus as "the son of David, the son of Abraham," proclaim Him the King whom God has set upon His holy hill of Zion; and it will be remembered that the last words are those in which the Lord declares : "All authority is given unto Me in heaven and in earth." The same peculiarity is specially seen in Mark. That Gospel takes as its title " The Beginning of the Gospel of Jesus Christ, the Son of God "; that is the commencement of the evangel—the proclamation of the good tidings. The last words show us how the evangel was continued; " they went forth and preached everywhere, the Lord working with them and confirming the Word with signs following. Amen." Luke tells us in the commencement of his Gospel that his purpose is to give assurance through the Spirit's revelation of the

Saviour; in other words, to make known the certainty of "those things most surely believed among us" and in which Theophilus had been instructed. His Gospel concludes with showing us the ascending Saviour, blessing the disciples; and the last words display the assurance and its fruits: "And they worshipped Him, and returned to Jerusalem with great joy: and were continually in the temple, praising and blessing God. Amen " (xxiv. 52, 53).

Now, if this law holds also in the fourth Gospel, then the difficulty of these last words has been pointing to one of the most resplendent of the Redeemer's glories. The Gospel begins by telling us that He is the Word given for our reading and comprehending. It is our destiny to know and to comprehend Him. He is the window by which we look out upon the infinite glory—the doorway by which we pass to all the treasures of wisdom and knowledge. John then reminds us that the Word has expressed Himself in act before He tabernacled in the flesh. "In the beginning was the Word, and the Word was with God, and the Word was God. The same was in the beginning with God. All things were made by Him; and without Him was not anything—was not one thing—made that was made " (i. 1-3). And not only have the first of all things created, and with them the first parents of the human race, been formed by His hands, but He has also come into touch with every one of us. "That was the true Light which enlighteneth every man that cometh into the world."

Let it be borne in mind that it is to set forth Jesus in this relationship—the Maker of all things, the Giver of life to all things living, He Himself being the Life and the Light of men—that this Gospel is written. Should we not, then, expect to find at the close just such a word as that about the "many other things?" So far they have not been touched upon; surely, then, the Evangelist will tell us why this mighty field has not been entered. And here *is* his explanation. He reminds us that the many other things are there, but they are not recorded. If they *were* "written every one, I suppose," he says, "that even the world itself could not contain the books that should be written. Amen." But if they were not to be told us, why was Jesus thus disclosed at the beginning of the Gospel, and why were these things thus referred to in the end of it? Is it not because the Spirit will remind us that we do not yet know everything about the Friend of our soul, and that the future fellowship has revelations for us grander even than these that have been told us in the Evangelist's pages? This hint completes the work and crowns the purpose of the Fourth Gospel. As it speaks its last word, it kindles the lamp of our hope; and we press on with joy and eagerness anticipating that time when we shall know even as we are known.

The very difficulty experienced in understanding the concluding words of the Gospel ought to have warned believing men that they had failed to understand them. And, taking them weighted with this new significance, we become ashamed of our talk about exaggeration and hyperbole. We know how science has multiplied its books ; and of all these books it is the work of specialists that is regarded as the most valuable. Sir Charles Bell, for example, wrote a book upon the hand. Had he known *everything* about it, the work might well have been extended. Suppose that, instead of the gropings of science among the indications of design in the human frame, scientific men saw everything in the light of a full revelation. Say that they saw man's frame to be that almost endless world of design that it is—that they saw it in its marvellous harmony and the equally marvellous wisdom displayed in its minutest parts. Say that, possessed of this new fulness of material, they addressed themselves to the task of explaining it to mankind. Say that this great field was divided among a host of writers, and that each set forth all the details that had been revealed in his section. Can we sum up the number of the books that should be written ? But the human body is only one of myriads of organisms which people the earth, the air, and the sea. Let the full light of revelation fall upon each one of these. Let nothing in it, however slight, be left without a discovery of it that shall be full and entrancing. Let multitudes of new writers divide these new fields among them. Let them become the exponents of all these things to mankind. Where shall we place the fast accumulating books, for each of the many thousands of species will have its library ?

But we have only begun to enter this great world of created existences. The rocks beneath our feet enshrine the relics of other creations that have passed away. Let these, so to say, revive again. Let the light of an equally full revelation display every one of *them.* Let these new, and not less marvellous arrangements, be made equally plain; and let new pens be busy, and new libraries be written. Then from the animal kingdom let us pass to the vegetable, and to the mineral, kingdoms. Let past and present be revealed. Let each organism, and each mineral, and each crystal, and each chemical combination be also fully manifested so that all, and more than all, that science has ever desired to know, is fully disclosed. Let the pens of ready writers again fly along the pages. And then, when this earth has been exhausted, and there is nothing left that has not been recorded, let us pass to the planets, and let the like be done for each of them. And from the planets, with their sun and moons, let us travel through the starry universe, and do the same for these suns innumerable, and all their planets, and all their moons. Where now shall we bestow our books. It will not be enough to say, "we shall pull down our libraries and build greater;" for every fresh revelation is piling fresh libraries around us. There is but one utterance that will express our labouring thought. It is this which the Spirit of God has provided: "And there are also many other things which Jesus did, the which, if they should be written everyone, I suppose that even the world itself could not contain the books that should be written."

But even that survey shows us merely a part of His ways. What a field is covered by the words,

which are also embraced in the wondrous beginning
to which those last words make answer : "That was
the true Light which enlighteneth every man that
cometh into the world" (i. 9). The marvels of the
Providence of Jesus are not less than those of His
creative work. His hand has been laid upon every
human being that has breathed this common air.
From the days of tenderest infancy the Lord has
been with each. When He lifted the little ones in
His arms and laid His hands upon them and blessed
them, the curtain was lifted for a moment from the
hidden but unending ministry of the Friend of the
soul. At each moment of the earthly pilgrimage he
whose eye was opened would exclaim : "Thou hast
beset me behind and before, and laid Thine hand
upon me" (Psalm cxxxix. 5). Say now that we enter
this new domain. Every one is aware that there is
nothing more entrancing than a life-story. Let the
tale of each one's life, his thought and experiences,
his striving and attaining, be written. Above all, let
the entire record of the Great Shepherd's guiding
of each, with its gain or loss, be penned by those
from whose eyes not a single thing is hid. Let this
be done for every dweller in every hamlet, village,
town, and city in our land, and in every land under
the sun. Let the service be repeated for every generation in the past. Let the vanished civilisations
re-appear with their countless millions. Let the life
of no child of humanity be left unrecorded. Where
shall we place the books? Again we thank God for
the words: "I suppose that even the world itself

could not contain the books that should be written."
And it was well, let me repeat, that the Gospel of the
Friend should leave us with these words upon its lips.
They tell us of the treasures of wisdom and knowledge
yet to be possessed, of the unending revelations of
love and glory which will make the heavenly life the
boundless joy and the unending praise that we have
been told it is.

CHAPTER X.

WHAT THESE THINGS MEAN.

IN setting out upon our study of the Gospels, we
asked at the close of chapter ii. was it possible for
us to know whether these Gospels are the gift of God
or are merely a loving service rendered by Christian
men ?

We have now before us the materials for a reply.
That each of the four Gospels sets forth the Lord
Jesus from first to last in one special aspect will be
admitted by anyone who has read the foregoing
chapters. So plainly is this being now seen, that the
recognition of these distinct tendencies is entering
into ordinary exposition. Here, then, the great and
complicated problem of the origin of the Gospels finds
an easy but complete solution. The agreements,
which are without parallel in any other books claiming to be independent, point to a common source.
But, as we have seen, the differences between them
wreck every theory which criticism has devised.

Every possible explanation of their origin, treating them as merely human documents, has been tried; and all have been weighed in the balances and been found wanting. The view to which any critic clings to-day, he has accepted simply because it is the best among a number of suggestions, none of which is wholly satisfactory. It is merely a more solid patch in a bog; and too much weight must not be put upon it, or it also will go under!

The problem is one, therefore, *which criticism has given up.* It cannot solve it upon the supposition that these Books have had a merely natural origin. That, let me say, is a momentous confession. Faced by facts, the critical attack owns itself defeated. It started with the most perfect confidence that there was nothing in the Scripture the origin of which could not be explained in a perfectly natural way. The Books of the Bible, said the critics, originated in the same way as the other books of the nations. We were jubilantly told, that one proof of the correctness of this view was the light which it shed upon the Bible. The darkness, consequent upon ages of superstitious reverence for the Bible and of an impossible theory of its inspiration, was past. What the Bible had lost in authority, it had gained, we were assured, in intelligibility and in real power. Criticism, by bringing the Books of the Bible into connection with the movements of their times, had invested them with a fresh charm, and had made the Bible, in fact, a new Book for multitudes!

That was the boast: and now in these four memoirs

of the Lord Jesus criticism meets its fate.   It approached the Gospel problem, as has just been said, with the most absolute confidence.   The very plurality of the Gospels was a proof, to begin with, that the conviction of criticism, that it had to do with merely ordinary productions, was right.   It was perfectly natural that a life like our Saviour's should have attracted many pens.   And now we learn that the facts resist every solution which criticism can suggest or imagine.   In other words, these four Gospels cannot possibly be explained as merely human documents.   Does the problem find a solution, then, in the belief which criticism has attempted to displace?   That the Books become intelligible the moment we admit that they are Divine, it requires but a word, as we have seen, to show.   The striking agreements in words, some of them quite unusual, and in phrases are at once explained (as is universally agreed) by a common source.   When we say that this Source is the Holy Spirit, the real Author of all the four Books, we present a solution to which no possible objection can be taken on the ground of its not meeting the case in hand.   Words and phrases are alike, for the simple and sufficient reason that behind them all there is one Mind.

That belief is consequently commended by its fitness to meet one part of this two-fold Gospel problem. It triumphantly explains the agreements. And when we come to the other part of the problem—the differences—the truth of this explanation is also demonstrated.   These differences are all in accord with the distinct aim of each Gospel. The purpose of each is carried on and completed by means of those very variations. They exist solely on account of each individual Gospel's purpose. And now by the side of this fact we have to place another. These purposes are so woven into the texture of the Gospels that they are by no means apparent to a casual reader. It is only when they are suggested that they are detected and traced even by a studious reader of the Gospels; and it is only within the last sixty or seventy years that attention has been drawn to what we have now to admit are nevertheless deeply marked characteristics. If it is asked why these were not seen earlier, especially by the great thinkers and scholars of past ages, a reply lies close at hand. Why had so many ages to elapse before Newton's discovery was made? Why was it that the true theory of light and so much besides were hid even from him?

That there is a Providence in all these things we firmly believe. The discoveries are made at the right time. And this of the purposes of the Gospels has come just when it was needed. Faith found the key which a so-called science was to seek in vain. But what we have to note now is this. If it has taken eighteen centuries to discover these distinctions, how were they at the first conceived and executed? No one will imagine that these four men made any such arrangement. They held no meeting at which the great work was arranged and divided. No one suggested that Matthew should present the Lord as the King, Mark as the Servant, Luke as the Saviour, and

John as the Friend. And yet, that it has been so arranged, it is impossible to deny. It is also equally plain
that this four-fold picture is marvellously complete.
It has shown the glory of Christ : it has met the needs
of the Church. The boldness and the completeness
of the plan, and the ever-present control which shapes
the work of each Evangelist are a manifestation of
that miracle which we call " Inspiration." For the
thought which has faced this problem has to confess
that it finds its only solution in the statement that the
Gospels are the work and the gift of the Spirit of God.

E. Goodman and Son, Phœnix Printing Works, Taunton.

INDEX.